DESERT

Also by J. M. G. Le Clézio in English
from Verba Mundi Books and
David R. Godine · *Publisher*

THE PROSPECTOR
a novel,
translated by Carol Marks

*Hypnotic and mythic . . . Le Clézio brilliantly
conveys the sublime and terrible beauty of
life and its twin, death, in devastating
evocations . . . a remarkable work.*
ALA Booklist (starred review)

*A gentle portrayal of a man haunted by
visions of his ideal childhood . . .
[Le Clézio's] writing is deeply
evocative and descriptive.*
Publishers Weekly

J. M. G. LE CLÉZIO

DESERT

*Translated from the French
by C. Dickson*

A Verba Mundi Book
David R. Godine · Publisher · Boston

This is a Verba Mundi Book
published in 2009 by
DAVID R. GODINE, *Publisher*
Post Office Box 450
Jaffrey, New Hampshire 03452
www.godine.com

Originally published in French in 1980 as *Désert*
by Editions Gallimard, Paris

Copyright © 1980 by Editions Gallimard
Translation copyright © 2009 by C. Dickson

Cet ouvrage, publié dans le cadre d'un programme d'aide à la publication,
bénéficie du soutien du Ministère des Affaires étrangères et du
Service Culturel de l'Ambassade de France aux Etats-Unis.

This work, published as part of a program of aid for publication,
received support from the French Ministry of Foreign Affairs and the
Cultural Services of the French Embassy in the United States.

LIBRARY OF CONGRESS CATALOGING-IN-PUBLICATION DATA

Le Clézio, J.-M. G. (Jean-Marie Gustave), 1940–
[Désert. English]
Desert / by J.M.G Le Clezio.
p. cm.
ISBN 978-1-56792-386-5
I. Title.
PQ2672.E25D413 2009
843´.914–dc22
2009003264

FIRST U.S. EDITION
Printed in the United States of America

DESERT

Saguiet al-Hamra, winter 1909–1910

T HEY APPEARED as if in a dream at the top of the
dune, half-hidden in the cloud of sand rising from
their steps. Slowly, they made their way down into the
valley, following the almost invisible trail. At the head
of the caravan were the men, wrapped in their woolen
cloaks, their faces masked by the blue veil. Two or three
dromedaries walked with them, followed by the goats
and sheep that the young boys prodded onward. The
women brought up the rear. They were bulky shapes,
lumbering under heavy cloaks, and the skin of their arms
and foreheads looked even darker in the indigo cloth.

They walked noiselessly in the sand, slowly, not
watching where they were going. The wind blew relent-
lessly, the desert wind, hot in the daytime, cold at night.
The sand swirled about them, between the legs of the
camels, lashing the faces of the women, who pulled the
blue veils down over their eyes. The young children ran
about, the babies cried, rolled up in the blue cloth on
their mothers' backs. The camels growled, sneezed. No
one knew where the caravan was going.

The sun was still high in the stark sky, sounds and
smells were swept away on the wind. Sweat trickled slowly
down the faces of the travelers; the dark skin on their
cheeks, on their arms and legs was tinted with indigo.
The blue tattoos on the women's foreheads looked like
shiny little beetles. Their black eyes, like drops of molten

1

metal, hardly seeing the immense stretch of sand, searched for signs of the trail in the rolling dunes.

There was nothing else on earth, nothing, no one. They were born of the desert, they could follow no other path. They said nothing. Wanted nothing. The wind swept over them, through them, as if there were no one on the dunes. They had been walking since the very crack of dawn without stopping, thirst and weariness hung over them like a lead weight. Their cracked lips and tongues were hard and leathery. Hunger gnawed their insides. They couldn't have spoken. They had been as mute as the desert for so long, filled with the light of the sun burning down in the middle of the empty sky, and frozen with the night and its still stars.

They continued to make their slow way down the slope toward the valley bottom, zigzagging when loose sand shifted out from under their feet. The men chose where their feet would come down without looking. It was as if they were walking along invisible trails leading them out to the other end of solitude, to the night. Only one of them carried a gun, a flintlock rifle with a long barrel of blackened copper. He carried it on his chest, both arms folded tightly over it, the barrel pointing upward like a flagpole. His brothers walked alongside him, wrapped in their cloaks, bending slightly forward under the weight of their burdens. Beneath their cloaks, the blue clothing was in tatters, torn by thorns, worn by the sand. Behind the weary herd, Nour, the son of the man with the rifle, walked in front of his mother and sisters. His face was dark, sun-scorched, but his eyes shone and the light of his gaze was almost supernatural.

They were the men and the women of the sand, of the wind, of the light, of the night. They had appeared as if in a dream at the top of a dune, as if they were born of the cloudless sky and carried the harshness of space in their limbs. They bore with them hunger, the thirst of bleeding lips, the flintlike silence of the glinting sun, the cold nights, the glow of the Milky Way, the moon; accompanying them were their huge shadows at sunset, the waves of virgin sand over which their splayed feet trod, the inaccessible horizon. More than anything, they bore the light of their gaze shining so brightly in the whites of their eyes.

The herd of grayish-brown goats and sheep walked in front of the children. The beasts also moved forward not knowing where, their hooves following in ancient tracks. The sand whirled between their legs, stuck in their dirty coats. One man led the dromedaries simply with his voice, grumbling and spitting as they did. The hoarse sound of labored breathing caught in the wind, then suddenly disappeared in the hollows of the dunes to the south. But the wind, the dryness, the hunger, no longer mattered. The people and the herd moved slowly down toward the waterless, shadeless valley bottom.

They'd left weeks, months ago, going from one well to another, crossing dried torrents lost in the sands, walking over plateaus, climbing rocky hills. The herd ate stubby grasses, thistles, euphorbia leaves, sharing them with the tribe. In the evening, when the sun was nearing the horizon and the shadows of the bushes grew inordinately long, the people and animals stopped walking. The men unloaded the camels, pitched the large tent of brown wool, standing on its single cedar wood pole. The women lit the fire, prepared the mashed millet, the sour milk, the butter, the dates. Night fell very quickly, the vast cold sky opened out over the dark earth. And then the stars appeared, thousands of stars stopped motionless in space. The man with the rifle who led the group called to Nour and showed him the tip of the Little Dipper, the lone star known as Cabri, and on the other side of the constellation, Kochab, the blue. To the east, he showed Nour the bridge where five stars shone: Alkaïd, Mizar, Alioth, Megrez, Fecda. In the far-eastern corner, barely above the ash-colored horizon, Orion had just appeared with Alnilam, leaning slightly to one side like the mast of a boat. He knew all the stars, he sometimes called them strange names, names that were like the beginning of a story. Then he showed Nour the route they would take the next day, as if the lights blinking on in the sky plotted the course that men must follow on earth. There were so many stars! The desert night was full of those sparks pulsing faintly as the wind came and went like a breath. It was a timeless land, removed from human history perhaps, a land where nothing else could come to be or die, as if it were already beyond other lands, at the pinnacle of earthly existence. The men often watched the stars, the vast white swath that is like a sandy bridge over the earth. They talked a little, smoking rolled *kif* leaves; they told each other stories of journeys, rumors of the war with the Christians, of reprisals. Then they listened to the night.

The flames of the twig fire danced under the copper teakettle, making a sound of sizzling water. On the other side of the brazier, the women were talking, and one was humming a tune for her baby who was falling asleep at her breast. The wild dogs yelped, and the echoes in the hollows of the dunes answered them, like other wild dogs. The smell of the livestock rose, mingled with the dampness of the gray sand, with the acrid odor of the smoke from the braziers.

Afterward, the women and children went to sleep in the tent, and the men lay down in their cloaks around the cold fire. They melted into the vast stretch of sand and rock – invisible – as the black sky sparkled ever more brilliantly.

They'd been walking like that for months, years maybe. They'd followed the routes of the sky between the waves of sand, the routes coming from the Drâa, from Tamgrout, from the Erg Iguidi, or farther north – the route of the Aït Atta, of the Gheris, coming from Tafilelt, that joins the great *ksours* in the foothills of the Atlas Mountains, or else the endless route that penetrates into the heart of the desert, beyond Hank, in the direction of the great city of Timbuktu. Some died along the way, others were born, were married. Animals died too, throats slit open to fertilize the entrails of the earth, or else stricken with the plague and left to rot on the hard ground.

It was as if there were no names here, as if there were no words. The desert cleansed everything in its wind, wiped everything away. The men had the freedom of the open spaces in their eyes, their skin was like metal. Sunlight blazed everywhere. The ochre, yellow, gray, white sand, the fine sand shifted, showing the direction of the wind. It covered all traces, all bones. It repelled light, drove away water, life, far from a center that no one could recognize. The men knew perfectly well that the desert wanted nothing to do with them: so they walked on without stopping, following the paths that other feet had already traveled in search of something else. As for water, it was in the *aiun*: the eyes that were the color of the sky, or else in the damp beds of old muddy streams. But it wasn't water for pleasure or for refreshment either. It was just a sweat mark on the surface of the desert, the meager gift of an arid God, the last shudder of life. Heavy water wrenched from the sand, dead water from crevices, alkaline water that caused colic, vomiting. They must walk even farther, bending slightly forward, in the direction the stars had indicated.

But it was the only – perhaps the last – free land, the

5

land in which the laws of men no longer mattered. A land for stones and for wind, and for scorpions and jerboas too, creatures who know how to hide and flee when the sun burns down and the night freezes over.

Now they appeared above the valley of Saguiet al-Hamra, slowly descending the sandy slopes. On the floor of the valley, traces of human life began: fields surrounded by drystone walls, pens for camels, shacks made of the leaves of dwarf palms, large woolen tents like upturned boats. The men descended slowly, digging their heels into the sand that crumbled and shifted underfoot. The women slowed their pace and remained far behind the group of animals, suddenly frantic from the smell of the wells. Then the immense valley appeared, spreading out under the plateau of stones. Nour looked for the tall, dark green palms rising from the ground in close rows around the clear freshwater lake; he looked for the white palaces, the minarets, everything he had been told about since his childhood whenever anyone had mentioned the city of Smara. It had been so long since he'd seen trees. His arms hung loosely from his body as he walked down toward the valley bottom, eyes half shut against the sun and the sand.

As the men neared the floor of the valley, the city they had glimpsed briefly disappeared, and they found only dry, barren land. The heat was torrid, sweat streamed down Nour's face, making his blue clothing stick to his lower back and shoulders.

Now other men, other women also appeared, as if they'd suddenly sprung up from the valley. Some women had lit their braziers for the evening meal, children, men sitting quietly in front of their dusty tents. They'd come from all parts of the desert, beyond the stony Hamada, from the mountains of Cheheïba and Ouarkziz, from Siroua, from the Oum Chakourt Mountains beyond even

6

the great southern oases, from the underground lake of Gourara. They'd come through the mountains at Maïder Pass, near Tarhamant, or lower down where the Drâa joins the Tingut, through Regbat. All of the southern peoples had come, the nomads, the traders, the shepherds, the looters, the beggars. Perhaps some of them had left the Kingdom of Biru or the great oasis of Oualata. Their faces bore the ruthless mark of the sun, of the deathly-cold nights deep in the desert. Some of them were a blackish, almost red color, tall and slender, they spoke an unknown language; they were Tubbus come from across the desert, from Borku and Tibesti, eaters of kola nuts, who were going all the way to the sea.

As the troop of people and livestock approached, the black shapes of humans multiplied. Behind twisted acacias, huts of mud and branches appeared, like so many termite mounds. Houses of adobe, pillboxes of planks and mud, and most of all, those low, drystone walls, barely even knee-high – dividing the red soil into a honeycomb of tiny patches. In fields no larger than a saddle blanket, the *harratin* slaves tried to raise a few broad beans, peppers, some millet. The irrigation canals extended their parched ditches across the valley to capture the slightest drop of moisture.

They had arrived now in the environs of the great city of Smara. The people, the animals, all moved forward over the desiccate earth, along the bottom of the deep gash of the Saguiet Valley.

They had been waiting for so many hard flintlike days, so many hours, to see this. There was so much suffering in their aching bodies, in their bleeding lips, in their scorched gaze. They hurried toward the wells, impervious to the cries of the animals or the mumbling of the other people. Once they reached the wells and were before the stone wall holding up the soggy earth, they stopped. The children shooed off the animals by throwing stones, while the men knelt down to pray. Then each of them dipped his face in the water and drank deeply.

It was just like that, those eyes of water in the desert. But the tepid water still held the strength of the wind, the sand, and the great frozen night sky. As he drank, Nour could feel the emptiness that had driven him from one well to the next entering him. The murky and stale water nauseated him, did not quench his thirst. It was as if the silence and loneliness of the dunes and the great plateaus were settling deep inside of him. The water in the wells was still, smooth as metal, with bits of leaves and animal wool floating on its surface. At the other well, the women were washing themselves and smoothing their hair.

Near them, the goats and dromedaries stood motionless, as if they were tethered to stakes in the mud around the well.

Other men came and went between the tents. They were blue warriors of the desert, veiled, armed with daggers and long rifles, striding along, not looking at anyone; Sudanese slaves, dressed in rags, carrying loads of millet or dates, goatskins filled with oil; sons of great tents with almost black skin – dressed in white and dark blue – known as Chleuhs; sons of the coast with red hair and freckles on their skin; men of no race, no name; leprous beggars who did not go near the water. All of them were walking over the stone-strewn red dust, making their way toward the walls of the holy city of Smara. They had fled the desert for a few hours, a few days. They had unrolled the heavy cloth of their tents, wrapped themselves in their woolen cloaks, they were awaiting the night. They were eating now, ground millet mixed with sour milk, bread, dried dates that tasted of honey and of pepper. Flies and mosquitoes danced around the children's heads in the evening air, wasps lit on their hands, their dust-stained cheeks.

They were talking now, very loudly, and the women in the stifling darkness of the tents laughed and threw little pebbles out at the children who were playing. Words gushed from the men's mouths as if in drunkenness, words that sang, shouted, echoed with guttural sounds. Behind the tents near the walls of Smara, the wind whistled in the branches of the acacias, in the leaves of the dwarf palms. And yet, the men and women whose faces and bodies were tinted blue with indigo and sweat were still steeped in silence; they had not left the desert.

They did not forget. The great silence that swept constantly over the dunes was deep in their bodies, in their entrails. That was the true secret. Every now and again, the man with the rifle stopped talking to Nour and looked back toward the head of the valley, from where the wind was coming.

Sometimes a man from another tribe walked up to the tent and greeted them, extending his two open hands. They exchanged but a few brief words, a few names. But they were words and names that vanished immediately, simply vague traces that the wind and the sand would cover over.

When night fell over the well water there, the star-filled desert sky reigned again. In the valley of Saguiet al-Hamra, nights were milder, and the new moon rose in the dark sky. The bats began their dance around the tents, flitting over the surface of the well water. The light from the braziers flickered, giving off a smell of hot oil and smoke. Some children ran between the tents, letting out barking sounds like dogs. The beasts were already asleep, the dromedaries with their legs hobbled, the sheep and the goats in the circles of drystone.

The men let down their guard. The guide had laid his

rifle on the ground at the entrance to the tent and was smoking, gazing out into the night. He was hardly listening to the soft voices and laughter of the women sitting near the braziers. Maybe he was dreaming of other evenings, other journeys, as if the burn of the sun on his skin and the aching thirst in his throat were only the beginning of some other desire.

Sleep drifted slowly over the city of Smara. Down in the south, on the great rocky Hamada, there was no sleep at night. There was the numbing cold, when the wind blew on the sand, laying the base of the mountains bare. It was impossible to sleep on the desert routes. One lived, one died, forever peering out with a steady gaze, eyes burning with weariness and with light. Sometimes the blue men came across a member of their tribe sitting up very straight in the sand, legs stretched out in front, body stock still in the shredded clothing stirring in the wind. In the gray face, the blackened eyes were set on the shifting horizon of dunes, for that is how death had come upon him.

Sleep is like water, no one could truly sleep far from the springs. The wind blew, just like the wind up in the stratosphere, depriving the earth of all warmth.

But there in the red valley the travelers could sleep.

The guide awoke before the others, he stood very still in front of the tent. He watched the haze moving slowly up the valley toward the Hamada. Night faded with the passing haze. Arms crossed on his chest, the guide was barely breathing, his eyelids did not move. He was waiting for the first light of dawn, the *fijar*, the white patch that is born in the east, above the hills. When the light appeared, he bent over Nour and woke him gently, putting a hand on his shoulder. Together they walked away in silence; they walked along the sandy trail that led to the wells. Dogs barked in the distance. In the gray dawn light, the man and Nour washed themselves according to the ritual, one part after another, starting over again three times. The well water was cold and pure, water born of the sand and of the night. The man and the boy washed their faces and their hands once more, then they turned toward the east for the first prayer. The sky was just beginning to light the horizon.

In the campsites, the braziers glowed in the last shadows. The women went to draw water; the little girls ran through the water shouting a little, then they came teetering back with the jars balanced on their thin necks.

The sounds of human life began to rise from the campsites and the mud houses: sounds of metal, of stone, of water. The yellow dogs gathered in the square, circling each other and yapping. The camels and the herds pawed the ground, raising the red dust.

The light on the Saguiet al-Hamra was beautiful at that moment. It came from the sky and the earth at once, a golden and copper light that shimmered in the blank sky, without burning or blinding. The young girls, drawing back a flap of the tent, combed their heavy manes of hair, picking out lice, tying up their buns and attaching their blue veils to them. The lovely light shone on their copper faces and arms.

Squatting very still in the sand, Nour was also watching the light filling the sky over the campsites. Flights of partridges passed slowly through the air, making their way up the red valley. Where were they going? Maybe they would go all the way up to the head of the Saguiet, all the way to the narrow valleys of red earth between the Agmar Mountains. Then when the sun went down, they'd come back toward the open valley, over the fields where human houses look like termite houses.

Perhaps they had already seen Aaiún, the town of

mud and planks where the roofs are sometimes made of
red metal; perhaps they had even seen the emerald and
bronze-colored sea, the free and open sea?

Travelers began arriving in the Saguiet al-Hamra,
caravans of people and animals coming down the dunes
raising clouds of red dust. They went past the campsites
without even turning their heads, still distant and lonely
as if they were in the middle of the desert.

They walked slowly toward the water in the wells, to
soothe their bleeding mouths. The wind had begun
to blow up on the Hamada. Down in the valley it lost
momentum in the dwarf palms, the thorn bushes, the
labyrinths of drystone. Still, the world far from the
Saguiet glittered in the travelers' eyes; plains of razor-
sharp rocks, jagged mountains, crevasses, blankets of sand
glinting blindingly in the sunlight. The sky was boundless, of such a harsh blue that it burnt the face. Still farther out, men walked through the maze of dunes, in a
foreign world.

But it was their true world. The sand, the stones, the
sky, the sun, the silence, the suffering, not the metal and
cement towns with the sounds of fountains and human
voices. It was here – in the barren order of the desert –
where everything was possible, where one walked shadow-
less on the edge of his own death. The blue men moved
along the invisible trail toward Smara, freer than any
creature in the world could be. All around, as far as the
eye could see, were the shifting crests of dunes, the waves
of wide open spaces that no one could know. The bare
feet of the women and children touched the sand, leaving light prints that the wind erased immediately. In the
distance, mirages floated, suspended between the earth
and the sky, white cities, fairs, caravans of camels and
donkeys loaded with provisions, busy dreams. And the

men themselves were like mirages, born unto the desert earth in hunger, thirst, and weariness.

The routes were circular, they always led back to the point of departure, winding in smaller and smaller circles around the Saguiet al-Hamra. But it was a route that had no end, for it was longer than human life.

The people came from the east, beyond the Aadme Rieh Mountains, beyond Yetti, Tabelbala. Others came from the south, from the al-Haricha oasis, from the Abd al-Malek well. They walked westward, northward till they reached the shores of the sea, or else through the great salt mines of Teghaza. They had come back to the holy land, the valley of Saguiet al-Hamra, loaded with food and ammunition, not knowing where they would go next. They traveled by watching the paths of the stars, fleeing the sandstorms when the sky turns red and the dunes begin to move.

That is how the men and women lived, walking, finding no rest. One day they died, taken by surprise in the sharp sunlight, hit by an enemy bullet, or else consumed with fever. Women gave birth to children, simply squatting in the shade of a tent, held up by two other women, their bellies bound with wide cloth belts. From the first minute of their lives, the men belonged to the boundless open spaces, to the sand, to the thistles, the snakes, the rats, and especially to the wind, for that was their true family. The little girls with copper hair grew up, learned the endless motions of life. They had no mirror other than the fascinating stretches of gypsum plains under the pure blue sky. The boys learned to walk, talk, hunt, and fight simply to learn how to die on the sand.

* * *

13

Standing in front of the tent on the men's side, the guide remained still for a long time, watching the caravans moving toward the dunes, toward the wells. The sun shone on his brown face, his aquiline nose, his long, curly, copper-colored hair. Nour had spoken to him, but he wasn't listening. Then when the camp had calmed down, he motioned to Nour and together they walked away along the trail leading north, toward the center of the Saguiet al-Hamra. At times they encountered someone walking toward Smara, and they exchanged a few words.

"Who are you?"

"Bou Sba. And you?"

"Yuemaïa."

"Where are you from?"

"Aaïn Rag."

"I'm from the South, from Iguetti."

Then they separated without saying goodbye. Farther along, the almost invisible trail led through the rocks and straggly stands of acacia. Walking was difficult due to the sharp stones jutting up from the red earth, and Nour had a hard time following his father. The light was brighter, the desert wind blew the dust up under their feet. The valley wasn't wide there, it was a sort of gray and red crevasse that gleamed like metal in places. Stones cluttered the dry bed of the torrent, white and red stones, black flints glinting in the sun.

The guide walked with his back to the sun, bent forward, his head covered with his woolen cloak. The thorns on the bushes tore at Nour's clothing, lashed his naked legs and feet, but he paid no attention. His eyes were fixed straight ahead on the shape of his hasting father. All of a sudden, they both stopped: the white tomb had appeared between the stony hills, shining in the light from the sky. The man stood still, bowing slightly as if greeting the tomb. Then they started walking again on the stones that rolled underfoot.

Slowly, without turning his eyes away, the guide climbed up to the tomb. As they drew nearer, the domed roof seemed to rise out of the red rocks, grow skyward. The lovely pure light illuminated the tomb, inflated it in the furnace-hot air. There was no shade in that place, only the sharp stones of the hill, and beneath, the dry bed of the torrent.

They came up in front of the tomb. It was just four whitewashed walls set on a foundation of red stones. There was only one door, like the opening to an oven, obstructed by a huge red rock. Above the walls, the white dome was shaped like an eggshell and ended in a spearhead. Now Nour saw nothing but the entrance to the tomb, and the door grew larger in his eyes, becoming the door to an immense monument with walls like cliffs of chalk, with a dome as high as a mountain. Here, the desert wind and heat, the loneliness of day stopped: here, the faint trails ended, even those where lost people walk, mad people, vanquished people. Perhaps it was the center of the desert, the place where everything had begun long ago, when people had come here for the very first time. The tomb shone out on the slope of the red hill. The sunlight bounced off the tamped earth, burned down on the white dome, caused small trickles of red powder to sift down along the cracks in the walls from time to time. Nour and his father were alone next to the tomb. A heavy silence hung over the valley of the Saguiet al-Hamra.

From the round door, as he tipped the large rock away, the guide saw the powerful cold shadows and it seemed to him that he felt a sort of breath on his face.

Around the tomb was an area of red earth, tamped with the feet of visitors. That is where the guide and

Nour stopped first – to pray. Up there on top of the hill, near the tomb of the holy man, with the valley of the Saguiet al-Hamra stretching its dry streambed into the distance and the vast horizon upon which other hills, other rocks appeared against the blue sky, the silence was even more striking. It was as if the world had stopped moving and talking, had turned to stone.

From time to time, Nour could nevertheless hear the cracking of the mud walls, the buzzing of an insect, the wailing of the wind.

"I have come," said the man kneeling on the tamped earth. "Help me, spirit of my grandfather. I have crossed the desert, I have come to ask for your blessing before I die. Help me, give me your blessing, for I am of your own flesh. I have come."

That is the way he spoke, and Nour listened to his father's words without understanding. He spoke, sometimes in a full voice, sometimes in a low murmuring singsong, swaying his head, constantly repeating those simple words, "I have come, I have come."

He leaned down, took up some red dust in the hollow of his hands and let it run over his face, over his forehead, his eyelids, his lips.

Then he stood up and walked to the door. In front of the opening, he knelt down and prayed again, his forehead touching the stone on the threshold. Slowly, the darkness inside of the tomb dissipated, like a night fog. The walls of the tomb were bare and white, the same as on the outside, and the low ceiling displayed its framework of branches mixed with mud.

Nour went in now too, on all fours. He felt the hard cold floor of earth mixed with sheep's blood under his hands. The guide was lying on his stomach at the back of the tomb on the mud floor. Palms on the ground, arms stretched out before him, melting in with the earth. Now he was no longer praying, no longer singing. He was breathing slowly, his mouth against the ground, listening to the blood beating in his throat and ears. It was as if something unknown were entering him, through his mouth, through his forehead, through the palms of his hands, and through his stomach, something that went very deep inside of him and changed him imperceptibly. Perhaps it was the silence that had come from the desert, from the sea of dunes, from the rock-filled mountains in the moonlight, or from the great plains of pink sand where the sunlight dances and wavers like a curtain of rain, the silence of the green waterholes, looking up at the sky like eyes, the silence of the cloudless, birdless sky where the wind runs free.

The man lying on the ground felt his limbs growing numb. Darkness filled his eyes, as it does before one drifts into sleep. Yet at the same time new strength came to him through his stomach, through his hands, creeping into each of his muscles. Everything inside of him was changing, being fulfilled. There was no more suffering, no more desire, no more revenge. He forgot all of that, as if the water of the prayer had washed his mind clean. There were no more words either, the cold darkness in the tomb made them pointless. Instead there was this strange current pulsing in the earth mixed with blood, this vibration, this warmth. There wasn't anything like it on earth. It was a direct force, without thought, that came from the depths of the earth and went out into the depths of space, as if an invisible bond united the body of the man lying there and the rest of the world.

Nour was barely breathing, watching his father in the dark tomb. His fingers were spread out on the cold earth which was pulling him through space on a dizzying course.

They remained like that for a long time, the guide

lying on the ground and Nour crouching, eyes wide, staying very still. Then when it was all over, the man rose slowly and helped his son out. He went to sit down against the wall of the tomb. He seemed exhausted, as if he had walked for hours without eating or drinking. But there was a new strength deep within him, a joyfulness that lit his eyes. Now it was as if he knew what he needed to do, as if he knew in advance the path he must follow.

He pulled the flap of his woolen cloak down over his face, and he thanked the holy man without uttering a word, simply moving his head a little and humming in his throat. His long blue hands stroked the tamped earth, closed over a handful of fine dust.

Before them, the sun followed the curve of the sky, slowly descending on the other side of the Saguiet al-Hamra. The shadows of the hills and rocks grew long in the valley bottom. But the guide didn't seem to notice. Sitting very still, his back leaning against the wall of the tomb, he had no sense of the passing day, or hunger, or thirst. He was filled with a different force, from a different time that had made him a stranger to the order of man. Perhaps he was no longer waiting for anything, no longer knew anything, and now he resembled the desert – silence, stillness, absence.

When night began to fall, Nour was frightened and he touched his father's shoulder. The man looked at him in silence, with a slight smile on his face. Together they started down the hill toward the dry torrent. Despite the gathering night, their eyes stung and the hot wind burned their faces and hands. The man staggered a little as he walked on the path, and he needed to lean on Nour's shoulder.

Down at the bottom of the valley, the water in the wells was black. Mosquitoes hung in the air, trying to get at the children's eyelids. Farther on, near the red walls of Smara, bats skimmed over the tents, circled around the braziers. When they reached the first well, Nour and his father stopped again to carefully wash each part of their bodies. Then they said the last prayer, turning toward the approaching night.

T HEN GREATER and greater numbers of them came to the valley of the Saguiet al-Hamra. They came from the south, some with their camels and horses, but most of them on foot, because the animals died of thirst and disease along the way. Every day the young boy saw new campsites around the mud ramparts of Smara. The brown woolen tents made new circles around the walls of the city. Every evening at nightfall, Nour watched the travelers arriving in clouds of dust. Never had he seen so many human beings. There was a constant commotion of men's and women's voices, of children's shrill shouts, the weeping of infants mingled with the bleating of goats and sheep, with the clattering of gear, with the grumbling of camels. A strange smell that Nour wasn't really familiar with drifted up from the sand and floated over in short wafts on the evening wind; it was a powerful smell, both acrid and sweet at the same time, the odor of human skin, of breathing, of sweat. The fires burning charcoal, bits of straw, and manure were being lit in the twilight. The smoke from the braziers rose up over the tents. Nour could hear the soft voices of women singing their babies to sleep.

Most of those who were arriving now were old people, women and children, exhausted from their forced march through the desert, clothing torn, feet bare or tied with rags. Their faces were black, burnt with the light, eyes like two pieces of coal. The young children went naked, wounds marking their legs, bellies bloated with hunger and thirst.

Nour wandered through the camp, weaving his way through the tents. He was astonished to see so many people, and at the same time he felt a sort of anxiety because, without really knowing why, he thought that many of those men, those women, those children would soon die.

He was constantly running into new travelers walking slowly down the aisles between the tents. Some of them, black like the Sudanese, came from farther south and spoke a language that Nour didn't understand. Most of the men's faces were hidden, wrapped in woolen cloaks and blue cloth; their feet were shod with sandals made of goat leather. They carried long, flintlock rifles with copper barrels, spears, daggers. Nour stepped aside to let them pass, and he watched them walk toward the gate to Smara. They were going to greet the great sheik, Moulay Ahmed ben Mohammed al-Fadel, who was called Ma al-Aïnine, Water of the Eyes.

They all went and sat down on the small benches of dried mud that circled the courtyard in front of the sheik's house. Then they went to say their prayer at sunset to the east of the well, kneeling in the sand, turning their bodies in the direction of the desert.

When night had come, Nour went back toward his father's tent and sat down beside his older brother. On the right side of the tent his mother and sisters were talking, stretched out on the carpets between the provisions and the camel's packsaddle. Little by little, Smara and the valley fell silent again; the sounds of human voices and animal cries faded out one after the other. The magnificently round white disk of the full moon appeared in the black sky. Despite all the heat of day accumulated in the sand, the night was cold. A few bats flew across the moon, dove suddenly toward the ground. Nour, lying on

21

his side with his head resting against his arm, was watching them as he was waiting to doze off. He fell abruptly to sleep, without realizing it, eyes wide open.

When he awoke he had the odd impression that time had stood still. He looked around for the disk of the moon and upon seeing that it had begun its descent to the west, he realized he had slept for a long time.

The silence hanging over the campsites was oppressive. All that could be heard was the distant howling of wild dogs somewhere out on the edge of the desert.

Nour got up and saw that his father and brother were no longer in the tent. He could only make out the vague shapes of the women and children rolled up in the carpets on the left side of the tent. Nour started walking along the sandy path between the campsites toward the ramparts of Smara. The moonlit sand was very white against the blue shadows of stones and bushes. There was not a single sound, as if all the men were asleep, but Nour knew that the men weren't in the tents. Only the children were sleeping, and the women were lying very still, rolled up in their cloaks and carpets, looking out of the tents. The night air made the young boy shiver, and the sand was cold and hard under his bare feet.

When he neared the city walls, Nour could hear the murmuring of men's voices. A little farther on, he saw the motionless shape of a guard squatting in front of the gate to the city, his long rifle propped against his knees. But Nour knew of a place where the mud rampart had collapsed, and he was able to enter Smara without going past the sentinel.

He immediately discovered the men assembled in the courtyard of the sheik's house. They were sitting in groups of five or six on the ground around braziers where large copper kettles held water for making green tea. Nour slipped silently into the gathering. No one looked at him. All the men were watching a group of warriors standing in front of the door to the house. There were a few soldiers from the desert, dressed in blue, standing absolutely still, staring at an old man dressed in a simple cloak of white wool that was pulled up over his head, and two armed young men who took turns speaking out vehemently.

From where Nour was seated, it was impossible to understand their words, due to the sounds of the men who were repeating or commenting on what had already been said. When his eyes had adjusted to the contrast of the darkness and the red glow of the braziers, Nour recognized the figure of the old man. It was the great sheik Ma al-Aïnine, the man he'd already caught a glimpse of when his father and older brother came to pay their respects after their arrival at the well in Smara.

Nour asked the man next to him who the young men beside the sheik were. He was told their names: "Saadbou and Larhdaf, the brothers of Ahmed al-Dehiba, he who is called Particle of Gold, he who will soon be our true king."

Nour didn't try to hear the words of the two young warriors. All of his attention was focused on the frail form of the old man standing motionless between them, with the moon lighting his cloak and making a very white patch.

All the men were looking at him too, as if with the same set of eyes, as if he were the one really speaking, as if he would make a single gesture and everything would suddenly be transformed, for the very order of the desert emanated from him.

Ma al-Aïnine did not move. He didn't seem to hear the words of his sons, or the endless murmur coming from the hundreds of men sitting in the courtyard before him. At times he would cock his head slightly, look out over the men and the mud walls of his city toward the dark sky, in the direction of the rocky hills.

Nour thought that perhaps he simply wanted the men to return to the desert, from where they had come, and his heart sank. He didn't understand the words of all the men around him. Above Smara the sky was unfathomable, frozen, its stars dimmed in the white haze of moonlight. And it was a bit like a sign of death, or abandonment, like a sign of the terrible absence that was hollowing out the tents that stood so still near the city walls. Nour felt this even more strongly when he looked at the fragile shape of the great sheik, it was as if he were entering into the very heart of the old man, entering his silence.

Other sheiks, chieftains of great tents, and Tuareg warriors came to join the group one after another. They all spoke the same words, their voices cracking from fatigue and from thirst. They spoke of the soldiers of the Christians who made incursions into the southern oases bringing war to the nomads; they spoke of fortified towns the Christians were building in the desert barring access to wells all the way to the seashore. They spoke of lost battles, of the men who had died, so many of them that their names could no longer be remembered, of swarms of women and children fleeing northward through the desert, of the carcasses of dead livestock strewn everywhere along the way. They spoke of caravans that were cut short when the soldiers of the Christians liberated the slaves and sent them back to the south, and how the Tuareg warriors received money from the Christians for each slave they had stolen from the convoys. They spoke of merchandise and livestock being seized, of bands of brigands that had forayed into the desert along with the Christians. They spoke also of troops of soldiers marching for the Christians, guided by the black men from the south, so numerous that they covered the sand dunes from one end of the horizon to the other. And the horsemen who encircled the camps and killed anyone who resisted them on the spot, and then took the children away to put them into Christian schools in the forts on the coast. So when the other men heard this, they said it was true, by God, and the clamor of voices swelled up and heaved in the square like the sound of a rising wind.

Nour listened to the clamoring of voices growing louder, then subsiding, like the passage of the desert wind over the dunes, and there was a knot in his throat because he knew a terrible danger was threatening the city and all the men, a danger he was unable to understand.

Now, almost without blinking, he was watching the white shape of the old man standing very still between his sons in spite of the weariness and the cold night air. Nour thought that he alone, Ma al-Aïnine, could change the course of this night, calm the anger of the crowd with a wave of his hand or, on the contrary, unleash it with just a few words that would be passed from mouth to mouth and make the wave of rage and bitterness seethe. Like Nour, all the men were looking at him, eyes bright with fatigue and fever, minds tense with suffering. They could all feel their skin, leathered from the burning sun, their lips, blistered from the desert wind. They waited, almost without moving, eyes fixed, searching for a sign. But Ma al-Aïnine didn't seem to notice them. In his eyes there was a steady remote look as he gazed out over the men's heads, out beyond the dried mud walls of Smara. Maybe he was looking for the answer to the men's anxiety in the depths of the nocturnal sky, in the strange blur of light swimming around the disk of the moon. Nour looked up at the place where he could usually see the seven stars of the Little Dipper, but he saw nothing. Only the planet Jupiter was visible, frozen in the

25

icy sky. The haze of moonlight had covered everything. Nour loved the stars, for his father had taught him their names ever since he was a baby; but on this night, it was as if he couldn't recognize the sky. Everything was immense and cold, engulfed in the white light of the moon, blinded. Down on earth, the fires in the braziers made red holes that lit up the men's faces oddly. Maybe it was fear that had changed everything, that had emaciated the faces and hands and filled the empty eye sockets with inky shadows; it was night that had frozen the light in the men's eyes, that had dug out the immense hole in the depths of the sky.

When all the men had finished speaking, each standing up beside Sheik Ma al-Aïnine in turn – all the men whose names Nour had heard his father utter in the past, chieftains of warrior tribes, the men of the legend, the Maqil, the Arib, Oulad Yahia, Oulad Delim, Aroussiyine, Icherguiguine, the Reguibat whose faces were veiled in black, and those who spoke the Chleuh languages, the Idaou Belal, Idaou Meribat, Aït ba Amrane, and even those whose names were not familiar, come from the far side of Mauritania, from Timbuktu, those who had not wanted to sit near the braziers, but who had remained standing near the entrance to the courtyard, wrapped in their cloaks, looking at once guarded and contemptuous, those who hadn't wanted to speak – Nour observed each of them, one after the other, and he could feel a terrible emptiness hollowing out their faces, as if they would soon die.

Ma al-Aïnine didn't see them. He hadn't looked at anyone, except maybe once when his eyes had fallen briefly on Nour's face, as if he were surprised to see him amidst so many men. Since that barely perceptible moment – quick as a flash in a mirror, even though Nour's heart had begun beating faster and harder – Nour had been waiting for the sign that the old sheik was to give to the men grouped together before him. The old man stood still, as if he were thinking about something else, while his two sons, leaning toward him, spoke in hushed tones. At last he took out his ebony beads and squatted down very slowly in the dust, head bowed. Then he began to recite the prayer he had written for himself, while his sons sat down on either side of him. Soon afterward, as if that simple act had sufficed, the muttering of voices ceased and silence fell over the square, a cold and heavy silence in the overly white light of the full moon. Distant, barely perceptible sounds from the desert, from the wind, from the dry stones on the plateaus began to fill up the space again. Without saying goodbye, without a word, without making a sound, the men stood up, one after another, and left the square. They walked along the dusty path, one by one, because they didn't feel like talking to one another anymore. When his father touched his shoulder, Nour got up and also walked away. Before leaving the square, he turned back to look at the strange, frail figure of the old man, all alone now in the moonlight, chanting his prayer with the top part of his body rocking back and forth like someone on horseback.

In the following days anxiety began to mount again in the Smara camp. It was incomprehensible, but everyone could feel it, like a pain in the heart, like a threat. The sun burned down hard during the day, bouncing its brutal light off the edges of rocks and the dried beds of torrents. The foothills of the rocky Hamada shimmered in the distance, and there were always mirages over the Saguiet Valley. New bands of nomads arrived each hour of the day, haggard with weariness and thirst, coming in forced marches from the south, and their silhouettes melted into the horizon along with the scintillating mirages. They walked slowly, feet bandaged with strips of goatskin, carrying their meager loads on their backs. Sometimes they were followed by half-starved camels and limping horses, goats, sheep. They set up their tents hastily on the edge of the camp. No one went to greet them or ask them where they came from. Some bore the marks of wounds from battles they had fought against the soldiers of the Christians or the looters in the desert; most were on the verge of collapse, spent from fevers and stomach ailments. Sometimes all that was left of an army arrived, decimated, bereft of a leader, womanless, black-skinned men, almost naked in their ragged garments, their glassy eyes bright with fever and folly. They went to drink at the spring in front of the gate to Smara, then they lay down on the ground in the shade of the city walls, as if to sleep, but their eyes remained wide open.

Since the night of the tribal assembly, Nour hadn't seen Ma al-Aïnine or his sons again. But he distinctly felt that the great clamor of discontent that had been assuaged when the sheik had begun his prayer had not really stopped. It was no longer a matter of words, now. His father, his older brother, his mother said nothing, and they turned their heads away as if they didn't want to be asked any questions. But the anxiety was still mounting, in the sounds of the camp, in the bleating of the livestock that were growing impatient, in the sound of the footsteps of newcomers arriving from the south, in the harsh words that men spit out at one another or at their children. Anxiety was also present in the sharp odors of sweat, of urine, of hunger – so much acridity seeping up from the ground and from the hidden recesses of the camp. It mounted as food became scarcer, a few pepper dates, sour milk, and oatmeal to be swallowed hastily at the crack of dawn, when the sun had not yet risen from the dunes. Anxiety was in the murky water of the well that the tramping of humans and beasts had disturbed and that green tea could not improve. Sugar had been rare for a long time, and honey too, and the dates were as dry as rocks, and the tough pungent meat came from camels that had died of exhaustion. Anxiety was rising in the dry mouths and bloody fingers, in the weight that bore down on the heads and shoulders of the men, in the heat of day, and then in the cold of night, making children shiver in the folds of worn carpets.

Each day as he walked past the campsites, Nour heard the sound of women crying because someone had died in the night. Each day people edged a little further into despair and anger, and Nour felt his throat growing tighter. He thought of the sheik's distant gaze drifting out over the invisible hills in the night, then coming to rest on him for a brief moment, like a flash in a mirror that lit him up inside.

All of them had come to Smara from so far away, as if it would be the end of their journey. As if nothing else could be lacking. They had come because there was a lack of land under their feet, as if it had crumbled away behind them, and now it was no longer possible to turn back. And now they were here, hundreds, thousands of them, on land that could not provide for them, land without water, without trees, without food. Their eyes endlessly scoured every point in the circle of the horizon, the jagged mountains to the south, the desert to the east, the dry streambeds of the Saguiet, the high plateaus to the north. Their eyes were also lost in the empty cloudless sky, in which the blaze of the sun was blinding. Then anxiety turned to fear, and fear to anger, and Nour felt a strange ripple pass over the camp, an odor perhaps that rose from the tent tops and circled around the city of Smara. It was also a light-headed feeling, the dizzy feeling of emptiness and hunger that transformed the shapes and colors of the earth, that changed the blue of the sky, that generated great lakes of fresh water in the scorching bottoms of the salinas, that brought the sky to life with clouds of birds and flies.

Nour would go and sit in the shade of the mud wall when the sun was going down and watch the spot where Ma al-Aïnine had appeared that night in the square, the invisible spot where he had squatted down to pray. Sometimes other men would come, as he did, and stand motionless at the entrance to the square to see the wall of red earth with narrow windows. They said nothing, they just looked. Then they went back to their campsites.

Then, after all those days of anger and fear on the earth and in the sky, after all those freezing nights in which one slept very little and awoke suddenly for no particular reason, eyes feverish, body soaked with rank sweat, after all that time, the long days that slowly killed off elderly people and infants, suddenly, without anyone knowing why, the people knew that the time to depart had come.

Nour heard about it even before his mother mentioned anything, even before his brother laughed and said, as if everything had changed, "We're leaving tomorrow, or day after tomorrow – now listen, we'll be heading north, that's what Sheik Ma al-Aïnine said, we're going far away from here!" Maybe the news had come in the air, or in the dust, or else maybe Nour had heard it as he was gazing at the tamped earth in the square in Smara.

It spread through the whole camp very quickly, and the air was ringing as if with music. The voices of men, the shouts of children, the sound of copper clanging, camels grumbling, horses farting and pawing the ground, and it was like the sound rain makes as it approaches, sweeping down the valley and sending the red waters of the torrents rolling along with it. Men and women went running down the alleyways, horses stamped, tethered camels bit at their leads, for there was a great deal of impatience. Despite the burn of the sky, women remained standing in front of their tents, talking and shouting. No one could have explained how the news had first come, but everyone kept repeating the words that elated them, "We're leaving, we're going north."

Nour's father's eyes shone with a feverish kind of joy.

"We're leaving soon, our sheik has spoken, we're leaving soon."

"Where?" Nour had asked.

"North, across the Drâa Mountains, around the Souss, Tiznit. Up there, there is water and land for all of us, just waiting for us. Moulay Hiba, our true king, the son of Ma al-Aïnine said so, and so did Ahmed al-Shems."

Groups of men walked down the alleys toward the city of Smara, and Nour was caught up in their wake. Red dust rose under the men's feet and under the shuffling hooves of the livestock, it formed a cloud over the camp. Already the first rifle shots could be heard and the acrid smell of gunpowder drove out the odor of fear that had prevailed in the camp. Nour moved forward blindly, pushed along by the men, bumped against the sides of the tents. The dust made his throat dry and burned his eyes. The heat of the sun was unbearable, shooting white flashes through the thick dust. Nour walked on like that for a short time, blindly, arms outstretched. Then he stumbled to the ground and crawled into a tent for shelter. In the half-light, he was able to regain his bearings. An old woman was there, sitting against the lower part of the tent, wrapped in her blue cloak. When she first saw Nour she took him for a thief and screamed curses at him and threw stones at his face. Then she drew nearer and saw that his cheeks were smudged with dust in which tears had left red streaks.

"What's wrong? Are you sick?" she asked more gently.

Nour shook his head. The old woman crawled over to him on her hands and knees.

"You must be sick," she said. "I'll get you some tea."

She poured the tea into a copper goblet.

"Drink this."

The unsweetened, scalding tea made Nour feel better.

"We're going to leave here soon," Nour said in a slightly hesitant voice.

The woman looked at him. She shrugged her shoulders.

"Yes, that's what they say."

"This is a very memorable day for us," said Nour.

But the old woman didn't seem to think it was all that important, maybe simply because she was old.

"You might reach the place they speak of, up there in the north. But I will die before."

She repeated this: "I will die before reaching the north."

Later, Nour left the tent. The alleyways of the camp were deserted once again, as if all the inhabitants were gone. But in the shadows of the tents, Nour could make out human shapes: old people, sick people who were shivering with fever in spite of the sweltering heat, young women holding babies in their arms and staring out with blank, sad eyes. Once again Nour felt his throat tighten because the shadow of death was under those tents.

As he was nearing the wall of the city, he heard the sound of music growing louder. Men and women were gathered together in front of the gate to Smara, forming a large semicircle around the musicians. Nour heard the shrill sound of flutes rising, falling, rising again, then stopping, while the drums and rebecs repeated the same phrase incessantly. A man's deep monotone voice was intoning an Andalusian song, but Nour didn't recognize the lyrics. Above the red city, the sky was smooth, very blue, very hard. The travelers' celebration was going to begin now; it would last through to the next day at dawn and maybe even the day after. Flags would float on the wind, and horsemen would ride around the ramparts shooting off their long rifles while young women would cry out, making their voices tremor like bells.

Nour felt light-headed from the music and dancing, and he forgot the deathly shadow lingering under the tents. It was as if he were already making his way toward the tall cliffs in the north, out where the plateaus begin, out where the torrents of clear water are born, water no one had ever set eyes on. And yet the anxiety that had taken root when he had seen the troops of nomads arriving still remained somewhere deep within.

He wanted to see Ma al-Aïnine. He skirted the crowd, trying to get a glimpse of him over by the men who were singing. But the sheik wasn't with the crowd. So then Nour went back toward the gate of the ramparts. He entered the city through the same break in the wall he had used on the night of the Assembly. The large square of tamped earth was completely empty. The walls of the sheik's house shone in the sunlight. Around the door of the house, strange marks had been painted with clay on the white wall. Nour stood there looking at them and at the wind-worn walls for a long time. Then he walked toward the center of the square. The earth was burning and hard under his bare feet, like the slabs of stone in the desert. The sound of the flute music wasn't audible here in this deserted square, as if Nour were at the other end of the world. Everything became immense as the young boy walked toward the center of the square. He could distinctly feel the pulsing of blood in his temples and in the arteries of his neck, and the beating of his

33

heart seemed to thud down into the ground beneath the soles of his feet.

When Nour drew near to the clay wall and the place where the old man had squatted to say his prayer, he threw himself face down on the ground and remained immobile, not thinking of anything. His hands clutched at the earth as if he were hanging from the wall of a very high cliff, and the ashen taste of dust filled his mouth and nose.

After a long time, he was bold enough to lift his face, and he saw the white cloak of the sheik.

"What are you doing here?" asked Ma al-Aïnine. His voice was very gentle and distant, as if he were at the other end of the square.

Nour hesitated. He pulled himself up to his knees, but his head remained bowed because he didn't dare look at the sheik.

"What are you doing here?" asked the sheik again.

"I – I was praying," said Nour, and added, "I wanted to pray."

The sheik smiled.

"And you weren't able to pray?"

"No," Nour said simply. He took hold of the old man's hands.

"Please, give me your holy blessing."

Ma al-Aïnine ran his hands over Nour's head, rubbed the back of his neck gently. Then he brought the young boy to his feet and he embraced him.

"What is your name?" he asked. "You are the one I saw the night of the Assembly, aren't you?"

Nour said his name, his father's and his mother's names. When Ma al-Aïnine heard this last name, his face lit up.

"So, your mother is a descendant of Sidi Mohammed, he whom we called al-Azraq, the Blue Man?"

"He was my grandmother's maternal uncle," said Nour.

"Then you are truly the son of a sharifa," said Ma al-Aïnine. He remained silent for a long time, his gray eyes staring at Nour as if he were trying to remember something. Then he spoke of the Blue Man, whom he had met in the oases in the south on the other side of the rocks of the Hamada, back in the days when nothing here, not even the city of Smara, existed yet. The Blue Man lived in a hut of stones and branches on the edge of the desert, having nothing to fear from man or wild beast. Every morning, he found a plate of dates and a bowl of sour milk as well as a jug of fresh water in front of the door to his hut, for God watched over and provided for him. When Ma al-Aïnine came to ask to receive his teachings, the Blue Man refused to take him in. He made him sleep in front of the door, never meeting his eyes or saying a word to him for one whole month. He would simply leave him half of the dates and milk, and Ma al-Aïnine had never tasted more succulent food; as for the water in the jug, it quenched his thirst instantly and filled him with joy, for it was undefiled water that came from the purest dew drops.

After a month, however, the sheik was very sad, for al-Azraq had still not looked at him. So he decided to go back home to his family because he thought that the Blue Man did not deem him worthy of serving God. He was walking despondently down the path that led to his village when he saw a man waiting for him. It was al-Azraq who asked him why he had left. Then the Blue Man invited Ma al-Aïnine to stay with him in the very spot he had stopped. He remained at al-Azraq's side for many months, and one day the Blue Man said he had nothing more to teach him. "But you haven't yet bestowed your teachings upon me," said Ma al-Aïnine.

35

Then al-Azraq pointed to the plate of dates, the bowl of milk, and the jug of water: "Haven't I shared this with you, every day since your arrival?" After that he pointed to the horizon in the north, over by the Saguiet al-Hamra, and he told him to build a holy city for his sons, and he even predicted that one of them would become king. So Ma al-Aïnine had left his village with his family, and he had built the city of Smara.

When the sheik had finished telling his story, he embraced Nour once again and returned to the cool shade of his home.

The next day as the sun was going down, Ma al-Aïnine came out of his house to say the last prayer. The men and women in the camp had hardly slept, for they hadn't stopped chanting and stamping their feet. But the great journey across the desert had already begun, and the feeling of abandonment inspired by the march along the trail of sand had already entered their bodies, its scorched breath was already filling them, making mirages shimmer before their eyes. No one had forgotten the suffering, the thirst, the relentless burning of the sun on the infinite stones and sand, or the ever-receding horizon. No one had forgotten the gnawing hunger, not only hunger for food, but all sorts of hunger. Hunger for hope and for freedom, hunger for everything that is missing and that digs out a dizzy hollow in the ground, hunger that pushes a man forward into the cloud of dust amongst the dazed animals, hunger that makes him climb all the way up hillsides until he must start back down again, with hundreds of other identical hills stretching out before him.

Again, Ma al-Aïnine was squatting on the tamped earth in the middle of the square in front of the white-washed houses. But this time the tribal chieftains were sitting by his side. He had placed Nour and his father very near to him, while Nour's older brother and mother remained in the crowd. The men and women of the camp had gathered in a semicircle, some of them squatting, wrapped in their woolen cloaks to stave off the chill of night, others standing or walking around the walls. The musicians plucked the chords of their guitars and struck the skins of small earthen drums with their index fingers, making a sad music echo through the square.

The desert wind was now blowing intermittently, pelting the people's faces with grains of sand that stung their skin. Above the square, the sky was dark blue, almost black already. The city of Smara was surrounded on all sides with absolute silence, the silence of the stony red hills, the silence of the deep blue night. It was as if there had never been any other humans but these, prisoners in their minuscule crater of dried mud, clinging to the red earth around their puddle of gray water. Out beyond was stone and wind, waves of dunes, salt, and then the ocean, or the desert.

When Ma al-Aïnine began reciting his *dzikr*, his voice rang out oddly in the silence of the square, like the distant bleating of a goat. He chanted in almost a whisper, rocking the top of his body back and forth, but the silence that was in the square, in the city, and lying over the entire valley of the Saguiet al-Hamra had its source in the barren desert wind, and the voice of the old man was as clear and steady as that of a living animal.

Nour shuddered as he listened to the long appeal. Every man and every woman in the square stood motionless, as if their eyes were turned inwards.

Already, above the broken rocks of the Hamada in the west, the sun had made a large red stain. Inordinately long shadows had crept out over the ground, then had all run together like rising floodwaters.

"Praise be to God, the living God, the undying God, praise be to God who has no father and no son, who stands alone, who is one and of himself, praise be to God who guides us, for the Messengers of God came to bring truth..."

The voice of Ma al-Aïnine wavered at the end of each invocation, breathless, frail as a flame, and yet with each long syllable distinct and pure, shattering the silence.

"Glory be to God who is the one and only provider, the one and only lord, he who knows, who sees, he who understands and commands, glory be to him, giver of good and evil, for his will is the only desire, for his word is the only safe haven from the evil that men commit, from death, from illness, from sorrow created along with the world..."

Night was gathering slowly, first on the earth and in the hollows of sand, around the foot of the mud walls in front of the motionless men, in the holes where dogs slept, under the roofs of the tents, in the murky depths of the well water.

"It is the name of the protector, the name of he who comes to me and gives me strength, for his name is the highest, his name is such that I have nothing to fear from my enemies, and I repeat his name within myself as I go into combat, for his name is the name that reigns on earth and in heaven..."

Up in the sky the sunlight was fleeing westward as the cold rose from the depths of the earth, seeped up through the hard sand and into the legs of the men.

"Glory be to God, the infinite, there is no strength or power but in God the most high, God the infinite, God the most high, God the infinite, he who is neither from the earth nor the heavens, he who lives beyond my sight, beyond my knowledge, he who knows me but whom I cannot know, God the most high, God the infinite..."

The voice of Ma al-Aïnine resounded far into the desert, as if it were reaching the outer edges of the desolate land, far beyond the dunes and the rifts, beyond the barren plateaus and the desiccate valleys, as if it had already carried out as far as the new lands on the other side of the Drâa Mountains, to the fields of wheat and millet where the people would at last find their nourishment.

"God the almighty, God the most perfect, for there is no other divinity but God, the wise gifted with power, the most high gifted with benevolence, the friend gifted with knowledge, the ever-providing, the only generous one, the forbearing who commands the armies of the heavens and the earth, the most perfect, the loving one. . ."

Yet the feeble, distant voice touched every man, every woman as if on the inside of their bodies, and it was also as if it were coming from their own throats, as if it were mingling with their thoughts and their words to make its music.

"Glory, praise be to the ever-living, glory, praise be to the one who does not perish, to the one whose existence is supreme, for it is he who hears and knows. . ."

The air entered Ma al-Aïnine's chest, then he breathed out forcefully almost without moving his lips, eyes closed, the top part of his body swaying like the trunk of a tree.

"Our God the lord, our God the highest good, our God the light of light, the night sun, the dark of dark, our God the sole truth, the sole word, glory and praise be to the one who holds battle in our battle, glory and praise be to the one whose name overthrows our enemies, the lord of God's land. . ."

Then, without even realizing it, the men and the women began reciting the words of the *dzikr*; their voice rose each time the voice of the old man came to a trembling halt.

"He is great, the all powerful, the most perfect, he who is our lord and our God, he whose name is written in our flesh, he the revered, the most holy, the manifest, he who knows no master, he who said: I was a hidden treasure, I wished to be found, and to that end, I created the living creatures. . .

"He is great, he knows no equal nor rival, he who preceded all existence, he who created existence, he who is everlasting, who owns all, who sees, who hears, and who knows, he who is perfect, he who is without equal. . .

"He is great, he is magnificent in the hearts of the faithful, he is pure in the hearts of those who recognize him, he is without equal in the souls of those who have reached him, he is our lord, the highest of all lords. . .

"He knows no equal nor rival, he is the one who dwells at the pinnacle of the highest mountain, the one who is in the desert sands, who is in the ocean, in the sky, in the water, the one who is the path, who is the night and the stars. . ."

Then without even realizing it, the musicians began to play, and their airy music spoke with the voice of Ma al-Aïnine, murmuring with the faint, sharp notes of the mandolins, with the fluttering beat of the small drums, then suddenly bursting forth like the cry of birds to accompany the pure melody of the reed flutes.

The voice of the old man and the pipe music were now answering each other, as if they were saying the same thing, over and above the voices of the men and the sound of feet thudding on the hardened earth.

"He knows no equal nor rival, for he is the all power-ful, he who was not created, the light which gave life to candles, the fire which lit other fires, the first sun, the first star in the night, he who is born before all births, he who brings life and death to all earthly things, he who fashions and breaks down the forms of creatures. . ."

Then the crowd was dancing and shouting, making a rending sound – "Houwa! Him!" – and shaking their heads and turning their uplifted palms toward the dark sky.

"He who brought the truth to all the saints, who blessed the Lord Mohammed, he who gave the power and the word to our Lord the Prophet, God's messenger on earth. . ."

"Ah! Him!"

"Glory be to God, praise be to God, the infinite, the most perfect, the heart of the secret, the one who is written in the heart, the all high, the infinite. . ."

"Houwa! Him!"

"Glory be to God for we are his creatures, we are poor, we are ignorant, we are blind, deaf, we are imperfect. . ."

"Ah! Houwa!"

"O he who knows, give us the truth! O you, the gentle, the loving one, the patient, the generous, you who needed no one in order to exist!"

"Ah! Him!"

"Glory be to God who is the king, the holy one, the powerful, the victorious, the magnificent, who exists before all life, the divine, the infinite, the one, victorious over all enemies, the one who knows, who sees, who hears, the divine, the wise, the infinite, the witness, the creator, the only one, the infinite, all-seeing, all-hearing, the magnificent, the generous, the strong, the most perfect, the most high, the infinite. . ."

Ma al-Aïnine's voice was shouting. Then it suddenly stopped, like a cricket singing in the night. Then the rumor of voices and drums stopped too, the guitar and flute music ceased, and again there was nothing but the long awful silence, tightening around the temples, making the heart beat faster. Eyes filled with tears, Nour

41

looked at the old man bowing toward the earth with his hands over his face, and deep inside, quick as a stab, he felt the uncharted threshold of anguish. Then Larhdaf, Ma al-Aïnine's third son, began to sing also. His strong voice rang out in the square, no longer with the pure clarity of Ma al-Aïnine's, but like a sound of anger, and the musicians immediately began playing again.

"O God, our God! Welcome the witnesses of faith and truth, the companions of Moulay bou Azza, of Bekkaïa, the companions of the Goudfia, listen to the words of remembrance as our lord Sheik Ma al-Aïnine has dictated them to us!"

The muttering of the crowd suddenly changed to shouts: "Glory be to our sheik, Ma al-Aïnine, glory be to the messenger of God!"

"Glory be to Ma al-Aïnine! Glory be to the companions of the Goudfia!"

"O God, listen to the remembrance of his son, Sheik Ahmed, he who is called al-Shems, the Sun, listen to the remembrance of his son Ahmed al-Dehiba, he who is called Particle of Gold, Moulay Hiba, our true king!"

"Glory be to them! Glory be to Moulay Hiba, our king!"

Now the feeling of exhilaration had once again taken hold of the crowd, and the hoarse voice of the young man seemed to awaken their anger and dispel their fatigue.

"O God, our God, may you be pleased with your companions and your followers! The men of glory and greatness, may God be pleased with them! The men of love and truth, may God be pleased with them! The men of faith and purity, may God be pleased with them! The lords, the nobles, the warriors, may God be pleased with them! The saints, the blessed, the servants of the poor, the homeless, the suffering, may God be pleased with them! May God grant us his great blessing!"

42

The din of the crowd rose, and the names being called out were echoing off the walls of the houses, were being indelibly inscribed in memory, in the cold bare earth and in the star-filled sky.

"May the great blessing of the Lord, Messenger of God, be bestowed upon us, O God, and that of the Messenger Ilias, the blessing of al-Khadir, who drank at the very source of life, O God, and the blessing of Ouways Qarni, O God, and that of the Great Abd al-Qâdir al-Jilani, the saint of Baghdad, the Messenger of God on earth, O God..."

The names burst forth in the silence of the night, over the music that murmured and swayed as imperceptibly as a soft breath. "All of the people of the earth, and the people of the sea, O God, the people of the North, the people of the South, O God, the people of the East, the people of the West, O God, the people of the sky, the people of the earth, O God..."

The words of remembrance were more and more beautiful, words that came from the farthest corners of the desert and had at last found their way back into the hearts of each man, each woman, like an old dream starting over again.

"Bestow upon us, O God, the great blessing of the lords Abou Yaza, Yalannour, Abou Madian, Maarouf, al-Jounaïd, al-Hallaj, al-Chibli, the great holy lords of the city of Baghdad..."

The light of the moon appeared slowly above the rocky hills to the east of the Saguiet, and Nour watched it, swaying his body, keeping his eyes rooted deep in the black sky. In the center of the square, Sheik Ma al-Aïnine was still bowed forward, very white, almost ghostlike. Only his thin fingers were moving, flicking his ebony beads.

"Bestow upon us, O God, the blessing of the lords,

al-Halwi, he who danced for the children, Ibn Haouari, Tsaouri, Younous ibn Obaïd, Basri, Abou Yazrd, Mohammed al-Saghir al-Souhaïli whose teachings revealed the words of the great God, Abdesselaam, Ghazâli, Abou Chouhaïb, Abou Mahdi, Malik, Abou Mohammed Abdelazziz al-Thobba, the saint of the city of Marrakech, O God!"

The names were the exaltation of remembrance itself, as if they were the eyes of the constellations, and from their far-away gaze, great strength descended, there, upon the freezing square where the people were gathered.

"God, O God, bestow upon us the blessing of all the lords, the companions, the followers, the army of your victory, Abou Ibrahim Tounsi, Sidi bel Abbas Sebti, Sidi Ahmed al-Haritsi, Sidi Jakir, Abou Zakri Yahia al-Nawâni, Sidi Mohammed ben Issa, Sidi Ahmed al-Rifaï, Mohammed bel Sliman al-Jazoûli, the great lord, God's messenger on this earth, the saint of the city of Marrakech, O God!"

The names came and went from mouth to mouth, the names of stars, the names of grains of sand in the desert wind, the names of the endless days and nights, beyond death.

"God, O God, bestow upon us the blessing of all the lords of the earth, those who have known the secret, those who have known life and forgiveness, the true lords of the earth, the sea, and the sky, Sidi Abderrhaman, he who was known as Sahabi, the prophet's companion, Sidi Abdelqâdir, Sidi Embarek, Sidi Belkheir who drew milk from a he-goat, Lalla Mansoura, Lalla Fatima, Sidi Ahmed al-Haroussi, who repaired a broken jug, Sidi Mohammed, he who was known as al-Azraq, the Blue Man, who showed the great Sheik Ma al-Aïnine the path, Sidi Mohammed al-Sheikh al-Kaamel, the perfect one, and all the lords of the earth, the sea, and the sky. . ."

Silence fell once again, filled with ecstasy and glimmers

of light. From time to time the pipe music would start up again, slip along, then cease. The men and women stood up and walked toward the gates of the city. Left alone, Ma al-Aïnine did not move, bowing over the earth, staring at the same invisible spot on the ground lit with white moonlight.

When the dance began, Nour stood up and joined the crowd. The men were stamping the hard ground under their bare feet, without moving forward or backward, closed into a tight crescent that reached across the square. God's name was exhaled forcefully, as if all the men were suffering and wrenching their insides at the same time. The earthen drum punctuated each cry – "Houwa! Him!" – and the women cried out and made their voices quaver.

It was music that seeped into the cold earth, that rose into the deepest reaches of the dark sky, that mingled with the halo of the moon. There was no more time then, no more suffering. The men and women were striking the ground with the tips of their toes and with their heels, repeating the invincible cry:

"Houwa! Him! . . . Hayy! . . . Living!"

Their heads turned to the right, to the left, right, left, and the music inside their bodies came up through their throats and leapt out to the farthest reaches of the horizon. The hoarse, jerky breaths carried them along on the night as if in flight, lifting them up over the immense desert, toward the light patches of dawn on the other side of the mountains, to the land of the Souss, to Tiznit, toward the plain of Fez.

"Houwa! Him! . . . God!" shouted the deep voices of the men, drunk with the dull sound of the earthen drums and the strains of reed flutes, as the squatting women rocked their torsos and slapped their heavy silver and bronze necklaces with the palms of their hands.

45

Their voices trembled at times like those of the flutes, on the very threshold of human perception, then suddenly stopped. Then the men took up their thudding again and the harsh sound of their heavy breathing echoed in the square: "Houwa! Him!... Hayy!... Living!... Houwa! Hayy! Houwa! Hayy!" Eyes half closed, head thrown backward. It was a sound that went beyond natural forces, a sound that split open reality and was soothing at the same time, the coming and going of a giant saw devouring the trunk of a tree. Each painful and deep exhalation widened the wound in the sky, the wound that tied the men to open space, that mingled their blood and their lymph. Each singer called out the name of God, faster and faster, head craned upward like that of a bellowing ox, the arteries of the neck like ropes under the strain. The light from the braziers and the white glow of the moon struck their swaying bodies as if lightning were flashing repeatedly through the clouds of dust. Breaths were panting faster and faster, letting out almost mute cries, lips unmoving, mouths half opened, and in the square, in the barren desert night, nothing could be heard now save the forgelike sound of labored breathing in the men's throats:

"Hh! Hh! Hh! Hh!"

Now there were no more words. It was like that, linked directly to the center of the sky and the earth, united by the heavy wind of the men's breath, as if, when accelerated, the rhythm of their breath abolished the days and nights, the months, the seasons, even abolished the hopelessness of space, and brought the end of all journeys, the end of all time, closer. The suffering was intense, and the drunkenness from their breathing made their limbs tingle, their throats open wider. In the center of the half-circle of men, the women danced with only their bare feet, not moving their bodies, their arms – held slightly out from their bodies – shaking almost imperceptibly. The dull beat of their heels penetrated the earth, making an unbroken rumble like that of an army passing. Near the musicians, the warriors from the south, faces veiled with black, were leaping up and down in the air raising their knees up very high, like great birds attempting to take flight. Then, little by little, as night went on, they stopped moving. One after the other the men and the women squatted down on the ground, arms outstretched before them, palms turned skyward; only their hoarse whispers echoed in the silence, endlessly repeating the same syllables:

"Hh! Hh! Houwa! Hayy! . . . Hh! Hh!"

The wrenching sound of breathing was so great, so powerful that it was as if they had all already traveled very far from Smara, through the sky, on the wind, mingling with the moonlight and the fine desert dust. There was no such thing as silence, or solitude. The sound of breathing had filled the entire night, covered all of space.

Sitting in the dust in the center of the square, Ma al-Aïnine wasn't looking at anyone. His hands were holding the beads of the ebony chaplet, letting one bead fall at each exhalation of the crowd. He was the center of the breathing, he who had shown the people the path in the desert, he who had taught them each rhythm. He expected nothing more now. He had no more questions for anyone now. He too was breathing, along with the rhythm of the prayer, as if he and the other men had but one throat, one chest. And their breathing had already cleared the way leading north, to new lands. The old man no longer felt his age, or weariness, or anxiety. Breath passed through him, coming from all of those mouths, the breath that was both harsh and sweet, that increased

47

his life. The men were no longer looking at Ma al-Aïnine. Eyes closed, arms outstretched, faces turned toward the night, they were soaring, gliding along the path to the north.

When day broke in the east, above the rocky hills, the men and women began to walk toward the tents. Despite all of those days and all of those nights of exaltation, no one felt tired. They saddled the horses, rolled up the large woolen tents, loaded the camels. The sun was not very high in the sky when Nour and his brother began to walk along the trail of dust, heading northward. They carried bundles of clothing and food on their shoulders. Before them, other men and other children were also walking on the trail, and the cloud of gray and red dust began to drift up into the blue sky. Somewhere near the gates of Smara, surrounded by blue-clad warriors on horseback, with his sons at his side, Ma al-Aïnine watched the long caravan stretching out across the deserted plain. Then he pulled his white cloak closed and nudged his camel's neck with his foot. Slowly, without looking back, he rode away from Smara toward his end.

HAPPINESS

THE SUN RISES over the earth, the shadows stretch over the gray sand, over the dust in the paths. The dunes stand motionless before the sea. The small succulent plants quiver in the wind. In the cold, deep blue sky there's not a bird, not a cloud. There's the sun. But the morning light wavers a little, as if it weren't quite sure.

Along the path sheltered by the line of gray dunes, Lalla walks slowly. From time to time she stops, looks at something on the ground. Or she picks a leaf from a fleshy plant, squishes it between her fingers to smell the sweet peppery odor of the sap. The plants are dark green, shiny, they look like seaweed. Sometimes a big golden bumblebee is sitting on a clump of hemlock, and Lalla runs to chase it. But she doesn't get too close because she's a little frightened all the same. When the insect flies away, she runs after it, hands outstretched, as if she really did want to catch it. But it's just for fun.

Out here, that's all there is: the light in the sky, as far as you can see. The dunes quake with the pounding sea that can't be seen but can be heard. The little succulent plants are shiny with salt, as if from sweat. There are insects here and there, a pale ladybug, a sort of wasp with such a narrow middle it looks like it is cut in two, a centipede that leaves tiny marks in the dust, and louse flies, the color of metal, that try to land on the little girl's legs and face to eat the salt.

Lalla knows all the paths, all the dips in the dunes. She could go anywhere with her eyes closed and she'd know where she was right away, just from feeling the ground with her bare feet. At times the wind leaps over the barrier of dunes, throwing handfuls of needles at the child's skin, tangling her black hair. Lalla's

51

dress clings to her moist skin, she has to pull at the cloth to make it come loose.

Lalla knows all the paths, the ones that follow the gray dunes through the scrub as far as the eye can see, the ones that curve around and double back, the ones that never go anywhere. Yet every time she walks out here, there is something new. Today it was the golden bumblebee that led her so far away, out beyond the fishermen's houses and the lagoon of stagnant water. A little later, in the brush, that sudden carcass of rusted metal with its threatening claws and horns uplifted. Then, in the sand on the path, a small tin can with no label and with two holes on either side of the lid.

Lalla keeps walking, very slowly, searching the gray sand so intently that her eyes are a little sore. She looks for things on the ground, without thinking of anything else, without looking up at the sky. Then she stops under a parasol pine, sheltered from the light, and she closes her eyes for a minute.

She clasps her hands around her knees, rocks slightly back and forth, then from side to side, singing a song in French, a song that says only, "*Méditerra-né-é-e. . .*"

Lalla doesn't know what it means. It's a song she heard on the radio one day, and she only remembers that one word, but it's a word that pleases her. So every now and again, when she's feeling good, when she doesn't have anything else to do, or when on the contrary, she's a bit sad without really knowing why, she sings the word, sometimes in a whisper just for herself, so faintly that she hardly hears herself, or sometimes very loudly, almost at the top of her lungs, to make echoes and drive the fear away.

Now she's singing the word in a whisper, because she's happy. The large red ants with black heads walk over the pine needles, hesitate, scale up twigs. Lalla nudges them away with a dead branch. The smell of the trees drifts over on the wind mixed with the acrid taste of the sea. Sometimes there are spurts of sand that shoot up into the sky, forming wobbly spouts that balance on the crest of the dunes and then suddenly break, sending thousands of sharp needles into the child's legs and face.

Lalla remains in the shade of the tall pine until the sun is high in the sky. Then she goes leisurely back toward town. She recognizes her own footprints in the sand. They seem smaller and narrower than her feet, but, turning around, Lalla checks to make sure they are really hers. She shrugs her shoulders and starts to run. The thorns on the thistles prick her toes. Sometimes after limping a few steps she has to stop to pick the thorns from her big toe.

There are always ants, wherever you stop. They seem to come out from between the stones and scurry over the gray sand burning with light, as if they were spies. But Lalla is quite fond of them anyway. She also likes the slow centipedes, the golden-brown June bugs, the dung beetles, stag beetles, potato beetles, ladybugs, the crickets – like bits of burnt wood. The large praying mantises scare her, and Lalla waits for them to go away, or else she makes a detour without taking her eyes from them while they pivot, brandishing their pincers.

There are even gray and green lizards. They skitter off toward the dunes, thrashing their tails widely to help them run faster. Sometimes Lalla succeeds in catching one, and she plays at holding it by the tail until it comes loose. She watches the piece of tail twisting around by itself in the dust. One day a boy told her that if you waited long enough, you'd see the legs and head grow back onto the lizard tail, but Lalla doesn't really believe that.

Mostly there are flies. Lalla likes them too, despite their noise and their bites. She doesn't really know why she likes them, but she just does. Maybe it's because of their delicate legs, their transparent wings, or maybe because they know how to fly fast, forwards, backwards, in zigzags, and Lalla thinks it must be great to know how to fly like that.

She lies down on her back in the sand on the dunes, and the louse flies land on her face, her hands, her bare legs, one after another. They don't all come at once because in the beginning they're a little afraid of Lalla. But they like to come and eat the salty sweat on her skin, and they soon grow bold. When they walk on her with their light legs, Lalla starts laughing, but not too loudly, so as not to scare them off. Sometimes a louse fly bites Lalla's cheek and a little angry cry breaks from her lips.

Lalla plays with the flies for a long time. These are louse flies that live in the kelp on the beach. But there are also black flies in the Project houses, on the oilcloths, on the cardboard walls, on the windows. The buildings in Les Glacières have big blue flies that fly over the garbage bins making a noise like bomber planes.

Suddenly Lalla stands up. She runs as fast as she can toward the dunes. She climbs up the slope of sand that slips down and shifts under her bare feet. The thistles prick her toes, but she ignores them. She wants to get to the top of the dunes to see the sea, as quickly as possible.

As soon as you're at the top of the dunes, the wind hits you hard in the face, and Lalla nearly falls over backward. The cold wind from the sea contracts her nostrils and burns her eyes, the sea is immense, blue-gray, dotted with foam, it rumbles quietly as the short waves fall on the flat expanse of sand where the vast, deep blue, almost black sky is mirrored.

Lalla is leaning forward into the wind. Her dress (in truth it is a boy's calico shirt that her aunt cut the sleeves off of) is clinging to her stomach and thighs, as if she'd just come out of the water. The sound of the wind and the sea is screaming in her ears, first the left, then the right, mixed with the faint sound made by little twists of her hair snapping against her temples. Sometimes the wind picks up a handful of sand and throws it at Lalla's face. She has to shut her eyes to keep from being blinded. But the wind ends up making her eyes water anyway, and there are grains of sand in her mouth that grit between her teeth.

So when she is good and giddy from the wind and the sea, Lalla goes back down the rampart of dunes. She squats for a minute at the foot of the dune, just long enough to catch her breath. The wind doesn't reach the other side of the dunes. It goes over them, heads inland, till it reaches the blue hills hung with mist. The wind doesn't wait. It does what it wants, and Lalla is happy when it's there, even if it does burn her eyes and ears, even if it does throw handfuls of sand in her face. She thinks of it often, and of the sea too, when she's in the dark house in the Project, and the air is so heavy and smells so strong; she thinks of the wind that is huge, transparent, that leaps endlessly over the sea, that crosses the desert in an instant, goes all the way to the cedar forests and then dances over there at the foot of the mountains, amidst the birds and flowers. The wind doesn't wait. It crosses the mountains, sweeping away dust, sand, ashes, it knocks over boxes, sometimes it comes all the way to the town of planks and tarpaper and plays at ripping off a few roofs and walls. But it doesn't matter. Lalla thinks it's beautiful, as transparent as water, quick as lightning, and so powerful it could destroy all the cities in the world if it wanted to, even those that have tall white houses with high glass windows.

Lalla knows how to say its name, she learned it all by herself when she was little, and she used to listen to it coming through the planking of the house at night. It's called *whoooooohhh*, just like that, with a whistle.

A little farther on, in amongst the shrubs, Lalla meets back up with it. It draws the yellow grasses aside like a hand passing over them.

A hawk hovers almost motionless above the grassy plain, its copper-colored wings spread in the wind. Lalla looks at it, she admires it, because it knows how to fly in the wind. The hawk barely moves the ends of its quill feathers, slightly fans out its tail, and glides effortlessly along with its cross-shaped shadow rippling over the yellow grass. From time to time it pules, saying only, *kaiiiik! kaiiiik!* and Lalla answers it.

Then it suddenly dives toward the earth, wings drawn in, skims interminably over the grass, like a fish slipping over sea-weed swaying on the ocean floor. That's how it disappears into the distance between the tousled blades of grass. Even though Lalla calls out many times with the plaintive cry, *kaiiiik! kaiiiik!* the bird doesn't come back.

But it remains in her eyes for a long time, a shadow in the shape of an arrow skimming over the yellow grass like a stingray, soundlessly, in its tide of fear.

Lalla stands still now, her head thrown back, eyes opened on the white sky, watching the circles swimming there – cutting into one another, like when you throw stones into a water tank. There are no insects or birds or anything of the kind, and yet thousands of specks can be seen moving in the sky, as if there were ant peoples, weevil peoples, and fly peoples up there. They aren't flying in the white air; they're walking around in all directions, animated with a feverish haste, as if they didn't know how to get away. Maybe they are the faces of all the people who live in the cities, cities so big you can never get out, where there are so many cars, so many people, and where you never see the same face twice. Old Naman talks about all that and at the same time he also says strange words, Algeciras, Madrid (he says: *Madris*), Marseille, Lyon, Paris, Geneva.

Lalla doesn't always see those faces. It's only on certain days, when the wind blows and drives the clouds over toward the mountains, and when the air is very white and quivering with sunlight; that's when you can see them, the people-insects, the ones that move, walk, and run and dance way up there, barely visible, like very young gnats.

Then the sea calls to her again. Lalla runs through the scrub till she reaches the gray dunes. The dunes are like cows lying down, heads low, spines curved. Lalla likes to climb up on their backs, making a path just for herself with her hands and feet and then roll head over heels down the other side to the sandy beach. The ocean unfurls on the hard sand making a loud ripping sound, the water recedes, and the foam melts in the sun. There is so much light and so much noise here that Lalla has to shut her eyes and mouth. The sea salt burns her eyelids and lips, and the gusting wind makes her breath catch in her throat. Yet Lalla loves being by the sea. She enters the water, the waves knock against her legs and her stomach, making the blue shirt cling to her skin. She feels her feet sinking into the sand like two wooden poles. But she doesn't go any farther out, because every now and again the sea will catch children up – just like that, without paying attention – and then bring them back a couple of days later, leaving them on the hard beach, their bellies and faces swollen with water, their noses, lips, fingertips, and genitals eaten by crabs.

Lalla walks on the sand along the ruff of foam. Her dress – drenched all the way up to her chest – dries in the wind. The wind braids her jet black hair, but only on one side, and her face is the color of copper in the sunlight.

Scattered about on the sand are beached jellyfish with their tendrils spread out around them like tresses. Lalla watches the holes that form in the sand each time a wave recedes. She also runs after the tiny gray crabs, like spiders, with their pincers raised, and it gives her a good laugh. But she doesn't try to catch them like the other children do; she lets them run off into the sea, disappear in the sparkling foam.

Lalla walks a little farther down the shore, singing that same song that says only one word, "*Méditerra-né-é-e...*"

Then she goes over to sit down at the foot of the dunes facing the beach, her arms around her knees and her face hidden in the folds of the blue shirt to avoid breathing in the sand that the wind throws at her.

She always goes to sit in the same place, right where a rotten wooden pole sticks out of the water in the hollows of the waves, and a large fig tree grows in the stones amid the dunes. She waits for Naman the fisherman there.

Naman the fisherman isn't like everyone else. He's a fairly tall, thin man, with wide shoulders, a bony face, and brick-colored skin. He always walks around barefoot, wearing blue cotton pants and a white shirt that's too big for him that flares in the wind.

But even like that, Lalla thinks he is very handsome and very elegant, and her heart always beats a little faster when she knows he's going to come. He has a face with distinct features, leathered from the sea breeze; the skin on his forehead and cheeks is very dark and drawn tight from the sun out at sea. He has thick hair, the same color as his skin. But most of all, his eyes are an extraordinary color – a blue-green mixed with gray, very pale and transparent in that dark face, as if they had captured the light and transparency of the sea. It's in order to see his eyes that Lalla loves to wait for the fisherman on the beach near the tall fig tree and also to see his smile when he catches sight of her.

She waits a long time for him, sitting in the fine sand of the dune, in the shade of the tall fig tree. She hums a little, holding her arms over her head so she won't swallow too much sand. She sings the name that she is so fond of, that is long and beautiful, that simply says, "*Méditerra-né-é-e...*"

She waits, watching the sea that's beginning to get rough – a grayish-blue, like steel – and a sort of pale mist that masks the line of the horizon. Sometimes she thinks she sees a dark spot dancing amid the reflections between the crests of the waves, and she straightens up a little, because she thinks it's Naman's boat coming. But the dark spot disappears. It's a mirage on the sea, or maybe the back of a dolphin.

Naman was the one who had told her about dolphins. He told her of groups of dark backs leaping joyfully through the waves in front of the boat stems, as if to greet the fishermen, then suddenly they'd be off, disappearing out toward the horizon. Naman likes to tell Lalla stories about dolphins. When he talks, the light of the sea makes his eyes even brighter, and it's as if Lalla can see the black creatures in the color of his eyes. But as hard as she searches the sea, she never sees any dolphins. They probably don't like to come too near the coast.

Naman tells the story of a dolphin that led a fisherman's boat back to the coast one day when he was lost at sea in a storm. Clouds had settled over the sea, covering it like a shroud, and the raging wind had broken the boat's mast. So the storm had carried the fisherman's boat far out to sea, so far that he didn't know where the coast was anymore. The boat drifted for two days through the rough seas that threatened to capsize it at any moment. The fisherman thought he was doomed and was saying his prayers when a large dolphin appeared amidst the waves. It jumped around the boat, playing in the waves as dolphins usually do. But this dolphin was all alone. Then suddenly it started guiding the boat. It was hard to believe, but that's what the dolphin did: it swam behind the boat and pushed it. Sometimes, the dolphin swam off, disappeared in the waves, and the fisherman thought he'd been abandoned. Then the dolphin came back and started pushing the boat with its head, thrashing the sea with its powerful tail. They continued along in that fashion for one whole day, and at nightfall, during a break in the clouds, the fisherman finally caught sight of the lights on the coast. He shouted and wept with joy because he knew he'd been saved. When the boat neared the harbor, the dolphin turned and swam back toward the open sea, and the fisherman watched it go, the dolphin's big, black back gleaming in the twilight.

Lalla quite likes that story. She often searches the surface of the sea to find the big black dolphin, but Naman told her that all that happened very long ago, and the dolphin must be very old now.

Lalla is waiting like she does every morning, sitting in the shade of the tall fig tree. She gazes at the gray and blue sea where the pointed crests of the waves bob. The waves break on the beach following a sort of slanted course; first they come rolling in on the eastern side over by the rocky headland, and then from the west, near the river. Last of all they break in the middle. The wind pounces, snatches up piles of foam and flings them out toward the dunes; the foam melts into the sand and dust.

When the sun is very high in the cloudless sky, Lalla goes back to the Project; she doesn't hurry because she knows she'll have work waiting for her when she arrives. First she'll have to go fetch the water at the fountain, carrying an old rusty tin balanced on her head, then wash the clothes in the river, but that – well, that's rather nice because you can chat with the others and listen to them telling all sorts of incredible stories, especially that girl whose name is Ikikr (which means "chickpea" in Berber) because of the wart on her cheek. But there are two things that Lalla doesn't like at all: going to gather twigs for the fire and grinding wheat to make flour.

So she goes back very slowly, dragging her feet a little along the path. She doesn't sing any more then because it's the time of day when you run into people on the dunes, boys who are going to check the bird traps or men on their way to work. Sometimes the boys make fun of Lalla because she doesn't know how to walk barefoot very well and because she doesn't know any curse words. But Lalla can hear them coming from a long way off, and she hides behind a thorn bush near a dune and waits till they've passed.

There's also that scary woman. She's not old, but she's very dirty, with tangled black and red hair, clothing torn from the thorns. When she appears on the path in the dunes you have to be very careful because she's mean and doesn't like children. People call her Aïsha Kondisha, but that's not her real name. No one knows her real name. They say that she kidnaps children to hurt them. When Lalla hears Aïsha Kondisha coming along the path, she hides behind a bush and holds her breath. Aïsha Kondisha goes by muttering incomprehensible phrases. She stops a moment, lifts her head because she senses that someone is there. But she's almost blind and can't see Lalla. So she strikes out again, hobbling and shouting out insults in her hideous voice.

On certain mornings there is something in the sky that Lalla really loves: it's a big white cloud, long and stringy, that crosses the sky right in the bluest spot. At the end of the white trail, you can see a little silver cross moving slowly through the sky with its head pointing upward. She loves to watch the cross moving across the huge blue sky, without a sound, leaving behind the long white cloud made of little cottony puffs that blend in with each other and spread out like a road, then the wind brushes over the cloud and washes the sky clean.

Lalla thinks she would love to be up there, in the tiny silver cross, above the sea, above the islands like that, heading out to the most distant of lands. She remains for a long time looking up at the sky after the airplane disappears.

The Project comes into view after a bend in the path when you're far from the sea and you've walked for half an hour in the direction of the river. Lalla doesn't know why it's called the Project, because in the beginning there were only about ten plank and tarpaper cabins on the other side of the river and the vacant lots that separate it from the real town. Maybe they called it that to make people forget they were living with dogs and rats in the dust.

This is where Lalla came to live when her mother died, so long ago that she doesn't remember very well when she came. It was very hot because it was in the summer, and the wind blew clouds of dust up over the plank shacks. She'd walked with her eyes shut behind the form of her aunt until they reached the windowless cabin where her aunt's sons lived. Then she'd felt like running away, taking off along the road that leads to the high mountains and never coming back.

Every time Lalla comes back from the dunes and sees the roofs of tarpaper and sheet metal, her heart sinks and she remembers the day she came to the Project for the first time. But that was so long ago now, it's as if everything that had come before didn't really happen to her, as if it were a story that she'd heard someone tell.

It's like her birth, in the mountains to the south, where the desert begins. Sometimes in winter, when there's nothing to do outside and the wind blows hard over the plain of dust and salt, whistling between the poorly fitted planks in Aamma's house,

Lalla sits down on the floor and listens to the story of her birth.

It's a very long and very strange story, and Aamma doesn't always tell it the same way. In her slightly singsong voice, her head nodding as if she were going to fall asleep, Aamma says: "When the day you were to be born came, it was just before summer, before the dry season. Hawa could feel you were coming, and since everyone was still asleep, she left the tent silently. She just bound up her belly with a piece of cloth and walked out as best she could until she reached a spot with a tree and a spring, because she knew that when the sun came up she would need shade and water. It's the custom down there, everyone must always be born near a spring. So she walked there and then she lay down near the tree and waited for the night to end. No one knew that your mother was outside. She could walk without making a sound, without making the dogs bark. Even though I was sleeping right next to her, I hadn't heard her moan or get up to leave the tent. . ."

"Then what happened, Aamma?"

"Then it was daybreak, so the women woke up and we saw that your mother wasn't there and we realized why she'd left. So I went looking for her by the spring and when I arrived she was standing against the tree with her arms hanging onto a branch and she was moaning softly to avoid alarming the men and the children."

"What happened after that, Aamma?"

"Then you were born, right away, just like that, in the dirt between the roots of the tree, and we washed you in the spring water and wrapped you in a cloak because the night chill had not yet lifted. The sun rose, and your mother went back to the tent to sleep. I remember there was nothing to wrap you in, and you slept in your mother's blue cloak. Your mother was happy because you came very quickly, but she was sad too, because of your father's death; she thought she wouldn't have enough money to raise you, and she was afraid she would have to give you to someone else."

Sometimes Aamma tells the story differently, as if she doesn't really remember very well. For example, she says that Hawa wasn't clinging to the branch of the tree, but she was hanging from the rope of a well, and she was pulling with all her might to fight the pain. Or else she says that a passing shepherd delivered the baby and wrapped it in his woolen cloak. But all of that is veiled in an incomprehensible fog as if it had happened in another world, a world on the other side of the desert, where a different sun shines in a different sky.

"After a few days your mother was able to walk out to the well for the first time to wash herself and comb her hair. She carried you wrapped in the same blue cloak that she tied around her waist. She walked cautiously because she wasn't yet as strong as before, but she was very happy that you had come and when we asked her your name she said it was the same as hers, Lalla Hawa, because you were the daughter of a sharifa."

"Please, tell me about the one who was called al-Azraq, the Blue Man."

But Aamma shakes her head.

"Not now, another day."

"Please Aamma, tell me about him."

But Aamma shakes her head without answering. She stands up and goes to knead the bread in the large earthen platter near the door. Aamma's like that; she never wants to talk for very long, and she never says very much about the Blue Man or Moulay Ahmed ben Mohammed al-Fadel, who was called Ma al-Aïnine, Water of the Eyes.

The odd thing here in the Project is that everyone is very poor, but no one ever complains. The Project is mostly this heap of plank and sheet metal shacks with those large sheets of tarpaper held down with stones that serve as roofs. When the wind blows too hard in the valley, you can hear all the planks banging and the sheet metal clanging, and the snapping of the tarpaper tearing in a strong gust. It makes a funny music that rattles and clatters, as if everyone were in a big, old, broken-down bus on a dirt road, or as if there were a bunch of animals and rats galloping over the roofs and through the alleys.

Sometimes the storm is very violent, it whisks everything away. The next day the whole town needs to be rebuilt. But the people laugh as they do it because they are so poor they aren't afraid of losing what they have. Maybe they're happy too, because after the storm the sky is even vaster, bluer, and the light even more lovely. In any case, all there is around the Project is very flat land, and the dusty wind, and the sea so huge that you cannot see the whole of it.

Lalla loves to look at the sky. She often goes over by the dunes to the place where the sand path leads away in a straight line. And she flops down on her back right in the middle of the sand and the thistles with her arms outspread. Then the sky opens out over her smooth face, it shines like a mirror – peaceful, so peaceful, not a cloud, not a bird, not a plane.

Lalla opens her eyes very wide, she lets the sky come inside of her. It makes a swaying motion, as if she were on a boat, or as if she'd smoked too much and her head were spinning. It's because of the sun. It burns down very brightly despite the cold wind from the sea: it burns so brightly that its warmth enters the little girl's body, fills her belly, her lungs, her arms and legs. It hurts too, hurts her eyes and her head, but Lalla remains motionless, because she so loves the sun and the sky.

When she's there, sprawled out on the sand, far from other children, far from the Project filled with its noises and smells, and when the sky is very blue like today, Lalla can think about what she loves. She thinks of the one she calls al-Ser, the Secret, he whose gaze is like the sunlight that envelops and protects you.

No one here in the Project knows him, but sometimes when the sky is very beautiful and the light sparkles on the sea and on the dunes, it's as if the name of al-Ser were everywhere, vibrating everywhere, even deep within her. Lalla believes she can hear his voice, hear the faint sound of his footsteps, she feels his burning gaze that sees all, penetrates all, on the skin of her face. It's a gaze that comes from across the mountains, beyond the Drâa, from the heart of the desert, and it shines like a light that can never die.

No one knows anything about him. When Lalla talks to Naman the fisherman about al-Ser, he shakes his head because he's never heard the name, and he never mentions him in his stories. Yet Lalla thinks it must surely be his true name, since it was the one she had heard. But maybe it was only a dream. Even Aamma probably doesn't know anything about him. Nevertheless, it's a very handsome name, thinks Lalla, a name that makes you feel good when you hear it.

It's in order to hear his name, to catch a glimpse of the light in his eyes, that Lalla always walks far into the dunes till she reaches the place where there is nothing but the sea, the sand, and the sky. For al-Ser cannot make his name heard, or let the warmth of his gaze be felt when Lalla is in the plank and tarpaper Project. He's a man who doesn't like noise or strong smells. He needs to be alone in the wind, alone like a bird hanging in the sky.

The people around here don't know why she goes off alone. Maybe they think she goes over to the shepherds' houses on the other side of the rocky hills. They don't say anything.

People here are waiting. In truth, that's all anyone ever does in the Project. They've come to a halt, not far from the seashore, in their plank and zinc shacks, lying motionless in the thick shadows. When day breaks over the stones and the dust, they come out for a minute, as if something were going to happen. They talk a little, the girls go to the fountain, the boys go to work in the fields, or else they go hang around in the streets of the real town across the river, or they go sit on the side of the road to watch the trucks go by.

Every morning, Lalla crosses the Project. She goes to fetch buckets of water from the fountain. As she walks along, she listens to the music coming from the radio sets, perpetuated from one house to another, always the same interminable Egyptian song that comes and goes through the narrow streets of the

Project. Lalla enjoys hearing that music, wailing and rasping in cadence, mingling with the sound of the girls' footsteps and the sound of the water in the fountain. When she gets to the fountain, she waits her turn, swinging the galvanized bucket at the end of her arm. She watches the girls; some are as black as negresses, like Ikikr, others are very white with green eyes, like Mariem. There are old women with veils who come to fetch water in a black pot and hurry away in silence.

The fountain is a brass faucet at the top of a long lead pipe that shakes and groans every time it is turned on and off. The girls wash their legs and faces in the icy jet. Sometimes they splash one another with the buckets, letting out shrill cries. There are always wasps buzzing about their heads, getting caught in their tangled hair.

Lalla brings the bucket of water back to Aamma's house on her head, walking nice and straight so she won't spill a drop. In the morning, the sky is lovely and clear as if everything were still completely new. But when the sun nears its highest point, a haze rises near the horizon, like a dust cloud, and the sky weighs more heavily upon the earth.

THERE IS ONE PLACE Lalla really likes to go. You have to take the paths that lead away from the sea and head eastward, then you go up the bed of the dried torrent. When the rocky hills come into view, you keep walking over the red stones, following the goat tracks. The sun shines bright in the sky, but the wind is cold because it comes from lands in which there are no trees or water; it's the wind that comes from the depths of space. This is the dwelling place of the one whom Lalla calls al-Ser, the Secret, because no one knows his name.

So she comes up facing the great plateau of white stones that spreads all the way out to the edge of the horizon, all the way out to the sky. The light is dazzling; the cold wind cuts your lips and brings tears to your eyes. Lalla opens her eyes and stares as hard as she can until her heart starts thudding heavily in her throat and in her temples, until a red veil covers the sky, and she can hear the unknown voices in her ears that are all talking and muttering at the same time.

Then she walks out to the middle of the plateau of stones, to the place where only scorpions and snakes live. There are no more paths up on the plateau. There are only large blocks of broken rock, sharp as knives, upon which the light is glittering. There are no trees or grass, only the wind coming from the center of space.

It is here that the man sometimes comes to meet her. She doesn't know who he is or where he comes from. At times he is frightening, and at other times he is very gentle and very calm, full of celestial beauty. All she sees of him are his eyes because his face is veiled with a blue cloth, like the faces of the desert warriors. He wears a long white cloak that scintillates like salt in the sun. In the shadow of the blue turban, his eyes burn with a strange dim flame, and Lalla can feel the warmth of his gaze moving over her face and body as if she were nearing a fire.

But al-Ser doesn't always come. The man from the desert only comes when Lalla wants to see him very badly, when she really needs him, when she needs him just as much as she needs to talk, or to cry. But even when he doesn't come, there is still a trace of him there on the plateau of stones, maybe it's that searing look of his that lights up the landscape, that reaches from one end of the horizon to the other. So then Lalla can walk down the middle of the vast stretch of broken stones without paying attention to where she's going, without thinking about it. On certain rocks there are strange signs that she doesn't understand, crosses, dots, stains in the shape of suns or moons, arrows carved into the stone. They might be magic signs; that's what the boys from the Project say, and that's why they don't like to come up as far as the white plateau. But Lalla isn't afraid of the signs, or of loneliness. She knows the Blue Man from the desert is protecting her with his gaze and she is no longer afraid of the silence, or the barrenness of the wind.

There's no one up in that place, not a soul. Only the Blue Man of the desert who is constantly watching her, without talking to her. Lalla doesn't really know what he wants, what he's asking for. She needs him, and he comes silently, with his powerful gaze. She is happy when she's up on the plateau of stones, in the light of that gaze. She knows that she shouldn't talk to anyone about it, not even to Aamma, because it's a secret, the most important thing that's ever happened to her. It's also a secret because she's the only one who isn't afraid to come up to the plateau of stones often, in spite of the silence and the barrenness of the wind. Except maybe the Chleuh shepherd, the one they call the Hartani, he also comes up on the plateau sometimes, but that's when one of the goats from his herd gets lost running along the ravines. He isn't afraid of the signs on the stones either, but Lalla never dared to talk to him about her secret.

That's the name she's given the man who sometimes appears

on the plateau of stones: al-Ser, the Secret, because no one should know his name.

He doesn't speak. That is to say, he doesn't speak the same language as humans. But Lalla hears his voice inside her ears, and in his language he says very beautiful things that stir her body inwardly, that make her shudder. Maybe he speaks with the faint sound of the wind that comes from the depths of space, or else with the silence between each gust of wind. Maybe he speaks with the words of light, words that explode in showers of sparks on the razor-edged rocks, with the words of sand, the words of pebbles that crumble into hard powder, and also the words of scorpions and snakes that leave tiny indistinct marks in the dust. He knows how to speak with all of those words, and his gaze leaps, swift as an animal, from one rock to another, shoots all the way out to the horizon in a single move, flies straight up into the sky, soaring higher than the birds.

Lalla loves coming up here, on the plateau of white stones, to hear those secret words. She doesn't know the man she calls al-Ser; she doesn't know who he is or where he comes from, but she loves to encounter him up here, because in his eyes and words, he bears the heat of the land of dunes and of sand, of the South, a treeless, waterless land.

Even when al-Ser doesn't come, it's as if she could see through his eyes. It's difficult to understand, because it's a bit like in a dream, as if Lalla weren't exactly herself, as if she'd entered the world that lies behind the Blue Man's eyes.

That's when beautiful and mysterious things appear. Things that she'd never seen elsewhere, that trouble and worry her. She sees the immense expanse of gold- and sulfur-colored sand, as vast as the sea, with huge still waves. There is no one on the stretch of sand, not a tree, not a wisp of grass, nothing but the shadows of the dunes growing long, touching one another, creating lakes of twilight. Here everything looks the same, and it's as if she were here and at the same time a little farther away, over where her eyes happen to fall, then still elsewhere, right out on the edge between the earth and the sky. The dunes move under her gaze, slowly, spreading their fingers of sand. There are golden brooks that run along the torrid valley bottoms. There are ripples, cooked hard in the relentless heat of the sun, and huge white beaches with flawless curves standing perfectly still before the sea of red sand. Light glistens and streams down everywhere, light coming from all sides at once, the light of the earth, the sky, and the sun. In the sky, there are no limits. Nothing but the dry haze shimmering out near the horizon, distorting reflections, dancing like wispy grasses of light – and the ochre and pink dust vibrating in the cold wind that rises up toward the very center of the sky.

All of this is strange and remote, and yet it seems familiar. As if Lalla is seeing, directly in front of her, the huge desert with the gleaming light through someone else's eyes. She can feel the south wind blowing on her skin, the burning sand of the dunes under her bare feet. Most of all she can feel, overhead, the immensity of the blank sky, the sky with not a single shadow in which the pure sun is shining.

Then, for a long time, she stops being herself and becomes someone else, someone far away, forgotten. She sees other shapes, silhouettes of children, men, women, horses, camels, herds of goats; she sees the outline of a city, a stone and clay palace, mud ramparts from which troops of warriors are coming. She sees all of that because it is not a dream, but a remembrance from another's memory that she has unknowingly entered. She hears the sound of men's voices, the chanting of women, music, and maybe she even dances too, spinning around, beating the earth with the tips of her bare toes and her heels, making her copper bracelets and heavy necklaces jangle.

Then suddenly, as if in a breath of wind, everything is gone. It's just that al-Ser's eyes are no longer upon her, they have glanced away from the plateau of white stone. Then Lalla is looking through her own eyes again, can feel her heart again, her lungs, her skin. She can make out each detail, each stone, each crack, each tiny little pattern in the dust.

She turns back. She climbs down toward the bed of the dry torrent, avoiding the sharp rocks and the thorn bushes. When she gets to the bottom, she is very weary from all of that light, from the barrenness of the incessant wind. Slowly, she walks along the sand paths till she reaches the Project where the shadows of men and women are still moving around. She walks over to the fountain and bathes her face with her hands, kneeling on the ground, as if she were returning from a long journey.

W HAT'S ALSO NICE are the wasps. They're all over the town with their long yellow bodies with black stripes and their transparent wings. They go everywhere, flying about heavily without paying any attention to people. They're hunting for food. Lalla really likes them, she often watches them hanging in the sunbeams over heaps of garbage, or around the meat stalls at the butcher's market. Sometimes they come close to Lalla when she's eating an orange; they try to land on her face, on her hands. Sometimes too, one of them stings her on the neck or on the arm, and it burns for several hours. But it doesn't matter, Lalla really likes the wasps anyway.

The flies aren't as nice. First of all they don't have that long yellow and black body, or the waist that is so slender when they're standing on the edge of a table. The flies go fast, they alight suddenly, all flat with their big red-gray eyes goggling on their heads.

In the Project, there's always a lot of smoke hanging over the plank shacks, along the alleys of tamped earth. There are women cooking meals on clay braziers, there are fires for burning garbage, fires for heating tar to put on the roofs.

When she has time, Lalla likes to stop and look at the fires. Or sometimes she goes over to the dried torrents to gather acacia twigs, she ties them together with a piece of string and brings the bundle back to Aamma's house. The flames flare up joyfully among the twigs, making the stems and thorns burst open and the sap boil. The flames dance in the cold morning air, making fine music. If you look into the flames, you can see genies, at least that's what Aamma says. You can also see landscapes, cities, rivers, all sorts of extraordinary things that appear and then hide, sort of like clouds.

Then the wasps come out, because they smell the odor of

mutton cooking in the iron pot. The other children are afraid of the wasps, they want to drive them away, they try to kill them by throwing stones. But Lalla lets them fly around her hair and tries to understand what they are singing when they make their wings buzz.

When it's mealtime, the sun is high in the sky, burning hotly. Whites are so white that you can't look directly at them, shadows are so dark that they seem like holes in the ground. So first Aamma's sons come. There are two of them, one who is fourteen, named Ali, and the other who is seventeen, whom everyone calls Bareki, because he was blessed on the day of his birth. Aamma serves them first, and they eat rapidly, greedily, without speaking. They always shoo the wasps away with the backs of their hands as they eat. Then Aamma's husband comes; he works in the tomato fields, to the south. His name is Selim, but he's called the Soussi, because he is from the Souss River region. He's very small and thin, with lovely green eyes, and Lalla really likes him, even though it's rumored almost everywhere that he's a little lazy. He doesn't kill the wasps; on the contrary, he sometimes holds them between his index finger and thumb and plays at making their stingers come out, then he sets them delicately back down and lets them fly away.

There are always people who are far from their homes, and Aamma puts a piece of meat aside for them. Sometimes Naman the fisherman comes to eat at Aamma's house. Lalla is always very pleased when she knows he's going to come, because Naman likes her too, and he tells her nice stories. He eats slowly, and from time to time he says something funny just for her. He calls her little Lalla because she's the descendent of a true sharifa. When she looks into his eyes, Lalla feels as if she were looking at the color of the sea, going across the sea, as if she were on the other side of the horizon, in those big cities where there are white houses, gardens, fountains. Lalla loves to hear the names of the cities, and she often asks Naman to say them for her, just like that, just their names, slowly, to have time to see the things they hide:

"Algeciras."

"Granada."

"Sevilla."

"Madrid."

Aamma's boys want to know more. They wait for Old Naman to finish eating, and they ask all sorts of questions about life over there, across the sea. They want to know serious things, not names to dream about. They ask Naman about the money that can be earned, the work to be had, how much clothes cost, food, the price of a car, if there are a lot of movie theaters. Old Naman is too old, he doesn't know those kinds of things, or maybe he's forgotten them, and anyway, life must have changed since he lived over there, before the war. So the boys shrug their shoulders, but they don't say anything because Naman has a brother who still lives in Marseille and who might be useful one day.

On certain days Naman feels like talking about everything he's seen, and Lalla is the one to whom he tells it all because she's his favorite and because she doesn't ask any questions.

Even if they're not exactly true, Lalla loves the tales he tells. She listens carefully to him when he speaks of large white cities by the sea, with all those rows of palm trees, gardens filled with flowers, with orange and pomegranate trees climbing all the way up to the hilltops, and those towering buildings as high as mountains, those avenues that are so long you can't see the end. She also likes it when he talks about the black automobiles driving along slowly, especially at night, with their headlights turned on, and the multicolored lights of the shop windows. Or the huge white ships that arrive in Algeciras in the evening, slipping slowly along the damp wharves, while the crowd shouts and waves to welcome the newcomers. Or even the railroad leading northward, from city to city, traveling through the misty countryside, over rivers, mountains, going into long dark tunnels, just like that, with all the passengers and their baggage, all the way to the big city of Paris. Lalla listens to all of that and she feels a little fretful shiver, but at the same time she thinks she'd like to be on that railroad, going from town to town, toward unfamiliar places, toward the lands where everyone has forgotten all about dust and starving dogs, about plank shacks through which the desert wind blows.

"Take me with you when you leave," says Lalla.

Old Naman shakes his head, "I'm too old now, little Lalla, I won't be going back again, I'd die on the way."

To console her, he adds, "You'll go. You'll see all those cities, and then you'll come back here, like I did."

She simply stares into Naman's eyes to see what he'd seen, like when you stare into the deep sea. She thinks of the lovely names of the cities for a long time, she hums them in her head as if they were the words to a song.

Sometimes it's Aamma who asks him to talk about those foreign lands. So then, once again, he tells all about his journey through Spain, the border, then the road along the coast, and the great city of Marseille. He talks about all the houses, the streets, the stairways, the endless wharves, the cranes, boats as big as houses, as big as cities, from which trucks, freight cars, stones, cement are unloaded, and which then glide away on the dark waters of the port, blowing their horns. The two boys don't listen much to that because they don't believe Old Naman. When Naman leaves, they say that everyone knows he was a cook in Marseille, and they call him Tayyeb, to make fun of him, because it means "he was a cook."

But Aamma listens to what he says. It doesn't matter to her that Naman was a cook over there, and a fisherman here. She asks him different questions each time, in order to hear the story of the journey again, the border, and life in Marseille. Then Naman also talks about street battles in which men attack Arabs and Jews in the dark streets, and you have to defend yourself with a knife, or by throwing stones and running as fast as you can to get away from the police vans that pick people up and take them off to prison. He also talks about the people who cross the borders illegally, in the mountains, walking by night and hiding during the day in caves and in the bushes. But sometimes the police dogs follow their trail and attack them when they come down on the other side of the border.

Naman talks about all of that in a gloomy way, and Lalla can sense a cold shadow pass over the man's eyes. It's a strange feeling that she's not very familiar with, but it's frightening, threatening, like the passage of death, of malediction. Maybe that was something Old Naman had also brought back from over there, from those cities on the other side of the sea.

When he's not talking about his travels, Old Naman tells stories he heard long ago. He tells them just for Lalla and for the very young children because they're the only ones who listen without asking too many questions.

On certain days, he sits down facing the sea in the shade of his fig tree and repairs his nets. That's when he tells the most beautiful stories, those that take place out on the ocean, on boats, in storms, those in which people are shipwrecked and end up on desert islands. Naman can tell a story about almost anything, that's what's so great. For example, Lalla is sitting next to him in the shade of the fig tree and she's watching him repair his nets. His long brown hands with broken nails work swiftly, know how to tie knots nimbly. At one point there is a big tear in the mesh of the net, and Lalla of course asks, "Did a big fish do that?"

Instead of answering, Naman thinks for a while and says, "I didn't tell you about the day we caught a shark, did I?"

Lalla shakes her head, and Naman starts a story. As in most of his stories, there is a storm, with lightning flashing from one end of the sky to the other, waves as high as mountains, torrential rain. The net is heavy, so heavy to pull up that the boat is leaning to one side and the men are afraid of capsizing. When the net comes up, they see that a gigantic blue shark is caught in it and is thrashing around and opening its jaws full of terrifying teeth. So the fishermen must fight against the shark that is trying to swim away with the net. They hack at it with gaffs, with hatchets. But the shark bites the edge of the boat and tears it apart as if it were just crate wood. Finally the captain manages to kill the shark with a club, and they hoist the beast onto the deck of the boat.

"Then we cut him open to see what was inside, and we found a golden ring set with a deep-red precious stone that was so beautiful no one could take his eyes from it. Naturally we each wanted the ring for ourselves, and soon everyone was ready to kill one another to possess that cursed ring. That was when I suggested we throw dice for it because the captain had a pair of bone dice. So we played dice on the deck in spite of the raging storm that threatened to turn the boat over at any minute. There were six of us, and we tossed the dice six times, the winner being the one who threw the highest number. After the first round, only the captain and I remained because we had both thrown eleven, six and five. Everyone was pushing close around us to see who would win. I threw, and I got a double six! So I was the one who won the ring, and for a few minutes I was happier than I'd ever been in my life. But I looked at the ring for a long time, and its red stone shone like the fires of hell, with a lurid glimmer, like blood. Then I saw that the eyes of my companions were glowing with that same evil light, and I realized the ring was cursed, as was the person who had worn it and had been eaten by the shark, and I knew that whoever kept the ring would be cursed in turn.

"After I had looked at it well, I took it off my finger and threw it into the sea. The captain and my companions were furious and wanted to throw me into the sea as well. So I asked them, 'Why are you angry with me? That which came from the sea has returned to the sea, and now it's as if nothing happened.' At that same moment the storm suddenly subsided and the sun started shining on the sea. So then the sailors also calmed down, and the captain himself who had so coveted the ring forgot about it at once and told me I had done the right thing in throwing it back into the sea. We threw the body of the shark overboard as well and returned to port to repair the net."

"Do you really think the ring was cursed?" asks Lalla.

"I don't know if it was cursed," answers Naman, "but what I do know is that if I hadn't thrown it back into the sea, one of my shipmates would have killed me that very day in order to steal it, and we would have all died in the same way, right down to the very last."

They're stories that Lalla loves to hear, sitting next to the old fisherman like that, facing out to sea, in the shade of the fig tree, when the wind is blowing and making the leaves rustle. It's sort of as if she could hear the voice of the sea, and Naman's words weigh on her eyelids and cause drowsiness to well up in her body. So then she curls up in the sand, her head against the roots of the fig tree, while the fisherman continues repairing his red twine nets, and the wasps hum above drops of salt.

"Hey-o! Hartani!"

Lalla shouts very loudly into the wind as she nears some rocky, briar-filled hills. Out here, there are always a fair number of lizards that go skittering off between the stones. Sometimes there are even snakes that dart away with a swish. There are tall grasses as sharp as knives and lots of those dwarf palms that are used for making baskets and mats. You can hear insects chirping everywhere because there are tiny waterholes between the rocks and great deep wells hidden in the sinkholes where cold water sits. In passing, Lalla throws stones into the crevices and listens to the sound echoing deeply into the darkness.

"Harta-a-ni!"

He often hides, to make fun of her, simply stretching himself out at the foot of a thorn bush. He's always wearing his long homespun robe, frayed at the sleeves and at the hem, and the long white cloth that he wraps around his head and neck. He is long and thin like a vine, with lovely brown hands and ivory-colored fingernails, and feet made for running. But it's his face that Lalla likes most of all because it doesn't resemble any of the people who live here in the Project. It's a very thin, smooth face, a rounded forehead and very straight eyebrows, and large dark eyes that are the color of metal. His hair is short, almost frizzy, and he doesn't have a mustache or a beard. Yet he seems strong and sure of himself, with a very direct way of looking at you, fearlessly examining you, and he knows how to laugh when he wants to, with a laughter that rings out and makes you happy right away.

Today Lalla finds him easily because he isn't hiding. He's simply sitting on a large rock, staring straight ahead in the direction of the herd of goats. He's not moving. The wind lightly flares his brown tunic away from his body, lifts the end of his white turban. Lalla walks over to him without calling out because she knows he heard her coming. The Hartani has a sharp ear, he can hear the leap of a hare on the far end of a hill and he will point out planes in the sky to Lalla long before she has detected the sound of their motors.

When she's very near to him, the Hartani stands up and turns around. The sun shines on his black face. He smiles and his teeth also shine in the light. Even though he's younger than Lalla, he's just as tall as she is. He's holding a small blade with no handle in his left hand.

"What are you doing with that knife?" Lalla asks.

Feeling tired from her long walk, she sits down on the rock. He remains standing in front of her, balancing on one leg. Then all of a sudden he leaps backward and starts running over the rocky hill. A few minutes later he brings back a handful of reeds that he cut in the swamps. Smiling, he shows them to Lalla. He's panting a little, like a dog who has run too fast.

"They're lovely," says Lalla. "Are they for making music?"

She doesn't really ask that. She murmurs the words, making gestures with her hands. Every time she speaks, the Hartani stands still and looks at her intently because he's trying to understand.

Lalla might be the only person he understands and she the only one who understands him. When she says "music," the Hartani jumps up and down, holding out his long arms as if he were going to dance. He whistles between his teeth so loudly that the goats and their buck startle on the slope of the hill.

Then he takes a few of the cut reeds and joins them between his hands. He blows into them, and it makes a strange, slightly husky music, like the call of nighthawks in the dark, a sad sort of music, like the chant of Chleuh shepherds.

The Hartani plays for a moment without catching his breath. Then he holds out the reeds to Lalla, and she plays in turn, while the young shepherd stands still, his dark eyes bright with pleasure. They continue playing like that, taking turns blowing into the reed tubes of different lengths, and the sad music seems to be stemming from the land, drenched in white light, from the holes of the underground caves, from the sky itself in which the slow wind is stirring.

From time to time they stop, breathless, and the young boy bursts out with his ringing laughter, and Lalla starts laughing too, without knowing why.

Then they walk across the fields of rocks, and the Hartani takes Lalla's hand, because there are so many sharp rocks that she doesn't know about between the tufts of brush. They jump over the little drystone walls, zigzagging through the thorn bushes. The Hartani shows Lalla everything there is in the fields of stones and on the slopes of the hills. He knows all the hiding places better than anyone: those of the praying mantises and of leaf insects. He also knows all the plants, the ones that smell good when you crinkle their leaves between your fingers, the ones with roots filled with water, the ones that taste like anise, like pepper, like mint, like honey. He knows which seeds are crunchy, the tiny berries that dye your fingers and lips blue. He even knows the hiding places where you can find small petrified snails, or tiny star-shaped grains of sand. He leads Lalla far away with him, beyond the drystone walls, along paths she doesn't know, all the way out to the hills from where you can see the beginning of the desert. His eyes shine brightly; the skin on his face is dark and glistening with sweat when he gets to the top of the hills. Then he shows Lalla the way leading southward, toward the place of his birth.

The Hartani isn't like the other boys. No one really knows where he comes from. Only that one day, a long time ago, a man came riding in on a camel. He was dressed like the warriors of the desert, in a large sky-blue cloak with his face veiled in blue. He stopped at the well to water his camel, and he also took a long drink of the well water. It was Yasmina, the wife of the goat herder, who saw him when she was going to fetch water. She waited, to let the stranger quench his thirst, and when he left again on his camel, she saw that the man had left a very young infant wrapped in a piece of blue cloth at the edge of the well. Since no one wanted him, Yasmina kept the child. She brought him up, and he lived with her family as if he were her son. That child was the Hartani; he was given that nickname because he had black skin like the slaves from the south.

The Hartani grew up in the very spot where the warrior of the desert had left him, near the hills and the fields of stone, right where the desert begins. He was the one who watched over Yasmina's goats; he became like the other shepherd boys. He knows how to take care of animals; he knows how to lead them where he wants, without hitting them, just whistling between his fingers, for animals are not afraid of him. He also knows how to speak to swarms of bees, simply by whistling a little tune between his teeth, guiding them with his hands. People are a little frightened of the Hartani, they say he's *mejnoun*, that he has special powers that come from demons. They say that he knows how to tame snakes and scorpions, that he can send them out to kill other shepherds' livestock. But Lalla doesn't believe that; she's not afraid of him. Maybe she's the only person who knows him well, because she speaks to him in a different way than with words. She looks at him and reads the light in his black eyes, and he looks deep into her amber eyes; he doesn't only look at her face, but really deep down into her eyes, and it's as if he understands what she wants to say to him.

Aamma doesn't like Lalla going up into the hills and fields of stone to see the shepherd so often. She tells her he's an abandoned child, a stranger, that he's not a boy for her. But as soon as Lalla finishes her work at Aamma's house she runs along the path leading to the hills, and she whistles between her fingers like the shepherds do and shouts,

"Hey-o! Hartani!"

Sometimes she stays up there with him until nightfall. Then the young boy herds his animals together to lead them to the corral lower down, near Yasmina's house. Often, since they don't speak to each other, they remain sitting still on the boulders facing the rocky hills. It's difficult to understand what they're doing just then. Maybe they're looking out into the distance as if they could see across the hills, all the way out to the other side of the horizon. Lalla herself doesn't really understand how that happens, for time doesn't seem to exist anymore when she's sitting next to the Hartani. Words flow freely, go out toward the Hartani and come back to her, full of new meaning, like in certain dreams when you're two people at once.

The Hartani is the one who taught her how to sit still like that, just looking at the sky, the stones, the bushes, looking at the wasps and the flies flying, listening to the song of hidden insects, feeling the shadows of birds of prey and the trembling of hares in the scrub.

Like Lalla, the Hartani doesn't really have a family, he doesn't know how to read or write, he doesn't even know the prayers, he doesn't know how to speak, and yet he's the one who knows all those things. Lalla loves his smooth face, his long hands, his dark metallic eyes, his smile, she loves the way he walks, quick and agile as a hare, and the way he leaps from rock to rock, and disappears in the wink of an eye into one of his hiding places.

He never comes into the city. Maybe he's afraid of the other boys, because he's not like them. When he goes away, he always heads southward, toward the desert, to the place where the nomads atop their camels have left their tracks. He goes away for several days like that, without anyone knowing where he is. Then one morning he returns and goes back to his post in the field of stones with the she-goats and their buck as if he'd only been gone a few minutes.

When she's sitting there on a rock like that next to the Hartani, and they're both looking out at the vast stretch of stones in the sunlight, with the wind blowing from time to time, with the wasps humming over the little gray plants, and the sound of the goats' hooves slipping on loose stones, there's really no need for anything else. Lalla can feel the heat deep down inside of her, as if all the light of the sky and the stones were going straight into the very quick of her body, expanding. The Hartani takes Lalla's hand in his long, brown, slender fingers, he holds it so tight that it almost hurts. Lalla can feel the current of heat pass through the palm of her hand, like an odd, feeble vibration. She doesn't want to talk or think. She feels so good sitting there that she could stay all day long, right up until night fills the ravines, without moving. She stares straight out ahead, she can see each detail of the stone landscape, each tuft of grass, can hear each snapping sound, each insect call. She can feel the slow movement of the shepherd's breathing, she is so close to him that she is seeing through his eyes, feeling things with his skin. It lasts a brief instant, but it seems so long that, head spinning, she forgets everything else.

Then all at once, as if he were afraid of something, the young shepherd jumps to his feet, lets go of Lalla's hand. Without even looking at her, he starts running fast, like a dog, jumping over the rocks and the dried ravines. He leaps over the drystone walls, and Lalla sees his pale silhouette disappearing between the thorn bushes.

"Hartani! Hartani! Come back!"

Lalla shouts, standing up on the boulder, and her voice cracks because she knows it won't do any good. The Hartani disappears suddenly, swallowed up by one of those dark hollows in the limestone. He won't show himself again today. Maybe tomorrow, or some other time? So then Lalla also goes down the hill, slowly, from one rock to another, clumsily, and she looks back from time to time to try to catch a glimpse of the shepherd. She leaves the fields of stone and the drystone walls, makes her way back down toward the valley bottom, not far from the sea, where people live in houses made of planks, sheet metal, and tarpaper.

DAYS ARE THE SAME every day, here in the Project, and sometimes you're not really sure what day you happen to be living. It's an already remote time, and it's as if there were nothing written in the cards, nothing certain. As a matter of fact, no one really thinks about it here, no one really wonders who he is. Yet Lalla thinks about it often, when she goes up to the plateau of stones where the Blue Man dwells, the man she calls al-Ser.

It might be due to the wasps as well. There are so many wasps in the Project, many more than there are men and women. From dawn to dusk they go humming through the air searching for food, dancing in the sunlight.

Yet in one sense, the hours are never the same, like the things Aamma says, like the faces of the girls who gather around the fountain. There are torrid hours, when the sun burns your skin through the clothing, when the light sticks pins in your eyes and makes your lips bleed. That's when Lalla wraps herself up in blue cloth, ties a large handkerchief behind her head that covers her face up to the eyes, and wraps another thin blue cloth around her head that hangs down to her chest. The burning wind comes in from the desert, blowing hard grains of dust. Outside, the streets of the Project are empty. Even the dogs are hiding in holes in the earth, at the foot of the houses, against empty oil drums.

But Lalla loves being outdoors on days like that, maybe precisely because there is no one around. It's as if there were nothing left on earth, nothing that belonged to humans. That's when she feels most divorced from herself, as if nothing she had ever done could count, as if all memory had been erased.

So she goes over toward the sea, to the place where the dunes begin. She sits down in the sand, wrapped in the blue cloths; she looks at the dust rising in the air. Above the earth, at the zenith,

85

the sky is a very deep blue, almost the color of night, and when she looks over at the horizon just above the line of dunes, she can see that pink ashen color, like at dawn. On those days you are free too from flies and wasps because the wind has driven them back into the hollows in the rocks, into their nests of dried mud, or into the dark corners of the houses. There are no men, or women, or children. There are no dogs, no birds. There is only the wind whistling in the branches of the shrubs, in the leaves of the acacias and the wild fig trees. There are only the thousands of stone particles lashing at your face, parting around Lalla, forming long ribbons, snakes, plumes. There is the sound of the wind, the sound of the sea, the swishing sound of sand, and Lalla leans forward to breathe, the blue veil plastered against her nostrils and lips.

It's great because it's as if you'd sailed away on a boat, like Naman the fisherman and his companions, lost in the middle of a huge storm. The sky is blank, extraordinary. The earth has disappeared, or almost, barely visible through the cracks in the sand, ragged, worn, a few dark patches of reefs surrounded by the sea.

Lalla doesn't know why she goes out on those days. She just can't help it, she can't stay closed up in Aamma's house, or even go walking through the narrow streets of the Project. The burning wind dries out her lips and her nostrils; she can feel the flame descending inside her. It might be the flame of the light in the sky, the flame that comes from the East and that the wind is forcing into her body. But light doesn't only burn, it also liberates, and Lalla can feel her body getting lighter, swifter. She resists, clinging to the sand dune with both hands, her chin against her knees. She barely breathes, in short little gasps, so as not to become too light.

She tries to think of the people she loves, because that can keep the wind from blowing her away. She thinks of Aamma, of the Hartani, of Naman most of all. But on those days, nothing really counts, not even any of the people she knows, and her thoughts slip immediately away, escape, as if the wind had torn them from her and carried them out among the dunes.

Then suddenly she feels the eyes of the Blue Man from the desert upon her. It's the same look that was up there on the plateau of stones at the edge of the desert. It is a blank, imperious gaze that pushes down on her shoulders with all the weight of the wind and the light, a look filled with unbearable dryness that is painful, a look that has been hardened like the particles of stone that are hitting her face and clothing. She doesn't understand what he wants, what he's asking for. Maybe he wants nothing of her, he's just simply passing over the coastline, the river, the Project, and he's going even farther out, to burn up the cities and the white houses, the gardens, the fountains, the wide avenues in the lands on the other side of the sea.

Now Lalla is frightened. She would like to stop that gaze, to stop it on herself, so that it wouldn't go out beyond that horizon, so it would cease its revenge, its flames, its violence. She doesn't understand why the storm of the man from the desert wants to destroy those cities. She closes her eyes to block out the sight of the snakes of sand coiling around her, those dangerous plumes. Then she hears the voice of the desert warrior in her ears, the one she calls al-Ser, the Secret. She's never heard him so clearly, even when he appeared before her on the plateau of stones wearing his white cloak, his face veiled in blue. It's a strange voice that she hears inside of her head, mingling with the sound of the wind and the hissing of the sand. It's a distant voice that is saying words she doesn't really understand, endlessly repeating the same sounds, the same words.

"Make the wind stop!" says Lalla out loud, without opening her eyes. "Don't destroy the cities, make the wind stop and the sun stop burning, make everything be at peace!"

Then again, in spite of herself, "What do you want? Why do you come here? I'm nothing to you, why do you talk to me, and only to me?"

But the voice is still murmuring, still fluttering inside of Lalla's body. It is only the voice of the wind, the voice of the sea, of the sand, the voice of the light that dazzles and numbs people's willpower. It comes at the same time as the stranger's gaze, it shatters and uproots everything on earth that resists it. Then it goes farther out, toward the horizon, gets lost out at sea on the mighty waves, it carries the clouds and the sand toward the rocky coasts on the other side of the sea, toward the vast deltas where the smokestacks of refineries are burning.

"TELL ME ABOUT the Blue Man," says Lalla.

But Aamma is busy kneading bread on the large earthenware platter. She shakes her head. "Not now."

Lalla insists. "Yes, now, Aamma, please."

"I already told you everything I know about him."

"It doesn't matter, I want to hear you talk about him again, and about the man called Ma al-Aïnine, Water of the Eyes."

So Aamma stops mashing the dough. She sits on the floor and starts talking, because deep down, she really likes to tell stories.

"I already told you about this, it was long ago, in a time that neither your mother nor I knew, for it was when your mother's grandmother was a child that the great al-Azraq, he who was called the Blue Man, died, and Ma al-Aïnine was just a young man in those days."

Lalla knows all of their names well, she's heard them often since she was a small child, and still, each time she hears them, it gives her a little shiver, as if something deep down inside of her had been stirred.

"Al-Azraq was from the same tribe as your mother's grandmother, he lived far to the south, beyond the Drâa, even beyond the Saguiet al-Hamra, and in those days, there wasn't a single foreigner in the land; the Christians weren't allowed in. In those days, the warriors of the desert were undefeated, and all of the territories south of the Drâa belonged to them, for a very long way, deep into the heart of the desert, all the way down to the holy city of Chinguetti."

Each time Aamma tells the story of al-Azraq, she adds a new detail, a new sentence, or else she changes something, as if she didn't want the story to ever finish. Her voice is loud, somewhat singsong, it rings out oddly in the dark house with the sound of the corrugated iron cracking in the sunlight and the humming of wasps.

"He was called al-Azraq because before becoming a saint, he'd been a desert warrior far to the south, in the region of Chinguetti, because he was a nobleman and the son of a sheik. But one day, God called upon him, and he became a saint, he abandoned the blue attire of the desert and dressed himself in a woolen robe like the poor, and he walked barefoot through the land from city to city with a staff as if he were a beggar. But God wanted him to stand out from other beggars, and so God made the skin of his hands and face remain blue, and the color could never be washed away no matter the amount of water he used. The blue color remained on his face and hands, and when the people saw it, despite the worn woolen robe, they understood he wasn't a beggar, but a true warrior of the desert, a blue man that God had called upon, and that is why they gave him that name. Al-Azraq, the Blue Man. . ."

As she speaks, Aamma rocks back and forth lightly, as if she were marking the beat to music. Or sometimes she is quiet for a long time, leaning over the large earthenware platter, busily breaking up the dough and bringing it back together again to flatten it out with her closed fists.

Lalla waits, without saying anything, for her to go on.

"No one from back in those days is still alive," says Aamma. "Everything that is said about him comes from tales, his legend, what can be remembered. But now there are people who don't want to believe that anymore, who say it's all lies."

Aamma hesitates because she's choosing what she's going to say carefully.

"Al-Azraq was a great saint," she says. "He knew how to heal sick people, even those who were sick in their heads, those who had lost their minds. He would live anywhere, in the shacks of shepherds, small sheds of leaves built around the foot of trees, or even in caves high in the mountains. People came from far and wide to see him and ask for his help. One day, an old man brought his son who was blind, and he said, 'Heal my son, you who have received God's blessing, heal him and I will give you everything I have.' And he showed him a bag full of gold that he had brought with him. Al-Azraq said, 'Of what use can your gold be here?' and he motioned out toward the desert, without a drop of water, without a piece of fruit. And he took the old man's gold and threw it on the ground, and the gold turned into scorpions and snakes that fled into the distance, and the old man began to tremble with fear. Then al-Azraq said to the old man, 'Are you willing to go blind in place of your son?' The old man answered, 'I am very old, what use are my eyes to me? Let my son see, and I will be happy.' Immediately, the young man recovered his sight and was dazzled by the sunlight. But when he saw that his father was blind, he was no longer happy. 'Give my father his sight back,' he said, 'for it was I whom God condemned.' Then al-Azraq granted them both the gift of sight, because he knew they were good-hearted. And he continued his journey toward the sea and stopped to live in a place just like this, near the dunes by the seaside."

Aamma remains silent for a moment. Lalla thinks of the dunes, the place where al-Azraq lived, she hears the sound of the wind and the sea.

"The fishermen gave him food every day because they knew that the Blue Man was a saint, and they sought his blessing. Some came from very far away, from the fortified towns in the South; they came to hear him speak. But al-Azraq did not teach the Sunna with words, and when someone came to ask of him, 'Teach me the Way,' he simply told his beads for hours without saying anything else. Then he said to the visitor, 'Go and gather wood for the fire, go and fetch some water,' as if the visitor were his servant. He would say to him, 'Fan me,' and he even spoke to him with harsh words, accusing him of being lazy and lying, as if the visitor were his slave."

Aamma speaks slowly in the dim house, and Lalla believes she can hear the voice of the Blue Man.

"That's how he taught the Sunna, not with spoken words, but with gestures and prayers, to force the visitors to become humble in their hearts. But when simple people came, or children, al-Azraq was very kind to them, he said very gentle words to them, he told them marvelous tales, because he knew their hearts were not hardened and that they were truly close to God. They were the ones for whom he sometimes performed miracles, to help them because they had no other recourse."

Aamma hesitates. "Did I ever tell you about the miracle of the source he made spring up from under a stone?"

"Yes, but tell me again," says Lalla.

That's the story she loves most in the whole world. Every time she hears it, she feels something strange, like a feverish chill, moving deep down inside of her, as if she were going to cry. She thinks about how it all happened, very long ago, at the gates to the desert, in a village of mud and palm trees with a large empty square where the wasps hum and the water from the fountain shines in the sun, smooth as a mirror reflecting the clouds in the sky. There's no one in the village square because the sun is burning down very hard, and all the people have taken shelter in the shade of their homes. From time to time, a slow ruffle of scorched air passes over the still water of the fountain, like an open eye watching the sky, and casts a fine white powder on its surface, forming an imperceptible milky veil that melts quickly away. The water is clear and deep, blue-green, silent, very still in the hollow of red earth in which women's feet have left glistening prints. Only the wasps come and go over the water, skimming the surface, then turn back toward the houses from which the smoke of the braziers is rising.

"It's the story of a woman who went to fetch a jug of water at the fountain. No one remembers her name now because it all happened so long ago. But she was a very old woman who had very little strength left, and when she reached the fountain she began to weep and lament because it was such a long way for her to carry the water back home. She remained there, squatting on the ground, weeping and moaning. Then all of a sudden, without her hearing him come, al-Azraq was standing beside her. . ."

Lalla can see him clearly now. He is tall and thin, wrapped in his sand-colored cloak. His face is hidden behind his veil, but his eyes are shining with a strange light that is both soothing and invigorating, like the flame of a lamp. She recognizes him now. He's the one who appears up on the plateau of stones, up where the desert begins, the one who envelops Lalla in his gaze so firmly and with such insistence that it makes her dizzy. He appears just like that, as silently as a shadow, he knows how to be there when he's needed.

"The old woman continued to cry, so al-Azraq asked her gently why she was weeping."

Yet you can't be frightened when he appears silently, as though he's sprung up from the desert. His eyes are filled with kindness, his voice is slow and calm, light even streams from his face.

"The old woman told him of her sorrow, her loneliness, because her house was so far away from the water, and she hadn't the strength to get home carrying the jug of water. . ."

His voice and his gaze are one and the same thing, as if he already knew what the future held, as if he knew the secret of people's destinies.

"'Don't weep over that,' said al-Azraq. 'I'll help you get back to your house.' And he led her back home by the arm, and when they had arrived in front of her house, he simply said to her, 'Pick up that stone by the side of the path, and you will never again be in need of water.' And the old woman did as she was bidden, and under the stone, a source of very clear water sprang forth, and the water spread out until it formed a fountain, purer and more beautiful than any other in the land. So then the old woman thanked al-Azraq, and later, people from all parts came to see the fountain and taste its water, and everyone praised al-Azraq who had received such powers from God."

Lalla thinks about the fountain that sprang up under the stone, she thinks about the very clear, smooth water shining in the sunlight. She thinks about it for a long time in the half-light, while Aamma continues kneading the bread. And the shadow of the Blue Man recedes, silently, just as it had come, but his forceful gaze remains hovering over her, enveloping her like a breath.

Aamma is quiet now, she says nothing more. She continues to punch and knead the dough in the large, wobbling, earthenware platter. Maybe she too is thinking of the lovely fountain of deep water that sprang up under a stone on the path, like the true words of al-Azraq, the true path.

THE LIGHT IS beautiful here every day on the Project. Lalla had never really paid attention to the light until the Hartani taught her how to look at it. It's a very clear light, especially in the morning, just after sunrise. It shines down on the red rocks and the earth, brings them to life. There are places for seeing the light. One morning, the Hartani takes Lalla to one of those places. It's a chasm that opens at the bottom of a rocky ravine, and the Hartani is the only one who knows about this hiding place. You have to know where the passageway is. The Hartani takes Lalla's hand and leads her along the narrow tunnel that descends into the earth. Immediately you can feel the cool dampness of the shadows, and sounds cease, like when you put your head under water. The tunnel burrows deep into the earth. Lalla is a little frightened because it's the first time she's ever gone inside of the earth. But the shepherd squeezes her hand tightly and that gives her courage.

All of a sudden, they stop: the long tunnel is bathed in light because it opens right out into the sky. Lalla doesn't understand how that is possible because they never stopped going down, but it's true nevertheless: the sky is right there in front of her, immense and weightless. She stands motionless, breathless, wide-eyed. Here, all that's left is the sky, so clear that you think you're a bird flying through the air.

The Hartani motions for Lalla to come closer to the opening. Then he sits down on the stones, slowly, so as not to start a rock-slide. Lalla sits down a little behind him, trembling with dizziness. Down at the bottom, all the way down at the bottom of the cliff in the haze, she can make out the great barren plain, the dried torrents. Out on the horizon, an ochre mist spreads: it's the beginning of the desert. That's where the Hartani goes sometimes, all alone, taking nothing with him but a little bread wrapped in a handkerchief. It's in the east, where the sunlight is the most beautiful, so beautiful that you'd like to go running barefoot through the sand, leaping over the sharp stones and the ravines, pressing ever onward in the direction of the desert, just like the Hartani does.

"It's beautiful, Hartani!"

Sometimes Lalla forgets that the shepherd can't understand. When she speaks to him, he turns his face toward her, and his eyes are bright, his lips try to imitate the movements of language. Then he grimaces, and Lalla starts laughing.

"Oh!"

She points to a still black spot in the middle of the air. The Hartani looks at the spot for a moment and makes the sign of a bird with his hand, crooking the index finger, and spreading the last three fingers out like the feathers of a bird. The spot glides slowly along in the center of the sky, circling back on itself a little, dropping, coming closer. Now Lalla can see its body clearly, its head, its wings with spread quill feathers. It's a hawk in search of its prey, sailing silently along on the wind, like a shadow.

Lalla watches for a long time, her heart pounding. She's never seen anything as beautiful as that bird tracing its circles in the sky, so very high up above the red earth, solitary and silent in the wind, in the sunlight, and tipping down toward the desert at times as if it were going to fall. Lalla's heart beats even harder, because the silence of the tawny bird is making its way inside of her, giving rise to fear. Her eyes are riveted on the hawk, she can't tear them away. The awful silence in the center of the sky, the chill of the open air, most of all the burning light, daze her, dig out a dizzying void. She steadies herself, leaning her hand on the Hartani's arm to keep from falling forward into the emptiness. He too is watching the hawk. But it's as if the bird were his brother and nothing separated them. They both have the same look in their eyes, the same courage; they share the same interminable silence of the sky, the wind, and the desert.

When Lalla realizes that the Hartani and the hawk are one and the same, a shiver runs up her spine, but the dizziness has left her. The sky spreading before her is immense, the earth is a gray- and ochre-colored mist floating out on the horizon. Since all of this is familiar to the Hartani, Lalla is no longer afraid to enter the silence. She closes her eyes and allows herself to glide out on the air, into the center of the sky, holding on to the young shepherd's arm. Together, they slowly trace large circles up above the earth, so high up that not a single sound can be heard, only the light ruffling of the wind in the quill feathers, so high up that the rocks, the thorn bushes, the houses of planks and tarpaper are hardly visible.

Then, after having flown together for a long time and having become inebriated on the wind, the light, and the blue of the sky, they return to the mouth of the cave at the top of the red cliff; they touch down lightly, without causing a single stone to roll, without moving a grain of sand. Those are the things that the Hartani knows how to do, just like that, without talking, without thinking, with his eyes alone.

He knows of all sorts of places where you can see lights, because there isn't only one light, but many different lights. At first, when he used to lead Lalla over the rocks, into the hollows, toward the old dried-up crevices, or else high up on a red rock, she thought it was to go and hunt lizards or rob birds' nests, like the other boys do. But then, his eyes bright with delight, the Hartani would show her with a flourish of his hand – and at the end of his sweeping gesture, there would be nothing but the sky, immense, dazzlingly white, or else the dance of sunlight along the sharp broken rocks, or still yet those sorts of moons that the sun makes through the leaves of the shrubs. Those things were more beautiful when he looked at them, newer, as if no one had ever seen them before him, as in the beginning of the world.

Lalla likes to follow the Hartani. She walks behind him along the path he is opening up. It's not really a path because there aren't any traces, and yet when the Hartani moves forward you

97

can tell that this is exactly where the passageway is, and nowhere else. Maybe these are paths for goats and foxes, not for people. But the Hartani, he's just like one of them, he knows things that people don't, he sees them with his whole body, not only with his eyes.

It's the same with smells. Sometimes the Hartani walks a very long way out onto the rocky plain toward the east. The sun burns down on Lalla's shoulders and face, and she has a hard time keeping up with the shepherd. At times like that, he pays no attention to her. He's looking for something, almost without stopping, bent slightly toward the ground, leaping from rock to rock. Then all of a sudden he stops and puts his face against the earth, lying flat on his stomach as if he were drinking. Lalla draws quietly near when the Hartani lifts himself up a little. His metallic eyes are brimming with joy, as if he had found the most precious thing in the world. Between the stones, in the powdery dirt, there is a green and gray tuft, a very small shrub with scrawny leaves, like so many others out here, but when Lalla brings her own face closer, she smells the scent, very weak at first, then deeper and deeper, the scent of the most beautiful flowers, the smell of mint and of *chiba* weed, and that of lemons too, the smell of the sea and the wind, of prairies in summer. There is all of that and a lot more, in that dirty, fragile, minuscule plant growing in the shelter of two stones in the middle of the great arid plateau; and the Hartani is the only one who knows it.

He's the one who shows Lalla all of the lovely smells, because he knows their hiding places. Smells are like stones and animals, they each have their hiding place. But you have to know how to look for them, like dogs, picking up the tiniest scents on the wind, then pouncing without hesitation on the hiding place.

The Hartani showed Lalla how to do it. Before, she didn't know how. Before, she could pass right by a shrub, or a root, or a honeycomb, without picking up a thing. The air is so full of smells! They're constantly moving, like breaths, they rise, they fall, encounter one another, mingle, separate. A strange odor of fear hovers over the trail of a hare; a little farther along, the Hartani motions to Lalla to come closer. At first there is nothing on the red earth, but little by little, the young girl detects something acrid, intent; the smell of urine and sweat, then suddenly she recognizes it: it's the smell of a wild dog, starving, hair bristling, running over the plateau in pursuit of the hare.

Lalla loves spending her days with the Hartani. He shows all of those things to her alone. He's wary of the others, because they don't have time to wait, to seek out smells, to see desert birds fly. He's not afraid of people. It's rather they who are afraid of him. They say he's *mejnoun*, possessed by demons, that he's a magician, that he has the evil eye. The Hartani, he's the one who has no father or mother, because he came out of nowhere; he's the one a desert warrior left near the well one day, without saying a word. He's the one who has no name. Sometimes Lalla would really like to know who he is; she'd like to ask him, "Where are you from?"

But the Hartani doesn't understand the language of human beings; he doesn't answer questions. Aamma's eldest son says that the Hartani doesn't know how to speak because he's deaf. Anyway that's what the schoolmaster told him one day, it's called deaf-mute. But Lalla knows very well that isn't true, because the Hartani hears better than anyone. He knows how to hear sounds so subtle, so faint, that you can't even hear them by putting your ear to the ground. He can hear a hare jump on the far side of the plateau of stones, or else a man who is coming along the path at the other end of the valley. He can find the place where the cricket sings or the partridge nests in the tall grasses. But the Hartani doesn't want to hear the language of human beings because he comes from a land where there are no humans, only the sand dunes and the sky.

Sometimes Lalla speaks to the shepherd, for example she says, "Biluuu-la!" slowly, looking deep into his eyes, and a strange glimmer lights up his dark metallic eyes. He places his hand on Lalla's lips and follows their movement when she says things like that. But he never utters a word himself.

Then after a while, he's had enough, and he looks away; he goes to sit a little farther off, on another rock. But that's not very important, because now Lalla knows that words don't really count. It's only what you mean to say, deep down inside, like a secret, like a prayer; that's the only thing that counts. And the Hartani doesn't speak in any other way; he knows how to give and receive that kind of message. So many things are conveyed through silence. Lalla didn't know that either before meeting the Hartani. Other people expect only words, or acts, proof, but the Hartani, he looks at Lalla with his handsome metallic eyes, without saying anything, and it is through the light in his eyes that you hear what he's saying, what he's asking.

When he's worried, or on the contrary, when he's very happy, he stops, he puts his hands on Lalla's temples, meaning he holds them out on either side of the young girl's head, without touching her and he stays like that for a long time, his face filled with light. And Lalla can feel the warmth of his palms on her cheeks and temples as if there were a fire warming her. It's a strange feeling that fills her with happiness too, that creeps deep down inside of her, that releases and calms her. That's especially why she likes the Hartani, because he has that power in the palms of his hands. Maybe he really is a magician.

She looks at the shepherd's hands trying to understand. They are long hands with slender fingers, with pearl-colored nails, with thin skin that is brown, almost black on top, and pink, tinged with yellow underneath, like the leaves of those trees that have two colors.

Lalla likes the Hartani's hands very much. They're not like the hands of the other men in the Project, and she thinks there aren't any others like them in all the land. They are nimble and light, full of strength too, and Lalla thinks that they are the hands of a nobleman, the son of a sheik maybe, or maybe even a warrior from the Orient, from Baghdad.

The Hartani knows how to do everything with his hands, not just pick up a stone or break a piece of wood, but make slipknots with palm fibers, traps for catching birds, or else whistle, make music, imitate the call of the partridge, the hawk, the fox, and imitate the sound of the wind, the storm, the sea. Most of all his hands know how to talk. That's what Lalla likes best. Sometimes, tucking his feet under his large homespun robe, the Hartani sits down in the sun on a big flat rock to talk. His clothes are very light-colored, almost white, and you can only see his dark face and hands, and that is how he begins to talk.

It isn't really stories that he tells Lalla. Rather, it's images that he makes appear in the air, with only his gestures, his lips, with the light in his eyes. Furtive images that appear in flashes, flickering on and off, but never has Lalla heard anything more beautiful, more true. Even the stories that Naman the fisherman tells, even when Aamma talks about al-Azraq, the Blue Man of the desert, and the fountain of clear water that sprang up from under a stone, it's not that beautiful. The things that the Hartani says with his hands are preposterous, just like he is, but it's like a dream, because every image that he makes appear comes at a time when you're least expecting it, and yet it is just what you were expecting. He talks in that way for a long time, making birds with spread feathers appear, rocks clenched like fists, houses, dogs, storms, airplanes, giant flowers, mountains, wind blowing over sleeping faces. None of that means anything, but when Lalla looks at his face, the play of his black hands, she sees these images appear, so lovely and new, bursting with light and life, as if they actually sprang from the palms of his hands, as if they were coming from his lips, along the beam of his eyes.

The most beautiful thing when the Hartani is talking in this way is that nothing disturbs the silence. The sun burns down on the plateau of stones, on the red cliffs. The wind blows at times, slightly chilly, or you can hear the faint swish of sand running down the grooves in the rocks. With his long hands and agile fingers, the Hartani makes a snake slipping along the bottom of a ravine appear, then it stops, head uplifted. That's when a large white ibis takes flight, flapping its wings. In the night sky, the moon is round, and with his index finger the Hartani lights up the stars, one, one more, still another. . . In summer, the rain begins to fall; the water runs into the streams, filling out a round pond where mosquitoes hover. Straight into the center of the blue sky, the Hartani throws a triangular stone that rises, rises, and – *whish!* – it suddenly opens and turns into a tree with infinite foliage filled with birds.

Sometimes the Hartani uses his face to imitate people or animals. He can do the turtle really well, squinching up his lips, head down between his shoulders, back rounded. It makes Lalla laugh every time. Just like the first time. Or sometimes he does the camel, lips pushed out in front, front teeth bared. He also does a very good job of imitating the heroes he's seen in the movies. Tarzan, or Maciste, and all of the comic book characters.

Every now and again, Lalla brings him pocket-sized comics that she takes from Aamma's eldest son or that she buys with her savings. There are the stories of Akim, of Roch Rafal, stories that are set on the moon or on other planets, and small Mickey Mouse or Donald Duck comic books. She can't read what's written, but she has Aamma's son tell her the story two or three times, and she knows them by heart. But at any rate, the Hartani doesn't feel like hearing the story. He takes the small books, and he has a strange way of looking at them, holding them diagonally and cocking his head a little to one side. Afterwards, when he's looked at all the pictures closely, he leaps to his feet and imitates Roch Rafal or Akim on the back of an elephant (a rock plays the part of the elephant).

But Lalla never stays with the Hartani for very long, because there always comes a time when his face seems to close up. She doesn't really understand what happens when the face of the young shepherd turns sullen and stiff, and there is such a faraway look in his eyes. It's like when a cloud passes in front of the sun, when the night falls very suddenly on the hills in the valley bottoms. It's terrible, because Lalla really wants to hold on to the moment the Hartani seemed happy, to his smile, the light that gleamed in his eyes. But it's impossible. All of a sudden the Hartani is gone, like an animal. He jumps up and disappears in the wink of an eye, without Lalla being able to tell where he's gone. But she doesn't try to hold him back anymore. There are even certain days, when there's been so much light up on the plateau of stones, when the Hartani has been talking with his hands and making so many extraordinary things appear, that Lalla prefers to leave first. She stands up and without running, without looking back, makes her way down to the path that leads to the plank and tarpaper Project. Maybe from having spent so much time with the Hartani, she has grown to be like him now.

As a matter of fact, people don't like it very much that she goes to see the Hartani so often. Perhaps they're afraid she'll become *mejnoun* too, that she'll catch the evil spirits that are in the shepherd's body. Aamma's eldest son says that the Hartani is a thief, because he has gold in a small leather bag that he wears around his neck. But Lalla knows that's not true. The Hartani found that gold one day in the bed of a dried-up torrent. He took Lalla by the hand and guided her down to the bottom of the crevice and down there, in the gray sand of the torrent, Lalla had seen the gold dust shining.

"He's not the right kind of boy for you," says Aamma when Lalla comes back from the plateau of stones.

Lalla's face is now just as black as the Hartani's, because the burning sun is stronger up there.

Sometimes Aamma adds, "After all, you don't want to marry the Hartani, do you?"

"Why not?" Lalla answers. And she shrugs her shoulders.

She doesn't want to get married; she never even thinks about it. The idea of getting married to the Hartani makes her start laughing.

Nevertheless, whenever she can, once she's decided she's finished her work, Lalla leaves the Project and heads toward the hills where the shepherds are. It's east of the Project, up where the lands without water, the high cliffs of red stone, begin. She enjoys walking along the very white path that snakes through the hills, listening to the shrill music of the crickets, observing the marks left by snakes in the sand.

A little farther along, she hears the whistling of shepherds. They are mostly young children, boys and girls who are scattered about almost everywhere in the hills with herds of goats and sheep. They whistle like that to call to one another, to talk to one another, to scare off the wild dogs.

Lalla enjoys walking through the hills, eyes squinted tight because of the white light, with all of those whistling sounds echoing out on all sides. It makes her shiver a bit, in spite of the heat; it makes her heart beat faster. Sometimes she plays at answering them. The Hartani showed her how to do that, by putting two fingers in her mouth.

When the young shepherds come to see her on the path, they keep their distance from her at first, because they're rather wary. They have smooth faces, the color of burnt copper, with rounded foreheads and an odd color of hair, almost red. It's the desert sun and wind that have burnt their skin and hair. They are ragged, dressed only in long cream-colored canvas shirts, or dresses made from flour sacks. They don't come close because they speak Chleuh, and they don't understand the language that the people from the valley speak. But Lalla likes them, and they aren't afraid of her. Sometimes she brings them things to eat, whatever she was able to sneak out of Aamma's house, a little bread, some biscuits, dried dates.

Hartani is the only one who can keep them company, because he's a shepherd like them, and because he doesn't live with the people from the Project. When Lalla is with him, far out in the middle of the plateau of stones, they approach, jumping from one rock to another, without making a sound. But they whistle every now and again just to let you know. When they arrive, they gather round the Hartani, talking very rapidly in their strange language that makes a sound like birds. Then they leave again very quickly, leaping over the plateau of stones, still whistling, and sometimes the Hartani takes off running along with them, and even Lalla tries to follow them, but she can't jump as fast as they can. They all laugh real hard when they see her, and they start running again, letting out great bursts of joyful laughter.

They share a meal on the white rocks in the middle of the plateau. Under their shirts, they carry a bit of cloth that contains a little black bread, a few dates, figs, some dried cheese. They give a piece to the Hartani, a piece to Lalla, and in exchange she gives them some of her white bread. Sometimes she brings a red apple that she bought at the Cooperative. The Hartani takes out his little knife with no handle and cuts the apple into slivers so everyone can have a piece.

It's fine up on the plateau of stones in the afternoon. The sunlight is constantly bouncing off the sharp-edged stones; you're surrounded with sparkles. The sky is deep blue, dark, without that white haze that comes from the sea and the rivers. When the wind blows hard, you have to sink down into the holes in the rocks to protect yourself from the cold, and then you can hear nothing but the sound of the air whistling over the earth, through the bushes. It makes a sound like the sea, but slower, longer. Lalla listens to the shepherds and the distant bleating of the herds. Those are the sounds she loves most in the world, along with the calls of gulls and the crashing of the waves. They're sounds as if nothing bad could ever happen on earth.

One day, just like that, after having eaten some bread and dates, Lalla followed the Hartani all the way to the foot of the red hills, over where the caves are. That's where the shepherd sleeps in the dry season when the herd of goats needs to go farther out to find new grazing lands. In the red cliff, there are those black holes, half-hidden by thorn bushes. Some of those holes are hardly as large as a foxhole, but when you go inside, the cave opens out and becomes as large as a house, and so cool.

That's how Lalla went in, on her belly, following the Hartani. At first she couldn't see anything at all, and she got frightened. Suddenly, she started shouting, "Hartani! Hartani!"

The shepherd turned back, and took her by the arm and pulled her up into the cave. Then when she recovered her sight, Lalla saw the large room. The walls were so high you couldn't see the tops of them, covered with gray and blue stains, patches of amber, of copper. The air was gray because of the dim light coming from the holes in the cliff. Lalla heard the sound of wings beating heavily, and she pressed close to the shepherd. But it was only the bats that had been disturbed in their sleep. They went to perch a little farther off, squeaking and screeching.

The Hartani sat down on a large flat rock in the middle of the cave, and Lalla sat next to him. Together they watched the dazzling light coming through the opening of the cave in front of them. The inside of the cave is filled with darkness, with the dampness of everlasting night, but outside the light hurts your eyes. It's like being in another land, another world. It's like being at the bottom of the sea.

Lalla isn't talking now, she doesn't feel like talking. Like the Hartani, she is on the night side. The look in her eyes is as dark as night, her skin is the color of shadows.

Lalla can feel the warmth of the shepherd's body very near her, and the light of his eyes slowly creeps inside of her. She would so like to be able to reach him, enter his realm, be with him completely, so that he could hear her at last. She brings her mouth close to his ear, she smells the odor of his hair and his skin, and she says his name very softly, almost silently. The shadows of the cave are all around them, enveloping them like a fine yet sturdy veil. Lalla can hear very clearly the sound of water trickling down the walls of the cave and the small cries the bats are making in their sleep. When her skin touches that of the Hartani, it makes a strange wave of heat run through her body, a dizzy feeling. It's the heat of the sun that has been sinking into their bodies all day long and that is now flowing out in long feverish waves. Their breaths touch too, mingle, for there is no more need for words, only for what they feel. It's a dizziness she's never felt before, that has grown out of the shadows in the cave in just a few seconds, as if the stone walls and the damp shadows had been waiting a long time for them to come in order to release their powers. The dizziness is spinning faster and faster inside of Lalla's body, and she can distinctly hear the pulsing of her blood mixed with the sounds of drops of water on the walls and the small cries of the bats. As if their bodies were now one with the inside of the cave, or were prisoners in the entrails of a giant.

The Hartani's odor of goats and sheep mingles with the odor of the young girl. She can feel the warmth of his hands, sweat moistens her forehead and makes her hair stick to it.

Suddenly Lalla can't understand what's happening to her anymore. She is afraid, she shakes her head and tries to escape the embrace of the shepherd who is pinning her arms to the rock and knotting his long, hard legs against hers. Lalla wants to scream but, as in a dream, not a sound comes from her throat. The damp shadows are closed tightly around her, veiling her eyes, the weight of the shepherd's body is preventing her from breathing. Finally, she's able to wrench out a scream, and her voice echoes like thunder off the walls of the cave. The bats, abruptly awakened, begin whirling around the walls with the rushing sound of their wings and squeaking.

The Hartani is already on his feet atop the rock, he steps back a little. His long arms are flapping around to drive away the clouds of drunken bats swirling about him. Lalla can't see his face because the shadows in the cave have grown thicker, but she can sense the anxiety in him. A terrible feeling of sadness steals into her, rises steadily. She's not afraid of the shadows anymore, or of the bats. Now it is she who takes the Hartani's hand, and she can feel he is trembling dreadfully, that his whole body is jerking with spasms. He's just standing there. Torso leaning backwards, one arm over his eyes to keep from seeing the bats, he is trembling so hard that his teeth are chattering. Then Lalla guides him over to the opening of the cave, and she's the one who pulls him outside, until the sun floods down upon their heads and shoulders.

107

Out in the daylight, the Hartani's face looks so distraught, so pitiful that Lalla can't keep from laughing. She wipes the mud stains from her torn dress and from the Hartani's long shirt. Then they go back down the slope toward the plateau of stones together. The sun shines brightly on the sharp stones, the ground is white and red beneath the nearly black sky.

It's like diving headfirst into cold water when you are very hot, and swimming a long time to cleanse your whole body. Then they start running across the plateau of stones, as fast as they can, leaping over the rocks until Lalla stops, out of breath, bending over with a pain in her side. The Hartani continues to leap from rock to rock like an animal; then he notices that Lalla is no longer behind him, and he makes a large circle to work his way back. Together they remain sitting in the sun on a rock holding hands tightly. The sun descends toward the horizon, the sky turns yellow. Off in the distant hills, in the hollows of the valleys, the scattered sharp whistles of the shepherds call out to one another, then answer.

LALLA LOVES FIRE. There are all sorts of fires here in the Project. There are the morning fires, when the women and the little girls are cooking the meal in large black pots, and the black smoke swirls along the ground mixing in with the morning mist, just before the sun appears over the red hills. There are fires of grasses and branches that burn for a long time all by themselves, almost smothered, with no flames. There are the fires of the braziers as afternoon draws to an end, in the lovely light of the declining sun, amid coppery reflections. The low smoke slithers around like a long, blurry snake, filling out from house to house, wafting gray rings in the direction of the sea. There are the fires people light under old tin cans to heat tar for plugging up the holes in the roofs and the walls.

Here, everyone loves fire, especially old people and children. Every time a fire is lit, they go and sit around it, squatting on their heels, and they watch the flames dancing with blank looks on their faces. Or else they throw in little dried twigs that flare up all of a sudden, crackling, and handfuls of grass that disappear, making blue swirls.

Lalla goes to sit in the sand by the sea, in the place where Naman the fisherman has lit his big fire of branches to heat up pitch with which to caulk his boat. It's near evening; the air is very mild, very calm. The sky is an airy color of blue, transparent, without a cloud.

Near the shore, there are always those somewhat scrawny trees, burned by the salt and the sun, whose foliage is made up of thousands of tiny blue-gray needles. As Lalla passes them, she pulls off a handful of needles for Naman the fisherman's fire, and she also puts a few in her mouth to chew on slowly as she walks. The needles' taste is salty, bitter, but it mixes in with the smell of smoke and is just right.

Naman builds his fire any old place, wherever he finds large dead branches washed up on the beach, and he stuffs all the holes with dried twigs that he goes to fetch in the flatlands on the other side of the dunes. He also uses dried kelp and dead thistles. That's when the sun is still high in the sky. Sweat runs down the old man's forehead and cheeks. The sand burns like fire.

Then he lights the fire with his tinderbox, being very careful to place the flame on the side where there is no wind. Naman is very good at building fires, and Lalla watches his every move closely, to learn. He knows how to find just the right place, neither too exposed, nor too sheltered, in the hollows of the dunes.

The fire starts up and then goes out two or three times, but Naman doesn't really seem to notice. Every time the flame dies, he roots around in the twigs with his hand, without being afraid of getting burned. That's the way fire is; it likes people who aren't afraid of it. So then the flame leaps up again, not very strong at first; you can barely see the tip of it glowing between the branches, then suddenly it blazes up around the whole base of the bonfire, throwing out a bright light and crackling abundantly.

When the fire is going strong, Naman the fisherman sets the tripod up over it and places the pot of pitch on it. Then he sits down in the sand and watches the fire, every once in a while throwing in another twig that the flames devour instantly. Then the children also come to sit down. Having smelled the smoke, they've come from afar, running along the beach. They shout, call to one another, burst out laughing, because fire is magic, it makes people want to run and shout and laugh. Right now the flames are very high and bright, they are waving around and crackling, they're dancing, and you can see all sorts of things in their folds. What Lalla loves most of all is the base of the fire, the very hot brands enveloped in flames, and that incandescent color which has no name and resembles the color of the sun.

She also watches the sparks floating up the column of gray

smoke, gleaming bright and then going out, disappearing into the blue sky. At night, the sparks are even more beautiful, like clusters of falling stars.

The sand flies have come out as well, drawn by the odor of burning kelp and hot pitch, irritated by the plumes of smoke. Naman doesn't pay any attention to them. He's looking only at the fire. Every now and again he stands up, dips a stick into the pot of pitch to see if it's hot enough; then he stirs the thick liquid, blinking his eyes against the whirling smoke. His boat is a few meters away, on the beach, keel pointing skyward, ready for caulking. The sun is descending quickly now, nearing the arid hills on the other side of the dunes. Darkness is spreading. The children are sitting on the beach, huddled close to one another, and their laughter has died down a little. Lalla looks at Naman; she tries to get a glimpse of that clear, water-colored light that shines in his eyes. Naman recognizes her, gives her a friendly little wave, then says immediately, as if it were the most natural thing in the world:

"Did I ever tell you about Balaabilou?"

Lalla shakes her head. She's happy because it's the perfect time for a story, just like that, sitting out on the beach, watching the fire that is making the pitch popple in the pot, the very blue sea, feeling the warm wind hustling the smoke along, with the flies and the wasps humming, and not far off, the sound of the waves washing all the way up to the old boat overturned on the sand.

"Ah, so I never told you the story of Balaabilou?"

Old Naman stands up to look at the pitch that is boiling very hard. He turns the stick slowly in the pot and seems to think everything is just right. Then he hands an old pot with a burnt handle to Lalla.

"Okay, you're going to fill this up with pitch and bring it to me over there when I'm near the boat."

He doesn't wait for an answer and goes over to set himself up on the beach beside his boat. He prepares all kinds of paintbrushes made out of bits of rags tied to wooden sticks.

"Come on!"

Lalla fills up the pot. The boiling pitch spatters and stings Lalla's skin, and the smoke burns her eyes. But she runs, holding the pot full of pitch in her outstretched hands. The children follow her, laughing, and sit down around the boat.

"Balaabilou, Balaabilou. . ."

Slowly Old Naman chants the name of the nightingale as if he were trying to remember all the details of the story. He dips the sticks into the hot pitch and starts painting the hull of the boat between the seams of the boards, where there are oakum plugs.

"It was a very long time ago," says Naman. "It happened in a day that neither I, nor my father, nor even my grandfather knew, and yet we remember the story very well. In those days people weren't the same as they are now, and we knew nothing of the Romans or anything that had to do with other countries. That's why there were still djinns back then, because no one had chased them away. So back in those days, in a large city in the Orient, there lived a powerful emir whose only child was a daughter named Leila, Night. The emir loved his daughter more than anything in the world, and she was the most beautiful, the most gentle, the most obedient young girl in the kingdom; she was destined to live the happiest of lives in the world. . ."

Evening is settling slowly in the sky, deepening the blue of the sea and making the froth of the waves seem even whiter. At regular intervals, Old Naman dunks his rag brushes into the pot of pitch and, with a twirling motion, runs them along the grooves filled with oakum. The boiling liquid sinks into the chinks and dribbles onto the sand of the beach. Lalla and all the children watch Naman's hands.

"Then something terrible happened in the kingdom," Naman goes on. "There was a great drought, God's curse over the whole kingdom, and there was no more water in the rivers or in the reservoirs, and everyone was dying of thirst, first the trees and the plants, then the herds of animals, the sheep, the horses, the camels, the birds, and finally the humans, who died of thirst in the fields by the side of the road; it was a dreadful sight to see, and that is why we still remember it. . ."

The louse flies come out; they alight on the children's lips, buzz about their ears. They are inebriated by the sharp smell of the pitch and the thick plumes of smoke swirling up between the dunes. There are wasps too, but no one tries to bat them away because when Old Naman tells a story, it's as if they too become a little magic, sort of like djinns.

"The emir of the kingdom was very sad, and he summoned the wise men to ask their advice, but no one knew what to do to stop the drought. It was then that a stranger appeared, an Egyptian traveler who was well-versed in magic. The emir summoned him as well, and asked him to break the curse upon the kingdom. The Egyptian gazed at an ink spot, and he became suddenly frightened, began to tremble and refused to speak. 'Speak!' said the emir. 'Speak and I will make you the richest man in the kingdom.' But the stranger refused to speak. 'My lord,' he said, 'allow me to go on my way, don't ask me to reveal this secret.'"

When Naman stops talking to dip his brushes in the pot, Lalla and the children are almost afraid to breathe. They listen to the fire crackling and the sound of the pitch boiling in the pot.

"Then the emir grew angry and said to the Egyptian, 'Speak or you are doomed.' And the executioners seized him and were already unsheathing their sabers to cut off his head. So the stranger cried out, 'Stop! I will tell you the secret of the curse, but know that you are damned!'"

Old Naman has a very particular, long, drawn-out way of saying *Mlaaoune* – damned by God – that makes the children shudder. He stops for a moment to use up the rest of the pitch in the pot. Then he hands it to Lalla without saying a word, and she has to run over to the fire to fill it with boiling pitch. Thankfully, he waits for her to come back before continuing the story.

"Then the Egyptian said to the emir, 'Did you not once punish a man for stealing gold from a merchant?'

"'Yes, I did,' said the emir, 'because he was a thief.'

"'Know that the man was innocent,' said the Egyptian, 'and falsely accused, and that he has put a curse on you. It is he who sent the drought, for he is the ally of spirits and demons.'"

When evening comes like this out on the beach, while you're listening to Old Naman's deep voice, it's sort of as if time no longer existed, or as if it had been turned back, to another very long and very gentle time, and Lalla wishes Naman's story would never end, even if it had to last for days and nights, and she and the other children would fall asleep, and when they awakened, they would still be there listening to Naman's voice.

"'What must be done to stop this curse?' asked the emir. The Egyptian looked him straight in the eyes: 'You must realize there is but one remedy, and I will tell you what it is since you have asked me to reveal it to you. You must sacrifice your only daughter, she whom you love more than anything in the world. Go, leave her to be eaten by the wild beasts of the forest, and the drought which has stricken your land will cease.'

"Then the emir began to weep and to cry out in pain and anger, but as he was a good man, he allowed the Egyptian to leave freely. When the people of the land learned all of this, they also wept, for they dearly loved Leila, the daughter of their king. But the sacrifice had to be made, and the emir decided to take his daughter into the forest to allow her to be eaten by the wild beasts. However, there was one young man in the kingdom who loved Leila more than any of the others, and he was determined to save her. He had inherited from one of his relatives, a magician, a ring that gave the one who possessed it the power to be transformed into an animal. However, once transformed he could never return to his original form, and he would be immortal. The night of the sacrifice came, and the emir went into the forest along with his daughter. . ."

The air is smooth and pure, the line of the horizon is infinite. Lalla looks out as far as she can see, as if she had been turned into a gull and were flying straight out over the sea.

"The emir reached the middle of the forest; he had his daughter dismount from the horse and tied her to a tree. Then he left her, weeping in sorrow, for the cries of the ferocious beasts could already be heard as they approached their victim. . ."

At times, the sound of the waves on the beach is more distinct, as if the sea were drawing nearer. But it's just the wind blowing, and when it coils round in the hollows of the dunes, it sends spurts of sand that shoot up and mix with the smoke.

"In the forest, tied to the tree, poor Leila was trembling with fright, and calling out to her father to save her because she couldn't bear to die like that, devoured by the wild beasts. . . Already a large wolf was moving toward her, and she could see his eyes glowing like flames in the night. Then all of a sudden a sweet music broke forth in the forest. It was such beautiful, pure music that Leila was no longer afraid, and all the ferocious beasts of the forest stopped to listen. . ."

Old Naman's hands take the brushes, one after the other, and with a slow twirling motion, run them along the hull of the boat. Lalla and the children watch them too, as if the brushes were telling a story.

"The celestial music resounded throughout the forest, and as they listened, the wild beasts lay down on the ground and became as gentle as lambs, for the song that came from the heavens bewildered them, troubled their souls. Leila also listened to the music with delight, and soon her bonds came loose on their own, and she began to walk through the forest, and wherever she went, the invisible musician was above her, hidden in the leaves of the trees. And the wild beasts were lying along the path, and they licked the princess's hands without causing her the slightest harm. . . ."

The air is so transparent now, the light so soft, that you think you're in another world.

"Thus Leila came back to her father's house in the morning, after having walked all night long, and the music followed her all the way to the gates of the palace. When the people saw this, they were very happy because they loved the princess dearly. And no one noticed a little bird flying discreetly from branch to branch. And that very same morning the rain began to fall upon the earth. . ."

Naman stops painting for a minute; Lalla and the children stare at his copper face in which his green eyes are shining. But no one asks any questions, no one utters a word.

"And the bird Balaabilou sang on in the rain, because he was the one who had saved the life of the princess he loved. And since he could not return to his original form, he came every night to perch on the branch of a tree next to Leila's window and sing his sweet music to her. It is even said that after her death, the princess was also turned into a bird, and she joined Balaabilou to sing in the forests and gardens with him forevermore."

When the story is finished, Naman says nothing more; he continues working on his boat, running his pitch paintbrushes with a twirling motion along the hull. The light wanes because the sun is slipping over to the other side of the horizon. The sky becomes very yellow, with a hint of green, the hills seem to be cut out of tarpaper. The smoke from the bonfire is thin, light, it can barely be seen against the sunlight, like the smoke of a single cigarette.

The children drift off, one after another. Lalla remains alone with Old Naman. He finishes his work without saying anything. Then he goes off as well, walking slowly along the beach, carrying his paintbrushes and his pot of pitch. Then the only thing left next to Lalla is the dying fire. Darkness quickly reaches deep into the sky, all of the intense blue of day is gradually turning into the black of night. The sea grows calm at this particular time, no one knows why. The waves fall very lazily on the sandy beach, extending their skirts of purple foam. The first bats begin to zigzag over the sea in search of insects. There are a few mosquitoes, a few gray moths that have lost their way. Lalla listens to the muffled cry of the nighthawk in the distance. All that is left of the fire are a few red embers still burning with no flame or smoke, like strange throbbing beasts hidden amidst the ashes. When the last ember goes out, after having flared for just a few seconds, like a dying star, Lalla rises to her feet and walks away.

THERE ARE TRACKS almost everywhere in the dust of the old paths, and Lalla plays at following them. Sometimes they don't lead anywhere, when they're bird or insect tracks. Sometimes they lead you to a hole in the ground, or else to the door of a house. It was the Hartani who had shown her how to follow the tracks without getting thrown off by the surroundings, the grass, the flowers, or the shiny stones. When the Hartani is following a track, he's exactly like a dog. His eyes gleam, his nostrils flare, his whole body tenses and leans forward. Sometimes he even lies down on the ground to better smell the trail.

Lalla really likes the paths around the dunes. She remembers the first few days after arriving in the Project, after her mother had died from the fevers. She remembers her journey in the tarp-covered truck, and her father's sister, the one named Aamma, being wrapped up in the large, gray, woolen cloak, with her face covered because of the desert dust. The journey had lasted several days, and every day Lalla had sat at the back of the truck under the stifling tarp, amidst dusty bags and bundles. Then one day, through the opening in the tarp, she had seen the deep blue sea stretching down the length of foam-fringed beach, and she'd started to cry, without knowing if it was from joy or fatigue.

Every time Lalla walks out on the path by the seaside, she thinks of the deep blue sea in the midst of all the dust from the truck and of those long silent waves unfurling sideways, way off in the distance along the beach. She thinks of everything she saw all at once, just like that, through the slit in the tarp of the truck, and she can feel tears in her eyes, because it's sort of like her mother's eyes falling upon her, enveloping her, making her shudder.

That's what she's looking for along the path of the dunes, heart pounding, her whole body straining forward, like the Har-

118

tani when he's on a trail. She's looking for the places she came to afterwards, so long ago that she can't remember by herself.

Sometimes she says, "Oummi," just like that, softly, in a murmur. Sometimes she talks to her all by herself, very quietly, in a whisper, gazing out at the deep blue sea between the dunes. She doesn't really know what she should say, because it was so long ago that she's even forgotten what her mother was like. Could she have even forgotten the sound of her voice, even the words that she used to like to hear back then?

"Where did you go, Oummi? I'd like you to come to see me here, I'd really like that. . ."

Lalla sits down in the sand facing the sea, and she watches the slow movements of the waves. But it's not really the same as the day she saw the sea for the first time, after the stifling dust of the truck on the red roads coming from the desert.

"Oummi, don't you want to come back to see me? See, I haven't forgotten you."

Lalla searches her memory for traces of words that her mother used to say, words she used to sing. But it's difficult to find them. You have to close your eyes and throw yourself back as far as you can, as if you were falling into a bottomless well. Lalla opens her eyes again, because there's nothing left in her memory.

She gets to her feet, walks down the beach watching the water pushing the froth farther up on the sand. The sun burns her shoulders and the back of her neck; the light blinds her. Lalla likes that. She also likes the salt that the wind leaves on her lips. She examines the seashells abandoned on the sand, straw-colored or pink mother-of-pearl, the old, worn, empty snail shells, and the long ribbons of greenish-black, gray, or purple seaweed. She's careful not to step on a jellyfish, or a ray. Every now and again there is a strange, frantic churning in the sand when the water recedes in the place where a flatfish has been. Lalla walks a very long way down the shore, spurred on by the sound of the waves. Sometimes she stops, stands still, looking at her shadow puddled at her feet, or the bright sparkling of the foam.

"Oummi," Lalla says again. "Can't you come back, just for a minute? I want to see you, because I'm all alone. When you died and Aamma came to get me, I didn't want to go with her, because I knew I would never be able to see you again. Come back, just for a minute, come back!"

By half-closing her eyes and staring at the light reverberating off the white sand, Lalla can see the large fields of sand that were all around the house, back there, in Oummi's country. She even startles suddenly, because for a second she thinks she sees the shriveled tree.

Her heart is beating faster, and she begins to run toward the dunes, up where the wind from the sea is cut off. She throws herself down on her stomach in the hot sand; the small thistles tear her dress a little and stick their tiny needles in her belly and thighs, but she doesn't notice. There is an excruciating pain deep in her body, such a sharp jab that she thinks she's going to faint. Her hands sink into the sand, her breath stops. She becomes very stiff, like a wooden board. Finally she's able to open her eyes, very slowly, as if she were really going to see the outline of the shriveled tree awaiting her. But there's nothing there, the sky is very vast, very blue, and she can hear the long, drawn-out sound of the waves behind the dunes.

"Oummi, oh, Oummi," Lalla says again, moaning.

But now she can see it all very clearly: there is a large field of red stones and dust, right there in front of the shriveled tree, a field so immense it seems to stretch out to the ends of the earth. The field is empty, and the little girl runs toward the shriveled tree in the dust, and she's so small that she is suddenly lost in the middle of the field near the black tree, unable to see which way to go. So then she screams as hard as she can, but her voice bounces off the red stones, trails away in the sunlight. She screams, and a terrible silence surrounds her, a vicelike, aching silence. Then the lost little girl walks straight ahead, falls, gets back on her feet; she scrapes her bare feet on the sharp stones, and her voice is all broken with sobs, and she can't breathe.

"Oummi! Oummi!" That's what she's screaming; Lalla can hear the voice distinctly now, the broken voice that cannot leave the field of stones and dust, that bounces back on itself and is muffled. But those are the words Lalla hears, from the other end of time, the words that hurt her so, because they mean that Oummi will not come back.

Then suddenly, standing in front of the lost little girl, in the very middle of the field of stones and dust, is that tree, the shriveled tree. It's a tree that has died of thirst or old age, or maybe it was struck by lightning. It is not very tall, but it is extraordinary because it is twisted every which way with several old branches bristling up like fish bones and a black trunk with twining bark, with long roots knotted around rocks. The little girl walks toward the tree, slowly, without knowing why, she goes up to the calcified trunk, touches it with her hands. And suddenly she is seized with fear: from the top of the shriveled tree, in a very long, slow movement, a snake uncoils and slips down. As it slithers interminably along the branches, its scales swish over the dead wood with a metallic sound. The snake comes down leisurely, moving its blue-gray body toward the little girl's face. She watches it without blinking, without moving, almost without breathing, and now not a cry can escape from her throat. Suddenly, the snake stops, looks at her. Then she leaps backward and starts running with all her might across the field of stones, she's running so hard it looks as if she'll go all the way around the world, her mouth dry, blinded with the light, wheezing, she runs over to a house, over to the shape of Oummi who holds her very tight and strokes her face; and she can smell the sweet smell of Oummi's hair, and she can hear her gentle words.

But today there is no one, no one at the other end of the stretch of white sand, and the sky is even vaster, emptier. Lalla is sitting doubled over in the hollow of a dune, her head pushed down between her knees. She can feel the sun burning on the back of her neck, in the place where her hair parts, and on her shoulders, through the stiff cloth of her dress.

She thinks about al-Ser, the one she calls the Secret, whom she met on the plateau of stones near the desert. Maybe he wanted to tell her something, tell her she wasn't alone, show her the path that leads to Oummi. Maybe it is his gaze once again that is burning her shoulders and neck right now.

But when she opens her eyes again, there is no one on the shore. Her fear has vanished. The shriveled tree, the snake, the vast field of red stones and dust have faded away, as if they'd never existed. Lalla goes back toward the sea. It is almost as beautiful as on the day she saw it for the first time through the opening in the tarp of the truck and started to cry. The sun has swept the air over the sea clean. There are sparkles dancing above the waves and huge, frothy rollers. The wind is mild, heavy with the scents of the ocean depths, seaweed, shellfish, salt, foam.

Lalla begins to walk slowly along the shore again, and she feels a sort of giddiness deep inside of her, as if a gaze really were coming from the sea, from the light in the sky, from the white beach. She doesn't quite understand what it is, but she knows there is someone all around who is watching her, who lights her way with his gaze. It worries her a little, yet at the same time it gives her a warm feeling, a wave radiating inside her body, going from the pit of her stomach all the way out to the ends of her limbs.

She stops, looks around: no one is there, no human form. Only the great motionless dunes scattered with thistles, and the waves rolling in, one by one, toward the shore. Maybe it is the sea that is always looking on in that way, the deep gaze of the waves of water, the dazzling gaze of the waves of salt and sand. Naman the fisherman says that the sea is like a woman, but he never explains it. The gaze comes from all sides at once.

Just then, a large flock of gulls and terns passes along the shore, covering the beach in its shadow. Lalla stops, her feet sunk deep in sand mixed with water, her head thrown back: she watches the sea birds pass.

They pass slowly overhead, flying against the warm wind, their long tapered wings plying the air. Their heads are craned out to the side a little, and odd wailing, squawking sounds are coming from their slightly open beaks.

In the center of the flock is a gull that Lalla knows well because it is entirely white, without a single black spot. It flies slowly over Lalla, stroking steadily against the wind, its wing feathers slightly spread, beak open; and as it is flying over like that, it looks at Lalla, its little head tilted toward the beach, its round eye gleaming like a droplet.

"Who are you? Where are you going?" asks Lalla.

The white gull looks at her and doesn't answer. It goes off to join the others, flies for a long time along the shore looking for something to eat. Lalla thinks that the white gull knows her but doesn't dare fly right up to her because gulls aren't made for living with humans.

Old Naman sometimes says that sea birds are the souls of men who died at sea in a storm, and Lalla thinks that the white seagull is the soul of a very tall and slim fisherman, with light skin and hair the color of sunlight, whose eyes shine like a flame. Maybe he was a prince of the sea.

Then she sits down on the beach, between the dunes, and watches the group of gulls flying along the shore. They fly easily, with little effort, their long curved wings leaning on the wind, heads craned out a little to the side. They're looking for food, because not far from there is the huge city dump where the trucks unload. They continue crying out, making their funny, uninterrupted wailing sounds, mixed with sudden, inexplicable shrill outbursts, yelps, laughs.

And then from time to time, the white gull, the one that is like a prince of the sea, comes over and flies around Lalla; it traces wide circles above the dunes, as if it has recognized her. Lalla makes waving motions at it with her arm; she attempts to call it, trying out different names in hopes of saying the right one, the one that might give it back its original form, cause the prince of the sea to appear amid the foam with his hair streaming light and his eyes as bright as flames.

"Souleïman!"

"Moumine!"

"Daniel!"

But the large white gull continues circling in the sky, out by the sea, grazing the waves with the tip of its wing, its sharp eye riveted on Lalla's silhouette, without answering. Sometimes, because she feels a little spiteful, Lalla runs after the gulls, waving her arms and shouting out names randomly, to annoy the one that is the prince of the sea.

"Chickens! Sparrows! Little pigeons!"

And even: "Hawks! Vultures!" Because those are birds the gulls don't like. But the white bird that has no name continues its very slow, indifferent flight, it sails away down the shoreline, gliding on the east wind, and run as she might over the sandy beach, Lalla can't catch up with it.

Off it flies, slipping in amongst the other birds strung out along the foam, off it flies; soon they are nothing but imperceptible dots melting into the blue of the sea and the sky.

THE WATER IS beautiful too. When it starts to rain in the middle of summer, the water streams over the metal and tarpaper roofs, making its sweet music in the large drums under the drainpipes. The rain comes at night, and Lalla listens to the sound of thunder building and rolling around in the valley or over the sea. Through the cracks between the planks, she watches the lovely white light constantly flashing on and off, making everything in the house shake. Aamma doesn't move on her pallet, she goes on sleeping with her head under the sheet, without hearing the sounds of the thunderstorm. But at the other end of the room, the two boys are awake, and Lalla can hear them speaking in hushed tones, laughing quietly. They are sitting up on their mattresses, and they too are trying to see outside through the cracks between the planks.

Lalla gets up, walks silently over to the door to see the patterns the lightning is making. But the wind has risen, and big cold drops are falling on the dirt and spattering on the roof; so Lalla goes back to lie in her blankets, because that's the way she loves to hear the sound of the rain: eyes opened wide in the dark, seeing the roof light up from time to time, and listening to all the drops pelting down violently on the earth and on the sheet metal, as if small stones were falling from the sky.

After a moment, Lalla hears the gush of water pouring out of the drainpipes and hitting the bottom of the empty kerosene drums; she's as happy as if she were the one drinking the water. At first it makes a crashing metallic sound, and then gradually the drums fill up and the sound becomes deeper. And water is gushing everywhere at once, over the ground, into the puddles, into the old pots left strewn around outside. The dry dust of winter rises into the air when the rain beats down on the earth, and it makes a strange smell of wet dirt, straw, and smoke, which is pleasant to breathe in. Children are running around in the night. They've taken off all of their clothing, and they're running naked along the streets in the rain, laughing and shouting. Lalla would like to do the same, but she's too old now, and girls of her age can't go out naked. So she goes back to sleep, still listening to the patter of the water on the sheet metal, still thinking of the two lovely gushes of water spurting out on either side of the house and making the kerosene drums overflow with clear water.

What is really fine, when water has fallen from the sky like that for days and nights on end, is that you can go take hot baths in the bathhouse across the river, in town. Aamma has decided to take Lalla to the bathhouse near the end of the afternoon, when the heat of the sun lets up a little, and the big white clouds start gathering in the sky.

It's women's day at the bathhouse, and everyone is walking in that direction along the narrow path that follows the river upstream. Three or four kilometers upstream there's the bridge, with the truck road, but before reaching that, there's the ford. That's where the women cross the river.

Aamma is walking ahead, with Zubida, and her cousin whose name is Zora, and other women that Lalla knows by sight but whose names she's forgotten. They hitch up their skirts to ford the river; they're laughing and talking very loudly. Lalla is walking a little behind, and she's very pleased because on afternoons like this, there aren't any chores to do at the house or any wood to gather for the fire. And also, she really likes the big white clouds, so low in the sky, and the green of the grass by the side of the river. The river water is icy, earth-colored; it ripples between her legs when Lalla is crossing the ford. When she reaches the canal, in the center of the river, there is a ledge, and Lalla falls into the water up to her waist; she hurries to get out, her dress clinging to her belly and thighs. There are boys on the other bank, whom the women bombard with stones for watching them pull up their skirts to cross the river.

The bathhouse is a large brick hangar built right beside the river. This is where Aamma brought Lalla when she first arrived in the Project, and Lalla had never seen anything like it. There is but one large room with tubs of hot water and ovens where the stones are heated. It's open one day for women, the next day for men. Lalla really likes this room because a lot of light comes through the windows set up high in the walls under the corrugated iron roof. The bathhouse is only open in summer because water is scarce here. The water comes from a large tank, built on a rise, and it runs down an open-air conduit to the bathhouse, where it cascades into a large cement pool that looks like a washtub. That's where Aamma and Lalla go to bathe later, after the hot tub, pouring large jugs of cold water over their bodies and letting out little gasps because it makes them shiver.

There is something else that Lalla also really likes about this place. It's the steam that fills up the whole room like white fog, piling up in layers all the way to the ceiling and escaping through the windows, making the light fluctuate. When you first walk into the room, you feel as if you're suffocating for a minute, because of the steam. Then you take off your clothes and leave them folded on a chair, at the back of the hangar. The first few times, Lalla was embarrassed; she didn't want to undress herself in front of the other women, because she wasn't used to baths. She thought the others were making fun of her because she didn't have any breasts and her skin was very white. But Aamma scolded her and made her take off all of her clothes; then she tied her long hair up in a bun, wrapping a strip of canvas around it. Now she doesn't mind getting undressed. She doesn't even pay any attention to the others anymore. At first, she thought it was horrid because there were very ugly and very old women, with skin wrinkled up like dead trees, or else fat fleshy ones, with breasts dangling down like waterskins, or still others who were sick, their legs covered with ulcers and varicose veins. But now Lalla doesn't see them in the same way any longer. She pities the ugly and sick women; she's not afraid of them anymore. And also, the water is so beautiful, so pure, the water that has fallen straight from the sky into the large tank, the water is so new that it must certainly heal the ill.

That's the way it is when Lalla enters the tub water for the first time after the long months of the dry season: it envelops her body all at once, closing so tightly over her skin, over her legs, over her belly, over her chest, that Lalla momentarily loses her breath.

The water is very hot, very heavy; it brings the blood to the surface of the skin, dilates the pores, sends its waves of heat deep into the body, as if it had taken on the force of the sun and the sky. Lalla slides down into the bathtub until the scalding water comes up over her chin and touches her lips, then stops just under her nostrils. Afterward, she remains like that for a long time without moving, gazing up at the corrugated roof that seems to be swaying under the trails of steam.

Then Aamma comes with a handful of soapwort and some pumice powder, and she scrubs Lalla's body to get the sweat and the dust off, scrubs her on the back, the shoulders, the legs. Lalla docilely submits, because Aamma is very good at soaping and scrubbing down; afterward she goes over to the washtub, and she submerges herself in the cool, almost cold water, and it closes up her pores, smooths her skin, tightens her nerves and muscles. This is the bath she takes with the other women, listening to the sound of the waterfall coming from the tank; this is the water Lalla prefers. It is clear like the water from the mountain springs, it is light, it slips over her clean skin like over a worn stone, it leaps up into the light, splashing back up in thousands of drops. Under the waterspout, the women wash their long heavy hair. Even the ugliest bodies grow beautiful through the crystal-clear water; the cold raises voices, makes shrill laughter ring out. Aamma throws huge armfuls at Lalla's face, and her extremely white teeth gleam in her copper face. The sparkling drops roll slowly down her dark breasts, her abdomen, her thighs. The water wears and polishes your skin, makes the palms of your hands very soft. It's cold, despite the steam filling the hangar.

Aamma envelops Lalla in a large towel, she wraps a sort of cloth around herself that she knots on her breast. Together, they walk toward the back of the hangar where their clothes were left folded on chairs. They sit down, and Aamma starts to slowly comb out Lalla's hair, one strand at a time, preening each of them carefully between the fingers of her left hand, to extract the nits.

That's great too, like in a dream, because Lalla is gazing straight out ahead, not thinking of anything, exhausted from all the water, drowsy from the heavy steam struggling up to the windows where the sunlight wavers, numbed from the noise of the voices and the laughter of the women, from the splashing water, the humming of the ovens where the stones are heating. So she is sitting on the metal chair, her bare feet resting on the cool cement floor, shivering in her large wet towel, and Aamma's adroit hands are combing tirelessly through her hair, pulling it out, preening it, while the last drops of water run down her cheeks and along her back.

Then, when everything is finished, and they've put their clothes back on, they go and sit down together outside, in the warmth of the setting sun, and they drink mint tea in small glasses decorated with gold designs, almost without speaking to one another, as if they had been on a long journey and had had their fill of the world's marvels. It's a long road back to the Project of planks and tarpaper on the other side of the river. The night is already blue-black, and the stars are shimmering between the clouds when they get home.

THERE ARE DAYS that aren't like all the others – feast days – and those are the days you sort of live for, wait for, hope for. When the day is near, no one speaks of anything else in the streets of the Project, in the houses, over by the fountain. Everyone is impatient and wants the feast day to come faster. Sometimes Lalla wakes up in the morning, her heart thumping, with a strange tingling in her arms and legs, because she thinks that today is the day. She jumps out of bed without even taking the time to run her hands through her hair and goes out into the street to run through the cold morning air, while the sun hasn't yet appeared and, except for a few birds, everything is gray and silent. But since there isn't a soul stirring in the Project, she realizes the day hasn't come yet, and all she can do is go back and get under her blankets again, unless she decides to make the most of it and go sit in the dunes to watch the first rays of sunlight touching the crests of the waves.

One thing that is long, and slow, that makes impatience seethe deep in the bodies of men and women, is fasting. Because throughout the days leading up to the feast, people eat very little, only just before and just after daylight, and they don't drink anything either. So, as time goes by, there is a kind of emptiness that spreads inside your body, that burns, that makes a buzzing sound in your ears. Even so, Lalla likes to fast, because when you don't eat or drink for hours on end, days on end, it's as if the inside of your body is being cleansed. The hours seem longer, and fuller, because you pay attention to the slightest little things. The children stop going to school, the women stop working in the fields, the boys stop going to the town. Everyone sits around in the shade of the shacks and the trees, conversing a little and watching the shadows move with the sun.

When you haven't eaten for days, the sky seems cleaner too, bluer and smoother over the white earth. Sounds ring out louder, and longer, as if you were inside a cave, and the light seems lovelier, purer.

Even the days are longer, it's hard to understand, but from the moment the sun rises until dusk, you'd think a whole month had gone by.

Lalla likes fasting in that way, when the sun burns down and dryness sweeps over everything. The gray dust leaves the taste of stone in your mouth, and from time to time you have to suck on the little lemon-flavored herbs or the bitter *chiba* leaves, being very careful to spit out your saliva.

During the fasting period, Lalla goes to see the Hartani up in the rocky hills every day. He too goes without eating or drinking all day long, but it doesn't change anything about the way he is, and his face is always the same burnt color. His eyes shine brightly in the shadow of his face, his teeth gleam in his smile. The only difference is that he covers himself up completely in his homespun robe, to prevent water loss from his body. He stands there on one leg like that, motionless in the sun, the other foot resting on his calf just under the knee, and he gazes out into the distance, over where the reflections are dancing in the air, over in the direction of the herd of goats and sheep.

Lalla sits down beside him on a flat stone, she listens to the sounds coming from all sides of the mountain, the insect calls, the whistling of the shepherds, and also the cracking sounds made by the heat dilating the stones and the wind passing. She's in no hurry, because during the fast, she doesn't have to go fetch water or dead wood for cooking.

It's great to be in the midst of all of this dryness when you're fasting because it is as if an intense feeling of suffering were stretched tight everywhere, like an insistent gaze. At night, the moon appears on the edge of the rocky hills, completely round, dilated. Then Aamma serves the chickpea soup with bread, and everyone eats quickly; even Selim, Aamma's husband, who is called the Soussi, eats hurriedly, without putting olive oil on his bread like he usually does. No one says a word, there are no stories. Lalla would rather like to talk, she'd have so many things to say, a little feverishly, but she knows that it's not possible, for one mustn't break the silence of the fast. That's the way it is when you fast, you also fast with words and with your whole head. And you walk slowly, dragging your feet a bit, and you don't point at things or people with your finger, you don't whistle with your mouth.

Sometimes the children forget that they're fasting because it's difficult to control yourself all the time. Then they burst out laughing, or they take off running through the streets, kicking up clouds of dust and making all the dogs start barking. But the old ladies shout after them and throw stones, and they soon stop running, maybe it's also because they lack strength due to the fast.

It all lasts for so long that Lalla doesn't really remember anymore what it was like before the fast began. Then one day Aamma goes off toward the hills to buy a sheep, and everyone knows that the day is drawing near. Aamma goes alone, because she says that Selim the Soussi is incapable of buying anything worthwhile. She walks away along the narrow path that snakes up toward the rocky hills, where the shepherds live. Lalla and the children follow her at a distance. When she reaches the hills, Lalla looks around to see if the Hartani is there, but she knows very well it's no use: the shepherd doesn't like people, and he flees when inhabitants of the Project come to buy sheep. The Hartani's adopted parents shear the sheep. They have built a corral of branches stuck into the ground, and they are sitting in the shade waiting.

Other sheep traders are there, and shepherds too. A strange odor of animal fat and urine hangs over the dry earth, and the sharp bleating of imprisoned animals can be heard coming from the pens of branches. A lot of people have come from the Project, even some from the towns; they left their cars at the entrance to the Project where the road ends and followed the path on foot. They're people from the North, with yellow skin, gentlemen dressed in suits, or else peasants from the South, Soussis, Fassis, people from Mogador. They know there are a lot of shepherds in the area, sometimes they know relatives or friends and hope to get a fine animal for a good price, clinch a good deal. So they are standing by the pens, haggling, making motions with their hands, leaning over the fences to get a better look at the sheep.

Aamma walks deliberately through the market. She doesn't stop, she just walks around the pens, looking rapidly at the animals, but she sees immediately what they're worth. When she's looked in all the pens, it's obvious she's chosen the sheep she wants. So then she goes to see the trader and asks his price. And since she wants that particular sheep and no other, she barely even haggles over the price and gives the owner his money right away. She was careful to bring a rope, and one of the shepherds puts it around the sheep's neck. That's it, now all that needs to be done is to bring the sheep back home. Aamma's eldest son, the one who is called Bareki, has the honor of leading the sheep back. It's a big strong sheep with a dirty yellow fleece that smells strongly of urine, but Lalla feels a little sorry for the sheep when it goes by, head hanging and eyes frightened because the boy is pulling with all his might on the rope and strangling it. Then they tie the sheep up behind Aamma's house in a shed of old boards made especially for it, and they give the sheep as much food and water as it wants for the last few days of its life.

So then one fine morning when Lalla wakes up, she knows immediately it's feast day. She knows it without needing anyone to tell her, just opening her eyes and seeing the cast of the light. She is on her feet in a second, out in the street with the other children, and already the rumor of the feast is beginning to run through the air, to rise over the houses of planks and tarpaper, like the sound of birds.

Lalla runs over the cold earth as fast as she can; she crosses fields, runs along the narrow path that leads to the sea. When she arrives at the top of the dunes, the sea wind hits her all at once, so hard that her nostrils close up, and she stumbles backward. The sea is dark and brutal, but the sky is still such a soft, light gray that Lalla isn't afraid anymore. She undresses quickly and, without hesitating, dives headfirst into the water. The unfurling wave covers her, rushes against her eyelids and eardrums, into her nostrils. The saltwater fills her mouth, runs down her throat. But on this day, Lalla isn't afraid of the sea; she drinks in large gulps of the saltwater and comes out of the wave staggering, as if drunk, blinded with the salt. Then she goes back into the wave that swells up around her.

Just then, the all-white seagull Lalla likes so much passes slowly overhead, mewing softly. Lalla waves at it, and she shouts out names at random to make it come:

"Hey! Kalla! Illa! Zemzar! Horriya! Habib! Cherara! Haïm. . ."

When she shouts that last name, the gull cocks its head and looks at her, and starts circling over the young girl.

"Haïm! Haïm!" shouts Lalla again, and now she's sure it's the name of the seafarer who was once lost at sea, because it's a name that means the Wanderer.

"Haïm! Haïm! Come here, please!"

But the white gull circles over once more and then flies away on the wind, down the beach, over to the place the other gulls gather every morning before taking flight for the city dump.

Lalla shivers a little because she's just this minute felt the chill of the wind and sea. The sun will soon be up. The pink and yellow flush is nascent behind the rocky hills where the Hartani lives. The light makes the drops of water on Lalla's skin sparkle, because she has goose bumps. The wind is blowing hard, and the sand has almost completely covered Lalla's blue dress. Without waiting to dry, she gets dressed and goes off half running, half walking, toward the Project.

Squatting in front of the door to her house, Aamma is cooking the flour fritters in the large pot filled with boiling oil. The earthen brazier is a red glow in the night shadows that still linger around the houses.

Now this just might be the very moment of the feast day that

Lalla likes best. Still shivering from the cold sea, she sits down in front of the burning brazier and eats the sizzling fritters, savoring the sweet dough and the harsh taste of the seawater that is still in the back of her throat. Aamma notices her wet hair and scolds her a little, but not much, because it's a feast day. Aamma's children also come and sit down near the brazier, their eyes still swollen with sleep, and later Selim the Soussi comes. They eat the fritters without saying anything, plunging their hands into the large earthenware platter filled with amber-colored fritters. Aamma's husband eats slowly, working his jaw as if he were chewing cud, and once in a while he stops eating to lick the drops of oil running down his hands. He does talk a little, saying trivial things that no one listens to.

There's something like the taste of blood about this day, because it's the day they have to kill the sheep. It's a funny feeling, as if there were something hard and tense, like the memory of a bad dream that makes your heart beat faster. The men and women are joyful, everyone is joyful because it's the end of the fast, and they're going to be able to keep eating and eating to their heart's content. But Lalla isn't able to be completely happy because of the sheep. It's hard to describe, it's like something hurried inside of her, a desire to flee. She thinks about that especially on feast days. Maybe she's like the Hartani, and she doesn't care much for feasts.

The butcher comes to kill the sheep. Sometimes it's Naman the fisherman because he's Jewish and can kill a sheep with no dishonor. Or sometimes it's a man who comes from far away, an Aissaoua with large muscular arms and a cruel face. Lalla hates him. With Naman it's different; he only does it when he's asked, to help out, and he won't accept anything but a piece of roast meat in return. But the butcher, he's cruel, and he'll only kill the sheep if he's given money. The man takes the animal away, pulling on the rope, and Lalla runs off to the sea, so she won't hear the wrenching cries of the sheep being dragged over to the square of tamped earth, not far from the fountain, and won't see the blood gushing out in spurts when the butcher cuts the animal's throat with his long, pointed knife, the steaming black blood filling up the enameled basins. But Lalla comes back soon, because deep down inside, there is that little tremor of desire, that hunger. When she nears Aamma's house again she can hear the clear sound of fire crackling, smell the exquisite odor of roasting meat. When roasting the choice pieces of mutton, Aamma doesn't want anyone to help her. She prefers to be left alone squatting in front of the fire, turning the spits – lengths of wire upon which the pieces of meat are strung. When the legs and chops are well done, she takes them off the fire and puts them on a large earthenware platter set directly on the coals. Then she calls Lalla, because now it's time for the smoking. This too is one of the moments of the feast day that Lalla prefers. She sits by the fire not far from Aamma. Lalla looks at her face through the flames and smoke. Once in a while, when Aamma casts a handful of moist herbs or green wood onto the fire, wafts of black smoke arise.

Aamma talks a little, at times, as she's preparing the meat, and Lalla listens to her along with the crackling of the fire, the shouts of children playing around them, and the voices of men; she smells the hot, strong odor soaking into the skin on her face, permeating her hair, her clothing. Lalla cuts the meat into fine strips with a small knife and places them on racks of green wood hanging above the fire, right where the smoke separates from the flames. This is also the moment when Aamma speaks of the old days, of life in the South, on the other side of the mountains, in the place where the desert sands begin and where the fresh-water springs are as blue as the sky.

"Tell me about Hawa, please, Aamma," Lalla says again.

And since the day is a long one, and there is nothing else to do but watch the strips of meat drying in the whirling smoke, using a twig to shift them from time to time, or else licking your fingers to keep from getting burned, Aamma starts talking. Her voice is slow and hesitant at first, as if she were making an effort to remember, and it goes well with the heat of the sun that is moving very slowly across the blue sky, with the crackling of the flames, with the smell of the meat and the smoke.

"Lalla Hawa" (that's what Aamma calls her) "was older than I, but I remember the first time she came to the house very well, accompanied by your father. She came from the South, from the open desert, and that's where he had met her, because her tribe was from the South, from the Saguiet al-Hamra, near the holy city of Smara, and her tribe belonged to the family of the great Ma al-Aïnine, the one who was called Water of the Eyes. But the tribe had to leave their lands because the soldiers of the Christians drove them all – men, women, and children – from their home, and they walked for days and months through the desert. That is what your mother told us later. In those days, people in the Souss Valley were poor, but we were happy to be together because your father loved Lalla Hawa very much. She laughed and sang, and she even played the guitar; she used to sit in front of the door to our house and sing songs. . ."

"What did she use to sing, Aamma?"

"Songs from the South, some of them in the language of the Chleuhs, songs about Assaka, Goulimine, Tan-Tan, but I wouldn't be able to sing them like she did."

"That doesn't matter, Aamma, just sing so I can hear it."

So then Aamma sings in a low voice, through the sound of the crackling flame. Lalla holds her breath to better hear her mother's song.

"One day, oh, one day, the crow will turn white, the sea will go dry, we will find honey in the desert flower, we will make up a bed of acacia sprays, oh, one day, the snake will spit no more poison, and rifle bullets will bring no more death, but that will be the day I will leave my love. . ."

Lalla listens to the voice murmuring in the fire without being able to see Aamma's face, as if her mother's voice were reaching her ears.

"One day, oh, one day, the wind will cease to blow in the desert, the grains of sand will become as sweet as sugar, under each white stone a spring will be awaiting me, one day, oh, one day, the bees will sing a song for me, for on that day I will have lost my love..."

But now Aamma's voice has changed, it is louder and more lilting, it goes up high like the voice of the flute, it rings out like copper bells; it isn't her voice anymore, it's a perfectly new voice, the voice of some unknown young woman who is singing through the curtain of flames for Lalla, just for Lalla.

"One day, oh, one day, the sun will shine at night, and puddles of moon water will gather in the desert, when the sky is so low I can touch the stars, one day, oh, one day, I'll see my shadow dancing before me, and that will be the day I will lose my love..."

The distant voice slips over Lalla like a shiver, envelops her, and her eyes get blurry as she watches the flames dance in the sunlight. The silence that follows the words of the song lasts a very long time, and in the background Lalla can hear the sounds of music and drums beating for the feast. Now she is alone, as if Aamma had gone, leaving her there with the strange voice singing the song.

"One day, oh, one day, I will look into the mirror and see your face, and I will hear the sound of your voice in the bottom of the well, and I will recognize your footsteps in the sand, one day, oh, one day, I will learn the day of my death, for that will be the day I will lose my love..."

The voice becomes deeper and more hushed like a sigh, it quivers a little in the flickering flame, is lost in the twirls of blue smoke.

"One day, oh, one day, the sun will be dark, the earth will split open to its very core, the sea will cover the desert, one day, oh, one day, my eyes will see no light, my lips will be unable to say your name, my heart will suffer no more, for that will be the day I will leave my love..."

The unknown voice fades away in a murmur, disappears in the blue smoke, and Lalla has to wait a long time without moving before she realizes that the voice won't come back. Her eyes are filled with tears, and her heart is aching, but she says nothing as Aamma resumes cutting off strips of meat and placing them on the wood lattices in the smoke.

"Tell me more about her, Aamma."

"She knew a lot of songs, Lalla Hawa did; she had a lovely voice, like you do, and she knew how to play the guitar and the flute and dance. Then when your father had the accident, she suddenly changed, and she never sang or played the guitar again, even when you were born, she never felt like singing again, except for you, when you cried in the night, to rock you and sing you to sleep. . ."

The wasps are out now. They're drawn by the smell of grilled meat, and they've come by the hundreds. They're humming around the fire, trying to land on the strips of meat. But the smoke drives them off, chokes them, and they fly drunkenly through the fire. Some fall onto the coals and blaze up with a short yellow flame, others fall to the ground, dazed, half burned. Poor wasps! They've come to get their share of the meat, but they don't know how to go about it. The bitter smoke makes them dizzy and infuriates them, because they can't land on the wood lattices. So they fly straight ahead, blinded, mindless as moths, and die. Lalla tosses them a piece of meat to stave off their hunger, to keep them away from the fire. But one of them hits Lalla, stings her on the neck. "Ouch!" Lalla shouts as she pulls it off and throws it away from her. She is stinging with pain, but feeling very sorry, because deep down inside she really likes the wasps.

Aamma pays no attention to the wasps. She bats them away with a wave of a rag and keeps turning the strips of meat on the lattices and talking.

"She didn't much like staying at home. . ." she said, her voice a little hushed as if she were relating a very old dream. "She would often go off, with you tied on her back with a scarf, and go far away, very far away. . . No one knew where she was going. She would get on the bus and go all the way to the ocean, or sometimes to the surrounding villages. She would go into the marketplaces, over by the fountains, where there were people she didn't know, and she would sit down on a stone and observe them. Maybe they thought she was a beggar... But she didn't want to work around the house because my family was hard on her, but I liked her a lot, she was like my sister."

"Tell me about her death again, Aamma."

"It's not right to speak of that on a feast day."

"It doesn't matter, Aamma, tell me about the day she died anyway."

Separated by the flames, Aamma and Lalla can't see each other very well. But it's as if there were other eyes touching them deep inside, right where it hurts.

The blue and gray plumes of smoke dance, swelling and shrinking like clouds, and on the lattices of green wood, the strips of meat have turned dark brown like old leather. In the background, the sun is slowly setting, the tide is rising with the wind, there is the song of crickets, the shouts of children running through the streets of the Project, the voices of men, music. But Lalla hardly hears any of that. She's totally absorbed in the whispering voice relating the death of her mother, long, long ago.

"We didn't know what was going to happen, no one knew. One day, Lalla Hawa went to bed because she was very tired, and she felt terribly cold all through her body. She remained in bed like that for several days without eating or moving, but she didn't complain. When we asked her what was wrong, she just said, nothing, nothing, I'm just tired, that's all. I was the one who was taking care of you then, feeding you, because Lalla Hawa couldn't even get out of bed... But there was no doctor in the village, and the dispensary was a long way away, and no one knew what to do. And then one day, it was on the sixth day, I think, Lalla Hawa called me, and her voice was very weak, she motioned to me to come closer and she simply said, 'I'm going to die,' that's all. Her voice was strange, and her face was all gray, and there was a burning look in her eyes. Then I became frightened and went running out of the house, and I took you as far away as I could, through the countryside until I reached a hill, and I stayed there all day long sitting under a tree while you played nearby. And when I came back to the house you were asleep, but I could hear the sounds of my mother and my sisters crying, and I came across my father in front of the house, and he told me that Lalla Hawa was dead. . ."

Lalla is listening with every fiber of her being, her eyes trained on the flames that are crackling and dancing before the twirls of smoke rising into the blue sky. The wasps continue their drunken flight, darting through the flames like bullets, falling to the ground, wings singed. Lalla is also listening to their music, the only true music of the plank and tarpaper Project.

"No one knew that would happen," said Aamma. "But when it happened, everyone cried, and I was filled with a cold feeling, as if I were going to die as well, and everyone was sad for you, because you were too young to understand. Later, I brought you here when my father died, and I had to come to the Project to live with the Soussi."

It will be a long time yet before the strips of meat are finished being smoked, so Aamma keeps on talking, but she says nothing more about Lalla Hawa. She talks about al-Azraq, who was called the Blue Man, who could tame the wind and the rain, who could make all things obey him, even the stones and the bushes. She talks about the hut made of branches and palm leaves that was his house, standing alone in the middle of the open desert. She says that the sky over the Blue Man's head would fill with birds of all sorts that sang celestial songs to accompany his prayer. But only those with a pure heart could find the house of the Blue Man. The others would get lost in the desert.

"Did he also know how to talk to wasps?" asks Lalla.

"To wasps and to wild bees, for he was their master, he knew the words to tame them. But he also knew the song to send clouds of wasps, bees, and flies to his enemies and he could have destroyed a whole city if he wanted to. But he was righteous and only used his powers to do good."

She also speaks of the desert, the wide open desert that commences south of Goulimine, east of Taroudant, beyond the Drâa Valley. It was there in the desert that Lalla was born, at the foot of a tree, as Aamma tells it. There in the open desert, the sky is immense; the horizon has no end because there is nothing for the eye to catch upon. The desert is like the sea, with the waves of wind over the hard sand, with the froth of rolling bramble bushes, with the flat stones, patches of lichen and plaques of salt, and the black shadows that dig out holes when the sun draws near to the earth. Aamma speaks of the desert for a long time, and while she speaks, the flames gradually grow smaller, the smoke gets lighter, transparent, and the embers slowly cover over with a kind of shimmering silver dust.

"Out there, in the open desert, men can walk for days without passing a single house, seeing a well, for the desert is so vast that no one can know it all. Men go out into the desert, and they are like ships at sea; no one knows when they will return. Sometimes there are storms, but nothing like here, terrible storms, and the wind tears up the sand and throws it high into the sky, and the men are lost. They die, drowned in the sand, they die lost like ships in a storm, and the sand retains their bodies. Everything is so different in that land; the sun isn't the same as it is here, it burns hotter, and there are men that come back blinded, their faces burned. Nights, the cold makes men who are lost scream out in pain, the cold breaks their bones. Even the men aren't the same as they are here . . . they are cruel, they stalk their prey like foxes, drawing silently near. They are black, like the Hartani, dressed in blue, faces veiled. They aren't men, but djinns, children of the devil, and they deal with the devil; they are like sorcerers. . ."

Then Lalla thinks again of al-Azraq, the Blue Man, master of the desert, he who could make water spring from under the desert stones.

Aamma thinks of him too and says, "The Blue Man was like the men of the desert, then he received God's blessing, and he left his tribe, his family, to live alone... But he knew the things that the people of the desert know. He was given the power of healing with his hands, and Lalla Hawa also had that power, and she knew how to interpret dreams, and tell the future, and find lost objects. And when people knew she was a descendant of al-Azraq, they would come to ask her advice, and sometimes she would tell them what they asked of her, and other times she didn't want to answer..."

Lalla looks at her hands and tries to understand what they hold. Her hands are large and strong, like the hands of boys, but the skin is soft and the fingers are tapered.

"Do I have the power too, Aamma?"

Aamma starts laughing, she rises to her feet and stretches.

"Don't think about that," she says. "The meat is ready now, it's time to put it on the platter."

When Aamma walks away, Lalla takes down the lattice rack and lays the strips of meat out on the earthenware platter, nibbling on a piece here and there. Since the fire has died down, the wasps have come back in droves; they're humming very loudly, dancing around Lalla's hands, getting tangled in her hair. Lalla isn't afraid of them. She shoos them away gently and throws them another piece of smoked meat, because today is a special day for them too.

Afterward, she goes down toward the sea following the narrow path that leads to the dunes. But she doesn't go as far as the water. She stays on the other side of the dunes, sheltered from the wind, and looks for a hollow in the sand in which to lie down. When she finds a place where there aren't too many thistles or ants, she lies down on her back, arms at her sides, and keeps her eyes on the sky. There are big white clouds scudding across. There is the slow sound of the sea scraping against the sand on the beach, and it's nice hearing it without being able to see it. There are the cries of the gulls slipping along on the wind, making the sunlight blink on and off. There are the sounds of dry shrubs, small acacia leaves, the rustling sound of the filao needles, like water. There are still a few wasps humming around Lalla's hands, because they smell of meat.

Then Lalla tries once again to hear the stranger's voice singing very far away, as if from another country, the voice that goes up and down agilely, clearly, like the sound of fountains, like the sunlight. The sky before her grows slowly dim, but night is a long time in coming because it is the end of winter and the beginning of the season of light. Dusk is first gray, then red, with huge clouds like flaming manes. Lalla remains stretched out in her hollow of sand between the dunes, without taking her eyes off the clouds and the sky. She really does hear, in the *whoosh* of the sea and the wind, in the sharp cries of the gulls seeking out a beach for the night, she hears the soft voice repeating its lament, the clear, yet somewhat shaky voice, as if it already knew death was coming to silence it, the voice which is as pure as the water you can never drink enough of after long scorching days. It's a music born of the heavens and of the clouds, it bounces off the sand of the dunes, spreads out and resonates everywhere, even in the dry thistle leaves. It's singing for Lalla, just for Lalla, it envelops her and cleanses her in its fresh waters, it runs its hand through her hair, over her forehead, across her lips, it declares its love, it descends upon her and gives her its blessing. So then Lalla turns away and hides her face in the sand, because something inside of her has come undone, has broken, and tears come silently. No one comes to put a hand on her shoulder and ask, "Why are you crying, little Lalla?" Yet the stranger's voice makes her warm tears flow, it stirs up images deep inside of her that have been still for years. The tears run into the sand and make a little wet spot under her chin, make the sand stick to her cheeks, her lips. Then suddenly it is gone. The voice deep in the sky has grown silent. Night has fallen now, a lovely, dark blue, velvet night in which the stars sparkle between the phosphorescent clouds. Lalla shivers as if with a passing fever. She wanders down along the dunes amidst the blinking lightning bugs. Because she is afraid of snakes, she goes back to the narrow path where she can still see her footprints and walks slowly toward the Project where the feast is still going on.

LALLA IS WAITING for something. She doesn't really know what it is, but she's waiting. The days are long in the Project, the rainy days, the windy days, the summer days. Sometimes Lalla thinks she's simply waiting for the days to come, but when they arrive, she realizes that wasn't it. She's waiting, that's all. People have a lot of patience, maybe they wait for something all their lives, and nothing ever comes.

The men often sit around on a stone in the sunshine, their heads covered with a flap of their coat or a bath towel. They just stare out into the distance. What are they looking at? The dusty horizon, the dirt tracks where the trucks are rolling along, like large multicolored beetles, and the outline of the rocky hills, the white clouds moving across the sky. That's what they are looking at. They have no desire for anything else. The women are waiting too, over by the fountain, not talking, veiled in black, their bare feet planted squarely on the ground.

Even the children know how to wait. They sit down in front of the store, and wait, just like that, without playing or shouting. Once in a while, one of them will get up and go turn in his coins for a bottle of Fanta or a handful of mints. The others watch him in silence.

There are days when you don't know where you're headed, when you don't know what might happen. Everyone keeps an eye on the street, and by the side of the highway, the ragged children are awaiting the arrival of the blue bus, or the passage of large trucks carrying diesel fuel, wood, cement. Lalla is very familiar with the sound of the trucks. Sometimes she goes and sits with the other children on the new stone embankment at the entrance to the Project. When a truck is coming, all the children turn toward the far end of the road, a long way off, out where the air dances over the asphalt and makes the hills shimmer. You can hear the sound of the motor long before the truck appears. It's a high-pitched droning, almost like a whistle with, every now and again, a sharp honk that blares out and echoes off the walls of the houses. Then a cloud of dust comes into view, a yellow cloud mingled with the blue exhaust of the motor. The red truck comes barreling down the paved road at top speed. Over the cab of the truck there is an exhaust pipe spitting out blue smoke, and the sun glints brightly off the windshield and the chrome. The tires are devouring the pavement and zigzagging a little due to the wind, and every time the tires of the semi slip off the pavement, a cloud of dust billows into the sky. Then the truck passes in front of the children, honking very loudly, and the earth shakes under its fourteen black tires, and the dusty wind and pungent odor of diesel fumes waft over them like a hot breath.

Long afterward, the children are still talking about the red truck and telling stories about trucks, red trucks, white tank trucks, and yellow crane trucks.

That's what it's like when you're waiting. You often go out and watch the roads, the bridges, and the sea, to see the people who haven't been left behind going by, those who are getting away.

Some days are longer than others, because you're hungry. Lalla knows those days well, when there's not a penny in the house, and Aamma hasn't found any work in town. Even Selim the Soussi, Aamma's husband, doesn't know where to try to find money anymore, and everyone gets gloomy, sad, almost mean. So Lalla stays outdoors all day long; she goes as far out as possible on the plateau of stones, out where the shepherds live, and looks for the Hartani.

It's always the same; when she really wants to see him, he appears in a dip in the ground, sitting on a stone, his head wrapped up in a white cloth. He's watching his goats and sheep. His face is black, his hands thin and strong like the hands of an old man. He shares his black bread and dates with Lalla, and he even gives a few pieces to the shepherds who have come forward.

147

But he's not proud about it; it's as if what he gives is of no importance.

Lalla glances over at him every once in a while. She loves his imperturbable face, the aquiline profile, and the light that glows in his dark eyes. The Hartani is also waiting for something, but he's perhaps the only one who knows what he's waiting for. He doesn't say what it is since he doesn't know how to speak the language of human beings. But you can guess from his eyes what he's waiting for, what he's looking for. It's as if part of him had been left behind in the place of his birth, beyond the rocky hills and the snow-capped mountains, in the immensity of the desert, and one day he would have to find that part of himself, in order to really be whole.

Lalla stays with the shepherd all day long, only she doesn't get too near to him. She sits on a stone, not far away, and gazes out in the distance; she looks at the air dancing and rushing over the arid valley, the white light making sparks, and the slow meandering of the goats and sheep through the white stones.

When the days are sad, anxious, the Hartani is the only one who can be there, and who doesn't need words. A look is enough, and he knows how to give bread and dates with nothing in exchange. He even prefers for you to stay a few steps away from him, just like the goats and the sheep, who never completely belong to anyone.

All day long, Lalla listens to the calls of the shepherds in the hills, whistling that bores through the white silence. When she goes back to the Project of planks and tarpaper, she feels freer, even if Aamma does scold her because she's brought nothing home to eat.

That's the kind of day it is when Aamma takes Lalla to the house of the woman who sells carpets. It's on the other side of the river in a poor part of the city, in a big white house with narrow screened windows. When she enters the room used as a workshop, Lalla hears the sound of weaving looms. There are twenty of them, maybe more, lined up one behind the other in the milky half-light of the large room where three neon tubes are flickering. In front of the looms, little girls are squatting or sitting on stools. They work rapidly, pushing the shuttle between the warp threads, taking the small steel scissors, cutting the pile, packing the wool down on the weft. The oldest must be about fourteen; the youngest is probably not yet eight. They aren't talking, they don't even look at Lalla when she comes into the workshop with Aamma and the merchant woman. The merchant's name is Zora; she is a tall woman dressed in black who always holds a flexible switch in her pudgy hands with which to whip the little girls on the legs and shoulders when they don't work fast enough or when they talk to their workmates.

"Has she ever worked?" she asks, without even glancing at Lalla.

Aamma says she's shown her how people used to weave in the old days. Zora nods her head. She seems very pale, maybe because of the black dress, or else because she never leaves the shop. She walks slowly over to a free loom, upon which there is a large dark red carpet with white spots.

"She can finish this one," she says.

Lalla sits down and starts to work. She works in the large dim room for several hours, making mechanical gestures with her hands. At first she has to stop, because her fingers get tired, but she can feel the eyes of the tall pale lady on her and starts working again right away. She knows the pale woman won't whip her with the switch because she is older than the other girls working there. When their eyes meet, Lalla feels something like a shock deep inside, and a glint of anger flares in her eyes. But the fat woman dressed in black takes it out on the smaller girls, the skinny ones who cower like she-dogs, daughters of beggars, abandoned girls who live at Zora's house year-round and who have no money. The minute their work slows down, or if they exchange a few words in a whisper, the fat pale woman descends upon them with surprising agility and lashes their backs with her switch. But the little girls never cry. All you can hear is the whistling of

149

the whip and the dull whack on their backs. Lalla clenches her teeth; she looks down at the ground to avoid seeing or hearing it, because she too would like to shout and lash out at Zora. But she doesn't say anything because of the money she's supposed to bring back to the house for Aamma. To get even, she just ties a few knots the wrong way in the red carpet.

Still, the following day Lalla just can't stand it anymore. When the fat pale woman resumes whipping Mina – a puny, thin little girl of barely ten – with the switch because she's broken her shuttle, Lalla stands up and says coldly, "Stop beating her!"

Zora looks at Lalla incredulously for a minute. Her pale flabby face has taken on such an idiotic expression that Lalla repeats, "Stop beating her!"

Suddenly, Zora's features screw up in hatred. She strikes out vehemently at Lalla's face with the switch, but only grazes her left shoulder, as Lalla manages to dodge the blow.

"You'll see the beating I'll give you!" Zora screams, and now there's some color to her face.

"You bully! You wicked woman!"

Lalla grabs Zora's switch and breaks it over her knee. Then it is fear that twists the fat woman's face.

She backs away stuttering, "Get out! Get out! Right now! Get out!"

But Lalla is already running across the large room; she leaps outside into the sunlight; she runs without stopping all the way back to Aamma's house. Freedom is beautiful. You can watch the clouds floating along upside down again, the wasps busying themselves around little piles of garbage, the lizards, the chameleons, the grasses quivering in the wind. Lalla sits down in front of the house, in the shade of the wall of planks, and listens eagerly to all the minute sounds.

When Aamma comes home around evening time, she simply says, "I'm not going back to work at Zora's, ever again."

* * *

Since that day, things here in the Project have really changed for Lalla. It's as if she'd grown up all of a sudden, and people have started noticing her. Even Aamma's sons aren't like they used to be, cold and scornful. Sometimes she sort of misses the days when she was very young, when she had just arrived in the Project, and no one knew her name, and she could hide behind a shrub, in a bucket, in a cardboard box. She really enjoyed that, being like a shadow, coming and going without being seen, without being spoken to.

Old Naman and the Hartani are the only ones who haven't changed. Naman the fisherman still tells incredible stories as he repairs his nets on the beach, or when he comes to eat corn cakes at Aamma's house. He hardly ever catches fish anymore, but people really like him and continue to invite him over. His pale eyes are as transparent as water, and his face is stitched with deep wrinkles like scars from ancient wounds.

Aamma listens to him talk about Spain, about Marseille, or Paris, and about all the cities where he has been, where he's walked, where he knows the names of the streets and the people who live there. Aamma asks him questions, asks him if his brother can help her find work over there.

Naman nods his head. "Why not?"

That's his answer to everything, but he promises to write his brother all the same. Leaving the country is complicated though. You need money, papers. Aamma remains pensive, a faraway look in her eyes; she's dreaming of white cities with so many streets, houses, automobiles. Maybe that's what she's waiting for.

Lalla doesn't think about that very much herself. It's all the same to her. She's watching Naman's eyes, and it's a little bit as if she had known those seas, those countries, those houses.

The Hartani doesn't think about it either. He's remained like a child still, even though he's as tall and strong as an adult. His body is slim and elongated, his face is pure and smooth like a piece of ebony. Maybe it's because he doesn't know how to speak the same language others do.

151

He still sits down on a rock, staring out into the distance, wearing his homespun robe, with the white cloth on his head drawn over his face. Around him there are still black shepherds just like him, wild, dressed in rags, whistling as they leap from rock to rock. Lalla likes coming out where they live, out to the place which is filled with white light, the place where time stands still, where you can't grow up.

THE MAN WALKED into Aamma's house one morning in the beginning of summer. He was a man from the city, wearing a gray suit with a green sheen, black leather shoes that were as shiny as mirrors. He came with a few gifts for Aamma and her sons, an electric mirror framed in white plastic, a transistor radio no larger than a box of matches, pens with gold-colored caps, and a bag full of sugar and canned food. When he came into the house he passed Lalla at the door but hardly looked at her. He lay all the presents on the floor; Aamma told him to sit down, and he looked around for a seat, but there were only cushions and Lalla Hawa's wooden trunk that Aamma had brought back from the South with Lalla. The man chose to sit on the trunk after having tested it a little with the palm of his hand. The man waited for tea and sweet cakes to be brought to him.

When she learned a little later that the man had come to ask for her hand in marriage, Lalla felt very frightened. It made her head spin, and her heart started beating wildly. It wasn't Aamma who told her about it, but Bareki, Aamma's eldest son.

"Our mother decided to have you marry him, because he is very rich."

"But I don't want to get married!" Lalla shouted.

"You have nothing to say about it, you must obey your aunt," Bareki said.

"Never! Never!" Lalla ran off shouting, her eyes filled with angry tears.

Then she went back to Aamma's house. The man with the gray-green suit was gone, but the gifts were there. Ali, Aamma's younger son, was even listening to music, holding the tiny transistor radio against his ear. When Lalla walked in, he gave her a knowing look.

"Why did you keep that man's gifts? I won't marry him," Lalla said to Aamma coldly.

Aamma's son snickered, "Maybe she wants to marry the Hartani!"

"Get out!" said Aamma. The young man went out with the transistor.

"You can't force me to marry that man!" Lalla says.

"He will be a good husband for you," responds Aamma. "He's no longer very young, but he's rich, he has a big house in the city, and he has lots of powerful relations. You must marry him."

"I don't want to get married, ever!"

Aamma remains silent for a long time. When she speaks again, her voice is softer, but Lalla stays on her guard.

"I raised you as if you were my own daughter, I love you, and today you would affront me in this way?"

Lalla looks angrily at Aamma, because for the first time she's seeing her dishonest side.

"I don't care," she says. "I don't want to marry that man. I don't want these ridiculous gifts!"

She motions toward the electric mirror on its stand on the dried mud floor. "You don't even have electricity!"

Then suddenly, she's had enough. She leaves Aamma's house and goes out to the sea. But this time she doesn't run along the path; she walks very slowly. Today, nothing is the same. It's as if everything has been dulled, worn down from being looked at so much.

"I'm going to have to leave," Lalla says out loud to herself. But she immediately thinks that she doesn't even know where to go. So then she crosses over to the other side of the dunes and walks along the wide beach, looking for Old Naman. She would so like for him to be there, as usual, sitting on a root of the old fig tree, repairing his nets. She would ask him all sorts of questions about those cities in Spain with magic names, Algeciras, Málaga, Granada, Teruel, Zaragoza, and about those ports from which ships as big as cities sail, about the roads upon which automobiles drive northward, about trains and airplanes departing. She'd like to listen to him talk for hours about those snow-capped mountains and those tunnels, those rivers that are as vast as the sea, those wheat-covered plains, immense forests, and most of all about those fragrant cities where there are white palaces, churches, fountains, stores glittering with light. Paris, Marseille, and all of those streets, houses so tall you can barely see the sky, the gardens, the cafés, the hotels, and the intersections where you meet people from all corners of the world.

But Lalla can't find the old fisherman. There is only the white gull gliding slowly along facing the wind, wheeling over her head.

"Hey-o! Hey-o! Prince!"

The white bird swoops over Lalla a few more times, then, caught up in the wind, flies quickly away in the direction of the river.

So Lalla stays on the beach for a long time, with only the sound of the wind and the sea in her ears.

The following days, no one said a word about anything in Aamma's house, and the man with the gray-green suit didn't come back. The little transistor radio was already demolished, and the cans of food had all been eaten. Only the plastic electric mirror remained where it had been placed, on the tamped earth near the door.

Lalla hadn't slept well any of those nights, trembling at the slightest sounds. She remembered stories she'd been told about girls who had been taken away by force, in the night, because they didn't want to get married. Every morning at daybreak, Lalla went out before anyone else, to wash herself and fetch the water at the fountain. That way, she could keep an eye on the entrance to the Project.

Then came the wind of ill fortune, which blew over the land for several days in a row. The wind of ill fortune is a bizarre wind that only comes once or twice a year, at the end of winter or in the fall. The strangest thing about it is that you don't really feel it at first. It doesn't blow very hard, and sometimes it stops altogether, and you forget about it. It's not a cold wind like those of the midwinter storms, when the sea unleashes its furious waves. It's not a hot desiccating wind either, like the one that comes from the desert and lights the houses with a red glow, the one that makes sand hiss over the metal and tarpaper roofs. No, the wind of ill fortune is a very mild wind that swirls around, tosses a few gusts about, and then settles heavily on the roofs of the houses, on people's shoulders and chests. When it's here, the air gets hotter and heavier, as if there were a gray veil over everything.

When that slow, mild wind comes, people fall sick, almost everywhere, especially small children and elderly people, and they die. That's why it's called the wind of ill fortune.

When it began to blow on the Project that particular year, Lalla recognized it right away. She saw the clouds of gray dust moving over the plain, blurring the sea and the mouth of the river. Then people only went out muffled up in their cloaks in spite of the heat. There were no more wasps, and the dogs went off to hide in the hollows at the feet of the houses, with their noses in the dust. Lalla was sad, because she thought of the people the wind would sweep away in its path. So when she heard that Old Naman was sick, there was a pang in her heart and she couldn't breathe for a minute. She'd never really had that feeling before, and she had to sit down to keep from falling.

Then she walked and ran all the way to the fisherman's house. She thought there would be people with him, helping him, caring for him, but Naman is all alone, lying on his straw mat, his head resting on his arm. He is shivering so hard that his teeth are chattering, and he can't even raise himself up on his elbows when Lalla comes into the house. He smiles a little, and his eyes shine brighter when he recognizes Lalla. His eyes are still the color of the sea, but his thin face has turned a white, slightly gray color that is frightening.

She sits down next to him and talks to him, almost in hushed tones. Usually he's the one who tells stories, and she listens, but today all that has changed. Lalla just talks to him about any old thing, to soothe her anxiety and impart a little human warmth to the old man. She talks to him about things that he used to tell her of in the past, things about his trips to the cities in Spain and France. She talks about it all as if she'd been the one who had seen those cities, who had taken those long journeys. She talks to him about the streets of Algeciras, narrow winding streets near the port, where you can smell the sea wind and the odor of fish, and the train station with blue tiled platforms, and the big railroad trestles straddling ravines and rivers. She talks to him about the streets of Cádiz, gardens with multicolored flowers, tall palm trees lined up in front of white palaces, and about all of those streets with crowds, with black automobiles, buses, coming and going amid mirrored reflections, past buildings as tall as marble cliffs. She talks about the streets of all the cities, as if she had walked through them, Sevilla, Córdoba, Granada, Almadén, Toledo, Aranjuez, and about the city that is so big, you could get lost for days on end – *Madris*, where people come from all corners of the earth.

Old Naman listens to Lalla without saying anything, without moving, but his clear eyes shine brightly, and Lalla knows he loves hearing those stories. When she stops talking, she can hear the old man's body trembling and his breath wheezing: so she quickly resumes to avoid hearing those terrible sounds.

Now she's talking about the big city of Marseille in France, about the port with immense wharves where boats from all the countries in the world are docked, freighters as big as citadels with incredibly high forecastles and masts thicker than trees, very white ocean liners with thousands of windows that have strange names, mysterious flags, names of cities, Odessa, Riga, Bergen, Limassol. In the streets of Marseille, the crowd hurries along, endlessly going in and out of giant stores, jostling in front of the cafés, restaurants, movie theaters, and the black automobiles drive down the avenues leading who knows where, and trains fly over the roofs on suspended bridges, and airplanes take off and circle slowly in the gray sky above the buildings and the vacant lots. At noon, the church bells ring, and the sound reverberates through the streets, over the esplanades, deep down in the underground tunnels. At night, the city is lit up, lighthouses sweep the sea with their long pencils, automobile headlights glitter. The narrow streets are silent, and thieves armed with jackknives hide in doorways waiting for late-night stragglers. Sometimes there are terrible battles in vacant lots, or on the wharves in the shadows of the sleeping freighters.

Lalla talks for such a long time and her voice is so soft that Old Naman falls asleep. When he is asleep, his body stops trembling, and his breathing becomes more regular. Then Lalla can leave the fisherman's house at last, her eyes stinging from the light outside.

Many people are suffering from the wind of ill fortune, poor people, infants. When she passes by their houses, Lalla can hear their laments, the moaning voices of women, children crying, and she knows that there too, perhaps, someone will die. She is sad; she wishes she were far away, across the sea, in those cities she invented for Old Naman.

But the man with the gray-green suit has come back. He probably doesn't know that the wind of ill fortune is blowing on the plank and tarpaper Project; in any case he wouldn't really care, because the wind of ill fortune doesn't affect people like him. He's a stranger to ill fortune, to all of this.

He's come back to Aamma's house, and he passes Lalla in front of the door. When she sees him, it startles her and she lets out a little shriek, because she knew he would come back and felt apprehensive about it. The man in the gray-green suit gives her a funny look. He has a hard steady gaze, like people who are used to giving orders, and the skin on his face is white and dry with the blue shadow of a beard on his cheeks and chin. He's carrying other bags containing gifts. Lalla steps aside when he passes her and looks at the packages. He mistakes her glance and takes a step toward her, holding out the gifts. But Lalla leaps back as fast as she can; she runs away without turning back until she can feel the sand of the path that leads up to the plateau of stones under her feet.

She doesn't know where the path ends. Eyes blurred with tears, a knot in her throat, Lalla is walking as fast as she can. Up here the sun is always hotter, as if you were closer to the sky. But the heavy wind is not blowing on the brick- and chalk-colored hills. The stones are hard, broken and sharp-edged, jagged; the black shrubs are covered with thorns upon which, here and there, tufts of sheep's wool have snagged; even the blades of grass are sharp as knives. Lalla walks for a long time through the hills. Some are high and steep, with cliffs like sheer walls; others are low, hardly more than a pile of stones, and you'd think they'd been made by children.

Every time Lalla enters this land, she feels as if she no longer belongs to the same world, as if time and space had expanded, as if the ardent light of the sky had penetrated her lungs and dilated them, and her whole body had taken on the proportions of a giant who would live for a very long time, very slowly.

Taking her time now, Lalla follows the bed of a dry torrent up toward the vast plateau of stones, where the one she calls al-Ser dwells.

She doesn't really know why she's heading in that direction; it's sort of as if there were two Lallas, one who didn't know, blinded with anxiety and anger, fleeing the wind of ill fortune, and the other who did know and was making her legs walk in the direction of al-Ser's dwelling place. So she's climbing up to the plateau of stones, her mind blank, not understanding. Her bare feet find the ancient traces that the wind and the sun weren't able to erase.

She is slowly climbing up toward the plateau of stones. The sun is burning her face and shoulders, burning her hands and legs. But she can barely feel it. It's the light that is liberating, that erases memories, that makes you as pure as a white stone. The light cleanses the wind of ill fortune, burns away sickness, evil spells.

Lalla is moving forward, eyes almost closed against the reverberating light, and sweat is making her dress stick to her abdomen, to her chest, to her back. Never, perhaps, has there been so much light on earth, and never has Lalla so thirsted after it, as if she had come from a dark valley in which death and shadows prevailed. The air up here is still, it is hovering, it flickers and pulsates, and you think you can hear the sound of light waves, the strange music that resembles the song of bees.

When she reaches the vast, deserted plateau, the wind blows against her again, making her stagger. It is a cold, hard, unrelenting wind that pushes against her and makes her shiver in her damp, sweaty clothing. The light is blinding; it explodes in the wind, glinting in starbursts off the peaks of the rocks. Up here, there is no grass, no trees, no water, only light and wind for centuries on end. There are no paths, no human traces. Lalla is moving forward aimlessly, in the middle of the plateau, where only scorpions and scolopendras live. It is a place where no one comes, not even the desert shepherds, and when one of their animals strays up here, they jump up and down, whistling and throwing stones to make it come running back.

Lalla is walking slowly along, eyes almost closed, putting the tips of her bare toes down on the burning rocks. It's like being in another world, near the sun, balancing precariously, ready to fall. She's moving forward, but the essence of her is absent, or rather, her whole being is preceding her, her vision, her acutely tuned senses, only her body remains behind, still hesitating on the sharp-edged rocks.

She's waiting impatiently for the one who is bound to come now, she's sure of it, he must come. As soon as she'd started running to escape the man with the gray-green suit, escape Old Naman's death, she knew someone was waiting for her up on the plateau of stones, up where there are no people. It is the desert warrior veiled in blue, of whom she knows only the razor-sharp gaze. He was watching her from high up in the deserted hills, and his eyes reached all the way out to her and touched her, pulled her straight up here.

Now she is standing still in the middle of the vast plateau of stones. Around her there is nothing, only the mounds of stones, the powdered light, the cold hard wind, the intense sky with not a cloud, not a trace of mist.

Lalla remains motionless, standing up on a large, slightly inclined slab of stone, a hard dry slab of stone that no water has ever polished. The sunlight is beating down upon her, pulsating on her forehead, on her chest, in her belly, the light which is a gaze.

The blue warrior will certainly come now. It won't be long. Lalla thinks she hears the soft tread of his feet in the dust, her heart is pounding hard. Whirls of white light envelop her, curling their flames around her legs, tangling in her hair, and she can feel the rough tongue of light burning her lips and her eyelids. Salty tears stream down her cheeks, run into her mouth, salty sweat runs down drop by drop from under her arms, stinging her ribs, trickles down the length of her neck, down between her shoulder blades. The blue warrior must come, now, his gaze will be white-hot like the light of the sun.

But Lalla remains alone in the middle of the deserted plateau, standing on her sloping slab of rock. The cold wind is burning her, the dreadful wind that shuns human life, it's blowing to abrade her, to pulverize her. The wind that blows up here hardly even cares for the scorpions and the scolopendras, the lizards or the snakes; it might have a slight penchant for the foxes with their burnt coats. Yet Lalla isn't afraid of it, because she knows that somewhere between the rocks, or maybe up in the sky, there is the gaze of the Blue Man, the one she calls al-Ser, the Secret, because he is hidden. He is surely going to come, his eyes will look straight into the deepest part of her being and give her the strength to fight against the man in the suit, against the death hovering over Naman, will transform her into a bird, throw her up into the center of space; then maybe she could at last join the big white gull who is a prince, and who flies untiringly over the sea.

When the gaze reaches her, it makes a whirlwind in her head, like a wave of light unfurling. The gaze of al-Ser is brighter than fire, a light that is blue and burning at once, like that of the stars.

Lalla stops breathing for a few moments. Her pupils are dilated. She squats down in the dust, eyes closed, head thrown backward, because there is a terrible weight in that light, a weight which is entering her and making her as heavy as stone.

He has come. Once again, without making a sound, slipping over the sharp stones, dressed like the ancient warriors of the desert, with his ample cloak of white wool, and his face veiled with a midnight-blue cloth. Lalla watches him moving forward in her dream with every fiber of her being. She sees his hands tinted with indigo, she sees the light pouring from his dark eyes. He doesn't speak. He never speaks. It is with his eyes that he speaks, for he lives in a world where there is no need for the words of men. There are great whirls of golden light around his white cloak, as if the wind were raising clouds of sand. But Lalla can hear only the beat of her own heart, pounding very slowly, far away.

Lalla has no need for words. She has no need to ask questions, or even to think. Eyes closed, squatting in the dust, she can feel the eyes of the Blue Man upon her, and the warmth penetrates her body, pulses through her limbs. That is the extraordinary thing. The warmth of the gaze finds its way into the smallest recesses of her body, driving out the pain, the fever, the blood clots, everything that can obstruct and cause pain.

Al-Ser does not move. Now he's standing in front of her, while the waves of light slip and swirl around his cloak. What is he doing? Lalla is no longer afraid, she can feel the warmth growing inside of her, as if it were radiating out through her face, illuminating her whole body.

She can see what is in the eyes of the Blue Man. It is all around her, out into infinity, the shimmering, undulating desert, showers of sparks, the slow waves of dunes inching into the unknown. There are towns, large white cities with towers as slender as palm trees, red palaces adorned with foliage, vines, giant flowers. There are vast lakes of sky-blue water, water so lovely, so pure that it exists nowhere else on earth. It is a dream that Lalla is having, eyes closed, head thrown backward in the sunlight, arms wrapped around her knees. It is a dream that has come from afar, that existed up here on the plateau of stones long before her, a dream in which she is now partaking, as if in sleep, and its realm is unfolding before her.

Where does the path lead? Lalla doesn't know where she's going, drifting along in the desert wind that is blowing, burning her lips and eyelids at times, blinding and cruel, and at other times cold and slow, the wind that obliterates people and makes rocks tumble to the foot of cliffs. It's the wind that is leading out to infinity, out beyond the horizon, beyond the sky, all the way out to the frozen constellations, to the Milky Way, to the sun.

The wind carries her along on the endless path, the immense plateau of stones where the light is whirling. The desert unfurls its empty, sand-colored fields, strewn with crevasses, as wrinkled as dead skin. The gaze of the Blue Man is everywhere, all the way out in the farthest reaches of the desert, and it is through his eyes now that Lalla is seeing the light. She can feel the burn of his gaze, the wind, the dryness on her skin, and her lips taste of salt. She sees the shapes of the dunes, large sleeping animals, and the high black walls of the Hamada, and the immense dried-up city of red earth. This is the land where there are no humans, no towns, nothing that stops and unsettles. There is only stone, sand, wind. Yet Lalla feels happy because she recognizes everything, each detail of the landscape, each charred shrub in the large valley. It's as if she had walked there, long ago, the ground scorching her bare feet, eyes trained out on the horizon shimmering in the air. Then her heart starts beating harder and faster and she sees signs appear, lost traces, broken twigs, bushes quivering in the wind. She waits, she knows she will get there soon, it is very near now. The gaze of the Blue Man guides her over the fissures, the rockslides, along dry torrents. Then all of a sudden she hears that strange, uncertain, nasal song, quavering way off in the distance; it seems to be coming up from the sand itself, mingling with the constant swish of wind over stones, with the sound of the light. The song makes Lalla's insides flutter; she recognizes it; it's Lalla Hawa's song, the one that Aamma sang, the one that went, "One day, oh, one day, the crow will turn white, the sea will go dry, we will find honey in the desert flower, we will make up a bed of acacia sprays..." But now Lalla can't understand the words anymore because someone is singing in a very distant voice, in the Chleuh language. Yet the song goes straight to her heart, and her eyes fill with tears, despite her holding them closed with all her might.

The music lasts for a long time; it lulls her for such a long time that the shadows under the stones stretch out on the desert sand. Then Lalla can also make out the red city at the end of the immense valley. It's not really a city like those with which Lalla is familiar, those with streets and houses. It's a city of mud, wasted by time and worn with the wind, like the nests of termites or wasps. The light is beautiful over the red city, forming a clear pure dome of tranquility in the eternal dawn sky. The houses are grouped around the mouth of the well, and there are several trees, white acacias, standing stock-still like statues. But what Lalla notices most of all is a white tomb, as simple as an eggshell set down upon the red earth. That is where the light of the gaze is coming from, and Lalla realizes it is the dwelling place of the Blue Man.

Something terrible, yet at the same time very beautiful is reaching out to Lalla. It's as if something deep down inside of her were being torn and broken and allowing death, the unknown to enter. The burn of the desert heat inside of her spreads, courses through her veins, mixes with her entrails. The gaze of al-Ser is terrifying and painful, because it is the suffering born of the desert: hunger, fear, death, which come, pass over her. The lovely golden light, the red city, the delicate white tomb from which the supernatural light is emanating, also carry with them sorrow, anxiety, abandonment. It is a long anguished gaze that comes because the earth is hard, and the sky wants nothing to do with men.

Lalla remains motionless, crumpled over on herself, knees on the stones. The sun is burning her shoulders and neck. She doesn't open her eyes. Two streams of tears make little furrows in the red dust caked on her face.

When she lifts her head and opens her eyes, her vision is blurred. She needs to make an effort to see straight. The sharp silhouettes of the hills appear, then the deserted stretch of the plateau, with not a blade of grass, not a tree, only the light and the wind.

So then she begins to walk, staggering, slowly making her way back down the path leading to the valley, to the sea, to the plank and tarpaper Project. The shadows are long now, the sun is near the horizon. Lalla can feel her face swollen from the burn of the desert, and she thinks no one will be able to recognize her, now that she's become like the Hartani.

When she gets back down near the mouth of the river, night has fallen on the Project. The electric lightbulbs make yellow dots. On the road, trucks are driving along throwing out the white beams of their headlights, idiotically.

At times Lalla runs, at other times she moves very slowly, as if she were going to stop, turn around, and flee. There are a few radios making their music mechanically in the night. The fires of the braziers are going out on their own, and in the houses of poorly fitted planks, the women and children are already rolled up in their blankets because of the night dampness. From time to time, the faint wind makes an empty can roll, a piece of corrugated iron flap. The dogs are hiding. Above the Project, the black sky is filled with stars.

Lalla walks silently through the alleys and thinks that no one here needs her, that everything is just perfect without her, as if she'd been gone for years, as if she'd never existed.

Instead of going toward Aamma's house, Lalla walks slowly to the other end of the Project, where Old Naman lives. She's shivering because the night air is very damp, and her knees are trembling beneath her because she hasn't eaten anything since the day before. The day was so long up there on the plateau of stones that Lalla has the impression she's been gone for days, maybe months. It's as if she barely recognizes the streets of the Project, the sounds of children crying, the smell of urine and dust. Suddenly she thinks maybe months really have gone by, up there on the plateau of stones, and it only seemed like one long day. Then she thinks of Old Naman, and her throat tightens. In spite of her weakness, she starts running through the empty streets of the Project. The dogs hear her running; it makes them growl and bark a little. When she arrives in front of Naman's house, her heart is beating very hard, and she can barely breathe. The door is cracked open; there is no light.

Old Naman is lying on his mat, just as she'd left him. He's still breathing, very slowly, with a wheeze, and his eyes are wide open in the dark. Lalla leans over his face, but he doesn't recognize her. His mouth is so busy trying to breathe, it can't smile anymore.

"Naman . . . Naman. . ." Lalla murmurs.

Old Naman has no strength left. The wind of ill fortune has given him a fever, the kind that weighs on your body and on your head and keeps you from eating. The wind might carry him away. Anxiously Lalla leans down near the fisherman's face.

She says, "You don't want to go now? Not now, not yet?"

She wants so much to be able to hear Naman talk to her, tell her the story of the white bird who was a prince of the sea once again, or the story of the stone the Archangel Gabriel gave to human beings, and which turned black with their sins. But Old Naman can't tell stories anymore; he barely has enough strength to raise his chest to breathe, as if there were an invisible weight upon him. Foul sweat and urine soak the thin body lying seemingly broken on the floor.

Lalla is too tired now to tell other stories, to continue talking about everything over there, across the sea, all of those cities in Spain and France.

So she sits down next to the old man and watches the night light through the open door. She listens to the wheezing breath, hears the evil sound of the wind outside, rolling tin cans around and making pieces of corrugated iron flap. Then she falls asleep, like that, sitting with her head resting on her knees. From time to time Old Naman's choked breathing awakens her, and she asks, "Are you there? Are you still there?"

He doesn't respond, he's not sleeping; his gray face is turned toward the door, but his shiny eyes don't seem to see anymore, as if they were contemplating what lies beyond.

Lalla tries to fight against sleep, because she's afraid of what will happen if she goes to sleep. It's like the fishermen, the ones who are far away, lost out at sea, who can't see anything, rocked on the waves, caught in the whirling winds of the storm. They can't ever fall asleep because then the sea will grab them, throw them down into the depths, swallow them up. Lalla wants to resist, but her eyelids close in spite of herself, and she feels herself falling backwards. She swims for a long time without knowing where she's going, borne along on the slow sound of Old Naman's breathing.

Then, before daybreak, she awakens with a start. She looks at the old man stretched out on the floor, his peaceful face resting against his arm. He's not making a sound now, because he has stopped breathing. Outside, the wind has stopped blowing, the danger has passed. Everything is peaceful, as if no one ever died, anywhere.

WHEN LALLA DECIDED to leave, she didn't say anything to anyone. She decided to leave because the man with the gray-green suit came back to Aamma's house several times, and each time he looked at Lalla with those eyes that were as shiny and hard as black stones, and he sat on Lalla Hawa's trunk to drink a glass of mint tea. Lalla isn't afraid of him, but she knows if she doesn't go away, one day he'll force her to go to his house and marry him, because he is rich and powerful and doesn't like anyone to resist him.

She left this morning at the crack of dawn. She didn't even glance into the back of the house at the shape of Aamma sleeping, rolled up in her sheet. She just took a piece of blue cloth in which she put some stale bread and a few dried dates, and a gold bracelet that had belonged to her mother.

She went out without making a sound, without even waking a dog. She walked barefoot over the cold earth, between the rows of sleepy houses. Before her, the sky is a little pale, because day is coming. The mist is coming in from the sea; it makes a big, soft cloud that floats up the river, spreading out two curving arms like a gigantic bird with gray wings.

For a minute, Lalla feels like going as far as Naman the fisherman's house, just to see it once more, because he's the only person that Lalla has felt sad about losing. But she's afraid of being late, and she walks away from the Project, along the goat path, toward the rocky hills. When she begins climbing up the rocks, she feels the cold wind cutting through her. There is no one up here either. The shepherds are still asleep in their huts of branches by the corrals, and it's the first time that Lalla has entered the region without hearing their sharp whistling. It makes her a little frightened, as if the wind had turned the earth into a desert. But little by little, the sunlight appears on the other side of the hills, a red and yellow patch mingling with the gray night. Lalla is glad to see it, and she thinks that is where she'll go later, to the place where the sky and the earth are filled with that huge patch of first light.

Thoughts are a bit jumbled in her mind as she walks over the rocks. It's because she knows she won't be coming back to the Project, that she'll never see all the things she is so fond of again, the vast arid plain, the stretch of white beach where the waves fall one after the other; she's sad because she's thinking of the still dunes where she used to sit and watch the clouds make their way across the sky. She'll never see the white bird who was the prince of the sea again, or the silhouette of Old Naman sitting in the shade of the fig tree by his upturned boat. So she slows down her pace a bit, and for a minute she feels like looking back. But before her are the silent hills, the sharp stones where the light is beginning to sparkle, and the little thorn bushes, where small droplets of moisture from the sky are trembling, and also the feather-light gnats drifting along on the wind.

So she walks on without turning around, holding the bundle of bread and dates tightly against her chest. When the path comes to an end, it means there are no more humans around. Then the sharp stones come up out of the ground, and you have to leap from rock to rock, making your way up to the highest hill. That's where the Hartani is waiting for her, but she can't see him yet. Maybe he's hiding in a cave over by the cliff, in the place where you can look out over the whole valley, all the way to the sea. Or else he's right nearby, behind a burnt bush, hidden up to his neck in some hole made from a stone, just like a snake.

He's always on the lookout, like the wild dogs, ready to jump away, take flight. Maybe today he doesn't want to leave anymore? Yet Lalla told him only yesterday that she would come, and she'd pointed to the long expanse in the distance, to the large block of limestone that seems to be holding up the sky, right where the desert begins. His eyes had shone brighter, because the idea has always been in his mind, since he was very small, and he has never stopped thinking about it for a second. You can tell by the way he looks out at the horizon, neck craning forward, eyes fixed. He never sits down; he squats on his heels, as if he were ready to leap up. He's the one who showed Lalla the path in the desert, the path you get lost on, the one no one ever comes back from, and the sky, so beautiful and pure out there.

The sun is up now, it appears before her like a huge disk of fire, dazzling, it rises slowly, ballooning out over the chaos of stone. Never has it seemed so beautiful. In spite of the pain and the tears pouring from her eyes and running down her cheeks, Lalla looks straight at it, without blinking, just like Old Naman said the princes of the sea did. The light goes deep inside of her, touches everything that is hidden in her body, especially her heart.

There's no longer any trace of the path now, and Lalla has to pick her way through the boulders. She jumps from rock to rock, over dried torrents, she skirts the cliff walls. The rising sun has made a big blind spot on her retinas, and she's moving along somewhat haphazardly, bent forward to keep from falling. She goes through the hills, one after the other, then walks down the middle of a vast field of stones. There isn't a soul. As far as she can see, there is nothing but the expanse of dry stone, with a few cactuses and tufts of euphorbia. The sun has depopulated the earth, burned it and worn it down until there is nothing left but these white stones, this brush. Lalla isn't looking straight at it anymore; it is too high in the sky, and her pupils would be burned in a second, as if by lightning. The sky is ablaze. It's blue and is burning like a huge flame, and Lalla has to squint up her eyes very tightly to be able to see ahead of herself. As the sun gradually rises in the sky, the things of the earth fill out, soak up light. There is no sound out here, but it seems as if you can hear the stones dilating, cracking from time to time.

She's been walking for a long time. How long? Hours probably, without knowing where she's going, simply in the opposite direction of her shadow, toward the other end of the horizon.

Out there, the tall red mountains seem to be hanging in the sky, there are villages, a river maybe, lakes of sky-colored water. Then suddenly, without her understanding where he's come from, the Hartani is there, standing in front of her. He isn't moving, dressed as he is every day in his homespun robe, his head wrapped in a piece of white cloth. His face is black, but his smile lights it up when Lalla walks up to him.

"Oh, Hartani! Hartani!"

Lalla presses herself against him; she recognizes the smell of his sweat and his dusty clothes. He too has brought a little bread and some dates in a damp rag tied to his belt.

Lalla opens her bundle and shares a little bread with him. They eat quickly, without sitting down, because they've been hungry for a long time. The young shepherd glances around. He is studying the landscape carefully, and he resembles a bird of prey with unblinking eyes. He motions to a point, far away, out on the horizon over by the red mountains. He puts the palm of his hand under his lips: there is water out there.

They start walking again. The Hartani is out front, jumping lightly over the rocks. Lalla tries to place her feet in his steps. The boy's frail, light-footed silhouette is forever out in front of her, he seems to be dancing over the white stones; she watches it like a flame, like a reflection, and her feet seem to move all by themselves, in rhythm with the Hartani.

The sun is beating down hard now, it weighs on Lalla's head and shoulders, it aches inside her body. It's as if the light that entered her in the morning was beginning to burn, to well up, and she can feel long painful waves moving up her arms and legs, becoming lodged in the cavity of her skull. The burn of the light is dry and dusty. There is not a drop of sweat on Lalla's body, and her blue dress rubs against her belly and thighs, crackling with static electricity. The tears in her eyes have dried; crusts of salt have made sharp little crystals like grains of sand in the corners of her eyelids. Her mouth is dry and hard. She runs the ends of her fingers over her lips and thinks that her mouth has become like that of a camel, and she'll soon be able to eat cactuses and thistles without feeling anything.

As for the Hartani, he's still springing from rock to rock without looking back. His nimble white silhouette is farther and farther away; it's like an animal fleeing, not stopping, not looking back. Lalla would like to catch up with him, but she hasn't enough strength left. She staggers haphazardly over the chaos of stones, eyes trained straight ahead. Her wounded feet are bleeding, and in falling down several times, she's skinned her knees. But she can hardly feel the pain at all. All she can feel is the withering reverberation of the light everywhere. It's as if there were a bunch of animals jumping all about her on the rocks, wild dogs, horses, rats, goats making tremendous leaps. . . There are also large white birds, ibises, secretary birds, storks, beating their long fiery wings, as if they were trying to take flight, and they begin an interminable dance. Lalla can feel the breeze from their wings in her hair; she can hear the rustling of their quill feathers in the thick air. So then she turns her head, looks back to see all of those birds, all of those animals, even the lions she glimpsed out of the corner of her eye. But when she looks at them, they instantly melt away, disappear like mirages, and recompose behind her.

The Hartani is barely visible. His light silhouette is dancing over the white stones, like a shadow detached from the earth. Lalla isn't trying to follow in his steps now, she can't even see the immobile red mass of the mountain in the sky at the other end of the plain any longer. Maybe she's not moving forward anymore? Her bare feet stub up against the rocks, bleed, stumble over holes. But it is as if the path is always undoing itself right behind her, like river water slipping through your legs. Most of all, it's the light which is flowing by, it runs down onto the vast empty plain, flows by on the wind, sweeping over the open space. The light is making a sound like water, and Lalla hears its song, without being able to drink. The light is coming from the center of the sky; it burns down on the earth in the gypsum, in the mica.

From time to time, in amidst the ochre dust between the white pebbles, there is an ember-colored flint, sharp as a fang. Lalla keeps her eye on its glint as she walks, as if the stone were giving her strength, as if it were a sign left by al-Ser, to show her which way to go. Or else, still farther out, a plaque of mica just like gold, with reflections that look like a nest of insects, and Lalla thinks she can hear the humming of their wings. But sometimes on the dusty ground, there just happens to be a dull, gray, round stone, an ordinary shingle from the sea, and Lalla looks at it as hard as she can; she takes it in her hand and holds it tight, to save herself. The stone is burning hot, all striped with white veins that make up a route in its center from which branch other routes as fine as baby hairs. Holding it in her fist, Lalla walks straight ahead. The sun is already going down toward the other end of the white plain. The evening wind is sweeping up flurries of dust that hide the tall red mountain at the foot of the sky.

"Hartani! Hartani!" Lalla shouts. She's fallen to her knees on the stones because her legs refuse to walk any farther. Above her the sky is blank, ever more vast, ever more blank. There isn't an echo to be heard.

Everything is clear and pure, Lalla can see the smallest pebbles, the slightest shrub, almost all the way out to the horizon. No one is moving. She'd love to see the wasps; she thinks she'd really like that, watch them making their invisible knots in the air around the children's hair. She'd really like to see a bird, even a crow, even a vulture. But there's nothing, no one. Only her dark shadow stretching out behind her, like a pit in the too-white earth.

So she lies down on the ground, and thinks that she is going to die soon, because there's no strength left in her body, and the fire of the light is burning her lungs and her heart up. Slowly, the light fades, and the sky becomes veiled, but perhaps it is the weakness inside of her that is dimming the sun.

Suddenly Hartani is there again. He's standing in front of her on one leg, balancing himself like a bird. He comes up to her, leans over. Lalla grabs onto his homespun robe, she clings to the cloth with all her might, she doesn't want to let go of it, and she almost makes the boy fall over. He squats down next to her. His face is dark, but his eyes are filled with intensity and are shining very brightly. He touches Lalla's face, her forehead, her eyes, he runs his fingers over her cracked lips. He motions to a point out on the stony plain, in the direction of the setting sun, over where there is a tree next to a rock: water. Is it near, is it far? The air is so pure that it's impossible to tell. Lalla tries to get back to her feet, but her body isn't responding anymore.

"Hartani, I can't go on. . ." murmurs Lalla, nodding toward her bleeding legs doubled up underneath her.

"Go away! Leave me, go away!"

The shepherd hesitates, still squatting next to her. Maybe he is going to go away? Lalla looks at him without saying anything; she feels like going to sleep, disappearing. But the Hartani puts his arms around Lalla's body, slowly lifts her up. Lalla can feel the muscles of the boy's legs trembling under the load, and she tightens her arms around his neck, tries to make her weight blend in with that of the shepherd.

The Hartani walks over the stones, he lopes along quickly as if he were alone. He runs along on his long wobbly legs, crossing ravines, striding over rifts. The sun and the dusty wind have stopped whirling over the stony plain, but there are still slow movements out on the red horizon throwing sparks off the flint stones. There is something like a huge funnel of light before them, out where the sun has plunged toward the earth. Lalla listens to the Hartani's heart beating in the arteries of his neck, she can hear his panting breath.

Before nightfall, they reach the rock and the tree, the place where there is an eye of water. It's just a hole in the stony ground with gray water in it. The Hartani sets Lalla down gently beside the water and helps her drink from his cupped hand. The water is cold, a little bitter. Then the shepherd leans over too, and drinks for a long time with his head near the water.

They wait for the night. It falls very rapidly out here, sort of like a curtain being drawn, with no mist, no clouds, nothing spectacular. It's almost as if there were no more air, or water, just the glow of the sun being gradually extinguished by the mountains.

Lalla is lying on the ground against the Hartani. She isn't moving. Her legs are bone tired, lacerated, and the clotted blood has made scabs covering the soles of her feet like black shoe leather. Sometimes the pain from her feet shoots up through her legs, running along the bones and muscles to her groin. She moans a little, teeth clenched to keep from crying out, her hands squeeze the young boy's arms. He doesn't look at her; he's looking straight out at the horizon, over in the direction of the dark mountains, or maybe he's watching the huge night sky. His face has grown very black due to the shadows. Is he thinking about something? Lalla would really like to go inside of him to find out what he wants, where he's going. . . She starts to talk, more for herself than for him. The Hartani listens to her in the way a dog does, lifting its head and following the sound of the syllables.

She talks to him about the man with the gray-green suit, about his hard black eyes like bits of metal, and then about the night spent with Naman, when the wind of ill fortune was blowing over the Project. She says, "Now that I've chosen you for my husband, no one can take me away, or force me to go before a judge to get married. . . We're going to live together now and we'll have a child, and no one else will want to marry me, you understand, Hartani? Even if they catch us, I'll say that you are my husband, and that we are going to have a child, and they won't be able to stop that. So then they'll let us go, and we can go and live in the lands to the south, far away, in the desert. . ."

She no longer feels the fatigue, or the pain, only the exhilaration of that freedom, in the middle of the field of stones, in the silent night. She holds the body of the young shepherd very tightly until their odors and their breaths have completely mingled. Very slowly, the boy enters and possesses her, and she can hear the sound of his heart quickening against her chest.

Lalla turns her face up toward the center of the sky, and looks out intently. The cold, beautiful night envelops them, holding them in its blue darkness. Never has Lalla seen such a beautiful night. Back there in the Project, or on the shores of the sea, there was always something that came between you and the night – mist or dust. There was always a veil dulling it, because there were people everywhere, with their fires, their food, their breathing. But here, everything is pure. Now the Hartani lies down beside her, and a very deep, dizzy feeling traverses them, widening their pupils.

The Hartani's face is taut, as if the skin on his forehead and cheeks was of polished stone. Above them, space slowly fills with stars, thousands of stars. They throw out bursts of white, pulse, trace their secret figures. The two fugitives watch them, almost holding their breath, eyes wide. They can feel the pattern of the constellations settling on their faces, as if they only existed through their gaze, as if they were drinking in the soft light of night. They aren't thinking of anything anymore, not of the path in the desert, not of the suffering they will know tomorrow or the other days; they can't feel their wounds anymore, or hunger or thirst, or anything earthly; they have even forgotten the burn of the sun that blackened their faces and bodies, that devoured the inside of their eyes.

The starlight falls gently down like rain. It makes not a sound, raises no dust, stirs up no wind. Now it is lighting the stony field, and the area around the mouth of the well, the charred tree becomes light and frail as a wisp of smoke. The earth is no longer really flat, it has been drawn out like the prow of a boat, and now it drifts slowly forward, glides along, rocking and rolling, moving slowly through the lovely stars, while the two children holding tightly to one another, bodies buoyed, carry out the gestures of lovemaking.

New stars appear every second, tiny, hardly even possible in the blackness, and the invisible threads of their light join the others. There are myriads of gray, red, white lights intermingling with the deep blue of the night, suspended like bubbles.

Later, as the Hartani is drifting peacefully off to sleep with his face against her, Lalla watches all the signs, all the bursts of light, everything that is pulsing, flickering, or remaining fixed, like an eye. Still higher up, directly above her, is the vast Milky Way, the path traced by the blood of Gabriel's lamb, according to what Old Naman used to say.

She drinks in the extremely soft light coming from the clusters of stars, and suddenly she has the feeling, like the words to the song Lalla Hawa's voice sang, that it is so very close, she could simply reach out her hand and take a handful of the beautiful shimmering light. But she doesn't move. Her hand is resting on the Hartani's neck and listening to the blood beating in his arteries, the tranquil passage of his breathing. Night has eased the fever of the sun and the dryness. Thirst, hunger, anxiety have all been relieved by the light of the galaxy, and on her skin, like droplets, are the marks of each star in the sky.

The two children can no longer see the earth now, holding tightly to one another, they are wheeling out through the open sky.

EACH DAY ADDED a little more land. The caravan had been divided into three sections, separated by a two- or three-hour march. The one headed by Larhdaf was on the left, over by the foothills of the Haua, on the route to Sidi al-Hach. Saadbou, the youngest son of the great sheik, was leading the one on the far right, following the dried riverbed of the Jang Saccum up through the middle of the valley of the Saguiet al-Hamra. In the middle, and hanging back, Ma al-Aïnine moved along with his warriors on camelback. Then came the caravan of men, women, and children prodding their livestock out in front, following the huge cloud of red dust rising into the sky ahead of them.

Each day, they walked along the bottom of the immense valley while the sun over their heads followed the opposite path. It was the end of winter, and the rains had not yet assuaged the earth. The bottom of the Saguiet al-Hamra was as hard and crackled as an old goatskin. Even its red color burned their eyes and the skin on their faces.

In the morning, before the sun was even up, the call for the first prayer rang out. Then the sounds of the animals arose. The smoke from the braziers filled the valley. In the distance, Larhdaf's soldiers called out their chants and were answered by Saadbou's men. But the blue men of the great sheik prayed in silence. When the first signs of red dust rose into the air, the men set the herds to moving. Everyone picked up their bundles and started walking again over the earth, which was still cold and gray.

Slowly, day broke on the horizon, up above the

Hamada. The men watched as the gleaming disk lit up the valley bottom and, already, they squinted their eyes and leaned slightly forward, as if to resist the weight and pain of the light on their brows and shoulders.

At times Larhdaf's and Saadbou's troops were so close that the sound of their horses' hooves and the grumbling of their camels could be heard. Then the three dust clouds blended together in the sky and almost obscured the sun.

When the sun was at its zenith, the wind rose and swept everything clean, driving away the high walls of red dust and sand. The men stopped their herds in half circles and took shelter behind the reclining camels or up against the thorn bushes. The earth seemed as vast as the sky, as barren, as blinding.

Nour walked behind the great sheik's troops, carrying his load of provisions in a large piece of canvas knotted around his chest. Each day from dawn to dusk, he walked in the tracks of horses and men without knowing where he was going, without being able to see his father, or his mother, or his sisters. Sometimes he would meet back up with them in the evening, when the travelers lit their twig fires for tea and porridge. He spoke to no one, and no one spoke to him. It was as if the fatigue and dryness had burned up the words in his throat.

When night was falling, and the animals had pawed out a hollow in which to sleep, Nour was able to take a look at the immense deserted valley surrounding him. Walking out a little ways from the camp, standing upon the desiccated plain, Nour felt as if he were as tall as a tree. The valley seemed boundless, an infinite expanse of stones and red sand, unchanged since the beginning of time. Scattered in the distance were the burnt shapes of small acacias, bushes, and tufts of cactuses and dwarf palms, in places where the moisture in the valley made faint dark marks. The earth took on a mineral color in the twilight. Nour stood absolutely still, waiting for darkness to descend and fill up the valley, slowly, like impalpable water.

Later, other parties of nomads came to join Ma al-Aïnine's group. They conferred with the chieftains of the tribes, asking them where they were going and then followed the same route. Now there were several thousand of them walking along the valley toward the wells of Hausa, al-Faunat, and Yorf.

Nour no longer knew how many days it had been since the journey began. Maybe it was only one single and interminable day unfolding like that, while the sun rose and set again in the blazing sky, and the cloud of dust swirled in on itself, churning like a wave. The men following Ma al-Aïnine's sons were far ahead; they had probably already reached the end of the Saguiet al-Hamra, beyond the tomb of Mohammed Embarek, the place where the lunar wasteland of the valley of Mesuar opens out on the plateau of the Hamada. Maybe their horses were already climbing the slopes of the rocky hills, and seeing the immense valley of the Saguiet al-Hamra opening out behind them with the billowing red-ochre clouds of Ma al-Aïnine's people and herds.

Now, the men and women in the last column were beginning to slow down. From time to time, Nour stopped to wait for his mother and sisters' group. He sat down on the hot stones, a flap of his cloak pulled over his head, and watched the horde moving slowly along the trail. The unmounted warriors walked bent over, staggering under the loads on their shoulders. Some of them were leaning on their rifles, their spears. Their faces were black, and through the crunching of their footsteps in the sand, Nour could hear the sound of their labored breathing.

Behind them came the children and the shepherds, pursuing the herds of goats and sheep, throwing stones to drive them onward. The swirls of dust enveloped them like a red fog, and Nour watched the strange, disheveled shapes that seemed to be dancing in the dust. The women walked alongside the pack camels, some were carrying babies in their cloaks, slowly making their way barefoot over the scorching earth. Nour could hear the clear tinkling of their gold and copper necklaces, the bangles on their ankles. They walked along humming a sad interminable song that came and went like the sound of the wind.

But at the very end came those who could not go on, the aged, the infants, the wounded, young women whose men were dead and who no longer had anyone to help them find food or water. There were many of them, scattered along the trail in the valley of the Saguiet, and they kept coming for hours after the soldiers of the sheik had passed. They were the ones Nour looked upon with special compassion.

Standing by the side of the trail, he saw them walking slowly past, hardly lifting their legs, heavy with weariness. They had emaciated gray faces, eyes shiny with fever. Their lips were bleeding; their hands and chests were marked with wounds where the clotted blood had mixed with golden particles of dust. The sun beat down on them as it did on the red stones of the path, and they received a real beating. The women had no shoes, and their bare feet were burned from the sand and eaten away with the salt. But the most painful thing about them, the most disquieting thing that made pity rise in Nour's breast, was their silence. Not one of them spoke or sang. No one cried or moaned. All of them, men, women, children with bleeding feet, plodded noiselessly forward, like a defeated people, not uttering a word. All that could be heard was the sound of their footsteps in the sand and the shallow panting of their breaths. Then they moved slowly away, bundles rocking on their backs, like strange insects after a storm.

Nour remained standing by the side of the trail, his bundle resting at his feet. From time to time, when an old woman or a wounded soldier walked in his direction, he tried to talk to them, drew near them saying, "Hello, hello, you aren't too terribly tired, are you? Would you like me to help you with your load?"

But they remained silent, they didn't even look at him, and their faces were as hard as the stones in the valley, closed tight against the pain and the light.

A group of men from the desert came, warriors from Chinguetti. Their ample sky-blue cloaks were in shreds. They had bound up their legs and feet with bloodstained rags. They were carrying nothing, not even a bag of rice, not even a flask of water. They had nothing left but their rifles and their spears and they struggled along, like the old people and children.

One of them was blind, and he was holding on to the group by a flap of cloak, staggering over the rocks in the path, tripping against the roots of shrubs.

When he passed near Nour and heard the voice of the young boy greeting them, he stopped and let go of his companion's cloak.

"Have we arrived?" he asked.

The others kept on walking without even looking back. The desert warrior's face was still young, but wasted with fatigue, and a dirty piece of cloth was tied across his burned eyes.

Nour gave him a little of his water to drink, put his load back on his shoulders, and placed the warrior's hand on his cloak.

182

"Come, I'll be your guide now."

They struck out walking on the path again, toward the end of the valley, pursuing the huge cloud of red dust.

The man did not speak. His hand was gripping Nour's shoulder so tightly it was painful. In the evening, when they stopped at the Yorf well, the boy was exhausted. They had now reached the foot of the red cliffs, where the mesas of the Haua and the valley leading northward began.

All the caravans had come together there: Larhdaf's, Saadbou's and the great sheik's, with his blue men. In the dusk light, Nour watched the thousands of men sitting on the dried earth around the dark stain of the well. The red dust was settling gradually, and the smoke of the braziers was already rising into the sky.

When Nour had rested, he picked up his bundle but didn't knot it around his chest. He took the blind warrior's hand, and they walked over to the well.

Everyone had already drunk, the men and women on the east side of the well, the animals on the west side. The water was murky, mixed with the red mud of the banks. Yet never had it seemed more beautiful to the people. The cloudless sky shone upon its black surface as if upon polished metal.

Nour leaned toward the water and drank deeply without catching his breath. Kneeling at the edge of the well, the blind warrior also drank, avidly, almost without even using his cupped hand. When he had had his fill, he sat down at the edge of the well, his face dark and his beard dripping with water.

Then they walked back, over near the animals. The sheik had given the order for everyone to stay clear of the well, so as not to trouble the water.

Night was falling quickly near the Hamada. Darkness crept into the bottom of the valley, leaving only the sharp peaks of red stone in the flaming sun.

Nour looked for his mother and father for a minute, without seeing them. Maybe they had already left for the first part of the northern trail with Larhdaf's soldiers. Nour chose a place for the night, near the livestock. He set his bundle down and shared a piece of millet bread and some dates with the blind warrior. The man ate quickly and stretched out afterward on the ground with his hands under his head. Then Nour spoke to him, to ask him who he was. The man began slowly, with his voice slightly hoarse from having remained silent, telling about everything that had happened back there, far away in Chinguetti, near the great salt lake of Chinchan, the soldiers of the Christians who had attacked the caravans, burned the villages, who had taken the children away to camps. When the soldiers of the Christians had come from the west, from the shores of the sea, or else from the south, warriors clad in white, mounted on camels, and black men from Niger, the desert peoples had had to flee northward. During one of the battles, he had been wounded with a rifle and had lost his sight. So his companions had brought him northward, to the holy city of Smara, because they said the great sheik knew how to heal wounds caused by the Christians, that he had the power of restoring sight. While he was talking, tears ran from his closed eyelids, because now he was thinking of everything he had lost.

"Do you know where we are now?" He was always asking that of Nour, as if he were afraid of being abandoned there, in the middle of the desert.

"Do you know where we are? Are we still a long way from the place where we'll be able to stop for good?"

"No," Nour would say, "we'll soon reach the lands the

sheik promised, the lands of plenty, where it will be like the kingdom of God."

But he had no idea, and deep down in his heart, he thought perhaps they would never reach that land, even if they did cross the desert, the mountains, and even the sea, all the way out to the place where the sun first appears on the horizon.

Now the blind warrior was starting to speak again, but he wasn't talking about the war. He was telling, in an almost hushed voice, about his childhood in Chinguetti, the salt road with his father and brothers. He was telling about his schooling in the Chinguetti mosque and then the departure of the huge caravans, through the expanse of the desert, heading for the Adrar, and even farther east, out by the Hank Mountains, around the Abd al-Malek well, where the miraculous tomb stands. He was talking about all of that softly, almost singing, lying on the ground, with the cool darkness of night covering his face and his burned eyes.

Nour lay down beside him, wrapped in his woolen cloak, his head resting upon the bundle, and he went to sleep with his eyes open, looking up at the sky and listening to the voice of the man who was talking to himself.

Desert nights were cold, but Nour's tongue and lips continued to burn, and it seemed as if red-hot coins were placed on his eyelids. The wind blew over the rocks, making the men shiver with fever in their rags. Somewhere in the midst of the sleeping warriors, the old sheik draped in his white cloak was looking out at the night, not sleeping, as he had done for months. His gaze wandered through the maze of stars bathing the earth in their soft light. Sometimes, he walked a short way among the sleeping men. Then he went back to sit in his place and drink some tea, slowly, listening to the coals crackling in the brazier.

185

Days passed in that way, burning and grueling, while the herds of men and animals made their way northward up the valley. Now they were following the trail to Tindouf, through the arid plateau of the Hamada. The sons of Ma al-Aïnine, along with the most able-bodied men, rode on ahead to scout out the narrow valleys of the Ouarkziz Mountains, but that route was too difficult for the women and children, and the sheik decided to follow the trail to the east.

Nour walked at the end of the caravan with the blind warrior clutching his shoulder. Each day the bundle of provisions grew lighter, and Nour knew there would not be enough to get to the end of the journey.

Now they were walking along the immense plateau of stones, very close to the sky. Sometimes they crossed crevasses, great black wounds in the white rock, slides of knifelike stones. The blind warrior squeezed Nour's shoulder and arm very tightly to keep from falling.

The men had worn out their goatskin shoes, and many of them had wrapped their feet in strips of their garments to stop the bleeding. The women went barefoot because they were used to it since their childhood, but at times a sharper stone cut into their skin, and they moaned as they walked.

The blind warrior never talked during the day. His dark face was hidden by his blue cloak and the bandage covering his eyes like the hood of a falcon. He walked without complaining, and ever since Nour had become his guide, he was no longer afraid of getting lost. Only when he could feel evening coming on, when Larhdaf and Saadbou's men, far out ahead in the valleys, called out in their chanting voices the signal to halt, the blind warrior would always ask with the same anxiousness, "Is

186

this the place? Have we arrived? Tell me, have we arrived in the place where we will stop at last?"

Nour looked around and saw nothing but the endless stretch of stone and dust, the changeless earth beneath the sky. He untied his bundle and simply said, "No, this isn't it yet."

Then, as he did every evening, the blind warrior would drink a few swallows from the waterskin, eat a few dates and some bread, stretch out on the ground, and continue to talk about things in his land, about the great holy city of Chinguetti, near Lake Chinchan. He talked about the oasis where the water is green, where the palm trees are immense and their fruit is as sweet as honey, where the shady groves are filled with the song of birds and the laughter of young girls on their way to fetch water. He talked about all of that in a sort of singsong voice, softly, as if he were rocking himself to ease the suffering. At times, his companions came to sit with him; they shared bread and dates with Nour, or they made tea from *chiba* weed. They listened to the blind warrior's monologue, then they too spoke of their land, of the wells in the South, Atar, Oujeft, Tamchakatt, and of the great city of Oualata. They spoke a strange, gentle language like that of the prayers, and their thin faces were the color of metal. When the sun was nearing the horizon, and the deserted plateau grew bright with light, they knelt down and prayed, foreheads in the dust. Nour helped the blind warrior bow down facing eastward, then he lay down, wrapped in his cloak, and listened to the sound of the men's voices until sleep crept over him.

That is how they crossed the Ouarkziz Mountains, following the fissures and the dried beds of torrents. The caravan was spread out across the entire plateau, from one end of the horizon to the other. The huge column of red dust rose each day in the blue sky, slanting in the wind. The herd of goats and sheep, the pack camels walked amidst the men, blinding them with dust. Far behind them, old people, sick women, abandoned children, wounded warriors walked in the excruciating light, heads bowed, legs wobbling, leaving drops of blood here and there in their tracks.

The first time Nour saw someone fall by the side of the trail without a sound, he wanted to stop; but the blue warriors and those who were walking with him pushed him onward, not saying anything, because there was nothing else to do. Now Nour no longer stopped. Sometimes there would be the shape of a body in the dust, arms and legs drawn in, as if it were asleep. It was an old man, or woman, that the pain and exhaustion had stopped there, by the side of the trail, struck in the back of the head as if with a hammer, the body already desiccated. The blowing wind would throw handfuls of sand over it, would soon cover it over, without anyone having to dig a grave.

Nour thought of the old woman who had given him some tea back there in the Smara camp. Maybe she too had fallen one day, struck down by the sun, and the desert sand had covered her over. But he didn't think about her for very long, because each step he took was like someone's death, wiping his memory clean, as if crossing the desert had to destroy everything, burn everything out of his memory, make him into a different boy. The hand of the blind warrior pushed him onward when Nour's legs slowed with fatigue, and perhaps, without that hand lying on his shoulder, he too would have fallen by the side of the trail, arms and legs drawn in.

There were always new mountains on the horizon; the plateau of stones and sand seemed endless, like the sea. Each evening, when he heard the signal for the halt being called, the blind warrior would say to Nour, "Is this it? Have we arrived?"

And then he would say, "Tell me what you can see."

But Nour simply answered, "No, this isn't it yet. There's nothing but desert, we have to keep walking."

Despair was beginning to spread amongst the people. Even the warriors of the desert, Ma al-Aïnine's invincible blue men, were exhausted, and their eyes looked shamed, like those of men who have lost faith.

They remained seated in small groups, rifles cradled in their arms, without talking. When Nour went to see his mother and father to ask them for water, it was their silence that frightened him the most. It was as if the threat of death had afflicted the people, and they no longer had the strength to love one another.

Most of the people in the caravan, the women, the children, were lying prostrate on the ground, waiting for the sun to die out on the horizon. They no longer even had the strength to say the prayer, despite the call of Ma al-Aïnine's religious men echoing over the plateau. Nour stretched himself out on the ground, resting his head upon his nearly empty bundle, and watched the fathomless sky changing color while he listened to the voice of the blind man singing.

Sometimes he felt as if it were all a dream, a terrible interminable dream he was having with his eyes open, a dream that was pulling him along the star routes, over the earth as smooth and hard as polished stone. Then all of the suffering was like thrusting spears, and he moved onward without understanding what was tearing at him. It was as if he had stepped outside of himself, abandoning his body on the burnt earth, his motionless body on the desert of stones and sand, like a stain, a pile of old forgotten rags, and his soul was venturing out into the icy sky, out amongst the stars, covering in the wink of an eye all of the space that his life would never be enough to apprehend. Then he saw, appearing like mirages, the extraordinary cities with palaces of white stone, towers, domes, large gardens streaming with pure water, trees laden with fruit, flower beds, fountains where young girls with tinkling laughter gathered. He saw it all distinctly, he slipped into the cool water, drank at the waterfalls, tasted each fruit, breathed in each smell. But what was most extraordinary was the music he heard when he left his body. He had never heard anything like it. It was the voice of a young woman singing in the Chleuh language, a gentle song that moved through the air and kept repeating the same words, like this:

"One day, oh, one day, the crow will turn white, the sea will go dry, we will find honey in the desert flower, we will make bedding of acacia sprays, oh, one day, the snake will spit no more poison, and rifle bullets will bring no more death, for that will be the day I will leave my love. . ."

Where was such a clear gentle voice coming from? Nour could feel his consciousness slipping still farther out, beyond this world, beyond this sky, toward the land where there are black clouds filled with rain, wide deep rivers where the water never stops flowing.

"One day, oh, one day, the wind will cease to blow over the earth, the grains of sand will be sweet as sugar, under each white stone on the path, a spring will be awaiting me, one day, oh, one day, the bees will sing for me, for that will be the day I will leave my love. . ."

Out there, the mysterious sounds of the storm rumble; out there cold and death reign supreme.

"One day, oh, one day, there will be the night sun, and puddles of moon water will gather upon the earth, the gold of the stars will rain from the sky, one day, oh, one day, I'll see my shadow dancing for me, for that will be the day I will leave my love. . ."

The new order is coming from there, the order that is driving the blue men from the desert, that is giving rise to fear everywhere.

"One day, oh, one day, the sun will go black, the earth will split open to its very core, the sea will cover the sand, one day, oh, one day, my eyes will see no light, my lips will be unable to say your name, my heart will stop beating, for that will be the day I will leave my love. . ."

The stranger's voice faded away in a murmur, and Nour could once again hear the slow sad song of the blind warrior talking to himself, his face turned toward the sky he could not see.

One evening Ma al-Aïnine's caravan arrived on the rim of the Drâa, on the far side of the mountains. There, as they descended toward the west, they caught sight of the smoke coming from Larhdaf's and Saadbou's camps. When they met back up with one another there was a surge of new hope. Nour's father came to see him and helped him carry his load.

"Where are we? Is this the place?" asked the blind warrior.

Nour explained to him that they had made it across the desert and that they weren't far from their goal.

That night there was a sort of celebration. For the first time in a very long time the sounds of guitars and drums were heard, and the clear song of flutes.

The night was milder in the valley, and there was grass for the animals. With his mother and father, Nour ate millet bread and dates, and the blind warrior also got his share. He spoke with them about the long road they had traveled from the Saguiet al-Hamra to the tomb of Sidi Mohammed al-Quenti. Afterward, they walked together, guiding the blind warrior through the fields of brush to the dried bed of the Drâa.

There were many people and animals, because the people and animals of the great sheik's caravan had been joined by the nomads of the Drâa, those of the wells of Tassouf, the people of Messeïed, of Tcart, of al-Gaba, of Sidi Brahim al-Aattami, everyone whom poverty and the threat of the arrival of the French had driven from the coastal regions and who had heard that the great sheik Ma al-Aïnine was en route for a holy war to expel the foreigners from the lands of the Faithful.

So the gaps in the ranks of men and women that death had made could no longer be seen. One no longer saw that most of the men were wounded or ill, or that the little children were slowly dying in their mothers' arms, burning up with fever and dehydration.

All that could be seen, on all sides of the black bed of the dried river, were human shapes walking slowly along, and herds of goats and sheep, and men riding their camels, their horses, all heading toward something, toward their destiny.

For days they walked up the huge Drâa Valley, over the tract of crackled sand, hard as kiln-baked clay, over the black bed of the river where the sun blazed at its zenith like a flame. On the other side of the valley, Larhdaf and Saadbou's men rode their horses up a narrow torrent, and the men, women, and herds followed the path they opened. Now it was Ma al-Aïnine's warriors who were going in last, mounted on their camels, and Nour was walking with them, guiding the blind warrior. Most of

Ma al-Aïnine's soldiers were on foot, using their rifles and spears to help themselves scale the ravines.

That same evening, the caravan reached the deep well, the one that was called Aïn Rhatra, not far from Torkoz, at the foot of the mountains. Just as he did every evening, Nour went to fetch water for the blind warrior, and they performed their ablutions and said their prayer. Then Nour settled in for the night not far from the sheik's warriors. Ma al-Aïnine didn't pitch his tent. He slept out of doors, like the men of the desert, simply wrapped in his white cloak, crouching on his saddle blanket. Night fell rapidly, because they were near the high mountains. The chill made the men shiver. Next to Nour, the blind warrior no longer sang. Maybe he didn't dare, due to the presence of the sheik, or maybe he was too exhausted to say anything.

When Ma al-Aïnine ate his evening meal with his warriors, he had a little food and tea brought over for Nour and his companion. It was the tea especially that made them feel better, and Nour thought he'd never had anything better to drink. The food and the fresh water of the well were like a light in their bodies that restored all of their strength. Nour ate the bread, watching the seated shape of the old man wrapped in the large white cloak.

From time to time, people approached the sheik to ask for his blessing. He welcomed them, had them sit down at his side, and offered them a piece of his bread, talked to them. They went away after having kissed a flap of his cloak. They were nomads from the Drâa, shepherds in rags, or blue women carrying their small children rolled up in their cloaks. They wanted to see the sheik, to glean a little strength, a little hope, to have him soothe the wounds on their bodies.

Later, during the night, Nour woke with a start. He saw the blind warrior leaning over him. The face filled with suffering glowed in the starlight. As Nour shrank back, almost frightened, the man said softly, "Will he restore my sight? Will I be able to see again?"

"I don't know," said Nour.

The warrior whimpered and fell back to the ground, head in the dust.

Nour looked around. On the floor of the valley, at the foot of the mountains, there was not a sign of movement, not a sound. Everywhere, people were sleeping, rolled up in their covers to stave off the cold. Alone, sitting on his saddle blanket, as if weariness did not exist for him, Ma al-Aïnine was motionless, eyes fixed on the night landscape.

So then Nour lay down on his side, cheek resting against his arm, and he watched the old man who was praying for a long time, and once again, it was as if he were slipping away into an interminable dream, a dream much greater than himself, which led him out toward another world.

Each day at sunrise the men were on their feet. They took up their burdens in silence, and the women rolled the young children up on their backs. The animals rose too, pawing the ground and making the first dust rise, for the old man's order had entered them, spreading through them along with the warmth of the sun and the giddiness of the wind.

They pursued their march northward, through the jagged mountains of the Taïssa, along narrow passes as blistering hot as the sides of a volcano.

Sometimes in the evening, when they arrived at a well, blue men and women, emerging from the desert, ran up to them with offerings of dates, sour milk, millet bread. The great sheik gave them his blessing, for they had brought their small children who had stomach ailments or eye infections. Ma al-Aïnine anointed them with a little dirt mixed with his saliva, he laid his hands on their fore-heads; then the women went off, returned to their red desert just as they had come. Men also came at times with their rifles and spears to join the troop. They were peas-ants with coarse features, with blond or red hair and strange green eyes.

On the other side of the mountains, the caravan arrived at the Taïdalt palm grove, where the Noun River and the trail to Goulimine begin. Nour thought they would be able to rest and drink to their heart's content, but the palm grove was small, shrunken from drought and the desert wind. The tall gray dunes had eaten into the oasis, and the water was mud-colored. There was hardly anyone in the palm grove, save a few old men, wasted with hunger. So Ma al-Aïnine's troop traveled on the next day, following the dried river toward Goulimine.

Before reaching the city, the troops of Ma al-Aïnine's sons rode out ahead. Two days later, they came back with bad news: the soldiers of the Christians had landed at Sidi Ifni, and they too were heading northward. Larhdaf wanted to go to Goulimine all the same, to fight against the Spanish and the French, but the sheik motioned toward the men camping on the plain and merely asked him, "Are those your soldiers?" Then Larhdaf bowed his head, and the sheik gave the order to depart, skirting Goulimine, toward the Aït Boukha palm grove, then across the mountains to reach the Bou Izakarn trail to the east.

Despite their exhaustion, the men and women made their way for weeks through the red mountains, along dry torrents. The blue men, the women, the shepherds with their herds, the pack camels, the horsemen, all had to weave their way through the blocks of stone, to find a passageway over the rockslides. That is how they reached the holy city of Sidi Ahmed ou Moussa, the patron saint of acrobats and jugglers. The caravan spread out over the arid valley to pitch camp. Only the sheik and his sons and members of the Goudfia stayed within the confines of the tomb while the noblemen came to show their allegiance.

That evening there was a collective prayer beneath the starry sky, and the men and women came together at the tomb of the saint. The silence around the fires was broken only by the crackling of dry branches, and Nour could see the slight frame of the sheik squatting on the ground, reciting the formula of the *dzikr* in a low voice. But that evening, it was a prayer without shouts or music, because death was too close, and fatigue had made their throats tight. There was nothing but the very gentle voice, light as a wisp of smoke, chanting in the silence. Nour looked around and saw the thousands of men sitting on the ground, draped in their woolen cloaks, lit by fires scattering out into the distance. They sat motionless in silence. It was the most intense, most painful prayer he had ever heard. No one moved except, from time to time, a woman breastfeeding her child to put it to sleep, or an old man coughing. In the steep-walled valley, there wasn't a breath of air, and the fires were burning very straight and bright. The night was ice-cold and beautiful, filled with stars. Then the glow of the moon appeared at the horizon, over the black cliffs, and the absolutely round silver disk rose hour by hour to its zenith.

The sheik prayed all night long as the fires went out, one after the other. The people, overcome with exhaustion, lay down to sleep right where they were. Nour only left the gathering two or three times, to go urinate behind the bushes in the valley bottom. He couldn't sleep, as if his body were burning with fever. Next to him, his father, mother, and sisters had dozed off, wrapped up in their cloaks, and the blind warrior was sleeping too, his head lying on the cold earth.

Nour continued to watch the old man sitting next to the white tomb, chanting softly in the silent night, as if he were rocking a child.

At daybreak, the caravan went on, accompanied by some of the Aït ou Moussa and mountain men from Ilirh, from Tafermit, the Ida Gougmar, the Ifrane, the Tirhmi, all those who wanted to follow Ma al-Aïnine in his war for the kingdom of God.

There were still many more days of crossing the deserted mountains, along dried torrents. Each day the burning sun, the thirst, the blinding, overly white sky, the all-too-red rocks, the dust that suffocated the animals and people started over again. Nour couldn't remember anymore what the world was like when he wasn't on the move. He couldn't remember the wells, where the women go to fetch water in their jugs and chatter like birds. He could no longer remember the song of the shepherds who allow their herds to wander, or the games children play in the sand of the dunes. It was if he had been walking forever, endlessly seeing identical hills, ravines, red rocks. At times he would have liked so much to sit down on a stone, just any stone by the side of the trail, and watch the long caravan going off, the dark shapes of the men and the camels in the shimmering air, as if it were a mirage fading away. But the hand of the blind warrior did not leave his shoulder, it pushed him onward, forced him to keep walking.

When they came in sight of a village, they stopped. The name of the village was passed from one person to the next, buzzing on everyone's lips, "Tirhmi, Anezi, Assaka, Asserssif. . ." Now they were walking along a real river, in which a thin trickle of water ran. Argans and white acacias grew along its banks. Then they walked over an immense sandy plain, as white as salt, where the sunlight was blinding.

One evening as the caravan was settling in for the night, a band of warriors arrived from the north, in the company of a man on horseback wearing a long white cloak.

It was the great sheik Lahoussine himself, who had come to bring the aid of his warriors and distribute food to the travelers. Then the people realized the journey was drawing to an end, because they were entering the valley of the great Souss River, the place where there would be water and pasture for the livestock, and land for all of the men.

When the news spread amongst the travelers, a feeling of emptiness and death came over Nour once again, as it had before leaving Smara. The people were running back and forth in the dust shouting out, calling to one another, "We've arrived! We've arrived!" The blind warrior was gripping Nour's shoulder very tightly, and he too was shouting, "We've arrived!"

But it wasn't until two days later that they arrived in the valley of the great river, before the city of Taroudant. For hours they followed the river upstream, walking in the thin streams of water running through the red stones. In spite of the river water, the banks were barren and dry, and the earth was hard, baked by the sun and the wind.

Nour walked over the smooth stones of the river, dragging the blind warrior behind him. In spite of the blaze of the sun, the water was as cold as ice. A few scraggly shrubs were growing in the middle of the river, on little pebble islands. There were also long white tree trunks that the floodwaters had brought down from the mountains.

Nour had already forgotten the presentiment of death. He was happy because he too believed it was the end of the journey, that this was the land Ma al-Aïnine had promised them before leaving Smara.

The hot air was laden with smells, for it was the beginning of spring. Nour breathed in that smell for the very first time. Insects danced over the streams of water, wasps, light flies. It had been so long since Nour had seen any wildlife that he was happy to see those flies and those wasps. Even when a horsefly suddenly stung him through his clothing, it didn't anger him, and he merely shooed it away with his hand.

On the other side of the Souss River, hugging the red mountain, was the large city of mud houses, looming up like a celestial vision. Unearthly, as if suspended in the sunlight, the city seemed to be waiting for the men of the desert, waiting to offer them refuge. Never before had Nour seen such a beautiful city. The high windowless walls of red stone and mud glowed in the light of the setting sun. A halo of dust was floating over the city like pollen, encompassing it in its magical cloud.

The travelers stopped in the valley, below the city, and gazed at it for a long time in both love and fear. Now, for the first time since the beginning of their journey, they felt how truly weary they were, their clothing in shreds, their feet wrapped in bloody rags, their lips and eyelids burned by the desert sun. They were sitting on the shingles of the river, and some had pitched their tents or had built shelters out of branches and leaves. As if he too were feeling the fear of the crowd, Ma al-Aïnine stopped with his sons and warriors on the bank of the river.

Now the large tents of the tribal chieftains were being raised; the pack camels were being unloaded. Night fell on the ramparts of the city; the sky went dark, and the red earth turned black. Only the high frost-covered peaks of the Atlas, Mount Tichka, Mount Tinergouet, still glistened in the sun when the valley was already sunk in darkness. The call for the evening prayer in the city could be heard, a voice that echoed out strangely like a lament. On the shingles of the river, the travelers were prostrating themselves and praying too, without raising their voices, accompanied by the soft gurgling of the stream.

When morning came, Nour was astounded. He had slept through the night without feeling the stones bruising his ribs, or the cold, or the dampness of the river. When he awoke, he saw the mist drifting slowly down the valley, as if the light of day were pushing it along. In the riverbed, amidst the sleeping men, the women were already up, going to fetch water, or gathering a few twigs. The children were looking for shrimp under the flat stones.

But it was when he looked at the city that Nour was filled with wonder. In the pure dawn air, at the foot of the mountains, stood the tall fortress of Taroudant. Its walls of red stone, its terraces, its towers were clear and distinct, seeming to have been sculpted out of the bedrock of the mountain itself. From time to time, the white mist passed between the riverbed and the city, half hiding it, as if the citadel were floating above the valley, a sort of earthen and stone vessel gliding slowly past the islands of the snow-capped mountains.

Nour stared at it without being able to turn away. His eyes were fascinated with the high windowless walls. There was something mysterious and threatening in those walls, as if the city wasn't inhabited by people, but by supernatural spirits. Slowly, the light appeared in the sky – pink, then amber-colored, just like that, until the intense blue was everywhere. The light sizzled on the mud walls, on the terraces, on the gardens of orange trees and on the tall palms. Lower down, the arid lands traversed by the irrigation canals were an almost dusky color of red.

Standing stock still on the beach in the silence, surrounded by the men of the desert, Nour watched the magical city awakening. Thin wisps of smoke lifted into the air, and – almost ethereal – the familiar sounds of life, voices, the laughter of children, a young woman singing could be heard.

For the men of the desert, sitting motionless in the bed of the river, those wisps of smoke, those sounds seemed immaterial, as if they were dreaming that fortified city on the mountainside, those fields, those palm and orange trees.

The sun had risen high in the sky, was already burning the stones of the riverbed. A strange odor wafted over to the nomad camp, and Nour had a hard time recognizing it. It wasn't the sharp and cold smell of the days of fleeing and fear, the smell he had been breathing in for such a long time across the desert. It was an odor of musk and oil, pungent, inebriating, the smell of braziers in which cedar coal is being burned, the smell of coriander, of pepper, of onions.

Nour breathed in that odor, without daring to move for fear of losing it, and the blind warrior also recognized that blissful smell. All the men remained motionless, their wide eyes looking on unblinkingly, achingly, at the high red wall of the city. They looked at the city which was so close and yet so distant at the same time, the city that might open its gates, and their hearts beat faster. Around them, the pebble beaches of the river were already shimmering in the heat of day. They watched the magical city without moving. Then, as the sun rose higher in the sky, each of the men, one after the other, covered his head with a flap of his cloak.

LIFE WITH THE SLAVES

LEANING ON THE RAILING, Lalla watches the strip of land that has appeared on the horizon like an island. In spite of her fatigue, all of her energy is turned toward scrutinizing the land; she's trying to make out the houses, the roads, maybe even the shapes of people. Next to her, the passengers are crowding up against the railing. They're shouting, gesticulating, talking excitedly; they're calling to one another in all different languages from one end of the afterdeck to the other. They've been waiting for this moment for such a long time! There are many children and teenagers. They're all wearing the same tag pinned to their clothing, with their name, date of birth, and the name and address of the person who is waiting for them in Marseille. The bottom of the tag has been stamped, signed, and marked with a small red cross circled in black. Lalla doesn't like the red cross; she has the feeling it's burning her skin through her smock, that it's gradually leaving its mark on her chest.

The cold wind is gusting over the deck, and the heavy waves are making the iron sides of the ship vibrate. Lalla feels nauseous because all night long, instead of sleeping, the children were passing around tubes of condensed milk that the Red Cross officials distributed before they embarked. And also, since there weren't enough deck chairs, Lalla had to sleep on the floor in the nauseating heat of the hold, surrounded with the smell of kerosene, of grease, shaken by the chugging of the engine. Now the first gulls are flying over the stern, they're screeching and squawking as if they were angry to see the ship arriving. They don't look like princes of the sea at all; they're a dirty gray color, with yellow beaks and a cruel gleam to their eyes.

Lalla hadn't seen the sun rise. She'd fallen asleep, overcome with fatigue on the tarpaulin in the hold, her head resting on a piece of cardboard. When she awoke, everyone was already up on deck, their eyes glued to the strip of land. The only person left in the hold was a very pale young woman holding a tiny baby in her arms. The baby was sick; it had vomited on the floor; it was whimpering softly. When Lalla drew near to ask what was wrong with it, the young woman looked at her without answering, glassy-eyed.

Now land is very near, it is floating on the green sea littered with trash. Rain is beginning to fall on the deck, but no one goes for shelter. The cold water runs over the children's frizzy hair, forming drops on the ends of their noses. They are dressed like paupers, in thin, short-sleeved shirts, blue cotton pants or gray skirts, sometimes in traditional long homespun robes. Their bare feet are stuck into black leather shoes that are too big. The adult men are wearing old worn suit jackets with pants that are too short, and woolen ski caps. Lalla looks at the children, the women, the men around her; they seem sad and frightened; their faces are yellow, swollen with weariness, their arms and legs nubbly with goose bumps. The smell of the sea mingles with that of fatigue and anxiety, and off in the distance, like a smudge on the green sea, the land also seems sad and weary. The sky is low; the clouds are hiding the tops of the hills; no matter how hard she looks, Lalla can't see the white city Naman the fisherman used to speak of, not the palaces or the church towers. Now there is nothing but endless stone- and cement-colored wharves, wharves opening out onto other wharves. The ship loaded with passengers is gliding slowly through the black water of the basins. Standing on the wharves, a few men are watching the ship go by indifferently. Though the children shout at the top of their lungs, waving their arms around, no one answers them. The rain continues to fall, a fine cold drizzle. Lalla looks at the water in the basin, the black greasy water, where refuse even the gulls don't want floats.

Maybe there is no city? Lalla looks at the rain-soaked wharves, the shapes of the docked freighters, the cranes, and still farther out, the long white buildings making a wall at the far end of the harbor. Little by little, the merriment of the children on the International Red Cross ship begins to subside. From time to time, a few shouts ring out, but they don't last. The officials and female assistants are walking over the deck, shouting out orders that no one understands. They succeed in grouping the children together and begin to call out names, but their voices are lost in the noise of the engine and the clamor of the crowd.

"... Makel..."

"... Séfar..."

"Ko-di-ki..."

"Hamal..."

"... Lagor..."

It doesn't make any sense and no one answers. Then the loudspeaker starts talking, as if it were barking over the heads of the passengers, and a kind of panic occurs. Some people run up toward the front, others try to climb the stairs to the upper deck, where the officers push them back. Finally, everyone calms down because the ship has just docked and the engines have been cut. On the wharf there is an ugly cement structure with lit windows. The children, the women, the men lean over the railing trying to get a glimpse of a familiar face amongst the people that can be seen walking around over there, no larger than insects, on the other side of the structure.

The process of disembarkment begins, meaning that for several hours, the passengers remain on the deck of the International Red Cross ship, waiting to be given some kind of signal. As time goes by, the children who are crowded together on the deck grow more and more restless. The small children begin to cry, with a continual high-pitched whining, which doesn't help matters. The women shout, or sometimes the men. Lalla is sitting on a pile of rope, with her suitcase beside her, in the shade of the bulkhead of the officers' deck, and is waiting, watching the gray gulls in the gray sky.

Finally the time comes to go ashore. The passengers are so tired of waiting that it takes them quite some time to get moving.

Lalla follows the drove up to the large gray structure. There, three policemen and some interpreters are asking questions of the people arriving. It is a bit quicker for the children, because the policeman simply reads what is written on their tags and copies it on the forms.

When he's finished, the man looks at Lalla and asks, "Do you intend to work in France?"

"Yes," Lalla says.

"What job?"

"I don't know."

"Housemaid," the policeman says, and writes that on his form. Lalla picks up her suitcase and goes over to wait with the others, in the large dirty room with gray walls where the electric light shines brightly. There's nothing to sit on, and in spite of the cold and the rain outside, the room is stiflingly hot. The youngest children have fallen asleep in their mothers' arms, or else on the floor, lying on a pile of clothing. Now it's the older children who are complaining. Lalla is thirsty; her throat is dry; her eyes are burning with fever. She's too tired to think of anything. She's waiting, leaning up against the wall, standing first on one leg, then the other. At the other end of the room, in front of the police lines, is the very pale young woman with a blank look, holding her baby in her arms. She's standing in front of the officer's desk looking haggard, not saying anything. The policeman talks to her for a long time, shows the papers to the interpreter from the International Red Cross. Something isn't right. The policeman asks questions that the interpreter repeats to the young woman, but she just looks at them, not seeming to understand. They don't want to let her through. Lalla looks at the young woman who is so pale, holding her baby. She is holding it so tightly in her arms that it wakes up a little and starts screaming, then calms down when its mother quickly uncovers her breast and offers it for the baby to suck on. The policeman looks embarrassed. He turns away, glances around. His eyes meet those of Lalla, who has just walked up.

"Do you speak her language?"

"I don't know," says Lalla.

Lalla says a few words in Chleuh, and the young woman looks at her for a minute and then answers.

"Tell her that her papers aren't in order, the authorization for the baby is missing."

Lalla tries to translate the sentence. She thinks the young woman hasn't understood, then all of a sudden she collapses and begins to weep. The policeman says a few more words, and the interpreter from the International Red Cross lifts the young woman to her feet as well as he can and guides her over to the back of the room, where there are two or three imitation leather armchairs.

Lalla is sad because she realizes that the young woman will have to take the boat back in the opposite direction with her sick baby. But she is too weary herself to think about it much, and she goes back to lean up against the wall next to her suitcase. At the other end of the room, high up on the wall, there is a clock with numbers inscribed on rotating flaps. Each minute, a flap turns with a sharp click. The people in the room aren't talking anymore. They're waiting, sitting on the floor, or standing against the wall, eyes fixed, faces tense, as if with each click, the door in the back is going to open and let them go.

Finally, after such a long time that no one is hoping for anything anymore, the men from the International Red Cross walk across the large room. They open the door in the back and start calling out the names of the children again. The muttering of voices resumes, the people crowd up near the exit. Lalla, carrying her cardboard suitcase, cranes out her neck to see over the heads of the others; she is so impatient for her name to be called that her legs begin to tremble. When the man from the Red Cross says her name, he sort of barks it out, and Lalla doesn't understand. Then he repeats himself, shouting, "Hawa! Hawa ben Hawa!"

Lalla runs, her suitcase banging around at the end of her arm, and makes her way through the crowd. She stops in front of the door while the man checks her tag, then she leaps out, as if someone had shoved her from behind. There is so much light outside, after all those hours spent in the large gray room, that Lalla staggers, overcome with dizziness. She moves forward through the rows of women and men without seeing them, walks aimlessly straight ahead, until she feels someone taking her by the arm, hugging her, kissing her. Aamma pulls her over toward the exit from the wharves, toward the city.

Aamma lives alone in an apartment in the old town, near the port, on the top floor of a dilapidated house. There's just a living room with a sofa, a dark bedroom with a folding bed, and a kitchen. The windows of the apartment open onto an inner courtyard, but you can see the sky pretty well above the tile roofs. In the morning, up until noon, there's even a little sunshine that comes in through the two windows of the room with the sofa. Aamma tells Lalla that she was very lucky to have found the apartment, and also to have found work as a cook at the hospital cafeteria. When she arrived in Marseille, several months ago, she was first housed in a furnished apartment in the outskirts, where there were five women to each room, and the police came by every morning, and there were fights in the street. Two men even had a knife fight, and Aamma had to flee, leaving one of her suitcases behind, because she was afraid of being picked up by the police and deported.

Aamma seems quite happy to see Lalla, after all this time. She doesn't ask her any questions about what happened when Lalla ran away into the desert with the Hartani and was later taken to the hospital in the city, because she was dying of thirst and fever. The Hartani had continued his journey southward alone, toward the caravans, because that was what he was always meant to do. Aamma has aged a lot in a few months' time. She has a thin weary face, a gray complexion, and her eyes are ringed with dark circles. In the evening, when she gets home from work, she nibbles on cookies and drinks mint tea while she talks about her journey by car across Spain with other men and women who were going to look for work. They drove along the roads for days, passing through villages, over mountains, rivers. And one day, the driver of the car showed them a city with a lot of identical brick houses, with black roofs. He said, this is it, here we are. Aamma got out of the car along with the others, and, since the entire trip had been paid in advance, they took their belongings and started walking through the streets of the town. But when Aamma showed the envelope with the name and address of Naman's brother, people started laughing and told her she wasn't in Marseille, but Paris. So then she had to take the train and travel all night again before she got here.

When Lalla hears that story, it gives her a good laugh, because she can imagine the passengers of the car walking around in the streets of Paris thinking they were in Marseille.

This city is really big. Lalla never thought there could be so many people living in the same place. Ever since she got here, she has been spending her days walking around town, from north to south, and from east to west. She doesn't know the names of the streets; she doesn't know where she's going. At times she walks along the wharves, looking at the silhouettes of the freighters; other times she walks up the main avenues, toward the center of town, or else she follows the labyrinth of narrow streets in the old town, climbs the stairways, going from square to square, from church to church, until she reaches the large esplanade from where you can see the fortified castle overlooking the sea. Or still other times, she'll go sit on the benches in the parks and watch the pigeons walking round on the dusty paths. There are so many streets, so many houses, stores, windows, cars; it makes your head spin, and the noise and the smell of gasoline fumes are inebriating and give you a headache. Lalla doesn't speak to anyone. Sometimes she sits on the steps of the churches, well hidden in her brown woolen coat, and watches the passersby. There are men who look at her, then stop on a street corner and pretend to be smoking a cigarette while they keep an eye on her. But Lalla knows how to disappear very quickly, she learned that from the Hartani; she goes across two or three streets, through a store, weaves around the stopped cars, and no one can follow her.

Aamma would like for her to work at the hospital with her, but Lalla is too young; you have to be eighteen. And also, it's hard to find work.

A few days after she arrived, she went to see Old Naman's brother, whose name is Asaph, but everyone calls him Joseph. He has a grocery store in Rue des Chapeliers, not far from the police station. He seemed happy to see Lalla, and he hugged her and talked about his brother, but Lalla was wary of him right away. He doesn't look anything like Naman. He's small, almost bald, with repulsive, bulging gray-green eyes, and a smile that augurs nothing good. When he learned that Lalla was looking for work, his eyes lit up, and he got nervous. He told Lalla that he just happened to need a young girl to help with the grocery store, putting things away, cleaning, and maybe even being in charge of the cash register. But as he was talking about all that, he was constantly staring at Lalla's abdomen and breasts with his repulsive watery eyes, so she told him she would come back tomorrow, and left immediately. Since she didn't go back, he came to Aamma's place one evening. But Lalla went out as soon as she saw him, and took a long walk through the narrow streets of the old town, making herself as invisible as a shadow, until she was sure the grocer had gone back to his place.

This city is a strange land, with all of these people, because they don't really pay any attention to you if you don't show yourself. Lalla learned how to slip silently along the walls, up the stairways. She knows all the places where you can see without being seen, hiding places behind trees, in big parking lots filled with cars, in doorways, in vacant lots. Even in the middle of very straight avenues, where there is a constant flow of cars and people going up, going down, Lalla knows she can become invisible. In the beginning, she still bore the marks of the burning desert sun, and her long, black curly hair was full of sparkling sunshine. So people would look at her in surprise, as if she were from another planet. But now months have gone by, and Lalla has been transformed. She cut her hair short; it is dull, almost gray. In the shadows of the narrow streets, in the damp chill of Aamma's apartment, Lalla's skin has grown dull too; it's become pale and gray. And then there's the brown coat Aamma found in a Jewish thrift store, near the cathedral. It reaches almost down to her ankles, the sleeves are too long and the shoulders sag, and the best thing is that it's made out of a sort of wool carpeting, worn and shiny with age, the color of city walls, of old paper; when Lalla puts on her coat, she really feels as if she becomes invisible.

Now she's learned the names of the streets by listening to people talking. They're strange names, so strange that sometimes she recites them under her breath as she's walking along between the houses:

> La Major
> La Tourette
> Place de Lenche
> Rue du Petit-Puits
> Place Vivaux
> Place Sadi-Carnot
> La Tarasque
> Impasse des Muettes
> Rue du Cheval
> Cours Belsunce

There are so many streets, so many names! Each day, Lalla goes out before her aunt wakes up; she puts an old piece of bread in the pocket of her brown coat and starts walking, first making circles around the Panier neighborhood until she reaches the sea by way of the Rue de la Prison, with the sun lighting up the walls of the city hall. She sits down for a moment to watch the cars going by, but not for too long, because the police will come along and ask her what she's doing there.

Then she continues going northward, walking up the wide, noisy avenues, La Canebière, Boulevard Dugommier, Boulevard

Athènes. There are people from countries all over the world, who speak all sorts of languages; people who are very black with narrow eyes, wearing long, white robes and plastic slippers. There are people from the north, with light hair and pale eyes, soldiers, sailors, and also corpulent businessmen who walk briskly and carry around odd little black suitcases.

Lalla likes to sit down there too, in a doorway, to watch all of those people coming and going, walking, running. When there are a lot of people, no one pays any attention to her. Maybe they think she's like them, that she's waiting for someone, for something; or maybe they think she's a beggar.

In crowded neighborhoods, there are lots of poor people, and those are the ones that Lalla watches most closely. She sees women in rags, very pale in spite of the sunshine, holding very small children by the hand. She sees old men, wearing long patched robes, drunks with blurry eyes, bums, foreigners who are hungry carrying cardboard suitcases and empty grocery bags. She sees children alone, faces grimy, hair disheveled, wearing old clothes too large for their scrawny bodies; they walk along quickly as if they were going somewhere, and their eyes are shifty and unpleasant like those of stray dogs. From her hiding place behind the parked cars, or else in the shadow of a carriage entrance, Lalla watches all of those people who look lost, who are walking along as if they were half asleep. There's an odd gleam in her dark eyes as she watches them, and perhaps just at that moment, a bit of the great desert light falls upon them, but they hardly even feel it, not knowing where it's coming from. They might get a slight shudder, but they walk quickly away, melt into the crowd of strangers.

On some days she goes out a very long way, walks for such a long time through the streets that her legs ache, and she has to sit down on the curb to rest. She walks eastward along the main avenue lined with trees, with a multitude of cars and trucks driving past, then crosses over hills and glens. In those neighborhoods, there are a good many vacant lots, buildings as tall as

214

cliffs, entirely white, with thousands of small identical windows; farther out, there are villas surrounded with laurels and orange trees, with vicious dogs that run along the fence barking as loud as they can. There are also lots of stray cats, thin, ill-kempt, that live atop the walls and under parked cars.

Lalla keeps walking, aimlessly, following the roads. She crosses distant neighborhoods through which canals snake, swarming with mosquitoes; she goes into the cemetery, as large as a city, with its rows of gray stones and rusty crosses. She climbs up to the very top of the hills, so far away you can barely even glimpse the sea, like a dirty blue smudge between the cubes of the buildings. There is a strange haze floating over the city, a big gray, pink, and yellow cloud where the light pales. The sun is already going down in the west, and Lalla can feel weariness stealing over her body, sleepiness. She looks at the city glittering in the distance; she can hear it humming like a motor, trains rolling along, entering the black holes of the tunnels. She's not afraid, and yet something is spinning inside of her, like a dizzy feeling, like a wind. Maybe it's the *chergui*, the desert wind that is coming all the way over here, which has crossed the whole sea, the mountains, the cities, the roads, and is on its way? It's hard to know. There are so many different forces here, so many sounds, movements, and maybe the wind has gotten lost in the streets, on the stairways, on the esplanades.

Lalla is watching a plane lifting slowly into the pale sky, making a thundering sound. It veers up over the city, passing in front of the sun, blinking it out for a fraction of a second, and then flies off in the direction of the sea, growing smaller and smaller. Lalla stares at it very hard, until it is nothing more than an imperceptible dot. Maybe it's going to fly out over the desert, over the expanses of sand and stones, out where the Hartani is walking?

So then Lalla goes off as well. Legs wobbling a little, she walks back down toward the city.

There's something else that Lalla really likes to do: she goes to sit on the steps of the wide flight of stairs in front of the train station and watches the travelers going up and down. There are the ones who are arriving, all out of breath, eyes tired, hair mussed, and who go teetering down the stairs into the light. There are the ones who are leaving, who are in a hurry because they're afraid of missing their trains; they run up the stairs two at a time, and their suitcases and bags knock against their legs, and their eyes are trained straight ahead on the entrance to the station. They stumble on the last steps, they call out to one another for fear of getting lost.

Lalla really likes hanging around the train station. It's as if the big city wasn't quite finished yet, as if there were still that large hole through which people keep coming and going. She often thinks that she would really like to go away, get on a train headed northward, with all of those names of lands that are intriguing and a little frightening, Irun, Bordeaux, Amsterdam, Lyon, Dijon, Paris, Calais. When she has a little money, Lalla goes into the station, buys a Coca-Cola at the refreshment stand and a platform ticket. She goes into the large departure hall, and wanders around on all the platforms in front of the trains that have just come in or that are leaving soon. Sometimes she even gets on one of the cars and sits down for a minute on the green moleskin seat. The people arrive one after the other and settle down in the compartment, they even ask, "Is it taken?" and Lalla gives a little shake of her head. Then when the loudspeaker announces that the train is going to leave, Lalla quickly gets off the car, jumps down onto the platform.

The train station is also one of the places where you can see without being seen, because there is too much agitation and hurriedness to pay much attention to anyone. There are all sorts of people in the station, cruel people, violent people with bright red faces, people who shout at the top of their lungs; there are very sad and very poor people too, old people who are lost, anxiously searching for the platforms their trains are leaving from, women with too many children who hobble along with their loads by the cars that are too high. There are all of the people

216

that poverty has brought to this city, blacks who have come off boats, heading for the cold countries with their colorful short-sleeved shirts and a lone beach bag serving as luggage; dark-skinned North Africans, layered with old jackets, wearing ski caps or hats with ear flaps; the Turks, the Spaniards, the Greeks, all looking worried and weary, wandering around on the plat-forms in the wind, bumping into one another in the midst of the crowd of indifferent travelers and jeering soldiers.

Lalla watches them, just barely hidden between the telephone booth and the information board. She's backed into the shad-ows pretty well, and her copper-colored face is shielded with the collar of her coat. But from time to time, her heart starts beat-ing faster and a flash of light darts from her eyes, like the reflec-tion of the sun off the stones in the desert. She watches all the people who are headed for other cities, for hunger, cold, misfor-tune, those who will be humiliated, who will live in solitude. They go by, stooping slightly, eyes blank, clothing already worn from nights of sleeping on the ground, like so many defeated soldiers.

They are headed for black cities, for low skies, for smoke-stacks, for the cold, the sickness that rips your chest apart. They're headed for their shantytowns in muddy lots, down below the freeways, for rooms like graves dug into the ground, surrounded by high walls and fences. Maybe those men, those women, pass-ing by like ghosts, dragging their bags and their too-heavy chil-dren, will never come back, maybe they'll die in those countries they don't even know, far from their villages, far from their fam-ilies? They're headed into those foreign countries that will take their lives, that will crush and devour them. Lalla is standing very still in her dark corner, and her vision blurs because that's what she thinks. She would so like to go away from here, walk through the streets of the city until there were no more houses, no more gardens, not even any roads, or shoreline, just a path like before, that would lead out, growing ever narrower till it reached the desert.

Night falls on the city. Lights flicker on in the streets, around the train station, on the iron pylons, and on the long red, white, and green bars over the cafés and the movie theaters. Lalla is walking through the dark streets without making a sound, slipping along hugging the walls. Men's faces are terrifying when night falls, and they are only partially lit by the streetlamps. Their eyes shine cruelly, the sound of their footsteps echoes in the corridors, under the carriage entrances. Lalla is walking quickly now, as if she were trying to flee. From time to time, a man follows her, tries to come up to her, take her arm, so Lalla hides behind a car, then disappears. Once again, she starts slipping along like a shadow; she wanders around in the streets of the old town until she reaches the Panier neighborhood, where Aamma lives. She takes the unlit stairway, so no one will see which door she's gone in. She knocks lightly on the door, and when she hears her aunt's voice, she says her name with relief.

That's what Lalla's days are like, here, in the big city of Marseille, along all the streets, with all of the men and all of the women she'll never be able to know.

THERE ARE A LOT of beggars. In the beginning, when she'd just arrived, Lalla was quite surprised. Now she's gotten used to it. But she doesn't forget to see them, like most people in the city, who just make a little detour so as not to step on them, or who even step over them when they're in a hurry.

Radicz is a beggar. That's how she met him, walking along the main avenues near the train station. One day, she'd left the Panier early, and it was still dark, because it was winter. There weren't many people in the narrow streets and stairways of the old town, and the main avenue below the general hospital was still deserted, with only trucks driving along with their headlights on and a few men and a few women on their mopeds all muffled up in their overcoats.

That was where she saw Radicz. He was sitting scrunched up in a doorway, doing his best to keep out of the wind and drizzling rain. He looked as if he were very cold and when Lalla came up beside him, he gave her a funny look, not at all like boys usually do when they see a girl. He looked at her without lowering his eyes, and there wasn't much you could read in that look, like the eyes of animals. Lalla stopped in front of him; she asked, "What are you doing here? Aren't you cold?"

The boy shook his head without smiling. Then he held out his hand.

"Give me something."

Lalla had nothing but a piece of bread and an orange that she'd brought along for her lunch. She gave them to the boy. He snatched the orange from her without saying thank you and began eating it.

That's how Lalla got to know him. After that, she saw him often, in the streets, near the train station, or else on the wide flight of stairs when the weather was nice. He can remain sitting for hours, staring straight ahead, without paying attention to anyone. But he likes Lalla quite a bit, maybe because of the orange. He told her his name was Radicz; he even wrote the name on the ground with a twig, but he seemed astonished when Lalla told him she didn't know how to read.

He has pretty hair, very black and straight, and a copper complexion. He has green eyes and a little moustache like a shadow over his lips. Most of all, he has a lovely smile sometimes, which makes his very white front teeth sparkle. He wears a small ring in his left ear, and he claims it's made of gold. But he's clothed shabbily, in an old pair of stained, torn pants, a bunch of old sweaters that he wears one on top of the other, and a man's suit jacket, which is too big for him. He wears a pair of black leather shoes with no socks.

Lalla likes to run into him by chance in the street, because he's never exactly the same. Some days his eyes are sad and veiled, as if he were lost in some dream and nothing could pull him out of it. Other days, he's happy, and his eyes shine; he tells all sorts of absurd stories that he makes up as he goes along, and he starts laughing for a long time, noiselessly, and Lalla can't help but laugh along with him.

Lalla would like for him to come to see her at her aunt's house, but she doesn't dare, because Radicz is a gypsy, and that would certainly not please Aamma. He doesn't live in the Panier neighborhood, or even nearby. He lives very far away, somewhere west of the city, near the railroad, over where there are the big vacant lots and large gasoline storage tanks, and smokestacks that burn day and night. He said so himself, but he never talks for long about his house or his family. He simply says that he lives too far away to come to town every day, and when he does come, he sleeps outside instead of going back to his house. He doesn't mind; he says he knows some good hiding places, where you're not cold, where you can't feel the wind and where no one, absolutely no one, could find him.

For example, there are the places under the stairs in the broken-down customs buildings. There's a hole, just the size of a kid, and you slip inside and plug up the hole with a piece of cardboard. Or else there are tool sheds on the building sites, or tarp-covered trucks. Radicz knows all about those kinds of things.

Most of the time, you can find him somewhere around the train station. When the weather's fine, and the sun is nice and warm, he sits on the steps of the wide flight of stairs, and Lalla comes over to sit by him. They watch the people going by together. Sometimes Radicz picks someone out, says, "Watch this." He goes straight over to the traveler who's leaving the train station, a little dazed by the light, and asks for some change. Since he has a handsome smile and something sad about his eyes too, the traveler stops, searches his pockets. It's mostly men of around thirty, well-dressed, without much baggage, who give Radicz money. With women it's more complicated, they want to ask questions, and Radicz doesn't like that.

So when he sees a nice-looking young woman he prods Lalla and says, "Go ahead, you ask her."

But Lalla is reluctant to ask for money. She's a little ashamed. Yet there are times when she'd like to have a little money, to eat a piece of pastry or go to the movies.

"This is the last year I'll be doing this," says Radicz. "Next year I'm leaving, I'm going to work in Paris."

Lalla asks him why.

"Next year I'll be too old, people won't give you anything when you're too old, they say you should go out and get a job."

He looks at Lalla for a minute, then he asks her if she works, and Lalla shakes her head.

Radicz points out someone walking past, over by the buses.

"He works with me too, we've got the same boss."

It's a young, very skinny black teenager, who looks like a shadow; he goes up to people and tries to take their suitcases, but it doesn't seem to work very well. Radicz shrugs his shoulders.

"He doesn't know how to go about it. His name is Baki, I don't

221

know what it means, but it makes the other black people laugh when he says his name. He never brings much money back to the boss."

Since Lalla is looking at him in surprise, he says, "Oh yeah, you don't know, the boss is a gypsy like me, his name is Lino, and the place where we all live – we call it the hotel – is a big house where there are lots of children, and they all work for Lino."

He knows the names of all the beggars in the city. He knows where they live, and who they work with, even those who are more or less bums and who live alone. There are some children who work as a family, with their brothers and sisters, and who also shoplift in the department stores and the supermarkets. The youngest ones learn how to keep a lookout or distract the shopkeepers; sometimes they're used as relays. Above all, there are the women, gypsy women dressed in their long flowered dresses, faces covered with a black veil, and all you can see are their shiny, black eyes, like those of birds. And then there are also the old men and women, poverty-stricken, hungry, who cling to the jackets and skirts of middle-class people and won't let go, mumbling incantations, until they are given a small coin.

Lalla gets a lump in her throat when she sees them, or when she runs into an ugly young woman with a small child hanging at her breast, begging on the corner of the main avenue. She didn't really know what fear was before, because back there in the Hartani's land, there were only snakes and scorpions or, at worst, evil spirits making shadowy motions in the night; but here it's the fear of emptiness, of need, of hunger, unnamed fear that seems to seep in from half-opened transoms into the horrid, stinking, basement rooms, well up from dark courtyards, enter rooms as cold as graves, or, like an evil wind, sweep along the wide avenues, where people are endlessly walking, walking, going away, pushing and shoving one another like that incessantly, day and night, for months on end, for years, through the unflagging sound of their rubber soles and, rising into the heavy air, the rumbling of their words, their motors, their grumbling, their gasping.

Sometimes your head starts spinning so fast that you have to sit down right away, and Lalla glances around for something to lean on. Her metal-colored face turns gray, her eyes blink out, she's falling, very slowly, as if into a huge well, with no hope of stopping her fall.

"What is it? Miss? Are you feeling okay? Are you all right?

The voice is shouting somewhere very far from her ear, she can smell the odor of garlic on the breath before her sight comes back. She's half-crumpled-up against the foot of a wall. A man is holding her hand and leaning over her.

". . . It's okay, it's okay. . ."

She's able to speak, very slowly, or maybe she's only thinking the words?

The man helps her walk, leads her over to the terrace of a café. The people who had gathered around move away, but even so, Lalla hears the voice of a woman saying very clearly, "She's simply pregnant, that's all."

The man has her sit down at a table. He's still leaning toward her. He's short and fat, with a pockmarked face, a moustache, hardly any hair.

"You need something to drink, it'll make you feel better."

"I'm hungry," Lalla says. She feels apathetic about everything, maybe she thinks she's going to die.

"I'm hungry." She repeats the words slowly.

The man panics and begins to stutter. He stands up and runs over to the counter, comes back soon with a sandwich and a basket of brioches. Lalla doesn't listen to him; she eats quickly, first the sandwich, then all the brioches, one after the other. The man watches her eat, and his fat face is still agitated with emotion. He speaks in bursts, then stops, for fear of tiring Lalla.

"When I saw you fall like that right in front of me, it really threw me! Is this the first time it's happened to you? I mean, it's awful with so many people in the avenue there, the ones just behind you almost walked over you, and they didn't even stop, it's – My name's Paul, Paul Estève, and you? Do you speak French?

You're not from here, are you? Have you had enough to eat? Would you like me to get you another sandwich?"

His breath reeks of garlic, tobacco, and wine, but Lalla is glad he's there; she thinks he's nice with his somewhat shiny eyes. He notices that, and starts talking again, like he does, every which way, asking questions and then answering them.

"You're not hungry anymore? Will you have a little something to drink? A cognac? No, better have something sweet, it's good for you when you're feeling weak, a Coke? Or some fruit juice? I'm not bothering you, am I? You know, that's the first time I've ever seen someone faint right in front of me like that, fall on the ground, and it – it really threw me. I work – I'm an employee for the Post and Telecommunications, you see, I'm not used to – well, I mean, maybe you should go and see a doctor all the same, would you like me to go and phone one?"

He's already getting up, but Lalla shakes her head, and he sits back down. Later, she drinks a little hot tea, and her exhaustion dissipates. Her face is once again copper-colored, light is shining in her eyes. She stands up and the man accompanies her out into the street.

"You're – you're sure you'll be all right now? Can you walk?"

"Yes, yes, thank you," Lalla says.

Before leaving, Paul Estève writes his name and address on a scrap of paper.

"If you need anything. . ."

He squeezes Lalla's hand. He's barely any taller than she is. His blue eyes are still all misty with emotion.

"Good-bye," says Lalla. And she walks away as quickly as she can without looking back.

THERE ARE DOGS almost everywhere. But they're not like the beggars, they prefer to live in the Panier, between Place de Lenche and Rue du Refuge. Lalla looks at them when she passes by, she's wary of them, their coats bristle up, they're very scrawny, but they don't look anything like the wild dogs that used to steal chickens and sheep back in the Project; these dogs are bigger and stronger, and there's something dangerous and desperate about the way they look. They go around scrounging for food in all the piles of garbage, they gnaw on old bones, fish heads, the waste the butchers throw out to them. There's one dog that Lalla knows well. He's always in the same spot every day, at the bottom of the stairway, near the street that leads to the big striped church. He's all black with a collar of white fur that grows down onto his chest. His name is Dib, or Hib, she's not sure, but in the end, his name isn't important at all because he doesn't really have a master. Lalla heard a little boy calling him that in the street. When he sees Lalla, he looks kind of glad and wags his tail, but he doesn't come near her, and he won't let anyone get near him. Lalla merely says a few words to him; she asks him how he is, but without stopping, just in passing, and if she has something to eat, she throws him a little piece.

Here in the Panier neighborhood, everyone knows everyone, more or less. It's not the same in the rest of the city, where there are those streams of men and women flowing along the avenues, creating that great din of shoes and motors. Here in the Panier, the streets are short; they twist and open into other streets, alleyways, stairways, and it's more like a big apartment with halls and rooms that fit together. Yet except for the big dog, Dib or Hib, and a few children whose names she doesn't know, most people don't even seem to see her. Lalla slips along without making a sound, going from one street to another, she follows the path of the sun and the light.

Maybe the people here are afraid? Afraid of what? It's hard to say; it's as if they feel they are being watched, and they have to be careful about everything they do and say. But no one is really watching them. So maybe it comes from the fact that they speak so many different languages? There are the people from North Africa, the Magrhebis, Moroccans, Algerians, Tunisians, Mauritanians, and then people from Africa, the Senegalese, the Malians, the Dahomeyans, and also the Jews, who come from all over, but never really speak the language of their country; there are the Portuguese, the Spaniards, the Italians, and also the odd people, who don't resemble the others, the Yugoslavians, the Turks, the Armenians, the Lithuanians; Lalla doesn't know what those names mean, but that's what everyone here calls them, and Aamma is quite familiar with all of those names. Most of all, there are the gypsies, like the ones who live in the house next door, so many of them you never know whether you've already seen them, or if they've just arrived; they don't like Arabs, or Spaniards, or Yugoslavians; they don't like anyone, because they're not used to living in a place like the Panier, so they're always ready to get into a fight, even the little boys, even the women, who, according to what Aamma says, carry razor blades in their mouths. Sometimes, at night, you're awakened by the sound of a battle in the alleyways. Lalla goes down the stairs to the street and, in the pale light of the streetlamp, sees a man crawling on the ground holding a knife stuck in his chest. The next day, there is a long gooey streak on the ground that the flies come buzzing around.

Sometimes people from the police come too; they stop their big black cars at the bottom of the stairways and go into the houses, especially those where the Arabs and the gypsies live. There are policemen with uniforms and caps, but those aren't the ones who are the most dangerous; it's the others, the ones who are dressed like everyone else, gray suits and turtleneck sweaters.

They knock on the doors very hard, because you have to open up right away, and they go into the apartments without saying anything, to see who's living there. At Aamma's, the policeman goes and sits on the vinyl sofa that Lalla uses as a bed, and she thinks he's going to make it sag and that tonight when she goes to bed the mark where the fat man sat down will still be there.

"Name? First name? Tribal name? Resident card? Work permit? Name of employer? Social security number? Lease, rent receipt?"

He doesn't even look at the papers Aamma gives him one after the other. He's sitting on the sofa, smoking a Gauloise, looking bored. He does look at Lalla though, who is standing at attention in front of the door to Aamma's room. He says to Aamma, "Is she your daughter?"

"No, she's my niece," Aamma says.

He takes all of the papers and examines them.

"Where are her parents?"

"They're dead."

"Ah," says the policeman. He looks at the papers as if he were thinking something over.

"Does she work?"

"No, not yet, sir," says Aamma; she says "sir" when she's afraid.

"But she's going to work here?"

"Yes, sir, if she finds work. It's not easy for a young girl to find work."

"She's seventeen?"

"Yes, sir."

"You must be careful, there are a lot of dangers here for a young seventeen-year-old girl."

Aamma doesn't say anything. The policeman thinks she hasn't understood and insists. He talks slowly, carefully articulating each word, and his eyes are shining as if he were more interested now.

"Be careful your daughter doesn't end up in Rue du Poids de la Farine, eh? There are lots of them over there, girls just like her, you understand?"

"Yes, sir," says Aamma. She doesn't dare repeat that Lalla isn't her daughter.

But the policeman feels Lalla's cold eyes on him, and it makes him feel uneasy. He says nothing more for several seconds, and the silence becomes unbearable. So then, in an outburst, the fat man starts over again with a furious voice, eyes squinted in anger.

"'Yes, I know, yes,' that's what you say, and then one day your daughter will be on the sidewalk, a whore at ten francs a pass, so then you'd better not come crying to me and say you didn't know, because I warned you."

He's almost screaming, the veins in his temples are bulging. Aamma stands still, paralyzed, but Lalla isn't afraid of the fat man. She looks at him coldly, walks up to him and simply says,

"Go away."

The policeman looks at her stunned, as if she'd insulted him. He's going to open his mouth, he's going to get up, maybe he's going to slap Lalla. But the young girl's stare is hard as steel, hard to hold. So the policeman suddenly stands up and is out of the apartment in an instant, rushing down the stairs. Lalla hears the door to the street slam shut. He's gone.

Aamma is crying now, holding her head between her hands, sitting on the sofa. Lalla goes over to her, puts her arms around her shoulders, kisses her cheek to comfort her.

"Maybe I should leave here," Lalla says softly, as one would speak to a child. "It might be best if I left."

"No, no," says Aamma, and cries even harder.

At night, when everything around her is asleep, when there's nothing but the sound of the wind on the zinc valleys of the roofs, and the water dripping somewhere into a gutter, Lalla lies on the sofa, eyes open in the half-light. She thinks about the house back there in the Project, so far away, when the cold night wind came. She thinks that she would like to push open the door and be outside right away, like before, engulfed in the deep night with thousands of stars. She would feel the hard, icy earth under her bare feet. She would hear the cracking sounds of the cold, the cries of the nighthawks, the owl hooting and the wild dogs barking. She thinks she would walk like that, alone in the night, until she reached the rocky hills, with the song of crickets all around her, or else out along the path in the dunes, guided by the breath of the ocean.

She searches the darkness as hard as she can, as if her eyes could open up the sky again, make the invisible shapes appear again, the outline of the sheet metal and tarpaper roofs, the walls of planks and cardboard, the crest of the hills, and all of the people, Naman, the girls at the fountain, the Soussi, Aamma's sons, and most of all, him – the Hartani, just as he'd been, motionless in the desert heat, standing on one leg, his body and face covered, without a word, without a sign of anger or fatigue, motionless before her as if he were awaiting death, while the men from the Red Cross came to get her and take her away. She also wants to see the one she used to call al-Ser, the Secret, the one whose gaze came from afar and enveloped her, penetrated her like sunlight.

But is it possible for them to come all the way over here, to the other side of the sea, to the other side of everything?

Can they find their way amongst all of those paths, find the gate amongst all of those gates? The darkness is still opaque; the emptiness in the room is immense, so immense that it is swirling around and hollowing out a funnel in front of Lalla's body, and the dizzy mouth clamps against her and sucks her toward it. She clings to the sofa with all of her might, resists, her body tensed to the breaking point. She would like to shout out, scream, in order to break the silence, throw off the weight of the night. But her tight throat will not let out a single sound, and merely breathing in requires a painful effort, makes a hissing sound like steam. For long minutes, hours maybe, she struggles, her whole body caught up in that spasm. Finally, all of a sudden, as the first light of dawn appears in the courtyard of the building, Lalla feels the whirlwind loosening, leaving her. Her limp shapeless body falls back onto the sofa. She thinks of the child she is carrying, and for the first time feels anxious about having hurt someone who is dependent upon her. She lays her two hands on each side of her belly, until the warmth goes very deep. She cries for a long time, without making a sound, with calm little sobs, like breathing.

THEY'RE PRISONERS of the Panier. Maybe they don't really realize it. Maybe they think they'll be able to leave one day, go somewhere else, go back to their villages in the mountains and in the muddy valleys, find the people they left behind, the parents, the children, the friends. But it's impossible. The narrow streets lined with old decrepit walls, the dark apartments, the cold dank rooms where the gray air weighs down on your chest, the stifling workshops where the girls work in front of their machines making pants and dresses, the hospital rooms, the construction sites, the roads with the deafening detonations of jackhammers, everything is keeping them here, grasping them, holding them prisoner, and they'll never get free.

Now Lalla has found work. She is a cleaning woman at the Hotel Sainte-Blanche, in the first part of the old town, to the north, not far from the main avenue where she met Radicz for the first time. She leaves early every day, before the shops open. She wraps herself up tightly in her brown coat because of the cold, and goes all the way across the old town; she walks through dark narrow streets, up stairways with dirty water trickling down one step at a time. There aren't many people out, just a few dogs with their hair bristling, looking for something to eat in the piles of garbage. Lalla keeps a piece of old bread in her pocket because they don't feed her at the hotel; sometimes she shares it with the old black dog, the one they call Dib or Hib. As soon as she arrives, the owner of the hotel gives her a bucket of water and a long-handled scrub brush for her to wash the stairs with, even though they are so dirty that Lalla thinks it's a waste of time. The owner is a fairly young man, but with a yellow face and swollen eyes as if he didn't get enough sleep. The Hotel Sainte-Blanche is a run-down, four-story house, with a funeral parlor on the ground floor. The first time Lalla went there, it frightened her and she almost left immediately; it was so dirty, cold, and smelly. But she's used to it now. It's like Aamma's apartment, or like the Panier neighborhood, it's just a matter of getting used to it. You just have to close your mouth and breathe slowly, in short breaths, to keep that odor from getting inside your body, that odor of poverty, of sickness, and of death that pervades the stairways, the halls, and all the nooks and crannies where the spiders and cockroaches live.

The owner of the hotel is a Greek, or a Turk, Lalla isn't quite sure. When he's given her the bucket and the scrub brush, he returns to his room on the first floor, the one with the glass door so he can watch who goes in and out from his bed. The people who live in the hotel are all menial workers, poor, men only. They're North Africans who work on the construction sites, black men from the Antilles, Spaniards too, who have no family, no home, and who are living there until they find something better. But they get used to it and stay, and often go back to their countries without ever having found anything else, because lodgings are expensive, and no one wants to have anything to do with them in the city. So they live in the Hotel Sainte-Blanche, two or three to a room, without knowing each other. Every morning when they leave for work, they knock on the owner's glass door, and pay for the night in advance.

When she's finished scrubbing the filthy stairs and the sticky linoleum in the hallways with the long-handled brush, Lalla scours down the toilets and the only shower room with the brush alone, but there again, the layer of filth is such that the hard bristles of the brush can't even put a dent in it. Then she cleans the rooms; she empties the ashtrays and sweeps up the crumbs and the dust. The owner gives her his passkey, and she goes from room to room. There's no one in the hotel. The rooms are easy to do because the men who live there are very poor, and they have practically no possessions. Just the cardboard suitcases, the plastic bags with their dirty laundry, a bit of soap wrapped in a

232

piece of newspaper. Sometimes there are a few photographs in an envelope on the table; Lalla looks at the blurred faces on the glossy paper for a moment, sweet faces of children, of women, half faded away, as if through a fog. There are letters too, sometimes, in large envelopes, or sometimes keys, empty coin purses, souvenirs purchased in bazaars near the old port, plastic toys for the children who are in the fuzzy pictures. Lalla looks at all of that for a long time; she holds the objects in her wet hands, looks at those precarious treasures as if she were half dreaming, as if she would be able to enter into the world of those murky photographs, hear the sound of the voices, laughter, glimpse the light in the smiles. Then it all suddenly vanishes, and she goes back to sweeping the room, cleaning up the crumbs left after the men's hasty meals, restoring the sad gray anonymity that the objects and the photographs had disturbed for an instant. Sometimes, on a bed with the sheets thrown back, Lalla finds a magazine full of obscene pictures, naked women with their legs spread, obese swollen breasts, like huge oranges, women with their lips painted light pink, with heavy eyes smeared with blue and green, with blond and red hair. The pages of the magazines are crumpled, stained with sperm, the photos are dirty and worn as if they had been left on the street under people's feet. Lalla also looks at the magazine for a long time, and her heart starts beating faster, from anxiety and uneasiness; then she puts the magazine down on the made bed, after having straightened out the pages and closed the cover, as if it too were a precious souvenir.

The whole time she's working in the stairways and the rooms, Lalla doesn't see anyone. She's never seen the faces of the men who live at the hotel; as for them, they're in a hurry when they leave for work in the morning and go past her without seeing her. In fact, Lalla is dressed so she won't be seen. Under her brown coat, she wears a gray dress that belongs to Aamma, which comes down almost to her ankles. She knots a large scarf over her head and slips her feet into black rubber sandals. In the dark corridors of the hotel, on the mud-colored linoleum, and in front of the dirty doors, she is barely visible, gray and black, like a pile of rags. The only people who know her here are the owner and the night watchman who stays until morning; he's a tall, very skinny Algerian, with a tough face and pretty green eyes like those of Naman the fisherman. He always greets Lalla, in French, and says a few nice words to her; since he always talks very ceremoniously in his deep voice, Lalla answers him with a smile. He is perhaps the only person here who has noticed that Lalla is a teenage girl, the only person who has seen, under the shadows of the rags, her handsome copper-colored face and her eyes filled with light.

When she's finished her work at the Hotel Sainte-Blanche, the sun is still high in the sky. So Lalla walks down the main avenue to the sea. She doesn't think of anything else then, as if she'd forgotten everything. In the avenue, on the sidewalks, the crowd is still rushing on, still rushing toward the unknown. There are men with glinting eyeglasses, striding hurriedly along; there are poor men wearing threadbare suits, going in the opposite direction, with guarded looks, like foxes. There are groups of young girls, wearing skintight clothing, who walk along clacking their heels, like this: *kra-kab, kra-kab, kra-kab.* The automobiles, the motorcycles, the mopeds, the trucks, the buses are all speeding past, going down to the sea, or up toward the higher part of the city, all filled with men and women with identical faces. Lalla is walking along on the sidewalk, looking at all of that, all of the movement, all of the shapes, the bursts of light, and it all goes inside of her and whirls around. She's hungry; her body is weary from having worked in the hotel, and yet she still feels like walking, to see more light, to drive out all the darkness that has remained deep inside of her. The icy winter wind blows in gusts along the avenue, raising dust and old newspaper pages. Lalla half closes her eyes, moves along bent slightly forward, just as she used to back in the desert, toward the source of light out there at the end of the avenue.

When she reaches the harbor, she feels a kind of drunkenness inside, stands teetering on the edge of the sidewalk. Here the wind is whirling about freely, driving the water in the harbor out ahead of it, making the riggings on the boats snap. The light is coming from even farther out, beyond the horizon, directly south, and Lalla walks along the wharves, toward the sea. The sound of humans and motors swirls around her, but she doesn't pay attention to it anymore. Sometimes running, sometimes walking, she heads for the large striped church; then even farther out, she enters into the derelict zone of the wharves, where the wind raises squalls of cement dust.

Here, suddenly, everything is silent, as if she really were going to enter the desert. Before her lies the white expanse of the wharves where the sunlight is shining brightly. Lalla walks slowly along beside the silhouettes of the huge freighters, under the metallic cranes, between the rows of red containers. There are no people here, or automobile motors, only white stone and cement, and the dark water in the basins. So then she picks out a place, between two rows of containers covered with blue tarps, and she sits down sheltered from the wind to eat some bread and cheese, gazing at the water in the harbor. At times big seabirds pass overhead shrieking, and Lalla thinks of her place between the dunes and the white bird that was a prince of the sea. She shares her bread with the gulls, but some pigeons also come. Here everything is calm, no one ever comes looking for her out here. From time to time, a fisherman walks down the wharf, holding his rod, looking for a good place to catch sea bream; but he hardly even glances at her out of the corner of his eye, and goes off to the back of the harbor. Or sometimes a child will walk along with his hands in his pockets, playing by himself at kicking a rusty tin can around.

Lalla feels the sunlight penetrating her, gradually filling her, driving out everything that is dark and sad deep inside. She no longer thinks about Aamma's place, about the dark courtyards with dripping laundry. She no longer thinks about the Hotel Sainte-Blanche, or even about all of those streets, avenues, boulevards, where people are endlessly walking, endlessly rumbling along. She becomes like a piece of rock, covered with moss and lichen, immobile, with no thoughts, dilated in the heat of the sun. Sometimes she even falls asleep, leaning against the blue tarpaulin, her knees pulled up under her chin, and she dreams she's in a boat gliding out on the still sea, all the way out to the other side of the world.

The huge freighters glide slowly through the black basins. They go over to the entrance of the harbor; they want to go back out to sea. Lalla plays at following them, running along the wharves as far as she can. She can't read their names, but she looks at their flags, the rust stains on their hulls, and their huge derricks folded back like antennae, and their chimneys decorated with stars, crosses, checkers, suns. In front of the freighters, the pilot boat sails out with a waddling motion like an insect, and when the freighters reach the high seas, they blow their horns, just once or twice, like that, to say good-bye.

The water in the harbor is lovely too, and Lalla often settles down with her back leaning up against a bollard, legs dangling over the water. She looks at the rainbow-colored oil slicks making and unmaking their clouds, and all the odd things drifting on the surface, beer bottles, orange peels, plastic bags, pieces of wood and rope, and that sort of brown foam that comes from who knows where, stretching like strings of spittle along the wharves. When a ship goes by, wavelets spread out from its wake, lapping up against the wharves. The wind blows very hard at times, driving wrinkles, shudders, over the basins, blurring the reflections of the freighters.

Some days in winter, when there is a lot of sunshine, Radicz the beggar comes to see Lalla. He walks slowly along the wharves, but Lalla recognizes him from a long way off; she comes out of her hiding place between the tarpaulins, and whistles between her fingers, as the shepherds used to back in the Hartani's land. The boy comes running up, sits down next to her on the edge of the wharf, and they look at the water in the harbor for a while, not saying anything.

Then the boy shows Lalla something she's never noticed before: on the surface of the black water, there are small silent explosions making circular ripples. At first Lalla looks up at the sky, because she thinks it's from raindrops. But the sky is blue. Then she realizes there are bubbles coming up from the bottom and bursting at the surface of the water. Together they have fun watching the bubbles explode.

"There! There's one! . . . Another one, another!"

"Over there, look!"

"And there! . . ."

Where are those bubbles coming from? Radicz says it's the fish breathing, but Lalla thinks it's probably the plants, and she thinks of those mysterious grasses swaying slowly at the bottom of the harbor.

After that, Radicz takes out his box of matches. He says it's to smoke, but in truth smoking isn't what he likes most; it's burning matches. When he has a little money of his own, Radicz goes into a tobacco shop and buys a big box of matches with an image of a gypsy woman dancing on it. He goes to sit down in a calm spot, and strikes his matches, one after the other. He does it very quickly, just for the pleasure of watching the little red match head flare up, making its rocket sound, and then the pretty orange flame dancing at the end of the little wooden stick, sheltered in his cupped hands.

Down by the harbor, there's a lot of wind, and Lalla has to act like a tent, holding out the flaps of her coat, and she can smell the pungent heat of the phosphorus stinging her nostrils. Every time Radicz strikes a match, they both laugh real hard, and they try to take turns holding the little piece of wood. Radicz shows Lalla how you can burn the whole match by licking the ends of your fingers and holding it by the burnt end. It makes a little hiss when Lalla takes the match by the end that's still red hot, and it burns her thumb and index finger, but it's not an unpleasant feeling; she watches the flame devouring the match, and the burnt wood twisting as if it were alive.

Then they smoke, one cigarette for the two of them, leaning their backs up against the blue tarp and gazing out into nothingness in the direction of the dark waters of the harbor and the cement-colored sky.

"How old are you?" Radicz asks.

"Seventeen, but I'll be eighteen soon," Lalla says.

"I'm going to be fourteen next month," Radicz says.

He thinks for a minute, furrowing his eyebrows.

"Have you ever . . . gone to bed with a man?"

Lalla is surprised at the question.

"No – I mean yes, why?"

Radicz is so preoccupied that he forgets to pass the cigarette to Lalla; he takes drag after drag, without inhaling the smoke.

"I haven't done it," he says.

"You haven't done what?"

"I've never gone to bed with a woman."

"You're too young."

"That's not true!" says Radicz. He gets angry and stutters a little. "It's not true! All my friends have done it, and there are even some who've got their own woman, and they make fun of me, they say I'm a faggot, because I don't have a woman."

He thinks some more, smoking his cigarette.

"But I don't care what they say. I don't think it's right to sleep with a woman like that, just to – to act big, to joke around. It's like cigarettes. You know, I never smoke in front of the others back at the hotel, so they think I've never smoked and that makes them laugh too. But that's because they don't know, but it's all the same to me, I'd rather they didn't know."

Now he gives the cigarette back to Lalla. It's smoked almost all the way down to the end. Lalla takes just one puff and then crushes it out on the ground on the wharf.

"You know I'm going to have a baby?"

She doesn't really know why she's telling that to Radicz. He looks at her for a long time without answering anything. There is something dark in his eyes, but it suddenly grows bright.

"That's good," he says seriously. "That's good, I'm very happy."

He's so happy he can't sit still anymore. He gets to his feet, paces around out by the water, then comes back toward Lalla.

"Will you come and see me over there, where I live?"

"If you like," says Lalla.

"You know, it's a long way away, you have to take the inter-city bus, and then walk for a long time, toward the storage tanks. We'll go together whenever you want to, because otherwise you'll get lost."

He runs off. The sun has gone down now; it's not far from the line of big buildings that can be seen on the other side of the wharves. The freighters are still motionless, like tall rusty cliffs, and flights of gulls are swooping slowly past them, dancing above the masts.

THERE ARE DAYS when Lalla can hear the sounds of fear. She doesn't really know what it is, like a heavy pounding on thick plates of metal, and also a muffled rumbling that doesn't come through her ears, but through the soles of her feet and echoes inside her body. Maybe it's loneliness, and hunger too, hunger for gentleness, for light, for songs, hunger for everything.

As soon as she goes out the door of the Hotel Sainte-Blanche, after finishing her work, Lalla feels the excessively white light of the sky falling upon her, making her stumble. She pulls the collar of her brown coat up as high as she can around her head, she covers her hair all the way down to her eyebrows with Aamma's gray scarf, but the whiteness of the sky still reaches her, and the emptiness of the streets also. It's like a feeling of nausea, rising from the pit of her stomach, coming up into her throat, filling her mouth with bitterness. Lalla sits down quickly, anywhere, without trying to understand, without worrying about the people looking at her, because she's afraid of fainting again. She fights against it with all her might, tries to slow the beating of her heart, the movements of her entrails. She puts both of her hands on her belly, so that the gentle warmth of her hands travels through her dress, goes inside of her, till it reaches the child. That's how she used to ease those terrible pains that would come to her lower abdomen, like an animal gnawing from the inside. Then she rocks herself a little, back and forth, sitting on the edge of the sidewalk like that, next to the stopped cars.

People go by her without stopping. They slow down a little, as if they were going to come over to her, but when Lalla looks up, there's so much suffering in her eyes that they hurry away, because it frightens them.

After a moment, the pain subsides under Lalla's hands. She

can breathe again more freely. In spite of the cold wind, she's covered with sweat, and her damp dress is sticking to her back. Maybe it's the sound of fear that you don't hear with your ears, but with your feet and your whole body, that is emptying the streets of the city.

Lalla goes back up toward the old town, slowly climbing the steps of the crumbling stairway where the stinking sewer runs. At the top of the stairway, she turns left, and walks down Rue du Bon-Jesus. On the old scabby walls, there are signs marked in chalk, letters and incomprehensible half-erased drawings. On the ground, there are several blood-red stains, drawing flies. The red color rings in Lalla's head, making a sirenlike noise, a sharp whistling that digs out a hole, empties her mind. Slowly, with great difficulty, Lalla steps over the first stain, the second, the third. There are strange white things mixed in with the red stains, like cartilage, broken bones, skin, and the siren rings even louder in Lalla's head. She tries to run down the sloping street, but the stones are damp and slippery, especially when you're wearing rubber sandals. Rue du Timon, there are more signs written in chalk on the old walls, words, maybe names? Then a naked woman with breasts like two eyes, and Lalla thinks of the obscene magazine unfolded on the unmade bed in the hotel room. A little farther along, there is a huge phallus drawn in chalk on an old door, like a grotesque mask.

Lalla keeps on walking, breathing laboriously. Sweat is still running down her forehead, between her shoulder blades, dampening her lower back, stinging her underarms. There's no one in the streets at this time of day, only a few dogs with their hair bristling, growling as they gnaw on their bones. The windows at street level have grilles or bars on them. Higher up, the shutters are closed, the houses look abandoned. A deathly cold emanates from the air vents, cellars, dark windows. It's like a breath of death blowing through the streets, filling the filthy recesses at the foot of the walls. Where should she go? Lalla is moving slowly again, she turns right once more, toward the wall of the old house.

Lalla is always a little frightened when she sees those large windows with bars over them, because she believes it is a prison where people have died in the past: they even say that at night you can sometimes hear the prisoners moaning behind the bars on the windows. Now she goes down Rue des Pistoles, which is always deserted, and takes Traverse de la Charité to see the strange pink dome she likes so much, through the gray stone gateway. Some days she sits down on the doorstep of a house and stares at the dome that looks like a cloud for a very long time, and she forgets everything, until a woman comes and asks her what she's doing there and makes her go away.

But today, even the pink dome frightens her, as if there were a threat behind its narrow windows, or as if it were a tomb. Without looking back, she walks hurriedly away, goes down along the silent streets, toward the sea again. The wind comes in gusts, making the laundry snap, large white sheets with frayed edges, children's clothing, men's clothing, blue and pink women's undergarments; Lalla doesn't want to look at them because they display invisible bodies, legs, arms, breasts, like corpses with no heads. She walks down Rue Rodillat, and there too, those low windows covered with grilles, closed off with bars, where men, women, and children are prisoners. Lalla hears snatches of sentences from time to time, sounds of dishes or of cooking, or at times that nasal music, and she thinks of all the people who are prisoners, in cold dark rooms, with the cockroaches and the rats, all the people who will never see the light again, never breathe in the wind again.

Over there, behind that window with cracked blackened panes, there's the fat infirm woman who lives alone with two scrawny cats, and who is always talking about her garden, her roses, her trees, about the tall lemon tree that produces the most beautiful fruit in the world – she, who has nothing but a cold dark cubbyhole and her two blind cats. This is Ibrahim's house; he's an old soldier from Oran who fought against the Germans, against the Turks, against the Serbs, out there in the places whose names he tirelessly repeats when Lalla asks him to: Thessalonica, Varna, Bjala. But won't he die too, trapped in his crumbling house in which the dark slippery stairs almost trip him up at every step, where the walls weigh down on his thin chest like a wet coat? Over there too, the Spanish woman with six children who all sleep in the same room with the narrow window, and who wander the Panier neighborhood, dressed in rags, pale, always starving. There, in the house with the walls that seem to be damp with sickly sweat, right where that lizard is running, is the sick couple who cough so hard that sometimes Lalla wakes up with a start in the night, as if she could really hear them through all of the walls. Then the foreign couple: he's Italian, she's Greek, and he's drunk every night, and every night he beats his wife, hits her hard in the head, just like that, without even getting mad, just because she's there and looking at him with those teary eyes in her face swollen with fatigue. Lalla hates that man; she clenches her teeth when she thinks about him, but she's also frightened of that calm and desperate drunkenness, of the woman's submission, because that's what can be seen in every stone and every stain in the cursed streets of this city, in every sign written on the walls of the Panier.

There is hunger everywhere, fear, cold poverty, like old, used, damp clothing, like old, withered, fallen faces.

Rue du Panier, Rue du Bouleau, Traverse Boussenoue, always the same scabby walls, the tops of the buildings brushed with cold light, the feet of the buildings where green water puddles, where piles of garbage rot. Here, there are no wasps or flies zooming freely through the air where the dust swirls. There is nothing but people, rats, cockroaches, everything that dwells in holes with no light, no air, no sky. Lalla prowls around the streets like an old black dog with its hair bristling, not being able to find its spot. She sits down for a minute on the steps of the stairway, next to a wall on the other side of which grows the only tree in town, an old fig tree rich with smells. She thinks for a second about the tree she used to love back when Old Naman would tell stories while he was repairing his nets. But, like an old arthritic dog, she can't stay in one place for very long. She strikes out again through the dark labyrinth, as the light from the sky grows slowly dimmer. She sits back down for a moment on the bench in the little square where there is a preschool. There are days she really likes sitting there, watching the small children toddling around in the square, legs wobbling, arms held out on either side. But now, there's nothing but shade, and on one of the benches, an old black woman in an ample colorful dress. Lalla goes over to sit beside her, tries to talk to her.

"Do you live here? Where are you from? What's the name of your country?"

The old woman looks at her without understanding, then she gets frightened and covers her face with the skirt of her colorful dress.

At the back of the square, there is a wall that Lalla is very familiar with. She knows every stain on the roughcast, every crack, every dribble of rust. All the way up at the top of the wall are black chimney stacks, gutters. Under the roof, little shutterless windows with dirty windowpanes. Under old Ida's window, laundry stiffened with rain and dust is hanging on a line. Under that, the windows of the gypsies. Most of the windowpanes are broken, some windows don't even have wooden frames anymore, they're nothing more than gaping black holes, like eye sockets.

Lalla stares at the dark openings, and once again she feels the cold and terrifying presence of death. She shudders. There is an immense void in this square, a whirl of emptiness and death that is coming from those windows, spiraling between the walls of the houses. On the bench next to her, the old mulattress isn't moving, isn't breathing. The only thing Lalla can see is her emaciated arm where the veins protrude like ropes, and her hand with long fingers stained with henna, holding the skirt of her dress up to her face on the side next to Lalla.

Maybe there's some kind of trap here too? Lalla would like to stand up and run away, but she feels riveted to the plastic bench, as if in a dream. Night falls gradually over the city, shadows fill the square, blotting out the corners, the cracks, slipping into the windows through the broken panes. It's cold now, and Lalla wraps herself tightly in her brown coat, she turns the collar up all the way to her eyes. But the cold creeps up through the rubber soles of her sandals, along her legs, to her bottom, to her lower back. Lalla closes her eyes to struggle against it, to stop seeing the emptiness whirling around the square, around the abandoned playground, before the blind eyes of the windows.

When she opens her eyes again, she's alone. The old mulattress in the colorful dress has left without her noticing. Oddly enough, the sky and the earth are not as dark as before, as if night had receded.

Lalla continues walking along the narrow silent streets. She goes down stairways where the pavement has been smashed in with jackhammers. Cold sweeps along the street, making the sheet metal on the toolsheds bang.

When she comes out facing the sea, Lalla sees the day isn't finished yet. There is a big bright spot above the cathedral, between the towers. Lalla runs across the avenue without even seeing the speeding automobiles, which honk their horns and flash their headlights. She slowly approaches the upper parvis, climbs the steps, slips between the columns. She remembers the first time she ever came to the cathedral. She was very frightened, because it was so huge and abandoned, like a cliff. Then Radicz the beggar showed her where he spends the night in summer, when the wind coming in from the sea is as warm as a breath. He showed her the place from where you can see the huge freighters coming into the harbor at night, with their red and green lights. He also showed her the place where you can see the moon and the stars, between the columns of the parvis.

But this evening it's empty. The green and white stone is ice-cold, the silence is heavy, disturbed only by the distant whishing of automobile tires and the screeching of bats flitting about under the vaulted ceiling. The pigeons are already sleeping, perched all around on the cornices, huddling together.

Lalla sits down for a moment on the steps, sheltered by the stone balustrade. She looks at the ground stained with guano and the dusty earth in front of the parvis. The wind is blowing violently, whistling through the gratings. There is great loneliness here, like on a ship on the high seas. It is painful; it tightens in your throat and temples, makes sounds echo strangely, makes lights flicker in the distance, along the streets.

Later, when night has come, Lalla goes back up into the city. She crosses Place de Lenche, where men are crowding around the doorways of bars, takes Montée Accoules, her hand resting on the polished double iron railing she so likes. But even there, the anxiety doesn't dissipate. It's behind her, like one of the big dogs with its hair bristling, with a starved look, which prowls around in the gutters looking for a bone to gnaw on. It's hunger, undoubtedly, hunger that gnaws at your belly, that hollows out its emptiness in your head, but hunger for everything, everything that is denied, inaccessible. It's been such a long time since people have eaten their fill, such a long time since they've had any rest, or happiness, or love, anything other than cold basement rooms, where the fog of anxiety floats, anything other than those dark streets overrun with rats, oozing with fetid water, filled with piles of refuse. Misery.

As she walks along in the narrow grooves of the streets, Rue du Refuge, Rue des Moulins, Rue de Belles-Ecuelles, Rue de Montbrion, Lalla sees all the detritus as if it had been washed up by the sea, rusted tin cans, old papers, bits of bone, wilted oranges, vegetables, rags, broken bottles, rubber rings, bottle caps, dead birds with torn-off wings, squashed cockroaches, dust, dirt, decay. These are the marks of loneliness, of abandon, as if humans had already fled this city, this world, left them in the grips of disease, death, oblivion. As if there were only a few people left in this world, the misfortunate, who continue to live in those run-down houses, in those already tomblike apartments, while the emptiness blows in through the gaping windows, the chill of night that tightens chests, that veils the eyes of old people and children.

Lalla continues to walk through the rubble; she walks over fallen plaster. She doesn't know where she's going. She goes down the same street several times, around the high walls of the general hospital. Maybe Aamma is there, in the big underground kitchen with greasy transoms, running her sponge mop over the black floors that nothing will ever be able to clean? Lalla doesn't want to go back to Aamma's place, ever again. She wanders along dark streets as a drizzle begins to fall from the sky, because the wind has fallen silent. Men walk past, dark faceless shapes that also seem lost. Lalla steps aside to let them pass, disappears into doorways, hides behind stopped cars. When the street is empty once again, she comes out, continues walking silently, exhausted, drunk with sleep.

Yet she doesn't want to sleep. Where would she be able to let herself go, forget herself? The city is too dangerous, and anxiety won't let poor girls sleep like the children of rich people.

There are too many sounds in the dark silence, sounds of hunger, sounds of fear, of loneliness. There is the sound of the sodden voices of bums in the shelters, the sound of Arab cafés with their endless, monotonous music, and the slow laughter of hashish smokers. There is the terrifying sound of the mad man punching his wife hard with his fist, every night, and the high-pitched voice of the woman screaming at first, then whimpering and moaning. Lalla is hearing all of those sounds now, very clearly, as if they echoed on endlessly. There is one sound in particular that follows her everywhere, that gets inside of her head and her belly and always repeats the same affliction: it's the sound of a child coughing, somewhere in the night, in the house next door, maybe it's the son of the Tunisian woman who is so fat and so pale, with sort-of-crazed green eyes? Or maybe it's some other child who's coughing in a house a few streets away, and then another who answers from somewhere else, in an attic room with a hole in the roof, still another who can't sleep in the freezing alcove, and another, as if there were scores, hundreds of sick children coughing in the night, making the same hoarse sound which is tearing up their throats and their lungs. Lalla stops, leaning her back against a door, and presses the palms of her hands against her ears with all of her might, to keep from hearing the coughing of the children barking out in the cold night from house to house.

Farther on, there is the curve in the street from where you can see, as though from a balcony, the intersection of the main avenues like the mouth of a river, and all the blinking, blinding lights. So Lalla climbs down the hill, following the stairways, she goes in through Passage de Lorette, walks across the large courtyard filled with the sound of radios and human voices, with walls blackened with smoke and poverty. She stops for a minute, her head turned toward the windows, as if someone were going to appear. But all that can be heard is the inhuman sound of a voice on the radio shouting something, slowly repeating the same sentence, "At the sound of this music the gods make their entrance!"

But Lalla doesn't know what that means. The inhuman voice drowns out the sound of the children coughing, the sound of drunken men, and the whimpering woman. Then there is another dark passageway, like a corridor, and you come out on the boulevard.

Out there, for a moment, Lalla doesn't feel the fear anymore, or the sadness. The crowd hurries along the sidewalks, eyes glittering, hands agile, feet pounding on the cement, hips swinging, garments rustling, charged with static electricity. Automobiles, trucks, motorcycles drive along on the pavement, headlights bright, and the reflections in the shop windows flash on and off constantly. Lalla lets herself be swept along by the movement of the people; she's not thinking about herself now; she's empty, as if she didn't really exist anymore. That's why she always comes back to the main avenues, to lose herself in the flow, to just drift along.

There are so many lights! Lalla watches them as she walks straight ahead. The blue, red, orangey, purple lights, the steady lights, the ones that move, the ones that dance in place like match flames. Lalla thinks about the star-filled sky, about the vast desert night, when she was lying on the hard sand next to the Hartani, and they were breathing softly, as if they had but one body. But it's difficult to remember. Out here, you have to keep walking, walking along with the others, as if you knew where you were going, but there's no end to the journey, no hiding place in a dip of the dunes. You have to keep walking so you won't fall, so you won't be trampled by the others.

Lalla goes all the way down to the end of the avenue, then walks back up another avenue, and yet another. There are still all the lights, and the sound of humans and their motors roars endlessly on. Then, all of a sudden, the fear returns, the anxiety, as if all the sounds of those tires and footsteps were tracing large concentric circles on the sides of a gigantic funnel.

Now Lalla can see them again: they're out there everywhere, sitting against the blackened walls, hunched over on the ground amidst the excrement and the garbage: the beggars, the old blind people with outstretched hands, the young women with chapped lips, a child hanging on their flaccid breast, the little girls dressed in rags, faces covered with scabs, who cling to the clothing of passersby, old women, the color of soot, with tangled hair, all the people whom the hunger and the cold have driven out of their hovels, and who are pushed along like flotsam by the waves. They are there, in the middle of the indifferent city, in the head-splitting din of motors and voices, rain-soaked, windblown, uglier and poorer still in the wan light of the electric lightbulbs. They look at the people passing by with blurry eyes, their sad moist eyes which are constantly fleeing and turning back toward yours, like those of dogs. Lalla walks slowly past the beggars, looking at them with a knot in her throat and again, that terrible void is hollowing out its whirlwind there, in front of those discarded bodies. She's walking so slowly that a beggar woman grabs her by the coat and tries to pull the young woman over to her. Lalla resists, forcefully pries away the fingers that are clutching at the cloth of her coat; she looks in pity and in horror at the face of the woman who is still young, cheeks swollen with alcohol, blotched red from the cold and, above all, those two blue, almost transparent, blind eyes, in which the pupils are no bigger than a pinhead.

"Come! Come here!" says the beggar woman, as Lalla is trying to unlock the fingers with broken nails. Then fear gains the upper hand, and Lalla yanks her coat out of the woman's grasp, and runs away, while the other beggars start laughing and the woman, rising to her knees on the sidewalk amidst her piles of rags, begins to scream insults at her.

Heart pounding, Lalla runs along the avenue; she bumps into people who are strolling around, going in and out of cafés, movie theaters; men in suits who have just had dinner and whose faces are still glistening from the effort they have made to eat and drink too much, perfumed boys, couples, soldiers out for a night on the town, foreigners with black skin and frizzy hair, who say words she doesn't understand, or who try to grab her, laughing very loud, as she runs by.

In the cafés, music blares incessantly, wild and throbbing music that reverberates deep in the ground, that vibrates all through your body, in your belly, in your eardrums. It's always the same music coming out of the cafés and the bars, colliding with the neon lights, with the red, green, orangey colors on the walls, on the tables, with the painted faces of women.

How long has Lalla been moving through the whirl of that music? She's not sure anymore. For hours, maybe for whole nights, nights with no days to interrupt them. She thinks about the expanse of the plateaus of stones in the night, of the mounds of razor-sharp rocks, of hare and viper tracks in the moonlight, and she glances about herself, here, as if she were going to see him appear. The Hartani, clothed in his homespun robe, with his eyes shining in his very black face, with his long slow movements like the gait of antelopes. But there is only this avenue, and still more of this avenue, and these intersections full of faces, of eyes, of mouths, these shrill voices, these words, these murmurs. The sounds of all these motors and horns, these glaring lights. You can't see the sky, as if there were a white veil covering the earth. How could they get all the way over here, the Hartani and he, the blue warrior of the desert, al-Ser, the Secret, as she used to call him? They would never be able to see her through the white veil separating the city from the sky. They would never be able to recognize her, in the midst of so many faces, so many bodies, with all of these automobiles, these trucks, these motorcycles. They would never even be able to hear her voice, here, with the sound of all of these voices speaking in all different languages, with this music reverberating, making the ground shake. That's why Lalla doesn't look for them anymore, doesn't talk to them anymore, as if they'd disappeared forever, as if for her, they were dead.

The beggars are out there in the night, in the very heart of the city. It has stopped raining, and the night is very white, distant, all the way through to midnight. There are very few people. Men go in and out of cafés and bars, but then they go speeding off in automobiles. Lalla turns right into the narrow street that climbs slightly uphill and she walks behind the stopped cars to keep from being seen. On the opposite sidewalk, there are a few men. They're standing still, not talking. They're looking up the street, at the entrance to a squalid building, a very small door painted green, half open on a lighted hallway.

Lalla stops too, and watches, hidden behind a car. Her heart is beating fast, and the great void of anxiety is blowing in the street. The building stands there like a dirty fortress, with its shutterless windows plastered with newspaper pages. Some windows are lit with a harsh ugly light, others an odd wan, blood-colored glow. It looks like a giant with scores of eyes standing stock still and watching, or sleeping, a giant filled with an evil force, who is going to devour the little men waiting in the street.

251

Lalla is so weak she needs to lean up against the hull of the car, shivering all over.

The evil wind is blowing in the street, that is what is creating the void over the city, the fear, the poverty, the hunger: that is what hollows out the whirling winds in the squares and makes silence weigh down in lonely rooms where children and old people are suffocating. Lalla hates that wind and all those giants with open eyes, reigning over the city, only to devour the men and women, crush them in their entrails.

Then the little green door of the building opens all the way, and now, on the sidewalk facing Lalla, a woman is standing motionless. That's what the men are staring at, without moving, smoking cigarettes. She's a very small woman, almost a dwarf, with a thick body and a swollen head set on neckless shoulders. But her face is childlike, with a tiny little cherry-colored mouth, and very black eyes with green rings around them. What is most surprising about her, apart from her small size, is her hair: cropped short, curly, it is a coppery red color that sparkles strangely in the light of the hallway behind her and makes a sort of flaming halo around her chubby doll's head, like a supernatural apparition.

Lalla looks at the little woman's hair, fascinated, not moving, almost not breathing. The cold wind is blowing hard all around her, but the little woman stands there in front of the entrance to the building, with the hair on her head ablaze. She's dressed in a very short black skirt that shows her heavy white thighs and a sort of low-necked purple pullover. She's wearing very high spike-heeled patent leather pumps. Because of the cold, she's pacing around a little in front of the door, and the sound of her heels echoes through the empty street.

Some men walk up to her now, smoking cigarettes. Most of them are Arabs with dark black hair, with gray complexions Lalla has never seen before, as if they lived underground and only came out at night. They don't say anything. They look tough, obstinate, tight-lipped, cold-eyed. The little woman with fiery hair doesn't even glance at them. She too lights a cigarette, and smokes rapidly, pivoting this way and that. When she turns around, she seems to be hunchbacked.

Then from the top of the street comes another woman. She's very tall by contrast, and very fleshy, already aged, withered with fatigue and lack of sleep. She's clothed in a long blue oilcloth raincoat, and her black hair is tousled with the wind.

She slowly descends the street, clacking her high-heeled shoes; she walks down to the dwarf and also stops in front of the door. The Arabs come up to her, talk to her. But Lalla doesn't understand what they're saying. One after the other, they walk away and stop a little farther off, eyes riveted on the two women standing there smoking. The wind gusts through the narrow street, plastering the women's clothes against their bodies, ruffling their hair. There is so much hate and despair in this street, as if it kept drifting endlessly down through the different degrees of hell, without ever reaching the bottom, without ever stopping. There is so much hunger, unsatisfied desire, violence. The silent men look on, standing motionless on the curb like lead soldiers, their eyes glued to the women's abdomens, to their breasts, to the curve of their hips, to the pale flesh of their throats, to their bare legs. Perhaps there is no love anywhere, no pity, no gentleness. Perhaps the white veil separating the earth from the sky has smothered the men, stopped the palpitations of their hearts, made all of their memories, all of their old desires, all of the beauty die?

Lalla can feel the relentless dizziness of the void entering her, as if the wind blowing in the street was part of a long spiraling movement. Maybe the wind is going to tear the roofs off the sordid houses, smash in the doors and windows, knock down the rotten walls, heave all the cars into a pile of scrap metal. It's bound to happen, because there's too much hate, too much suffering... But the big building remains standing, stunting the men in its tall silhouette. They are the immobile giants, with bloody eyes, with cruel eyes, the giants who devour men and women. In their entrails, young women are thrown down on dirty old mattresses, and possessed in a few seconds by silent men with members as hot as pokers. Then they get dressed again and leave, and the cigarette – left burning on the edge of the table – hasn't had time to go out. Inside the devouring giants, old women lie under the weight of men who are crushing them, dirtying their yellow flesh. And so, in all of those women's wombs, the void is born, the intense and icy void that escapes from their bodies and blows like a wind along the streets and alleys, endlessly shooting out new spirals.

Suddenly, Lalla can't wait any longer. She wants to scream, even cry, but that's impossible. The void and the fear are gripping her throat tightly, and she can barely breathe. So she breaks away. She runs as hard as she can down the alley, and the sound of her footsteps echoes loudly in the silence. The men turn and watch Lalla fleeing. The dwarf shouts something, but a man takes her by the neck and pushes her into the building with him. The void, disturbed for a moment, clamps shut over them, grasps them. Some men throw their cigarettes in the gutter and move off in the direction of the avenue, slipping along like shadows. Others arrive and stop at the curb and look at the tall woman with black hair standing in front of the door to the building.

Many beggars are sleeping around the train station, hunkered down in their tattered clothing, or surrounded by pieces of cardboard, in front of doorways. In the distance shines the edifice of the train station with its tall white streetlamps as bright as stars. In one doorway, sheltered by a stone milepost, in a large pool of damp shadows, Lalla has lain down on the ground. She's pulled her head and limbs into her big brown coat as well as she can, exactly like a turtle would. The stone is cold and hard, and the moist sound of the automobile tires makes her shiver. But at least she can watch the sky opening up, as she used to do out on the plateau of stones and, in keeping her eyes shut tightly, she can see the desert night once again between the edges of the veil that is parting.

LALLA IS LIVING at the Hotel Sainte-Blanche. She has a tiny little room, a dark cubbyhole up under the roof that she shares with the brooms, buckets, and old things left behind years ago. There's an electric lightbulb, a table, an old cot with canvas webbing. When she asked the owner if she could live there, he simply said yes, without asking her any questions. He didn't make any comments; he told her she could live there, that the bed wasn't being used. He also told her he would deduct the money for the electricity and the water from her salary, that was all. He went back to reading his newspaper, stretched out on his bed. That's why Lalla thinks the boss is okay, even if he is dirty and unshaven, because he doesn't ask questions. It's all the same to him.

With Aamma, it hadn't gone that smoothly. When Lalla told her she wasn't going to live at her place anymore, her face closed up, and she said all kinds of unpleasant things, because she thought Lalla was going away to live with a man. But she agreed to it anyway, since it worked out better for her in the end because of her sons who would soon be arriving. There wouldn't have been enough room for everyone.

Now Lalla knows the people in the Hotel Sainte-Blanche better. They're all very poor, and they've come from countries where there's nothing to eat, where there's almost nothing to live off of. They have hardened faces, even the youngest ones, and they aren't able to talk for very long. No one lives on the floor where Lalla is, because it's the attic, where the mice live. But directly under her, there's a room in which three black men live, three brothers. They aren't mean or sad. They're always cheerful, and Lalla loves to hear them laughing and singing on Saturday afternoons and Sundays. She doesn't know their names; she's not aware of what they do in the city. But she runs into them some-

256

times in the hallway, when she goes to the toilet, or when she comes down early in the morning to scrub the steps of the staircase. But when she goes to clean their room, they aren't there any longer. They hardly have any belongings, just a few boxes filled with clothing, and a guitar.

Next to the black men's room, there are two rooms occupied by North Africans working on the construction sites; they never stay for very long. They're nice enough, but taciturn, and Lalla doesn't talk to them for very long either. There's nothing in their rooms, because they keep all of their clothing in suitcases, and the suitcases under their beds. They're afraid of being robbed.

The person Lalla really likes is a young black African who lives with his brother in the small room on the second floor, at the very end of the hallway. It's the prettiest room, because it opens onto a bit of courtyard where there is a tree. Lalla doesn't know the older brother's name, but she knows that the young one's name is Daniel. He's very, very dark, with hair so frizzy that things are always getting caught in it, bits of straw, feathers, blades of grass. He has a perfectly round head, and an inordinately long neck. For that matter, everything about him is long; he's got long arms and legs, and a funny way of walking, as if he were dancing. He's always very merry when he talks to Lalla; he laughs all the time. She doesn't understand what he says very well, because he has a strange, singsong accent. But it doesn't really matter, because he makes very funny gestures with his long hands, and all sorts of grimaces with his wide mouth full of extremely white teeth. He's the one Lalla prefers, because of his smooth face, because of his laugh, because he looks a bit like a child. He works at the hospital with his brother, and on Saturdays and Sundays, he plays soccer. He's passionate about it. He's got posters and pictures all over his room, tacked to the walls, to the door, inside the closet. Every time he sees Lalla, he asks her when she's going to come and watch him play at the stadium.

She went once, on a Sunday afternoon. She sat all the way at the top of the bleachers, and watched. He made a little black spot on the green turf in the field, and that's how she was able to recognize him. He was the attacking right center midfielder. But Lalla never told him she'd gone to see him, maybe so he would keep asking her to come, with that laugh of his that rings out loudly in the halls of the hotel.

There's also an old man who lives in a very small room, at the other end of the hall. He never talks to anyone, and no one really knows where he comes from. He's an old man whose face has been eaten away by a terrible disease, with no nose or mouth, only two holes in place of his nostrils and a scar in place of his lips. But he has pretty eyes which are deep and sad, and he is always polite and kind, and Lalla likes him because of that. He lives on nearly nothing in that room, almost without eating, and he only goes out early in the morning to glean fruit that has fallen on the ground in the marketplace and to take a walk in the sunshine. Lalla doesn't know his name, but she likes him. He resembles Old Naman in a way; he has the same type of hands, strong and agile, hands burned by the sun and full of know-how. When she looks at his hands it's a little bit as if she could recognize the burning landscape, the stretches of sand and stones, the charred shrubs, the dried-up rivers. But he never talks about his country, or about himself; he keeps it locked up deep inside. He barely utters a few words to Lalla when he passes her in the hall, only about what the weather's like outside, or the news he heard on the radio. He might be the only one in the hotel who knows Lalla's secret, because he asked her twice, looking at her with his extremely profound eyes, if it wasn't too hard on her to be working. He didn't say anything else, but Lalla thought that he knew she had a baby in her belly, and she was even a little afraid the old man would tell the owner, because he wouldn't want to keep her at the hotel anymore. But the old man didn't say anything to anyone else. Every Monday, he pays for a week's lodgings in advance, without anyone knowing where his money comes from. Lalla is the only one who knows he's very poor, because there is never anything to eat in his room, save the bruised fruit that has fallen on the ground at the marketplace. So, sometimes, when she has a little extra money, she buys one or two nice apples, some oranges, and she puts them on the only chair in the small room, when she's doing the cleaning. The old man never thanks her, but she can tell from his eyes he's pleased when she runs into him.

Lalla knows the other lodgers by sight, but doesn't know anything about them. They're people who never stay long, Arabs, Portuguese, Italians, who only come to sleep. There are also a few who have stayed, but Lalla doesn't like them — two Arabs on the first floor who look cruel, and who get drunk on wood alcohol. There's the man who reads obscene magazines, and who leaves all those pictures of naked women on his unmade bed, so that Lalla will pick them up and look at them. He's a Yugoslavian, whose name is Gregori. One day, Lalla went into his room, and he was there. He took her by the arm and wanted to knock her onto the bed, but Lalla started yelling, and he got scared. He let her go, shouting insults at her. Ever since that day, Lalla has never gone into his room while he's there.

But none of those people really exist, except for the old man with his face eaten away. They don't exist because they leave no trace of their passage, as if they were nothing but shadows, ghosts. When they leave one day, it's as if they'd never come. The bed with canvas webbing is still the same, and the wobbly chair, the stained linoleum, the greasy walls where the paint is blistering, and the bare, flyspecked, electric lightbulb hanging at the end of its wire. Everything stays the same.

But most of all, it's the light coming from outside, through the dirty windowpanes, the gray light from the interior courtyard, the pale reflection of the sun, and the sounds: sounds of radios, sounds of automobile motors on the main avenue, the voices of men arguing. Sounds of pipes squeaking, the sound of the toilet flushing, the stairs creaking, the sound of the wind rattling the metal gutters.

Lalla listens to all of those sounds, at night, lying on her bed, looking at the yellow spot of the electric lightbulb burning. The men can't exist here, neither can children, nor any living thing. She listens to the sounds of the night as if she were inside a cave, and it's as if she herself didn't really exist anymore. In her belly, something is fluttering now, palpitating like an unfamiliar organ.

Lalla curls up in her bed, knees drawn up against her chin, and she tries to listen to the thing that is moving inside of her, that is beginning to take on life. There is still the fear, the fear that makes you flee through the streets and makes you bounce around from one corner to the next, like a ball. But at the same time, there is an odd wave of happiness, of warmth and light, that seems to be coming from far away, from beyond the seas and the cities, and binding Lalla to the beauty of the desert. Then, just as she does every night, Lalla closes her eyes, she breathes in deeply. Slowly, the gray light of the narrow room fades out, and the lovely night appears. It is inhabited with stars, cold, silent, lonely. She is resting on the boundless earth, on the stretch of immobile dunes. Next to Lalla is the Hartani, wearing his homespun robe, and his black copper face is shining in the starlight. It is his gaze that is coming all the way out to her, reaching her here, in this narrow room, in the sickly light of the electric lightbulb, and the Hartani's gaze is moving inside of her, in her belly, awakening life. It's been such a long time since he disappeared, such a long time since she went away, across the sea, as if she had been banished, and yet the gaze of the young shepherd is very forceful; she can feel him actually moving deep down inside, in the secrecy of her womb. Then they are the ones who disappear, the people in this city, the policemen, the men in the streets, the lodgers in the hotel, all of them disappear, and along with them, their city, their houses, their streets, their automobiles, their trucks, and there is nothing left but the stretch of desert where Lalla and the Hartani are lying together. They are both wrapped up in the large homespun robe, surrounded by the black night and the myriads of stars, and they are holding very tightly to one another, so as not to feel the cold creeping over the earth.

When someone dies in the Panier, the funeral shop on the ground floor of the hotel takes care of everything. At first Lalla thought it belonged to a relative of the hotel owner; but it's just a business like all the others. At first, Lalla thought that people came to die at the hotel, and afterward, they were sent to the funeral home. There aren't many people in the shop, only the boss, Mr. Cherez, two morticians, and the limousine driver.

When someone in the Panier is dead, the employees leave in the limousine, and they go to hang big black tapestries with silver teardrops on the door of the house. In front of the door, on the sidewalk, they set up a little table draped with a black cloth that also has silver tears on it. On the table, there is a saucer so that people can put a little card with their name on it when they go and visit the dead person.

When Mr. Ceresola died, Lalla knew right away, because she saw his son in the shop on the ground floor of the hotel. Mr. Ceresola's son is a short, chubby little man with a bristly mustache who doesn't have much hair, and he always looks at Lalla as if she were transparent. But Mr. Ceresola was different. He's someone Lalla really likes. He's an Italian, not very tall, but old and thin, and he walks painfully because of his rheumatism. He's always dressed in a black suit that must be pretty old too, because the fabric is threadbare at the elbows, at the knees. With the suit, he wears old black leather shoes that are always well polished, and in cold weather, he adds a wool scarf and a cap. Mr. Ceresola has a very dry, wrinkled face, quite leathered from the open air, short white hair, and funny tortoiseshell glasses, repaired with bandage tape and string.

People in the Panier really like him because he's polite and pleasant to everyone, and he has a dignified air about him with his old-fashioned black suit and his polished shoes. And also, everyone knows that he used to be a carpenter, a real master carpenter, and that he came from Italy before the war, because he

261

didn't like Mussolini. That's the story he sometimes tells when he runs into Lalla in the street on his way to the grocery. He says he arrived in Paris without any money, just enough to pay for two or three nights in a hotel, and that he didn't speak a word of French; so when he asked for some soap to wash with, he was shown a pot of hot water.

When Lalla runs into him, she helps him carry his packages because he has a hard time walking, especially when you have to go up the stairs leading to Rue du Panier. So as they walk along, he tells her about Italy, about his village, and the days when he worked in Tunisia, and the houses he built everywhere in Paris, in Lyon, in Corsica. He has a funny, somewhat loud voice, and Lalla has a hard time understanding his accent, but she enjoys hearing him speak.

Now he's dead. When Lalla realized that, she looked so sad that Mr. Ceresola's son glanced at her in astonishment, as if he were surprised that someone could care about his father. Lalla left very quickly, because she doesn't much like to breathe in the air in the funeral home, or see all of those celluloid wreaths, those coffins, and above all those morticians who have mean eyes.

So then Lalla followed the streets, slowly, head bowed, and that's how she ended up at the door to Mr. Ceresola's house. Around the door were the tapestries and the little table with its black cloth and saucer. There was also a big blackboard above the door with two crescent-shaped letters like this:

$$\text{\Huge $\smallsmile\kern-0.5em\smallsmile$}$$

Lalla goes into the house, she climbs the stairs with narrow steps, just as she used to do when she would carry Mr. Ceresola's packages, slowly, stopping on each landing to catch her breath. She is so tired today, she feels so heavy, as if she were going to fall asleep, as if she were going to die when she reached the top floor.

She stops in front of the door, hesitating a little. Then she pushes the door open and walks into the little apartment. At first she doesn't recognize the place, because the shutters are closed and it's dark inside. There isn't anyone in the apartment, and Lalla walks toward the large room where there's a table covered with an oilcloth, and a basket of fruit on it. At the back of the room is the alcove with the bed. When she draws near, Lalla can make out Mr. Ceresola, who is lying in the bed on his back, as if he were sleeping. He looks so peaceful in the half-light, with his eyes closed and his hands on either side of his body, that Lalla thinks for an instant that he's simply dozed off, that he'll soon wake up. She says, in a whisper, so as not to disturb him, "Mr. Ceresola? Mr. Ceresola?"

But Mr. Ceresola isn't sleeping. You can see that from his clothing, still the same black suit, the same polished shoes, but the jacket is on a little crooked, with the collar turning up behind his head, and Lalla thinks it's going to get wrinkled. There is a gray shadow on the old man's cheeks and chin, and blue rings around his eyes, as if he'd been beaten. Lalla thinks of Naman's eyes again, when he was lying on the floor in his house and couldn't breathe anymore. She thinks of him so hard that for a few seconds, he's the one she sees lying on the bed, his face sunk in sleep, his hands stretched out on either side of his body. Life is still quivering in the half-light of the room, with a very low, barely perceptible murmur. Lalla steps up very near to the bed, she looks more closely at the extinguished, wax-colored face, straight strands of white hair falling on the temples, mouth half opened, cheeks hollowed from the weight of the falling jaw. The thing that makes the face look odd is that it's no longer wearing the old tortoiseshell glasses; it looks naked, weak, because of the marks on the nose, around the eyes, along the temples, that are pointless now. Mr. Ceresola's body has suddenly become too small, too thin for those black clothes, and it's as if he'd disappeared, as if all that were left was this mask and these waxen hands, and these ill-fitting garments on hangers that are too narrow. Then suddenly fear surges back over Lalla, fear that burns her skin, that blurs her eyes. The half-light is suffocating, it's a paralyzing poison. The half-light comes from the back of the courtyards, flows down the narrow streets, through the old town, drowning everyone it encounters, the prisoners in the narrow rooms: small children, women, old people. It creeps into the houses, under the damp roofs, into the cellars, filling the smallest cracks.

Lalla stands motionless in front of Mr. Ceresola's corpse. She feels the cold creeping through her body, the funny waxen color covering the skin on her face and hands. She still remembers the wind of ill fortune that blew over the Project that night when Old Naman was dying, and the cold that seemed to seep out of all the holes in the earth to annihilate human beings.

Slowly, without taking her eyes from the dead body, Lalla backs toward the door of the apartment. Death is in the gray shadows floating between the walls, in the stairway, on the chipped paint in the hallways. Lalla goes down as fast as she can, heart pounding, eyes filled with tears. She leaps outside, and tries to run down to the lower part of town, down to the sea, wreathed in wind and light, but a pain in her belly forces her to sit down on the ground, doubled over. She groans, while people walk by, glance at her furtively, and move away. They too are afraid, you can tell by the way they walk, sort of sidling along, hugging the walls, the way dogs with their hair bristling do.

Death is upon them everywhere, thinks Lalla, they can't escape. Death is settled into the dark shop on the ground floor of the Hotel Sainte-Blanche, amongst the bouquets of plaster violets and the marble aggregate gravestones. That's where it lives, in the old decrepit house, in the rooms of the men, in the halls. They don't know it, they don't even have the slightest inkling. At night it leaves the shop of the funeral home in the form of cockroaches, rats, bedbugs, and spreads through all of the damp rooms, over all the doormats, it crawls and seethes over the floors, into the cracks, it fills everything like a poisonous shadow.

Lalla rises to her feet, staggers forward, her hands pushing against her lower abdomen, where a pain protrudes. She's not looking at anyone anymore. Where could she go? They're all alive, they eat, they drink, they talk, and in the meantime, the trap is closing in on them. They've lost everything, exiled, beaten, humiliated, they work on the roads, in the freezing winds, in the rain, they dig holes in the stony earth, they ruin their hands and their heads, driven mad by the jackhammers. They're hungry, they're frightened, they're frozen with solitude and emptiness. And when they stop, death wells up around them, right there, under their feet, in the shop, on the ground floor of the Hotel Sainte-Blanche. Down there, the morticians with mean eyes erase them, snuff them out, make their bodies disappear, replace their faces with masks of wax, their hands with gloves that stick out of their empty clothing.

Where can she go, where can she disappear to? Lalla would like to find a hiding place, like she had before in the Hartani's cave, up on top of the cliff, a place where all you can see is the sea and the sky.

She reaches the little square and sits down on the plastic bench, facing the wall of the broken-down house with empty windows like the eyes of a dead giant.

AFTER THAT, there was a sort of fever, almost everywhere in the city. Maybe it was because of the wind that had begun to blow at the end of the winter; it wasn't the wind of ill fortune and sickness, like the one when Old Naman had started to die, but a cold hard wind that blew down the main avenues of the city, raising the dust and the old newspapers, a wind that made you light-headed, that made you stagger. Lalla has never felt a wind like that before. It gets inside your head and whirls around, goes through your body like a cold draft, driving great shudders out ahead of it. So that afternoon, as soon as she gets outside, she starts running straight away, without even glancing at the shop of the funeral home, with the bored man in black.

Outside in the main avenues, there's a great deal of light because it's being carried in on the wind. It's leaping about, sparkling on the hulls of the automobiles, on the windows of the houses. It gets inside of Lalla's head too; it vibrates on her skin, makes her hair sparkle. Today, for the first time in ages, she can see the eternal whiteness of stone and sand all around her, shards as sharp as flint, the stars. Far out ahead of her, at the end of the large avenue, in the haze of light, mirages appear, domes, towers, minarets, and caravans mingling with the swarm of people and automobiles.

It's the wind of light, coming from the west, and blowing in the same direction as the shadows. Lalla can hear, just as she used to, the sound of the light sizzling on the asphalt, the long sound of it reflecting off the windows, all of the crackling sounds of the embers. Where is she? There's so much light it's as if she were alone in the midst of a network of needles. Maybe she's walking over the immense expanse of stones and sand right now, in the place where the Hartani is waiting for her, in the middle

266

of the desert? Maybe she's dreaming as she walks along, because of the light and the wind, and the big city will soon dissolve, evaporate in the heat of the rising sun after the horrid night?

At the corner of one street, near the flight of stairs leading up to the train station, Radicz the beggar is standing in front of her. His face is tired and anxious, and Lalla has a hard time recognizing him because the boy now looks like a man. He's wearing clothing Lalla isn't familiar with, a brown suit that sags around his bony body and big, black leather shoes that must certainly be wounding his bare feet.

Lalla would like to talk to him, tell him that Mr. Ceresola is dead, and that she's never going to go back to work at the Hotel Sainte-Blanche, or in any of those rooms where death can strike at any minute and turn you into a wax mask; but there's too much wind and too much noise to talk, so she shows Radicz the wad of rumpled banknotes in her hand.

"Look!"

Radicz opens his eyes wide, but he doesn't ask any questions. Maybe he thinks Lalla stole the money, or worse yet.

Lalla puts the bills back into her coat pocket. That's all that is left of the days she spent in the darkness of the hotel, scrubbing the linoleum with the couch-grass brush, sweeping the gray rooms that smell of sweat and tobacco. When she told the owner of the hotel she was leaving, he didn't say anything either. He got out of his old bed, which was never made, and walked over to the safe at the back of his room. He took out the money, counted it, added a week's advance, and gave it all to Lalla; then he went and lay back down again without saying anything else. He did all of that in a very leisurely fashion, in his pajamas, with his unshaven cheeks, and his dirty hair; then he went back to reading his newspaper again, as if nothing else were of any importance.

So now Lalla is drunk with freedom. She looks around, at the walls, the windows, the automobiles, the people, as if they were nothing but shapes, images, ghosts that the wind and the light would sweep away.

Radicz looks so unhappy that Lalla feels sorry for him.

"Come on!" She takes the boy by the hand, pulling him through the swirling crowd. Together they go into a very big store with bright light, not the beautiful light of the sun, but a harsh white glow, reflected in the profusion of mirrors. But that glare is also inebriating; it numbs and blinds you. With Radicz stumbling slightly behind her, Lalla goes through the perfume department, through cosmetics, wigs, and soaps; she stops almost everywhere, buys several different colored bars of soap that she has Radicz smell, then small bottles of perfume that she breathes in briefly as she walks along the aisles, and it makes her feel dizzy, almost nauseated. Red lipsticks, green eye shadow, black, ochre, foundation, brilliantine, creams, false eyelashes, false hair extensions – Lalla asks to be shown it all, and she shows it to Radicz, who doesn't say anything; then she takes a long time choosing a little square bottle of brick-colored nail polish and a tube of bright red lipstick. She's sitting on a tall stool, in front of a mirror, and trying out the colors on the back of her hand, while the salesgirl with strawlike hair gazes at her stupidly.

On the first floor, Lalla weaves through the clothing, still holding Radicz by the hand. She picks out a T-shirt, some blue denim work overalls, some canvas sandals, and red socks. She leaves her old, gray smock-dress and rubber sandals behind in the dressing room, but she holds on to the brown coat because she likes it. Now she walks more buoyantly, bouncing on the springy soles of the sandals, one hand in the pocket of her overalls. Her black hair falls in heavy curls on the collar of her coat, gleaming in the white electric light.

Radicz looks at her and thinks she's beautiful, but he doesn't dare tell her so. Her eyes are sparkling with joy. There's something like a fiery glow to Lalla's black hair and red copper face. Now it seems as if the electric light has brought the color of the desert sun back to life, as if she had stepped directly from the path out on the plateau of stones into the Prisunic store.

Maybe everything really has disappeared and the big store is standing alone in the midst of the boundless desert, just like a fortress of stone and mud. Yet it is the entire city that is surrounded by the sand, held tightly in its grips, and you can hear the superstructures of the concrete buildings snapping while cracks run up the walls and the plate glass mirrors of skyscrapers fall to the ground.

Lalla holds the burning force of the desert in her eyes. The light blazes on her black hair, on the thick tress she's braiding in the hollow of her collarbone as she walks along. The light blazes in her amber-colored eyes, on her skin, on her high cheekbones, on her lips. And so, in the big store full of noise and white electricity, people step aside, stop as Lalla and Radicz the beggar go by. The women, the men stop, surprised, because they've never seen anyone like them. Lalla strides along in the middle of the aisle, wearing her dark overalls, her brown coat which opens to show her throat and her copper-colored face. She isn't tall, and yet she seems huge as she moves down the center of the aisle and goes down the escalator to the ground floor.

It's because of all the light streaming from her eyes, her skin, her hair, the almost supernatural light. Behind her comes the strange, skinny boy, in his men's clothing, barefoot in his black leather shoes. His long black hair frames his hollow-cheeked, sunken-eyed triangular face. He tags behind silently, not moving his arms, walking a little bit sideways, the way cowering dogs do. People also look at him in surprise, as if he were a shadow detached from a body. Fear is visible on his face, but he tries to hide it with an odd smirking smile that looks more like a grimace.

At times, Lalla turns around, gives him a little wave, or takes his hand, "Come on!"

But the boy quickly lets himself fall behind. When they are outside again in the street, in the sun and the wind, Lalla asks him, "Are you hungry?"

Radicz looks at her with shiny feverish eyes.

"We're going to eat now," says Lalla. She shows him what's left of the handful of rumpled bills in the pocket of her new overalls.

Along the wide straight avenues, people are walking, some hurriedly, others slowly, dragging their feet. The automobiles are still driving along near the sidewalks, as if they were on the lookout for something or someone, a place to park. There are swifts up in the cloudless sky; they swoop down the valleys of the streets giving shrill cries. Lalla is happy to be walking like that, holding Radicz's hand, not saying anything, as if they were going off to the other side of the world and never coming back. She thinks about the lands across the sea, the red and yellow soil, the black rocks standing up tall in the sand like teeth. She thinks of the eyes of fresh water open on the sky, and of the taste of the *chergui*, which lifts up the thin skin of dust and makes the dunes move forward. She thinks of the Hartani's cave again, up on top of the cliff, the place where she'd seen the sky, nothing but the sky. Now it was as if she were walking toward that land, along the avenues, as if she were going back. People step aside to let them pass, eyes squinting in the light, not understanding. She moves past them without seeing them, as if through a crowd of shadows. Lalla isn't talking. She's squeezing Radicz's hand very tightly, walking straight ahead, toward the sun.

When they reach the sea, the wind is blowing even harder, heaving against them. The automobiles are honking aggressively, caught in the traffic jams around the harbor. Once again fear is visible on Radicz's face, and Lalla holds his hand firmly, to reassure him. She mustn't hesitate; if she does, the giddiness of the wind and the light will go away, leaving them on their own, and they won't be brave enough to be free.

They walk down the wharves not looking at the ships with hollow clanking masts. The reflections of the water dance on Lalla's cheek, setting her copper-colored skin, her hair aglow. The light around her is red, the red of burning embers. The boy looks at her, allows the heat emanating from Lalla to enter him, make him light-headed. His heart is pounding heavily, pulsing in his temples, in his neck.

Now the high white walls, the plate glass windows of the fine restaurant appear. That's where she wants to go. Over the door, colored flags are snapping in the wind on their masts. Lalla knows this place well; she's been noticing it from afar for quite some time now, very white, with its plate glass windows shooting off flashes in the setting sun.

She goes in without hesitating, pushing open the glass door. The large dining room is dark, but on the round tables, the cloths make dazzling splashes. Lalla sees everything in a glance, very clearly: the bouquets of pink flowers in the crystal vases, the silver utensils, the cut-glass goblets, the immaculate napkins, and the chairs covered with dark blue velvet, the waxed hardwood floor over which the waiters dressed in white slip by. It is unreal and remote, and yet this is the place she has come into, walking slowly, silently, over the parquet, and holding Radicz the beggar's hand very tightly.

"Come on," says Lalla. "We're going to sit over there."

She points out a table, near a plate glass window. They cross the dining room. Men and women sitting at the round tables lift their heads from their plates and stop chewing, stop talking. The waiters are stopped short, the spoon sunk into the dish of rice, or the bottle of white wine slightly tilted, pouring into the glass a very fine trickle of wine tailing off at the end like a flame going out. Then Lalla and Radicz sit down at the round table, on either side of the lovely white tablecloth, separated by a bouquet of roses. So the people start chewing, talking again, but in lower voices, and the wine starts pouring again, the spoon serves the rice, and the voices whisper a little, drowned out by the commotion of the automobiles passing in front of the large plate glass windows like monstrous fish in an aquarium.

Radicz doesn't dare look around. He's keeping his eyes trained solely on Lalla's face with all of his might. He has never seen a more beautiful, more luminous face. The light from the window shines on her heavy black hair, making a flame around Lalla's face, on her neck, on her shoulders, all the way down to her hands laying flat on the white tablecloth. Lalla's eyes are like two pieces of flint, the color of metal and fire, and her face is like a smooth copper mask.

A tall man is standing in front of their table. He's dressed in a black suit, and his shirt is as white as the tablecloths. He has a large, bored, flabby face, with a lipless mouth. He is precisely just about to open that mouth of his and tell the children to leave immediately, without making a scene, when his sad eyes meet those of Lalla, and he suddenly forgets what he was going to say. Lalla's stare is as hard as flint, filled with such strength that the man in black has to look away. He takes a step backward, as if he were going to leave, but then says, in a funny, slightly strangled voice, "Would . . . would you like something to drink?"

Lalla is still staring at him unblinkingly.

"We're hungry," she simply says. "Bring us something to eat."

The man in black walks away and comes back with the menu, which he lays on the table. But Lalla hands the piece of cardboard back and keeps her eyes trained on his. Perhaps later he'll remember his hatred and be ashamed of his fear.

"Bring us the same thing as they're having," Lalla orders. She motions to the group of people at the next table, the ones who are peering at them over their eyeglasses every now and again, turning halfway around in their seats.

The man goes and says something to one of the waiters, who comes up pushing a small cart loaded with dishes of all different colors. On the plates, the waiter places tomatoes, lettuce leaves, filets of anchovies, olives and capers, cold potatoes, eggs in a yellow powder, and still many more things. Lalla watches Radicz eating quickly, leaning over his plate like a dog gnawing at a bone, and she feels like laughing.

The light and the wind are still dancing for her, even here, on the glasses and the plates, in the mirrors on the walls, on the bouquets of flowers. The dishes are brought to the table one after the other, huge, flamboyant, filled with all sorts of delicacies with which Lalla isn't familiar: fish swimming in orange sauces, mounds of vegetables, plates full of red, green, brown, covered with silver domes, which Radicz lifts to sniff at the smells. The maître d'hôtel ceremoniously pours them an amber-colored wine, then in another wide, very fragile glass, a ruby-colored, almost black wine. Lalla dips her lips into the drink, but it is rather the color that she drinks, looking at it against the light. They are more inebriated with the light and the colors and smells of the food than with the wine. Radicz eats rapidly, everything at the same time, and he drinks the glasses of wine one after the other. But Lalla hardly eats anything; she just watches the boy eating, and the other people in the room, who seem to be frozen in front of their plates. Time has slowed down, or maybe it's her gaze, coupled with the light, that is immobilizing everything. Outside, the automobiles continue to drive past the windows, and you can glimpse the gray color of the sea between the boats.

When Radicz has finished eating everything in the dishes, he wipes his mouth with the napkin and leans back in the chair. He's a little red, and his eyes are very bright.

"Was it good?" asks Lalla.

"Yes," Radicz simply says. He's eaten so much that he's hiccupping a little. Lalla has him drink a glass of water and tells him to look her in the eye until his hiccups go away.

The big man in black comes over to their table.

"Coffee?"

Lalla shakes her head. When the maître d'hôtel brings the bill on a tray, Lalla holds it out to him.

"Read it."

She takes the wad of wrinkled bills out of her coat pocket and unfolds them one after the other on the tablecloth. The maître d'hôtel takes the money. He starts to walk away and then changes his mind.

"There is a man who would like to speak with you over there, at the table near the door."

Radicz takes hold of Lalla's arm, gives her a hard jerk.

"Come on, let's get out of this place!"

As she nears the door, Lalla sees a man around thirty with somewhat of a sad look about him sitting at a neighboring table. He stands and walks up to her. He stammers.

"I, excuse me for accosting you like this, but I – "

Lalla looks straight at him, smiling.

"You see, I'm a photographer, and I'd like to take some pictures of you, whenever you like."

Since Lalla doesn't answer, and keeps smiling, he gets more and more muddled.

"It's because – I saw you over there a little while ago, when you walked into the restaurant and it was – it was extraordinary, you are – it was really extraordinary."

He takes a ballpoint pen out of his suit jacket and quickly scribbles his name and address on a scrap of paper. But Lalla shakes her head and doesn't take the paper.

"I don't know how to read," she says.

"Then tell me where you live?" asks the photographer. He has very sad gray-blue eyes, very watery like those of dogs. Lalla looks at him with her eyes filled with light, and the man tries to think of something else to say.

"I live at the Hotel Sainte-Blanche," says Lalla. And goes out hurriedly.

Outside, Radicz the beggar is waiting for her. The wind is blowing his long hair over his thin face. He doesn't look happy. When Lalla talks to him he shrugs his shoulders.

Together, they walk till they reach the sea, not knowing where they are going. Here, the sea isn't the same as at Naman the fisherman's beach. It's a big cement wall that runs along the coast, clinging to the gray rocks. The short waves come crashing into the hollows of the rocks, making explosions; the foam rises up like mist. But it's great, Lalla loves to pass her tongue over her lips and taste the salt. She and Radicz climb down amongst the rocks till they get to a deep recess sheltered from the wind. The sun burns down very hot there; it sparkles out on the open sea and on the salty rocks. After the noise of the city, and after all those odd smells in the restaurant, it's good to be out here, with nothing before you but the sea and the sky. Slightly westward, there are some small islands, a few black rocks sticking up out of the sea like whales – that's what Radicz says. There are also some small boats with big white sails, and they look like children's toys.

When the sun starts going down in the sky, and the light is growing softer on the waves, on the rocks, and the wind is also blowing more gently, it makes you want to dream, to talk. Lalla is looking at the tiny succulent plants that smell of honey and pepper; they quiver at each gust of wind in the hollows of the gray rocks, facing the sea. She thinks she would like to become so small she could live in a grove of those little plants; then she would live in a hole in a rock, and she would have enough to drink for a whole day with just a single drop of water, and a single crumb of bread would be enough for her to eat for two whole days.

Radicz pulls a slightly crumpled pack of cigarettes out of the pocket of his brown suit jacket and gives one to Lalla. He says he never smokes in front of others, only when he's in a place he really likes. He says that Lalla is the first person he's ever smoked in front of. They're American cigarettes that have a piece of cardboard and cotton at one end, and they have a nauseating smell of honey. They both smoke slowly, looking out at the sea before them. The wind whisks the blue smoke away.

"You want me to tell you about the place I live in, over by the storage tanks?"

Radicz's voice is all different now, a little hoarse, as if emotion were making a lump in his throat. He talks without looking at Lalla, smoking the cigarette down until it burns his lips and fingertips.

"I didn't use to live with the boss before, you know. I lived with my father and mother in a trailer, we went from one fair to the next, we had a shooting stand, I mean, not with rifles, with balls and tin cans. Then my father died, and since there were a lot of us kids, and we didn't have enough money, my mother sold me to the boss and I came to live here in Marseille. At first, I didn't know that my mother had sold me, but one day, I wanted to leave, and the boss caught me and beat me, and he told me that I couldn't go back to live with my mother because she'd sold me and now he'd become like a father to me, so after that, I never left him again, because I didn't want to see my mother. At first I was really sad, because I didn't know anyone and I was all alone. But later I got used to it, because the boss is nice, he gives us as much as we want to eat, and it was better for me than staying with my mother since she didn't want to take care of me anymore. There were six of us boys living with the boss, well at first there were seven, and one of them died, he got pneumonia and he died right away. So we would go and sit in the places the boss had paid for, and we begged, and we brought the money back in the evening, we kept a little and the rest was for the boss. He bought our food with it. The boss always told us to be careful not to get picked up by the police, because then we'd be taken to child welfare, and he couldn't get us out of there. We never stayed for long in the same spot because of that, and the boss would take us someplace else afterward. First we lived in a hangar north of the city, then we had a trailer like my father's, and we went to pitch camp with the gypsies in the vacant lots just outside of town. Now we've got a big house for all of us, just before you get to the storage tanks, and there are other children, they work for a boss called Marcel, and there's Anita with still other children, two boys and three girls, I think the oldest one really is her daughter. We work around the train station, but not every day, so we won't get spotted, and we also go down to the harbor, and over to Cours Belsunce, or on La Canebière. But now the boss says I'm too old to beg, he says that's a job for little boys and girls, but he wants me to work a serious job, he's teaching me how to be a pickpocket, steal from stores, from the marketplace. Look, see this suit, this shirt, these shoes, he stole it all for me in a store while I was keeping watch. A little while ago, if you'd wanted to, you could have left with your outfit for nothing, it's easy, all you had to do was pick it out and I would have gotten it out of the store for you, I know the tricks. For example, for wallets, there have to be two of you, one takes it and passes it right away to the other, so you don't get caught with it. The boss says I've got a knack for it because I have long agile hands. He says that's good for playing music and for stealing. Now there are three of us boys doing it, along with Anita's daughter, we stop into the supermarkets all over. Sometimes the boss says to Anita, come on, we're going shopping at the supermarket, so he takes two boys, and sometimes Anita's daughter and another boy, well, the other boy is always me. You know, supermarkets are really big, there are so many aisles you can get lost, aisles with things to eat, clothes, shoes, soaps, records, everything. So you can work fast in pairs. We've got a bag with a false bottom for the smaller things, and the things to eat, and Anita puts the rest in her stomach, she has a round thing she puts under her dress as if she were pregnant, and the boss has a trench coat with pockets all over the inside, so we grab everything we want and leave! You know, at first I was scared of getting caught, but all you need to do is choose the right time, and not falter. If you falter, you'll get spotted by the detectives. I'm really good at recognizing detectives now, even from a long way off, they all have the same way of walking, of watching out of the corner of their eyes, I could pick them out a mile away. What I like best is working in the street with cars. The boss says he's going to teach me to work with cars, that's his specialty. Sometimes he goes into town and brings back a car so I can practice. He taught me how to pick the locked doors with a wire, or a fake key. Most cars can be opened with a fake key. Afterward, he shows me how to pull the wires out from under the dashboard and release the steering wheel lock. But he says I'm too young to drive. So I take whatever there is in the cars, and there's often a bunch of stuff in the glove compartment, checkbooks, papers, even money, and under the seats, cameras, radio sets. I like working real early in the morning, all alone, when there's no one in the streets, just a cat every now and again, and I really like to see the sun come up, and the nice clean sky in the morning. The boss also wants me to learn locks on the doors of houses, the rich villas around here, near the sea, he says that working in pairs, we could do some good jobs, because we're light and we can scale up walls easily. So he's teaching us the ropes, picking door locks, and opening windows too. He doesn't want to do it anymore, he says he's too old and that he couldn't run if he had to anymore, but that's not why, it's because he already got caught once and it scared him. I already went once with a guy called Rito, he's older than I am, he used to work for the boss and he took me along with him. We went into a street near the Prado, he'd scouted out a house, he knew no one was home. I didn't go in, I stayed out in the garden while Rito was taking everything he could, then we carried it all over to the car where the boss was waiting. I was scared, because I was the one who stayed in the garden standing watch, and I think I would have been less scared if I'd gone into the house to work. But you have to know everything before you start or you'll get caught. To get in, first of all you have to know how to find the right window, and then climb up a tree, or use the rainspout. You can't get dizzy. And if the police come, you can't panic, you have to stay still, or hide on the roof, because if you start running, they'll get you in two shakes. So the boss shows us all that at our place, at the hotel, he has us scale up the house, he has us walk on the roof at night, he even teaches us to jump like paratroopers, it's called rolling. But he says we're not going to stay here indefinitely, we're going to buy a trailer and leave for Spain. I'd rather go over to the area around Nice, but I think the boss prefers Spain. Wouldn't you like to come with us? You know, I'd tell the boss you were a friend, he won't ask you any questions, I'll just tell him you're my friend, and that you're going to live with us in the trailer, it'll be great. Maybe you could learn to work in the stores too, or else we could work the cars together, taking turns, that way people wouldn't suspect anything? You know, Anita is really nice, I'm sure you'd like her a lot, she's got blond hair and blue eyes, no one wants to believe she's a gypsy. If you came with us, I wouldn't mind not going to Nice, I wouldn't mind going to Spain, or anywhere. . ."

Radicz stops talking. He'd like to ask Lalla a few things, about the child in her belly, but he doesn't dare. He's lit up another cigarette, and is smoking, and from time to time, he passes the cigarette to Lalla so she can have a puff. The two of them are looking out at the lovely sea, at the black islands like whales, and the toy boats moving slowly over the shimmering sea. From time to time, the wind blows so hard you'd think the sea and the sky were going to go tumbling over.

Now Lalla is looking at her photographs in magazine articles, on the covers of fashion reviews. She looks at the reams of pictures, the contact sheets, the color layouts where her almost life-sized face appears. She thumbs through the magazines from back to front, holding them a little tilted, cocking her head to one side.

"Do you like them?" asks the photographer, sounding a little worried, as if it really mattered.

It makes her laugh, with her silent laughter that makes her extremely white teeth sparkle. She laughs about all of it, about the pictures, the magazines, as if it were a joke, as if it weren't her you could see on those sheets of paper. To begin with, it really isn't her. It's Hawa, the name she's given herself, the one she gave the photographer, and that's what he calls her; that's what he called her the first time he ran into her, in the stairways in the Panier, and brought her back to his place, to his big empty apartment on the ground floor of the new building.

Now Hawa is everywhere, on the pages of magazines, on the contact sheets, on the walls of the apartment. Hawa dressed in white, a black belt around her waist, alone in the middle of a shadeless rocky area; Hawa, in black silk, a scarf around her forehead, like an Apache; Hawa standing above the Mediterranean; Hawa in the midst of the crowd on Cours Belsunce, or else on the flight of stairs in front of the train station; Hawa dressed in indigo, barefoot on the asphalt of the esplanade, vast as a desert, with the outlines of storage tanks and smoking chimneys; Hawa walking, dancing; Hawa sleeping; Hawa with her handsome copper-colored face, with her long smooth body, shining in the light; Hawa eagle-eyed, with her heavy black hair cascading down over her shoulders, or smoothed back by the sea, like a Galalith helmet. But who is Hawa? Every day, when she wakes up in the large gray-white living room where she sleeps on an air mattress on the bare floor, she goes and washes up in the bathroom, not making a sound; then she climbs out the window and walks off aimlessly through the streets of the neighborhood; she walks as far as the sea. The photographer wakes up, opens his eyes but doesn't move; he acts as if he hasn't heard a thing, so as not to disturb Hawa. He knows that's the way she is, that he mustn't try to hold her back. He simply leaves the window open so she can come back in, like a cat. Sometimes she doesn't come back till after dark. She slips into the apartment through the window. The photographer hears her, comes out of his laboratory and sits down beside her in the living room, to talk with her a little. He's always moved when he sees her, because her face is so full of light and life, and he blinks his eyes a little, because in coming out of the dark laboratory, he's a bit dazzled. He always thinks he has a lot of things to tell her, but when Hawa is there before him, he can't recall what he wanted to say. She's the one who talks; she tells about the things she's seen, or heard, in the streets, and she eats a little as she's talking, some bread she's bought, some fruit, some dates that she brings back to the apartment by the pound.

The most extraordinary thing about it all is the letters: they come from all over, with Hawa's name on the envelopes. They're from magazines, fashion reviews that forward them after adding the photographer's name and address. He's both happy and unsettled at receiving all those letters. Hawa asks him to read them, and she always listens with her head cocked a little to one side, drinking mint tea (now the photographer's kitchenette is full of boxes of gunpowder tea and jasmine tea and little bundles of mint). Sometimes the letters say extraordinary things, or really dumb things written by young girls who have seen Hawa's picture somewhere and who talk to her as if they'd always known her. Or else letters from young boys who have fallen in love with her, and say she's as beautiful as Nefertiti or an Incan princess, and they would love to meet her one day.

Lalla starts laughing:

"What liars!"

When the photographer shows her the pictures he's just taken, Hawa with her almond-shaped eyes, shining like gems, and her amber-colored skin, sparkling with light, and her lips with a slightly ironic smile, and her sharp profile, Lalla Hawa starts laughing again, repeats, "What a liar! What a liar!"

Because she thinks it doesn't look like her.

There are also serious letters that speak of contracts, money, appointments, fashion shows. The photographer makes all the decisions, takes care of everything. He calls the fashion designers, notes the appointments in his agenda, signs the contracts. He's the one who chooses the designs, the colors, decides where the shots will be taken. Then he takes Hawa in his little red Volkswagen van, and they go far away, out where there are no houses, nothing but gray hills covered with thorny scrub, or to the delta of the great river, on the smooth beaches of the marshes, out where the water and the sky are the same color.

Lalla Hawa loves to travel in the photographer's van. She watches the landscape slipping around the windows, the black road winding toward her, the houses, the gardens, the fallow fields unraveling on the side, whipping away. People are standing on the side of the road, with blank looks on their faces, as if in a dream. Maybe it is a dream that Lalla Hawa is living, a dream in which there's no more day or night really, no more hunger or thirst, but shifting landscapes of chalk, brambles, crossroads, towns going by, with their streets, their monuments, their hotels.

The photographer never stops photographing Hawa. He changes cameras, measures the light, pushes the trigger. Hawa's face is everywhere, everywhere. It's in the sunlight, lit up as if with a halo in the winter sky, or in the depth of the night, it's vibrating over the waves of radio sets, in telephone messages. The photographer closes himself up all alone in his laboratory, under his little orange lamp, and looks indefinitely at the face taking form on the paper in the developing pan. First the eyes, immense, two stains growing deeper, then the black hair, the curve of the lips, the outline of the nose, the shadow under the chin. The eyes are looking elsewhere, as Lalla Hawa always does, elsewhere, out on the other side of the world, and every time, the photographer's heart speeds up, like the first time he caught sight of the light in her eyes in the Galères restaurant, or when he just happened to run into her again in the stairways of the old town.

She gives him her shape, her image, nothing else. Sometimes the contact of the palm of her hand, or an electric spark when her hair brushes against his body, and also her smell, slightly bitter, slightly stinging, like the smell of citrus fruit, and the sound of her voice, her clear laughter. But who is she? Maybe she's just a pretext for a dream he's chasing in his darkroom with his bellows cameras and his lenses that accentuate the shadow of her eyes, the shape of her smile a dream he and other men share about the pages of fashion reviews and glossy magazine pictures?

He takes Hawa by airplane to the city of Paris; they drive along in a taxi under the gray sky, by the Seine, on their way to business meetings. He takes pictures on the banks of the muddy river, on the large squares, on the endless avenues. He tirelessly photographs the handsome copper-colored face with the light flowing over it like water. Hawa wearing a black satin jumpsuit, Hawa wearing a midnight-blue trench coat, hair braided into a single thick tress. Every time his eyes meet Hawa's, it makes his heart skip a beat, and that's why he's hurrying to take pictures, always more pictures. He moves forward, backs up, changes his camera, puts one knee to the ground. Lalla makes fun of him: "You look like you're dancing."

He'd like to get angry, but it's impossible. He wipes the sweat from his forehead, from his eyebrow, which is slipping against the viewfinder. Then Lalla suddenly steps out of the light field because she's tired of being photographed. She walks away. To keep from feeling the emptiness, he'll continue to look at her for hours, in the darkness of his improvised laboratory in the bathroom of his hotel room, waiting – counting his heartbeats – for the handsome face to appear in the developing pan, most of all the eyes, that profound light flowing from the slanted eyes. That dusk-colored light, from ever so far away, as if someone else, someone secret, were looking out from those pupils, judging silently. And then, appearing later, slowly, like a cloud forming, the forehead, the line of the high cheekbones, the grain of the copper skin, weathered with the sun and the wind. There's something secret about her that sometimes just happens to be revealed on the paper, something you can see but never possess, even if you take pictures every second of her existence, until she dies. There's her smile too, very gentle, somewhat ironic, that makes little hollows at the corners of her mouth, and narrows the slanted eyes. It's all of this the photographer would like to capture with his cameras and bring back to life in the darkness of his laboratory. At times he's under the impression that it really is going to appear, the smile, the light in the eyes, the beauty of the features. But it only lasts a brief instant. On the paper plunged into the developer, the image moves, modifies, blurs, is covered with shadow, and it's as if the image erased the living person.

Maybe it's elsewhere, rather than in the image? Maybe it's in the way she walks, in her movements? The photographer watches Lalla Hawa's gestures, the way she sits down, moves her hands, palms open, making a perfect curve from the crook of her elbow to the tips of her fingers. He looks at the line of her neck, her lithe back, her wide hands and feet, her shoulders, and her heavy black hair with ashen reflections falling in thick curls on her shoulders. He looks at Lalla Hawa, and at times it's as if he can glimpse another face showing through the young woman's features, another body behind hers; barely perceptible, immaterial, ephemeral, the other person drifts up from deep within, then melts away, leaving a flickering memory. Who is it? Who is the girl he calls Hawa, what is her real name?

Sometimes Hawa looks at him, or she looks at people, in the restaurants, in the airport terminals, in the offices, she looks at them as if her eyes would simply erase them, send them back to the void they must belong to. When that strange look comes over her face, the photographer shudders, as if something cold has entered his body. He doesn't know what it is. Maybe it is the other being living inside Lalla Hawa, who is observing and judging the world through her eyes, as if in that very instant all of this – this gigantic city, this river, these squares, these avenues – disappeared, and let the vast stretch of the desert show through, the sand, the sky, the wind.

So the photographer takes Hawa to places that resemble the desert: wide-open rocky plains, marshes, esplanades, vacant lots. For him, Hawa walks around in the sunlight, and her eyes scan the horizon like those of birds of prey, searching for a shadow, a shape. She looks for a long time, as if she really were searching for someone; then she stands still on her shadow, while the photographer starts shooting.

What is she looking for? What does she want from life? The photographer looks at her eyes, her face, and he can feel the profound anxiety behind the force of her light. There is also wariness, the instinct to flee, that funny sort of glimmer that flits over the eyes of wild animals at times. She told him one day, right when he was expecting it, she spoke to him softly of the child she is carrying, who is rounding out her belly and making her breasts swell: "You know, one day I'll go away, I'll leave, and you mustn't try to hold me back, because I'll leave forever. . ."

She doesn't want money, it doesn't interest her. Every time the photographer gives her some money – wages for the hours of posing – Hawa takes the bills, picks out one or two, and hands him back the rest. Sometimes, she's even the one who gives him money, handfuls of bills and coins that she takes out of the pocket in her overalls, as if she didn't want to keep any of it for herself.

Or sometimes she wanders the streets of the city looking for beggars at the corners of buildings, and she gives them money, coins by the handful too, pressing her hand firmly into theirs so they won't lose anything. She gives money to the veiled gypsies who wander around barefoot in the main avenues, and to old women dressed in black squatting in the entrances to the post offices, to bums lying on benches in the squares, and to old men rummaging in rich people's garbage cans at nightfall. They all know her well, and when they see her coming their eyes get bright. The bums think she's a prostitute, because prostitutes are the only ones who give them that much money, and they make jokes and laugh real hard, but they look really happy to see her all the same.

Now, Hawa is being mentioned everywhere. In Paris, reporters come to see her, and one evening in the lobby of the hotel, a woman asks her questions.

"People are talking about you, about the mystery of Hawa. Who is Hawa?"

"My name isn't Hawa, when I was born I didn't have a name, so I was called Bla Esm, which means 'No name.'"

"So, why Hawa?"

"It was my mother's name, and I'm called Hawa, the daughter of Hawa, that's all."

"What country did you come from?"

"The country I come from has no name, like me."

"Where is it?"

"It's in the place where there is nothing, where there is no one."

"Why are you here?"

"I like to travel."

"What do you enjoy in life?"

"Life."

"Food?"

"Fruit."

"What's your favorite color?"

"Blue."

"Your favorite stone?"

"The pebbles on the path."

"Music?"

"Lullabies."

"They say that you write poems?"

"I don't know how to write."

"And films? Have you got any projects?"

"No."

"What is love to you?"

But suddenly Lalla Hawa has had enough, and she walks away very quickly, without looking back; she pushes open the door to the hotel and disappears into the street.

Now there are people who recognize her in the street, young girls who give her one of her photographs so she can put her signature on it. But since Hawa doesn't know how to write, she just draws the sign of her tribe, the one they mark the camels' hides with, which looks a little like a heart:

There are so many people everywhere, on the avenues, in the stores, on the streets. So many people jostling one another, looking at one another. But when Lalla Hawa's gaze passes over them, it's as if everything fades away, grows mute and deserted.

Lalla Hawa wants to get past these places very quickly to find out what comes next. One night, the photographer takes her to a dance hall called the Palace, the Paris-Palace, something like that. She has put on a black dress cut low in the back for dancing, because the photographer wants to take some shots.

This too is a place that resembles the wide-open, empty esplanades, where there are only the outlines of buildings and the parked cars in the sun. It's a dreadful and empty place, where men and women crowd together and grimace in the suffocating darkness, with electric lights flashing in clouds of cigarette smoke, and thundering noise pulsing, making the walls and the floor vibrate.

Lalla Hawa sits down on a step in a corner, and watches the people dancing, their faces glistening with sweat, their clothes glittering everywhere. At the back of the room, in a sort of cave, are the musicians: they're swinging their guitars, beating on the drums, but the sound of the music seems to come from elsewhere, like giants shouting.

Then she too gets up on the dance floor, surrounded by people. She dances the way she was taught to long ago, alone amongst the people, to hide her fear, because there is too much noise and too much light. The photographer remains sitting on the step, not moving, not even thinking to take pictures of her. At first the people don't pay any attention to Hawa, because the light is blinding. Then it's as if they've felt something extraordinary has happened, without their realizing it. They step aside, stop dancing, one after the other, to watch Lalla Hawa. She's all alone in the circle of light, she can't see anyone. She's dancing to the slow rhythm of the electric music, and it's as if the music were inside her body. The light is shining on the black fabric of her dress, on her copper-colored skin, on her hair. You can't see her eyes due to the shadows, but her gaze passes over the people, fills the room with all of its power, all of its beauty. Hawa is dancing barefooted on the smooth floor, her long flat feet are stamping to the rhythm of the drums, or rather it is she who seems to be imposing the rhythm of the music with the soles of her feet, and her heels. Her supple body is undulating; her hips, her shoulders, and her arms are held slightly out from her body, like wings. The light from the projectors is bouncing off of her, enveloping her, whirling about her feet. She's absolutely alone in the large room, alone as if she were in the middle of an esplanade, alone as if she were in the middle of a plateau of stones, and the electric music with its slow heavy rhythm is playing for her alone. Maybe they've all disappeared, all of those people who were there all around her, men, women, fleeting reflections in blinded mirrors, maybe they've been swallowed up? She can't see them anymore now, can't hear them anymore. Even the photographer sitting on his step has disappeared. They've become like rocks, like blocks of limestone. But she can move at last, she is free, she twirls around, arms outstretched, and her feet are hitting the floor, the tips of her toes, then her heels, as if on the spokes of a huge wheel whose axis reaches high up into the night.

She's dancing to get away, to become invisible, to rise up like a bird into the clouds. Under her bare feet, the plastic floor becomes burning hot, very lightweight, the color of sand, and the air is whirling around her body as fast as the wind. The dizziness of the dance is making the light appear now, not the hard cold beams of the spotlights, but the beautiful light of the sun, when the earth, the rocks, and even the sky are white. It's the slow heavy music of the electricity, of the guitars, of the organ, and the drums that is entering her; but maybe she's not even hearing it anymore. The music is so slow and deep that it covers her skin, her hair, her eyes with copper. The euphoria of the dance spreads out around her, and the men and women – stopped for a minute – take up the movements of the dance, following the rhythm of Hawa's body, tapping the floor with the tips of their toes, and their heels. No one is saying anything, no one is breathing. They're waiting, ecstatically, for the movement of the dance to enter them, sweep them up, like those waterspouts that go whirling over the sea. Lalla's heavy mane of hair is rising up and falling against her shoulders in cadence, her hands – fingers spread wide – are quivering. The men and women's bare feet are hitting the shiny floor faster and faster, harder and harder, as the rhythm of the electric music accelerates. In the large room, there are no more walls, mirrors, flashing lights. They've disappeared, been destroyed by the dizzying dance, overthrown. There are no more hopeless cities, abysmal cities, cities of beggars and prostitutes, where the streets are traps, where the houses are graves. There's none of that anymore; the elated look of the dancers has eradicated all the obstacles, all of the old lies. Now

Lalla Hawa is surrounded with an endless expanse of dust and stones, a living expanse of sand and salt, and the waves of the dunes. It's the same as in the old days, at the end of the goat path, in the place where everything seemed to end, as if you were at the end of the earth, at the foot of the sky, on the threshold of the wind. It's the same as when she felt the gaze of al-Ser for the first time, the one she calls the Secret. So then, at the very heart of her dizziness, while her feet continue to make her twirl around faster and faster, for the first time in a long time, she can feel the gaze settling upon her, examining her once again. In the middle of the immense and barren space, far from the dancing people, far from the smoggy cities, the gaze of the Secret enters her, touches her heart. The light suddenly begins to burn with unbearable intensity, a white-hot explosion sending its glaring rays through the whole room, a flash that will surely burst all the electric lightbulbs, the neon tubes, that will smite the musicians, their fingers on their guitars, and cause all the speakers to explode.

Slowly, still turning, Lalla slumps down, slips onto the polished floor, like a disarticulated mannequin. She remains alone for a long time, sprawled on the floor, her face hidden by her hair, before the photographer comes up to her as the dancers step aside, not understanding yet what has happened.

DEATH CAME. It began with the goats and sheep, and the horses too, left in the riverbed, bellies bloated, legs hanging open. Then it was the turn of the children and the old people; they became delirious and could no longer get back on their feet. So many died that a cemetery had to be made for them downstream, on a hill of red dust. They were carried away at dawn, unceremoniously, swathed in old pieces of canvas and buried in a simple hole dug hurriedly, over which a few stones were later placed to keep the wild dogs from digging them up. Along with death came the wind of the *chergui*. It blew in gusts, enveloping people in its burning folds, erasing all moisture from the earth. Every day, Nour wandered over the riverbed with other children, looking for shrimp. He also set snares made with grass nooses and twigs to catch hares and jerboas, but foxes usually got to them before he did.

It was hunger that was eating away at the people and making the children die. Since they'd arrived in front of the red city, days ago, the travelers had not received any food, and the provisions were nearly depleted. Each day, the great sheik sent his warriors out to the walls of the city to ask for food and land for his people. But the officials always made promises and never gave anything. They were so poor themselves, they said. The rains had been scarce and drought had hardened the earth, and the reserves from the harvest had run out. A few times, the great sheik and his sons went up to the ramparts of the city to ask for land, for seed, part of the palm grove. But there wasn't enough land for themselves, said the officials, from the head of the river all the way to the sea, the fertile lands had all been taken, and the soldiers of the Christians often went into the city of Agadir and took most of the harvest for themselves.

Each time, Ma al-Aïnine listened to the officials' answers without saying anything; then he went back to his tent in the bed of the river. But it was no longer anger or impatience that was growing in his breast. With the coming of death, each day, and the burning desert wind, he was sharing the feeling of desperation with his people. It was as if the people wandering along the empty banks of the river or squatting in the shade of their shelters were being confronted with their evident doom. That red soil, those desiccate fields, those meager terraces planted with olive and orange trees, those dark palm groves, were all foreign to them, remote, like mirages.

In spite of their despair, Larhdaf and Saadbou wanted to attack the city, but the sheik refused to use force. The blue men of the desert were too weary now; they had been walking and fasting for too long. Most of the warriors were feverish, sick with scurvy, their legs covered with festering wounds. Their weapons didn't even function anymore.

The people in the city were wary of the men from the desert, and the gates remained closed all day long. Those who tried nearing the ramparts had been met with gunfire: it was a warning.

So when he realized there was nothing left to hope for, that they would all die, one after the other, on the scorching riverbed, in front of the ramparts of the merciless city, Ma al-Aïnine gave the signal to move on northward. This time there was no praying or chanting or dancing. One after the other, slowly, like sick animals straightening up on their legs, teetering, the blue men left the riverbed, struck out again, walking toward the unknown.

Then the troop of the sheik's warriors no longer looked the same. They walked along with the convoy of men and animals, as haggard as they were, their clothing in tatters, their eyes blank and feverish. Maybe they'd stopped believing in the reasons for this long march; they continued moving forward simply out of habit, at the end of their strength, ready to collapse at any minute. The women bent over as they walked, their faces hidden by their blue veils, and many of them no longer had a child on her back, because he'd been left in the red earth of the Souss Valley. Then, at the end of the convoy, which stretched out over the whole valley, were the children, the old people, the wounded warriors, everyone who walked slowly. Nour was among them, guiding the blind warrior. He didn't even know where his family was anymore, lost somewhere in the cloud of dust. Only a few warriors were still mounted. The great sheik was traveling with them, on his white camel, wrapped in his cloak.

No one spoke. They walked on, each man keeping to himself, burned faces, feverish eyes trained on the red earth of the hills in the west, in order to spot the trail leading over the mountains to the city of Marrakech. They walked on with the light beating down on their skulls, their necks, making pain throb through their limbs, burning down into the very quick of their bodies. They could no longer hear the wind, or the sound of the people's feet scuffing over the desert. They could only hear the sound of their hearts, the sound of their nerves, the pain whistling and grating behind their eardrums.

Nour could no longer feel the hand of the blind warrior gripping his shoulder. He was just moving forward, without knowing why, with no hope of ever stopping. Maybe the day his mother and father decided to leave the camps in the South, they had been condemned to wander for the rest of their lives on this endless march, from well to well, along dried valleys? But were there other lands on earth apart from these infinite stretches in which the dust mingled with the sky, stark mountains, sharp stones, rivers with no water, thorn bushes, each of which could bring death with the slightest wound? Each day, off in the distance, on the hillsides near the wells, the people saw more houses, fortresses of red mud surrounded with fields and palm groves. But they saw them as one sees mirages, shimmering in the burning hot air, remote, inaccessible. The inhabitants of the villages didn't show themselves. They had fled into the mountains or they were hiding behind their ramparts, ready to combat the blue men of the desert.

At the head of the caravan, on their horses, the sons of Ma al-Aïnine pointed to the narrow opening of the valley surrounded by the chaos of the mountains.

"The trail! The trail to the North!"

So they walked through the mountains for days. The burning wind blew through the ravines. The blue sky was immense above the red rocks. There wasn't a soul up there, not a person or an animal, only the tracks of a snake in the sand once in a while, or, very high up in the sky, the shadow of a vulture. They walked on without looking for life, without seeing a sign of hope. Like blind people, the men and women made their way along in single file, placing their feet in the footsteps that preceded them, mixed in with the herd animals. Who was guiding them? The dirt trail snaked through ravines, over rockslides, merged with dried torrent beds.

Finally, the travelers arrived on the edge of Oued Issene, swollen with melting snow. The water was lovely and pure; it leapt between the arid banks. But the people looked at it without emotion, because the water was not theirs; they could not retain it. They stayed on the banks of the stream for several days, while the warriors of the great sheik, accompanied by Larhdaf and Saadbou, went up the Chichaoua trail.

"Have we arrived, is this our land?" the blind warrior always asked. The cold water of the stream tumbled down over the rocks in cascades, and the path was getting more difficult. Then the caravan arrived in front of a Chleuh village at the end of the valley. The sheik's warriors were waiting for them there. They had raised their large tent, and the sheiks of the mountains had sacrificed sheep to welcome Ma al-Aïnine. It was the village of Aglagla, at the foot of the high mountains. The people of the desert set up camp near the walls of the village, without even asking. That evening, children from the village came, bringing grilled meat and sour milk, and they were all able to eat their fill, which they hadn't done in a long time. Then they lit big fires of cedar wood, because the night was cold.

Nour watched the flames dancing in the pitch-black night for a long time. There was chanting too, strange music the likes of which he'd never heard, sad and slow, accompanied by the sound of the flute. The men and women of the village asked for Ma al-Aïnine's blessing, asked him to heal them of their illnesses.

Then the travelers started out for the other side of the mountains, in the direction of the holy city. It just might prove to be the place where the people of the desert would know an end to their suffering, according to what Ma al-Aïnine's blue warriors said, because it was in Marrakech that Ma al-Aïnine had given his oath of allegiance to Moulay Hafid, the Leader of the Faithful, fourteen years earlier. It was there that the king had given the sheik a piece of land, so that he could build the house for teaching the Goudfia. And it was also in the holy city that the eldest son of Ma al-Aïnine was waiting for his father in order to join the holy war; and everyone venerated Moulay Hiba, he who was called Dehiba, the Particle of Gold, he who was called Moulay Sebaa, the Lion, for it was he whom they had chosen to be king of the lands of the South.

In the evening, when the caravan stopped and the fires were being lit, Nour led the blind warrior over to where Ma al-Aïnine's warriors were sitting, and they listened to the stories of what had come to pass when the great sheik and his sons had arrived with the warriors from the desert, all mounted on swift camels, and how they had entered the holy city; they had been welcomed by the king along with Ma al-Aïnine's two sons, Moulay Sebaa, the Lion, and Mohammed al-Shems, he who was called the Sun; they also told of the offerings the king had made, so the sheik could build the ramparts of the city of Smara; and the journey they had undertaken with such large herds of camels, they covered the entire plain, while the women and the children and the equipment and the food supplies were all loaded aboard the big steamship called *Bashir*, and sailed several days and several nights from Mogador to Marsa Tarfaya.

They also recounted the legend of Ma al-Aïnine, in their slightly singsong voices, and it was as if they were telling about a dream they had once had. The voice of the warriors mingled with the sound of the flames, and every now and again, Nour caught a glimpse of the frail shape of the old man through the plumes of smoke, like a flame, in the center of the camp.

"The great sheik was born far from here, to the south, in the country that is called Hodh, and his father was the son of Moulay Idriss, and his mother was a descendant of the Prophet. When the great sheik was born, his father named him Ahmed, but his mother named him Ma al-Aïnine, Water of the Eyes, because she had wept with joy when he was born. . . ."

296

Nour listened in the night, beside the blind warrior, his head resting against a stone.

"When he turned seven, he recited the Koran without making a single mistake, so his father, Mohammed al-Fadel, sent him to the great holy city of Mecca, and on the way, the child performed miracles. . . He knew how to heal the sick, and to those who asked him for water, he said, the heavens will give you water, and immediately heavy rains streamed over the earth. . ."

The blind warrior was swaying his head slightly, as if he were marking time to the words, and Nour was drifting slowly off to sleep.

"Then people from all corners of the desert came to see the child who could perform miracles, and the child, the son of the great Mohammed Fadel ben Maminna, simply put a little saliva on the eyes of the sick person, he blew on his lips and the sick person immediately stood up and kissed the child's hand, for he had been healed. . ."

Nour could feel the body of the blind warrior trembling against him, as he rocked his head slowly from shoulder to shoulder. It was the monotone voice of the storyteller and the wavering of the smoke and the flames: the earth itself seemed to be moving in time with the rhythm of the voice.

"So then the great sheik settled in the holy city of Chinguetti, at the Nazaran well, near al-Dakhla, to give his teachings, for he knew the science of the stars and of numbers, and the word of God. So the men of the desert became his disciples, and they were called Berik Allah, those who have received the blessing of God. . ."

The voice of the blue warrior droned on in the night, before the leaping dancing flames, with the smoke enveloping the men and making them cough. Nour listened to the stories of the miracles, the springs gushing forth in the desert, the rainwater covering the arid fields, and the words of the great sheik in the square of Chinguetti, or in front of his home in Nazaran. He listened to the beginning of Ma al-Aïnine's long march through the desert, all the way to the *smara*, the brush land, where the great sheik had founded his city. He listened to the legend of his battles against the Spaniards, in al-Aaiún, in Ifni, in Tiznit, with his sons, Rebbo, Taaleb, Larhdaf, al-Shems, and the one who was called Moulay Sebaa, the Lion.

Thus, every evening, the same voice continued the legend, in the same way, half singing, and Nour forgot where he was, as if it were his own story that the blue man was telling.

On the other side of the mountains, they entered the great red plain, and walked northward, going from village to village. In each village, men with feverish eyes, women, children came to join the caravan and took the places of those who had died. The great sheik was out ahead on his white camel, surrounded by his sons and his warriors, and Nour could see the cloud of dust in the distance that seemed to be guiding them.

When they arrived before the great city of Marrakech, they did not dare go very close, so they set up camp near the dried river to the south. For two days the blue men waited, barely even moving, in the shelter of their tents and in huts of branches. The hot summer wind covered them with dust, but they waited, every last bit of their strength turned to waiting.

Finally, on the third day, Ma al-Aïnine's sons came back. Next to them, on horseback, was a tall man, clothed like the warriors from the North, and his name passed over everyone's lips: "Moulay Hiba, he who is called Moulay Dehiba, the Particle of Gold, Moulay Sebaa, the Lion."

When the blind warrior heard this name, he began to

tremble, and tears ran from his burnt eyes. He set off running straight ahead, arms outstretched, letting out a long cry, something like a high-pitched earsplitting wail.

Nour tried to catch him, but the blind man was running as fast as he could, tripping over stones, staggering over the dusty ground. The people of the desert stepped out of his path, and some were even frightened and turned their eyes away, because they thought the blind man was possessed by the devil. The blind warrior seemed to be consumed with immeasurable joy and suffering. Several times he fell to the ground, having stumbled over a root, or a stone, but each time he got back up and continued to run toward the place where Ma al-Aïnine and Moulay Hiba were, without being able to see them. Finally, Nour caught up with him, took him by the arm; but the man continued running and shouting, dragging Nour along with him. He ran straight ahead, as if he could see Ma al-Aïnine and his son, he was moving unfalteringly toward them. So then the sheik's warriors grew frightened, they grabbed their rifles to stop the blind man from coming closer. But the sheik simply said: "Let them come."

Then he dismounted his camel and walked up to the blind warrior.

"What do you want?"

The blind warrior threw himself on the ground, arms stretched out before him, and sobs wracked his body, choked him. Only the long, high-pitched wail still came from his throat, like a plaint. Then Nour spoke: "Grant him sight, great king," he said.

Ma al-Aïnine looked at the man lying on the ground for a long time, his body shaken with sobs, his clothing in rags, his hands and feet bleeding from the journey. Without saying anything, he knelt down next to the blind man, laid his hand on the back of his neck. The blue men and the sons of the sheik remained standing. The silence was so great at that moment, Nour felt dizzy. A strange, unknown force was welling up from the dusty earth, enveloping the men in its whirl. It was the light of the setting sun perhaps, or the power of the gaze that had fallen upon the place, that was trying to find its way out, like trapped water. Slowly, the blind warrior raised himself up, his face appeared in the light, caked with sand and the water of his tears. Taking a corner of his sky-blue haik, Ma al-Aïnine wiped off the man's face. Then he passed his hand over his forehead, over his burnt eyelids, as if he were trying to erase something. Moistening his fingertips with saliva, he rubbed the blind man's eyelids, and blew softly on his face, without uttering a word. The silence lasted for such a long time that Nour couldn't recall what had come before, what he had said. Kneeling in the sand next to the sheik, he was looking only at the blind warrior's face, in which a new light seemed to be dawning. The man was no longer wailing. He was sitting very still in front of the sheik, arms held slightly out from his body, his damaged eyes open very wide, as if he were slowly becoming inebriated by the gaze of the sheik.

Then Ma al-Aïnine's sons came, and Moulay Hiba also drew near, and they helped the old man to his feet. Very gently, Nour took the warrior by the arm, and had him stand also. The man started walking, leaning on the boy's shoulder, and the light of the setting sun shone upon his face like golden dust. He did not speak. He moved along very slowly, like a man who had gone through a long illness, placing his feet squarely on the stony ground.

He was teetering a little, but his arms were no longer held out, and his body was free of suffering. The people of the desert were standing still in silence, watching him walk out toward the other end of the plain. There was no more suffering, and now his face was calm and gentle, and his eyes were filled with the golden light of the sun, which was touching the horizon. And on Nour's shoulder, his hand had grown light, like that of a man who knew where he was going.

Oued Tadla, June 18, 1910

THE SOLDIERS LEFT Zettat and Ben Ahmed before dawn. General Moinier was in charge of the column that left from Ben Ahmed, two thousand foot soldiers armed with Lebel rifles. The convoy was moving slowly over the charred plain, in the direction of the Tadla River valley. General Moinier, two French officers, and a civilian observer were at the head of the column. A Moorish guide accompanied them, dressed like the warriors of the South, mounted on horseback, like the officers.

The same day, the other column, numbering only five hundred men, had left the city of Zettat, to form the other jaw of the pincers that were to close in on Ma al-Aïnine's rebels on their way north.

Before the soldiers, the bare earth stretched out as far as the eye could see, ochre, red, gray, gleaming under the blue of the sky. The scorching summer wind passed over the earth, raised the dust, veiled the light like a haze.

No one spoke. The officers up front spurred their horses on, trying to move ahead of the rest of the troop in the hopes of escaping the stifling cloud of dust. Their eyes scanned the horizon to see what would appear: water, mud villages, or the enemy.

General Moinier had been waiting for this moment for such a long time. Every time someone mentioned the South, the desert, he thought about him – Ma al-Aïnine – the intransigent, the fanatic, the man who had sworn to drive all Christians from the desert lands, him, the head of the rebellion, the man who assassinated Governor Coppolani.

"Nothing serious," they'd said at headquarters in Casablanca, at Fort-Trinquet, at Fort-Gouraud.

"A fanatic. A sort of witch doctor, a rainmaker, who's gathered all the ragpickers from the Drâa, from Tindouf, all the Negroes from Mauritania behind him."

But the old man of the desert was slippery. He was sighted in the North, near the first checkpoints in the desert. When someone was sent out to have a look, he had disappeared. Then people spoke of him again, this time on the coast, in Rio de Oro, in Ifni. Of course he was in a great position with the Spanish! What was going on down there in al-Aaiún, in Tarfaya, in Cape Juby? Once he had struck, the old sheik, wily as a fox, went back with his warriors to his "territory" down there south of the Drâa, in the Saguiet al-Hamra, to his "fortress" in Smara. Impossible to dislodge him. And there was also the mystery, the superstition. How many men had been able to cross over to that region? As he rode along beside the officers, the observer recalled the journey of Camille Douls in 1887. The account of his meeting with Ma al-Aïnine in front of his palace in Smara: clothed in his ample sky-blue haik, with a tall white turban on his head, the sheik had come up to him, had looked at him for a long time. Douls was a prisoner of the Moors; his clothing was in shreds, his face ravaged from fatigue and from the sun, but Ma al-Aïnine had looked at him without hatred, without contempt. It was that long look, that silence, which were still with him, which had made the observer shudder, every time he thought about Ma al-Aïnine. But maybe he was the only one who had felt that way, when he had read the Douls account long ago. "A fanatic," said the officers, "a savage, who thinks only of plundering and killing, of putting the southern provinces to fire and sword, as he had in 1904, when Coppolani was assassinated in the Tagant, as he had in August of 1905 when Mauchamp was assassinated in Oujda."

Yet, each day, as he marched with the officers, the observer had that uneasy feeling inside, that feeling of apprehension he could not understand. It was as if he were afraid – in rounding a hill, or in some dried stream-bed – of suddenly running into the gaze of the great sheik, alone in the middle of the desert.

"He's had it now, he can't hold out, it's a question of a few months, a few weeks perhaps, he'll have to surrender, or else he'll be forced to throw himself into the sea, or lose himself in the desert, no one is backing him anymore and he knows it. . ."

The officers and the army headquarters in Oran, in Rabat, even in Dakar, have been waiting for this moment for so long. The "fanatic" is backed into a corner, on one side is the sea, on the other, the desert. The sly old fox will be forced to capitulate. Hadn't he been abandoned by everyone? To the north, Moulay Hafid signed the Act of Algeciras, putting an end to the holy war. He had accepted the French protectorate. Then there was the letter of October 1909, signed by Ma al-Aïnine's own son, Ahmed Hiba, he who is called Moulay Sebaa, the Lion, in which he offers the sheik's submission to the law of Makhzen and asks for aid. "The Lion! He's quite alone right now, the Lion and the sheik's other sons, al-Shems, in Marrakech, and Larhdaf, the bandit, the plunderer of the Hamada. They've got no more resources, no more arms, and the population of the Souss Valley has abandoned them. . . They've only got a handful of warriors left, ragpickers, whose only arms are their old bronze-barreled rifles, their yataghans, and their spears! The Middle Ages!"

304

As he rides along with the officers, the civilian observer thinks of everyone who's waiting for the fall of the old sheik. The Europeans in North Africa, the "Christians," as the people from the desert call them – but isn't their true religion money? The Spanish in Tangiers, in Ifni, the English in Tangiers, in Rabat, the Germans, the Dutch, the Belgians, and all the bankers, all the businessmen awaiting the fall of the Arab empire, already making plans for the occupation, parceling out the arable lands, the forests of cork oaks, the mines, the palm groves; the brokers from the Banque de Paris et des Pays Bas, who keep track of the amount of customs duties collected in all the ports; Deputy Etienne's racketeers who created the "Emeralds of the Sahara Company," the "Gourara-Touat Nitrates Company," for whom the bare earth must make way for imaginary railroads, for trans-Saharan, trans-Mauritanian rails, and it will be the army which will clear the way with rifle shots.

What more can the old man from Smara do against this wave of money and bullets? What can his ferocious gaze of a hunted animal do against the speculators who covet the lands, the cities, against those who are after the riches that will ensure the poverty of these people?

Beside the civilian observer, the officers ride along, faces impervious, never uttering an unnecessary word. Their eyes are trained on the horizon, out beyond the rocky hills, over where the misty valley of the Oued Tadla stretches.

Maybe they aren't even thinking about what they're doing? They're riding along on the invisible trail which the Tuareg guide on his tawny horse is opening for them.

Behind them the Senegalese, the Sudanese infantry dressed in their dust-gray uniforms march heavily, leaning forward, lifting their legs up high, as if they were walking over furrows. Their steps make a steady scuffing sound on the hard earth. Behind them, the cloud of red and gray dust rises slowly, dirtying the sky.

It all began long ago. Now nothing can be done about it, as if this army were marching against phantoms. "But he will never agree to give himself up, especially not to the French. He would rather have every last one of his men killed, and be killed himself beside his sons, than be taken... And that would really be best for him, because believe me, the government will not accept his surrender, not after Coppolani's assassination, remember. No, he's a cruel wild fanatic who must disappear, he and all of his tribe, the Berik Allah, the 'blessed by God' as they call themselves... It's the Middle Ages, isn't it?"

The old fox had been betrayed, abandoned by his own people. One after the other, the tribes parted ways with him, because the chieftains realized that it was impossible to stop the advance of the Christians, in the north, in the south, they even came from the sea, they crossed the desert, they were at the gates of the desert in Tindouf, in Tabelbala, in Ouadane, they even occupied the holy city of Chinguetti, where Ma al-Aïnine had given his first teachings.

Perhaps the last great battle had taken place at Bou Denib, when General Vigny had crushed Moulay Hiba's six thousand men. That's when Ma al-Aïnine's son fled into the mountains, disappeared to hide his shame undoubtedly, because he'd become a *lakhme*, a spineless being, as they say, defeated. The old sheik was left alone, prisoner to his Smara fortress, not understanding that it hadn't been the arms but the money that had defeated him: the money of the bankers who had paid for Sultan Moulay Hafid's soldiers and their handsome uniforms; the money that the soldiers of the Christians came to exact in the ports, taking their part of the customs duties; the money from the plundered lands, usurped palm groves, forests given over to those who knew best how to take them. How could he have understood that? Did he know what the Banque de Paris et des Pays Bas was? Did he know what a loan for the construction of railroads was? Did he know what a company for mining nitrates from Gourara-Touat was? Did he even know that while he was praying and giving his blessing to the people of the desert, the governments of France and Great Britain were signing an agreement that gave to one of them a country named Morocco, and to the other a country named Egypt? While he was giving his word and his breath to the last free men, to the Izarguen, the Aroussi-yine, the Tidrarin, the Ouled Bou Sebaa, the Taubalt, the Reguibat Sahel, the Ouled Delim, the Imraguen, while he was bestowing his powers upon his own tribe, the Berik Allah, did he know that a banking consortium, whose principal member was the Banque de Paris et des Pays Bas, was granting King Moulay Hafid a loan of sixty-two million five hundred thousand gold francs, with a five percent interest rate guaranteed by the proceeds of customs duties from the ports on the coast, and that the foreign soldiers had entered the country to ensure that at least sixty percent of the daily intake of customs was paid to the Banque? Did he know that upon the signing of the Act of Algeciras, which put an end to the holy war in the North, King Moulay Hafid was indebted to the tune of two hundred and six million gold francs, and that it was already evident that he could never reimburse his creditors? But the old sheik didn't know all of that, because his warriors weren't fighting for gold, but simply for a blessing, and the land they were defending didn't belong to them, or to anyone, because it was simply the free open spaces over which their eyes swept, a gift from God.

"... A wild man, a fanatic, who tells his warriors before the battle that he will render them invincible and immortal, who sends them charging against rifles and machine guns armed only with their spears and their sabers. . ."

Now the troop of black infantrymen is occupying the whole valley of the Tadla River, at the ford, while the officials from Kasbah Tadla have come to acknowledge their submission to the French officers. Curls of smoke from the campfires rise into the evening air, and the civilian observer, as he does at every halt, watches the lovely night sky slowly unveiling. Again he thinks of Ma al-Aïnine's gaze, mysterious and profound, the gaze that fell upon Camille Douls disguised as a Turkish merchant, and scrutinized him to the very depths of his soul. Perhaps at the time he had guessed what the foreign man dressed in rags brought with him, the first image-stealer who wrote his travel log every evening on the pages of his Koran. But now it's too late, and nothing can stop destiny from being fulfilled. On one side, the sea, on the other, the desert. The horizons are closing in on the people of Smara, the last nomads are surrounded. Hunger, thirst are hemming them in, they are beset with fear, illness, defeat.

"We could have put an end to your sheik and his rag-pickers long ago if we'd wanted to. A 75-millimeter cannon in front of his cob palace, a few machine guns, and we would have been rid of him. Maybe they thought he wasn't worth the trouble. They told themselves it was best to wait for him to fall on his own, like a worm-eaten fruit. . . But now, after Coppolani's assassination, it's no longer a matter of war: it's a police operation against a band of brigands, that's all."

The old man had been betrayed by the same people he was trying to defend. It was the men from the Souss Valley, from Taroudant, Agadir, who had spread the news: "The great sheik Moulay Ahmed ben Mohammed al-Fadel, he who is called Ma al-Aïnine, Water of the Eyes, is marching northward with his warriors of the desert, those from the Drâa, the Saguiet al-Hamra valley, and even the blue men from Oualata, from Chinguetti. There are so many of them they cover an entire plain. They are marching northward toward the holy city of Fez, to overthrow the sultan and have Moulay Hiba appointed in his place, he who is called Sebaa, the Lion, the eldest son of Ma al-Aïnine."

But the general staff at headquarters hadn't believed the rumors. It gave the officers a good laugh.

"The old man of Smara has gone mad. As if he could, with his troop of ragpickers, overthrow the sultan and drive out the French army!" That's what I thought: the old fox is backed up against the sea and the desert, and he's chosen to commit suicide; it's his only way out now, to get himself killed along with his whole tribe.

Therefore, today, June 21, 1910, the troop of black infantrymen is en route with three French officers and the civilian observer at the head. They have veered south to meet up with the other troop that left from Zettat. The jaws of the pincers are closing in, to seize the old sheik and his ragpickers.

The light of the sun, mingled with the dust, burns the soldiers' eyes. In the distance, on the hill overlooking the stone-strewn plain, an ochre village suddenly appears, barely distinguishable from the desert. "Kasbah Zidaniya," the guide simply says. But he pulls his horse up short. In the distance, a group of warriors on horseback are galloping along the hills. The black foot soldiers take position while the officers move their horses aside. Scattered shots crash out, without a single bullet whistling or hitting a mark. The observer thinks it sounds more like hunters out in the brush. A wounded man is taken prisoner, an Arab from the Beni Amir tribe. Sheik Ma al-Aïnine isn't far; his warriors are marching on the al-Borouj trail, to the south. The troop sets out again, but now the officers stay close to the soldiers. Everyone is watching the brush closely. The sun is still high in the sky when the second skirmish takes place, on the al-Borouj trail. Shots ring out again in the torrid silence. General Moinier gives the order to charge toward the valley bottom. The Senegalese shoot, their knees to the ground, then run, with bayonets fixed. The Beni Moussa tribe has killed twelve black soldiers before fleeing through the bush, leaving scores of their dead on the ground. Then the Senegalese troops continue their charge toward the valley bottom. The soldiers flush out blue men everywhere, but they are not the invincible warriors everyone expected. They are men in rags, disheveled, weaponless, who run limping away, who fall on the stony ground. More like beggars, thin, scorched from the sun, consumed with fever, who run into one another, letting out cries of distress, while the Senegalese, gripped with a murderous desire for vengeance, fire their rifles into their midst, nail them to the red earth with their bayonets. In vain, General Moinier calls for them to fall back. Before the black soldiers, the men and women run helter-skelter, fall to the ground. The children run through the shrubs, speechless with fear, and the herds of goats and sheep run into one another bleating frantically. Everywhere the bodies of blue men are strewn over the ground. The last shots echo out, then there is nothing more to be heard; once again, the torrid silence weighs heavily over the landscape.

From atop a hill, motionless on their horses, which are pacing nervously, the officers watch the great expanse of brush into which the blue men have already disappeared, as if they had been swallowed up by the earth. The Senegalese foot soldiers come back, carrying their dead companions, without a glance at the hundreds of men and women in rags who are lying on the ground. Somewhere on the slopes of the valley, amidst the thorn bushes, a boy is sitting next to the body of a dead warrior, staring very hard at the bloody face whose eyes have grown dark.

IN THE STREET lit with the rising sun, the boy walks unhurriedly alongside the parked cars. His lean body glides past the shiny hulls, his reflection slips over the windows, the polished fenders, the headlights, but that's not what he's looking at. He leans slightly toward each automobile, and his eyes search the interior of the cab, the seats, the floor under the seats, the rear window, the glove compartment.

He moves silently forward, all alone in the wide empty street where the sun is lighting the first glimmer of morning, clear and pure. The sky is already very blue, limpid, without a cloud. The summer wind is blowing in from the sea, rushing through the streets, along the straight avenues, whirling about the small parks, shaking the palm trees and the tall araucarias.

Radicz quite likes the summer wind; it's not a malevolent wind like the one that tears up the dust, or the one that goes into your body and chills you to the bone. It's a mild wind, laden with sweet smells, a wind that smells of the sea and of grass, that makes you sleepy; Radicz is happy, because he slept out under the stars, in an abandoned garden, with his head between the roots of a tall parasol pine not far from the sea.

Before sunrise, he woke up and knew instantly that the summer wind had begun. So he rolled around in the grass a little, the way dogs do, and then he ran without stopping all the way to the edge of the sea. He looked at it for a long time from up on the road, so lovely and so calm, still gray with night, but already splashed in places with the blue and pink of dawn. For a second even, he almost felt like climbing down on the rocks – still cold with night – taking off all his clothes, and diving into the water. It was the summer wind that had called him out to the sea, had shown him the water. But he remembered he didn't have much time left, that he had to hurry because people would be getting up soon. So he went back up into the streets, looking for cars.

Now, he's nearing a large complex of buildings and gardens. He walks along the alleys of the park, where the cars are stopped. There isn't a soul in the gardens for as far as you can see. The shades on the buildings are still down; the balconies are empty. The summer wind is blowing on the façades of the buildings, making the shades snap. There's also the soft sound in the branches of the mimosas and the oleanders, and the tall palm trees rustling as they sway.

The light appears slowly, first up in the sky, then on the tops of the buildings, and the streetlamps grow pale. Radicz really likes this time of day because the streets are still silent, the houses closed up, without a soul, and it's as if he were alone in the world. He walks slowly along the alleys around the building, and he thinks the whole city is his, there's no one else left. Maybe, as in the aftermath of a catastrophe, while he was sleeping in the abandoned garden, the men and women had fled, had already left, running for the mountains, abandoning their houses and their cars. Radicz moves along beside the still hulls, looking inside, the empty seats, the motionless steering wheels, and he has the strange feeling that someone is observing him, threatening him. He stops, looks up in the direction of the high walls of the buildings. The dawn light has already lit the tops of the façades with its pink hue. But the shades and the windows remain closed, and the large balconies are empty. The sound of the wind passing is a very soft sound, very lazy, a sound which isn't meant for humans, and again Radicz feels the void which has hollowed out over the city, which has replaced human sounds and movements.

Maybe while he was sleeping, his head between the roots of the old parasol pine, the summer wind, as if coming from some other world, mysteriously put all the men and all the women in town to sleep, and they're lying in their beds, in their apartments with closed shutters, deep in a magical sleep that will never end.

So now the city can rest at last, breathe, the wide empty streets with stopped cars, the closed shops, the darkened streetlamps and traffic lights; so now the grass will be able to grow peacefully in the cracks of the pavement, the gardens will start looking like forests again, and the rats and birds will be able to go wherever they want fearlessly, as they did in the days before humans.

Radicz stops for a minute to listen. The birds just happen to be awakening in the trees, starlings, sparrows, blackbirds. It's the blackbirds especially that are calling out very loudly, and flying heavily from one palm tree to another, or else hopping along on the wet tar in the big parking lots. The boy really likes blackbirds. They have a lovely black coat and a bright yellow beak, and they have that peculiar way of hopping, with their head turned slightly to one side, keeping an eye out for danger. They look like thieves, and that's why Radicz likes them. They're like him, a bit careless, a bit crooked, and they know how to whistle shrilly to warn that danger is near; they know how to laugh, with a kind of resonant chuckling in their throats that really makes him laugh too. Radicz moves slowly through the parking lots, and from time to time, he whistles to answer the blackbirds. Maybe while the boy was sleeping in the abandoned garden, his head between the roots of the tall parasol pine, the men and women left the big city, just like that, without making a sound, and the blackbirds have taken their place. That idea really pleases Radicz, and he whistles even louder, using his fingers, to tell the blackbirds he's with them, that it's all theirs, everything, the houses, the streets, and even the shops and everything inside them.

The light in the park, around the buildings, is rapidly increasing. Dewdrops are glistening on the roofs of the cars, on the leaves of the shrubs. Radicz has to force himself not to stop and look at all those drops of light. In the emptiness of the big parking lot, with those high white walls, those shades rolled down, those empty balconies, they shine with heightened intensity, as if they were the only real and living things. They quiver a little in the wind from the sea, they look like thousands of unblinking eyes watching the world.

Then once again, Radicz vaguely feels the threat hanging over it all, here, in the parking lot of the buildings, the danger that is prowling. It's a gaze, or perhaps a light, that the boy can't see, can't understand. The threat is hidden under the tires of the stopped automobiles, in the reflections on their windows, in the wan glow of the streetlamps that are still lit in spite of the daylight. It makes a shudder run over his skin, and the boy feels his heart slowing down, then speeding up, and the palms of his hands grow moist with cold sweat.

The birds have disappeared now, except some flights of swifts that go rushing by at top speed, twittering. The blackbirds have fled over to the other side of the huge blocks of concrete, and the air has grown silent. Even the wind is gradually letting up. Dawn doesn't last very long over the big city; it shows its miracle for an instant, then fades away. Now day is coming. The sky is no longer gray and pink, the dull color is invading it. There's a sort of haze in the west, over where the tall chimneys of the storage tanks have undoubtedly begun spitting out their poisonous fumes.

Radicz sees all of that, everything that's happening, and his throat tightens. Soon the men and the women will open their shutters and doors, they'll roll up their shades and come out on the balconies; they'll walk through the streets of the city, and start the motors of their cars and trucks, and drive around look-ing at everything with their mean eyes. That's why there's that gaze, that threat. Radicz doesn't like the daytime. He only likes the night, and the dawn, when everything is silent, uninhabited, when there's nothing but bats and stray cats.

So, he keeps walking up the alleys of the big parking lot, looking a little more closely at the interiors of the parked cars. From time to time, he sees something that might be interesting, and he tries the door handles, just like that, rapidly in passing, just in case they should open. He's run across three cars whose doors aren't locked, but hasn't touched them yet, because he's not sure it's worth the trouble. He tells himself he'll come back a little later, when he's gone around the whole lot, because unlocked cars are a quick job.

The light of day is broadening rapidly up above the trees, but you still can't see the sun. All you can see is the lovely, warm light opening out, spreading through the sky. Radicz doesn't like the daytime, but he quite likes the sun, and he's happy at the idea of seeing it appear. It finally comes, an incandescent disk that shoots a glint deep into his eyes, and Radicz stops walking for a second, blinded.

He waits, listening to the sound of his heart beating in his arteries. The threat is all around, without his being able to say where it's coming from. The light increases, and fear weighs down all the more heavily, from atop the high white walls with hundreds of blue shades, from atop the flat roofs bristling with antennae, from atop the cement pylons, from atop the tall palm trees with smooth trunks. It's the silence that is most frightening. The silence of the day and the electric lights of the streetlamps that continue to shine with a shrill humming sound. It's as if the ordinary sounds of humans and their motors could never come back, as if sleep had stopped them short, locked them in stone, motors jammed, throats tight, faces with closed eyes.

"Okay, let's go."

It's Radicz talking out loud, to muster his courage. His hand tries the door handles again, his eyes search the cold interiors of the cabs. The sunlight is glittering on the drops of dew clinging to the hulls and the windshields.

"Nothing . . . nothing."

Haste now somewhat overrides his anxiety. The day is spread taut, white, the sun will soon be above the roofs of the tall buildings. It's undoubtedly already shining on the sea, lighting up sparkling reflections on the crests of the waves. Radicz is walking along not paying attention to his surroundings.

"Good, thanks."

A car door has opened. Without a sound, the boy slips his body into the car; his hands feel everywhere, under the seats, in the corners, in the door pockets, open the glove compartment. His hands feel quickly, agilely, like the hands of the blind.

"Nothing!"

Nothing: the inside of the car is empty, cold and damp as a cave.

"Bastards!"

Anxiety is followed by anger, and the boy goes back up the alley, alongside the building, searching inside each car. Suddenly a noise makes him start, the roaring of a motor and the crashing of metal. Hidden behind a green station wagon, Radicz watches the garbage truck pass and the collectors who are emptying the bins. The truck makes its way around the buildings, without entering the parking lot. It goes off, half hidden by the hedges of oleander and the palm trunks, and Radicz thinks it looks like a funny metallic insect, a dung beetle maybe, with its big rounded back lurching along.

When everything has fallen silent again, Radicz sees some shapes that could be interesting in the bed of the station wagon. He moves closer to the back window and can distinguish clothing, lots of clothing piled up in the back, in orange plastic sacks. There are also clothes in the front, shoe boxes and, on the floor, right next to the seat, difficult for someone with no experience to make out, the corner of a transistor radio set. The doors of the station wagon are locked, but the front window is cracked open; Radicz pulls with all his might, hangs on the edge of the window to enlarge the opening. Millimeter by millimeter, the window gives way, and soon Radicz can pass his long skinny arm through until his fingertips touch the door lock and pull it up. He opens the door and slips into the front of the car.

The station wagon is very spacious, with deep seats, covered in dark green vinyl. Radicz is glad to be inside the vehicle. He remains sitting on the cold seat for a minute, his hands resting on the steering wheel, and looks at the parking lot and the trees through the large windshield. The top part of the windshield is tinted emerald green, and it casts a strange hue on the white sky when you move your head. To the right of the steering wheel, there's a radio. Radicz turns the knobs, but the radio doesn't come on. His hand pushes the button on the glove compartment, and it opens; in the compartment there are papers, a ballpoint pen, and a pair of sunglasses.

Radicz passes over the back of the front seat to the rear. He examines the garments rapidly. They are new clothes, suits, shirts, women's suits and pants, sweaters, all folded up in their plastic sacks. Next to himself, Radicz makes a pile of clothing, then piles of shoe boxes, ties, scarves. He stuffs the clothes into the pants, knotting the legs to make bundles. Suddenly, he remembers the transistor radio. He slips onto the front seat, his head on the floor, and his hands feel the object, lift it a little. He turns a knob, and this time music blares out, guitar notes that glide and flow like the song of birds at dawn.

That's when he hears the sound of the police coming. He didn't see them coming, maybe he didn't even really hear them coming, the soft sound of tires on the tarred gravel of the circular alley, the rustling of a shade going up somewhere on the immense silent façade of the building, white with light; maybe it's something else that alerted him, while he was there with his head down listening to the transistor radio's bird music. Inside his body, behind his eyes, or else in his guts, something knotted up, clenched, and the void filled the body of the station wagon like a cold chill. So then he rose up and saw it.

The black police car is racing toward the alley of the parking lot. Its tires are making a wet sound on the tar and on the gravel, and Radicz can clearly see the faces of the policemen, their black uniforms. At the same time he feels the hard murderous look observing him from up on one of the balconies of the building, up where the shade has just gone quickly up.

Should he remain hidden in the large car, holed up like an animal? But he's the one the police are coming after, he knows it, he's sure of it. So his body suddenly uncoils, springs out of the front door of the station wagon, and he starts running on the sidewalk, in the direction of the wall surrounding the parking lot.

All at once, the black car accelerates, because the policemen have seen him. There's the sound of voices, brief shouts that echo through the park, bounce off the tall white walls. Radicz hears the whistle blowing shrilly, and he hunches his shoulder up, as if it were bullets. His heart is pounding so hard he can barely hear anything else, as if the whole surface of the parking lot, the buildings, the trees in the park, and the asphalt alleys were all throbbing, quivering, and aching fitfully along with it.

His legs are running, running, beating on the asphalt, beating on the loose earth of the flower beds. His legs are leaping over the planted shrubs, over the low walls around the lawns. They are tearing along as fast as they can, frantic, shaking with panic, not knowing where they're going, not knowing where they'll stop. Now there is the high wall separating the parking lot, and the legs can't take flight. They run along the wall, they zigzag between the still cars. The boy doesn't need to turn around to see that the black police car is still there, that it's very near, that it's taking the curves at top speed, making its tires screech and its motor race. Then it's behind him on a long straight stretch, at the end of which is the open avenue, and Radicz's tiny body is bolting like a flushed rabbit. The black police car grows larger, approaches, its wheels are devouring the tar and gravel alley. As he's running, Radicz hears the sound of shades going up, everywhere, on the façade of the building, and he thinks all the people are now out on their balconies to watch him run. And suddenly, there is an opening in the wall, a door maybe, and Radicz's body leaps through the opening. Now he's on the other side of the wall, all alone on the main avenue that leads to the sea, with maybe a three-, four-minute head start, the time it will take for the black police car to get to the parking lot exit, do a U-turn on the avenue. That too the boy knows without thinking about it, as if it were his frantic heart and his legs that were thinking for him. But where can he go? At the end of the avenue, less than a hundred yards away, is the sea, the rocks. That's the direction the young man is instinctively running in, so fast that the hot air of the day is making tears run from his eyes. His ears can't hear the sound of the wind, and he can't see anything but the black ribbon of the road where the sunlight is shining brightly, and, at the very end, above the wall of the coastal road, the milky color of the sea and the sky mingling together. He is running so fast he can't hear the tires of the black police car on the pavement anymore, or the two terrifying horn blasts that are filling up all of the space between the buildings.

Just a few more leaps, keep going, legs, a few more beats, heart, keep going, for the sea isn't very far now, the sea and the sky mingling together, where there are no more houses, or people, or cars. So in the same instant that the body of the young man bounds onto the pavement of the coastal road, heading straight for the sea and the sky mingling together, like a deer the pack hounds are catching up with, at that very instant, a large blue city bus with its headlights still lit arrives, and the rising sun hits its curved windshield like a flash of lightning when Radicz's body smashes up against the hood and the headlights with a terrific crash of metal and screeching brakes. Not far from there, on the edge of the palm tree park, stands a very somber young woman, still as a shadow, watching intently. She doesn't move, she just watches as people approach from all sides, gathering on the road around the bus, around the black car, around the blanket covering the thief's broken body.

Tiznit, October 23, 1910

O UT WHERE THE city melts in with the red earth
of the desert, old drystone walls, ruins of houses
made of adobe in amongst acacias, some of which have
burned, out where the dusty winds blow freely, far from
the wells, from the shade of the palm trees, that is where
the old sheik is in the process of dying.

He arrived here, in the city of Tiznit, at the end of his
long pointless march. To the north, in the land of the
defeated king, the foreign soldiers are advancing, from
city to city, destroying everything that resists them. To
the south, the soldiers of the Christians have entered the
holy valley of the Saguiet al-Hamra, they are even going
to occupy Ma al-Aïnine's empty palace. The wind of ill-
fortune has begun to blow on the stone walls, through
the narrow loopholes, the wind that wears everything
away, that empties everything out.

It's blowing here now, the malevolent wind, the warm
wind that comes from the north, that brings the mist in
from the sea. Scattered around Tiznit like lost animals, the
blue men are waiting, sheltered by their huts of branches.

Throughout the entire camp, no other sound can be
heard but that of the wind clicking in the acacia branches,
and from time to time the complaint of a hobbled animal.
There is a vast silence, a terrible silence that hasn't let up
since the attack of the Senegalese soldiers, in the valley
of the Oued Tadla. The voices of the warriors have been
stilled now; the chants have fallen silent. No one speaks

about what will happen anymore, maybe because nothing else will happen.

It's the wind of death that is blowing over the dried earth, the malevolent wind coming from the lands occupied by the foreigners, in Mogador, in Rabat, in Fez, in Tangiers. The warm wind, bearing with it the murmur of the sea, and even beyond, the humming of the big white cities where the bankers, the merchants rule.

In the mud house with the half-caved-in roof, the old sheik is lying on his cloak on the bare mud floor. The heat is stifling; the sound of flies and wasps fills the air. Does he know that all is lost, that it's all over now? Yesterday, day before yesterday, the messengers from the South came to bring him news, but he didn't want to listen to them. The messengers had kept their news of the South to themselves, the surrender of Smara, the flight of Hassena and Larhdaf, Ma al-Aïnine's youngest sons, in the direction of the plateau of Tagant, the flight of Moulay Hiba in the direction of the Atlas Mountains. But now they are taking away with them the news they will give to those who are awaiting them down there: "The great sheik Ma al-Aïnine will soon be dead. Already, his eyes can see no more, and his lips can speak no more." They will say that the great sheik is dying in the poorest house in Tiznit, like a beggar, far from his sons, far from his people.

A few men are sitting around the ruined house. They are the last blue warriors of the Berik Allah tribe. They fled across the plain of the Tadla River, without looking back, without trying to understand. The others turned back southward, back to their trails, because they realized there was no hope left, that the lands they had been promised would never be given to them. But it wasn't land they had wanted. They loved the great sheik, they venerated him as they would a saint. He had given them his divine blessing, and that had bound them to him, like the words of an oath.

Nour is with them today. Sitting on the dusty earth, sheltered by a roof of branches, he is staring steadily at the mud house with the half-caved-in roof, where the great sheik is closed up. He doesn't know yet that Ma al-Aïnine is dying. It's been several days since he's seen him come out, wearing his soiled white cloak, leaning on the shoulder of his servant, followed by Meymuna Laliyi, his first wife, the mother of Moulay Sebaa, the Lion. When he first arrived in Tiznit, Ma al-Aïnine sent messengers out for his sons to come and get him. But the messengers did not come back. Every evening, before the prayer, Ma al-Aïnine came out of the house to gaze northward at the trail upon which Moulay Hiba should have come. Now it is too late, and it is obvious his sons won't come.

He lost his sight two days ago, as if death had taken his eyes first. Even when he used to come out to look northward, it was no longer his eyes that were searching for his son, it was his whole face, his hands, his body that desired the presence of Moulay Hiba. Nour watched him, frail figure, almost ghostly, surrounded by his servants, followed by the black shadow of Lalla Meymuna. And he could feel the chill of death darkening the landscape, as if a cloud had hidden the sun.

Nour thought about the blind warrior lying in the ravine, on the bed of the Tadla River. He thought about the dead face of his friend who might have already been eaten by jackals, and he also thought about all the people who had died on the journey, left at the mercy of the sun and the night.

Later, he had met up again with the rest of the caravan that had escaped the massacre, and they had walked for days, dying of hunger and weariness. They had fled like outlaws along the most difficult trails, avoiding the cities, barely daring to taste the well water. Then the great sheik had fallen sick, and they had had to stop here, at the gates of Tiznit, on this dusty land over which the malevolent wind was blowing.

Most of the blue men had continued their aimless endless journey, toward the plateaus of the Drâa, to pick up the trails where they'd left off. Nour's mother and father had gone back to the desert. But he couldn't bring himself to follow them. Maybe he was still hoping for a miracle, the land that the sheik had promised them, where there would be peace and abundance, which the foreign soldiers could never enter. The blue men had left, one after the other, taking their rags with them. But so many had died on the way! Never would they find the peace they had known before, never would the wind of ill-fortune leave them in peace.

At times, the rumor would crop up: "Moulay Hiba is coming, Moulay Sebaa, the Lion, our king!" But it was only a mirage, which faded away in the torrid silence.

Now it is all too late, because the sheik Ma al-Aïnine is dying. Suddenly the wind stops blowing; the heaviness in the air causes the men to stand. They all heave to their feet, look westward, where the sun is descending toward the low horizon. The dusty earth, strewn with razor-sharp stones, is bathed in a glaring hue, bright as molten metal. The sky is veiled with a thin haze, through which the sun resembles an enormously dilated red disk.

No one understands why the wind has suddenly stopped, or why there is that strange, burnt color out on the horizon. But once again, Nour feels the chill enter him, like a fever, and he starts to tremble. He turns toward the ruins of the old house, where Ma al-Aïnine is. He walks slowly toward the house, drawn to it in spite of himself, his eyes trained on the black door.

Ma al-Aïnine's warriors, the Berik Allah, watch the boy

324

walking toward the house with dark faces, but none of them step forward to bar his way. Their eyes are blank and weary, as if they were living a dream. Perhaps they too have lost their sight during the pointless march, eyes burned by the desert sun and sand?

Slowly, Nour walks forward over the rocky earth, toward the house with mud walls. The setting sun is lighting up the old walls, deepening the dark shadow of the door.

It is through that door that Nour is now passing, just as he once had with his father, into the tomb of the saint. For an instant, he remains immobile, blinded by the darkness, feeling the damp coolness inside the house. When his eyes have adjusted, he sees the large, empty room, the mud floor. At one end of the room, the old sheik is lying on his cloak, his head resting on a stone. Lalla Meymuna is sitting next to him, wrapped in her black mantle, face veiled.

Nour doesn't make a sound, he holds his breath. After a long time Lalla Meymuna turns her face toward the boy, because she can feel his eyes upon her. The black veil pulls aside, uncovering her handsome, copper-colored face. Her eyes are shining in the half-light; tears are running down her cheeks. Nour's heart starts pounding very hard, and he feels a sharp pain in the center of his body. He is going to back away toward the door, leave, when the old woman tells him to come in. He walks slowly toward the center of the room, doubled over slightly because of the pain in the middle of his body. When he is before the sheik, his legs buckle under him, and he falls heavily to the floor, arms stretched out in front. His hands are touching Ma al-Aïnine's white cloak, and he remains lying with his face against the damp earth. He doesn't cry, doesn't say anything, doesn't think of anything, but his hands are clutching the woolen cloak and holding it so tightly that it hurts. Next to him, Lalla Meymuna is sitting still beside the man she loves, wrapped in her black mantle, and she can no longer see anything, no longer hear anything.

Ma al-Aïnine is breathing slowly, painfully. His breath lifts his chest with difficulty, making a hoarse sound that fills the entire house. In the half-light, his emaciated face seems even whiter, almost transparent.

Nour stares very hard at the old man, as if his eyes could slow down the march of death. Ma al-Aïnine's parted lips pronounce snatches of words that are quickly drowned out by the rales. Maybe he is chanting the names of his sons again, Mohammed Rebbo, Mohammed Larhdaf, Taaleb, Hassena, Saadbou, Ahmed al-Shems, he who is called the Sun, and above all the name of the one he searched for every evening on the northern trail, the one he is still waiting for, Ahmed Dehiba, he who is called Moulay Sebaa, the Lion.

With a corner of her cloak, Lalla Meymuna dries the sweat beading on Ma al-Aïnine's face, but he doesn't even feel the contact of the cloth on his forehead and cheeks.

At times his arms go stiff, and his torso strains, because he wants to sit up. His lips tremble, his eyes roll around in their sockets. Nour draws nearer, and helps Meymuna raise Ma al-Aïnine; they hold him in a sitting position. With incredible energy for such a frail body, the old sheik remains sitting upright for a few seconds, arms outstretched, as if he were going to stand. His thin face betrays intense anxiety, and Nour feels terrified because of that empty look, those pale eyes. Nour remembers the blind warrior, Ma al-Aïnine's hand that touched his eyes, his breath on the wounded man's face. Now Ma al-Aïnine is feeling that same kind of solitude, the kind from which there is no escape, and no one can appease the utter emptiness in his eyes.

The pain Nour feels is so great that he would like to get away, leave this house of shadows and death, go running out over the dusty plain, out toward the golden light of the setting sun.

But suddenly, he feels the power in his hands, in his breath. Slowly, as if he were trying to remember forgotten gestures, Nour runs the palm of his hand over Ma al-Aïnine's forehead, without saying a word. He wets his fingertips with his saliva, and touches the eyelids that are fluttering with anxiety. He blows softly on the old man's face, his lips, his eyes. He wraps his arm around his torso and slowly, the frail body lets go, reclines.

Now Ma al-Aïnine's face seems appeased, freed of its suffering. Eyes closed, the old man is breathing softly, noiselessly, as if he were going to fall asleep. Nour too feels peaceful inside, the pain in his body has relaxed. He moves back a little without taking his eyes off the sheik. Then he goes out of the house, as the dark shadow of Lalla Meymuna stretches out on the floor to sleep.

Outside, night is slowly falling. You can hear the cries of birds flying over the bed of the stream, toward the palm grove. The warm wind from the sea starts blowing again, in fits and starts, rustling in the leaves of the collapsed roof. Meymuna lights the oil lamp, she gives the sheik some water. In front of the door to the house, Nour's throat feels tight, burning; he can't sleep. Several times during the night, following a sign from Meymuna, he goes up to the old man, runs his hand over his forehead, blows on his lips and eyelids. But weakness and despair have destroyed his power, and he is no longer able to erase the anxiety that is making Ma al-Aïnine's lips tremble. Perhaps it is the pain inside his own body that is crippling his breath.

Just before the first dawn, when the air outside is completely still and silent, when there is not a sound, not a single insect call, Ma al-Aïnine dies. Meymuna, who is holding his hand, feels it, and she lies down on the floor next to the man she loves, and begins to cry, no longer holding back the sobs. Nour, standing by the door, looks once more at the frail figure of the great sheik, lying on his white cloak, so light that he seems to be floating above the ground. Then, backing away, he leaves, finds himself alone in the night, on the ash-colored plain lit with the full moon. Grief and fatigue prevent him from walking very far. He stumbles to the ground near some thorn bushes and falls immediately asleep, not hearing the voice of Lalla Meymuna weeping as if in song.

T HAT'S HOW SHE LEFT one day, without telling anyone. She got up one morning, just before dawn, as she used to do, back in her country, to go down to the sea, or out to the gates of the desert. She listened to the breathing of the photographer who was sleeping in his big bed, overwhelmed with the summer heat. Outside, the swifts were already letting out their high-pitched cries, and off in the distance, maybe the soft sound of the street cleaner's water hose. Lalla had hesitated, because she wanted to leave something for the photographer, a sign, a message, to say good-bye to him. Since she didn't have anything, she took a piece of soap and drew the well-known sign of her tribe, the one she used to sign her photographs with in the streets of Paris:

$$\mathbb{C}\mathbb{C}$$

because it's the oldest drawing she knows and because it looks like a heart.

Then she walked away, through the streets of the city, never to return.

She traveled by train for days and nights, from city to city, from country to country. She waited for trains in the stations for such a long time that her legs grew stiff and her back and buttocks ached.

People came and went, talked, looked. But they didn't pay any attention to the silhouette of the young woman with a weary face who, despite the heat, was wrapped up in a funny old brown coat that reached down to her feet. Maybe they thought she was poor, or sick. Sometimes people talked to her in the passenger cars, but she didn't understand their language, and simply smiled.

Then the ship sails slowly out over the smooth sea away from Algeciras; it's heading for Tangiers. On the deck, the sun and the salt burn, and the people are all crowded into the shade, men, women, children, sitting beside their boxes and suitcases.

Some sing from time to time, to ward off anxiety, a sad nasal song, then the song stops, and all that can be heard is the chugging of the engine.

Over the railing, Lalla is looking at the smooth, dark blue sea, out where the rollers curl slowly over the swell. Dolphins are leaping in the ship's white wake, chasing after one another, swimming away. Lalla thinks of the white bird, the one that was a true prince of the sea, the one that flew over the beach back in the days of Old Naman. Her heart quickens, and she looks up ecstatically, as if she were really going to see him, arms outstretched over the sea. She can feel the burn of the sun on her skin, the old burn, and she can see the light of the sky which is so lovely and so cruel.

Suddenly the voice of some men singing their nasal song troubles her, and she feels tears running from her eyes, without really understanding why. It's been such a long time since she's heard that song, as if in an old dream, half faded away. They are men with black skin, dressed only in camouflage shirts and cotton pants that are too short, barefoot in Japanese sandals. One after the other, they sing the sad nasal song, which no one else can understand, just like that, rocking themselves with their eyes half shut.

And when she hears their song, Lalla feels – deep down inside of herself, very secretly – the desire to see that white land again, the tall palm trees in the red valleys, the expanses of stones and sand, the wide lonely beaches, and even the villages of mud and planks, with sheet metal and tarpaper roofs. She squints her eyes a little and sees it before her, as if she hadn't left, as if she'd only fallen asleep for an hour or two.

Deep inside of her, inside her swollen belly, there is also that movement, those painful thrusts that are hitting the inside of

330

her skin. Now she thinks of the child who wants to be born, who is already living, who is already dreaming. She shivers a little and pushes her hands against her dilated stomach, lets her body fall in with the heavy rocking of the boat, her back leaning against the vibrating iron bulkhead. She even sings a little to herself, between her teeth, a little to the child who stops hitting her and listens, the old song, the one Aamma used to sing, that came from her mother:

"One day, the crow will be white, the sea will go dry, there will be honey in the desert flower, we will make up a bed of acacia sprays, one day, oh, one day, the snake will spit no more poison, and rifle bullets will bring no more death, for that will be the day I will leave my love. . ."

The chugging of the engines drowns out the sound of her voice, but inside her belly, the unknown child listens closely to the words, and falls asleep. So to make more noise, and to muster her courage, Lalla sings the words to her favorite song louder:

"*Méditerra-né-é-e. . .*"

The boat glides slowly over the smooth sea, under the heavy sky. Now there is an ugly gray splotch on the horizon, like a cloud snagging on the sea: Tangiers. All the faces are turned toward the spot, and the people have stopped talking: even the black men are no longer singing. Africa comes slowly into view – irresolute, deserted – in front of the stem of the ship. The seawater turns gray, shallower. In the sky, the first gulls are flying, gray as well, scrawny and fearful.

Has everything changed then? Lalla thinks of her first journey, to Marseille, when everything was still new, the streets, the houses, the people. She thinks of Aamma's apartment, of the Hotel Sainte-Blanche, of the vacant lots near the storage tanks, of everything that she left behind in the big deadly city. She thinks of Radicz the beggar, of the photographer, of the reporters, of all the people who have turned into shadows. She's got nothing left but her clothes now, and the brown coat that Aamma gave her when she arrived. The money too, the bundle of new banknotes held together with a pin that she took from the photographer's jacket pocket before leaving. But it's as if nothing had ever happened, as if she'd never left the Project of planks and tarpaper, or the plateau of stones and the hills where the Hartani lives, as if she'd simply fallen asleep for an hour or two.

She looks out at the empty horizon, off the stern of the ship, then at the spot of gray earth and the mountain where the houses, like smudges, in the Arab city are growing larger. She winces, because inside her abdomen, the child has started making rough movements.

In the bus, driving down the dust road, stopping to let on peasants, women, children, Lalla gets that strange, ecstatic feeling again. The light is enveloping her, so is the fine dust rising like a fog on either side of the bus, entering the passenger compartment, sticking in her throat, and gritting under her fingers, the light, the dryness, the dust: Lalla can feel their presence, and it's like a new skin covering her, like a new breath.

Is it possible that something else once existed? Is there another world, other faces, another light? The lie of memories cannot survive the noise of the coughing bus, or the heat, or the dust. The light cleanses everything, abrades everything, as it used to, out on the plateau of stones. Lalla feels the weight of the secret gaze upon her again, around her; no longer the gaze of men, filled with desire and yearning, but the gaze filled with mystery that belongs to the one who knows Lalla and who reigns over her like a god.

The bus drives along the dust track, lumbers up hills. Everywhere, there is nothing but dry burned earth, like an old snakeskin. Above the roof of the bus, the sky and the light burn fervently, and the passenger compartment grows as hot as the inside of an oven. Lalla feels the drops of sweat rolling down her forehead, along her neck, down her back. In the bus, the people are immobile, impassive. The men are wrapped in their woolen cloaks; the women are squatting on the floor, between the seats, covered with their blue-black veils. Only the driver is moving, grimacing, looking in the rearview mirror. Several times his eyes meet Lalla's, and she turns her face away. The plump man with a flat face adjusts the mirror to see her better, then, with an angry gesture, puts it back in place. The radio, volume turned all the way up, screeches and spits and, when passing near an electricity pylon, lets out a long trail of nasal music.

All day long, the bus drives along the tarred roads and dust tracks, crosses dried rivers, stops in front of mud villages where naked children are waiting. Skeletal dogs run along beside the bus, trying to nip at the wheels. At times, the bus stops in the middle of a deserted plain because the motor stalls. While the driver with a flat nose leans into the open hood to clean the idling jet, the men and women get off, sit down in the shade of the bus or go to urinate, squatting amid the euphorbia bushes. Some take small lemons out of their pockets to suck on, clacking their tongues.

Then the bus starts out again, bumping over the roads, climbing up hills, like that, interminably, in the direction of the setting sun. Night falls quickly on the stretch of deserted plains; it covers over the stones and turns the dust to ashes. Then, suddenly, the bus stops in the night, and Lalla can see lights in the distance, on the far side of the river. Outside, the night is hot, filled with the whirring of insects, the croaking of toads. But it seems like silence after the hours spent on the bus.

Lalla gets off, walks slowly along the river. She recognizes the building of the public bathhouse, then the ford. The river is black; the tide has pushed back the freshwater stream. Lalla crosses the ford with the water at mid-thigh, but the cool river soothes her. In the dusk light, Lalla sees the figure of a woman carrying a bundle on her head, her long cloak hitched up to her waist.

A little farther ahead, on the opposite bank, the path leading to the Project begins. Then the mud and plank houses, one, another one. Lalla doesn't recognize the houses anymore. There are new ones everywhere, even near the riverbank, where it floods when the water is high. The alleyways of tamped earth are poorly lit with electric lamps, and the plank and sheet metal houses look abandoned. As she walks down the streets, Lalla hears the sound of voices whispering, of babies crying. Somewhere, out beyond the town, the eerie yapping of a wild dog. Lalla's feet are treading upon ancient traces, and she takes off her canvas sandals to better feel the coolness and the grain of the earth.

The same gaze is still guiding her, here, in the streets of the Project; it's a very long and very gentle gaze, coming from all sides at once, from the depths of the sky, swaying in the wind. Lalla walks past the houses she's familiar with; she smells the odor of coal fires going out; she recognizes the sound of the wind in the tarpaper, on the sheet metal. It all comes back to her at once, as if she'd never left, as if she'd only fallen asleep for an hour or two.

So, instead of going toward Ikikr's house, over by the fountain, Lalla takes the path to the dunes. Weariness is making her body heavy, triggering a pain in her lower back, but it is the unknown gaze that is guiding her, and she knows she must go out of the village. Barefoot, she walks as quickly as she can between the thorn bushes and the dwarf palms, till she reaches the dunes.

Here, nothing has changed. She walks along the gray dunes, just as she used to. From time to time, she stops, looks around, picks a sprig of a succulent plant and squishes it between her fingers to smell the peppery odor she used to love. She recognizes all the hollows, all the paths, those that lead up to the rocky hills, those that go to the salt marsh, those that don't go anywhere. The night is deep and mild, and above her the stars are bright. How much time has gone by for them? They haven't changed places, their flame – like that of magic lamps – has not burned out. Perhaps the dunes have moved, but how could you tell? The old carcass that used to bare its claws and lift its horns and scare her so much has disappeared now. There are no more abandoned tin cans, and certain shrubs have burned; their branches have been broken to pieces for the brazier fires.

Lalla can't find her spot up on top of the dunes anymore. The passageway that led to the beach has filled with sand. Laboriously, Lalla scales the cold sand of the dunes till she reaches the crest. Her breath is wheezing in her throat, and the pain in her back is so sharp she's moaning, in spite of herself. In clenching her teeth, she changes the moaning into a song. She thinks of the song she used to love to sing, in the old days, when she was afraid:

"*Méditerra-né-é-e...*"

She tries to sing, but her voice is too weak.

Now she's walking over the hard sand of the beach, right along the sea foam. The wind isn't blowing very hard, and the waves are purling softly in the night, and Lalla feels the giddy thrill once again, just as she had on the ship and in the bus, as if it had all been waiting for her, expecting her. Maybe it's the gaze of al-Ser, the one she calls the Secret, that is on the beach, mixed in with the starlight, with the sound of the sea, with the whiteness of the foam. It is a night without fear, a remote night, the likes of which Lalla has never known.

Now she's nearing the place where Old Naman used to like to haul his boat up, to heat the pitch or mend his nets. But the place is empty, and the beach stretches on into the night, deserted. There is only the old fig tree, standing against the dune, with its thick branches thrown back from being accustomed to the wind. Lalla recognizes its heavy bland odor with delight; she watches the movement of its leaves. She sits down at the foot of the dune, not far from the tree, and looks at it for a long time, as if the old fisherman were going to appear any second.

Weariness weighs upon Lalla's body, pain has numbed her arms and legs. She lets herself fall slowly backward into the cold sand, and goes immediately to sleep, lulled by the sound of the sea and the smell of the fig tree.

The moon rises in the east, climbs into the night over the rocky hills. Its pale light shines on the sea and the dunes, bathes Lalla's face. Later in the night, the wind rises too, the warm wind that blows in from the sea. It passes over Lalla's face, over her hair, sprinkles sand on her body. The sky is so vast, and the earth absent. Below the constellations, things have changed, evolved. Cities have enlarged their rings, like mold stains in the valley bottoms, in the shelter of bays and estuaries. People have died, houses have fallen to ruin, in a cloud of dust and scattering cockroaches. And yet, on the beach, near the fig tree, in the place where Old Naman used to come, it's as if nothing had happened. It's as if the young woman had just gone on sleeping.

The moon moves slowly upward till it reaches its zenith. Then it descends in the west, out in the high seas. The sky is pure, without a cloud. In the desert, beyond the plains and the rocky hills, the cold wells up from the sand, spreads out like water. It's as if the whole earth, here, and even the sky, the moon, and the stars, had been holding their breath, had suspended their time.

Now they are all stopped, as the *fijar*, the first dawn, begins.

In the desert, the fox, the jackal, no longer chase after the jerboa or the hare. The horned viper, the scorpion, the scolopendra, are stopped on the cold earth, under the black sky. The *fijar* has seized them, has turned them to stone, to powdered stone, to mist, because this is the hour when the heavens spread celestial time over the earth, chilling bodies, and sometimes interrupting life and breath. In the dip of the dune, Lalla isn't moving. Her skin is shivering, in long shivers that shake her limbs and make her teeth chatter, but she doesn't wake up.

Then comes the second dawn, the *white*. The light begins to mix with the darkness of the air. Instantly, it sparkles in the sea foam, on patches of dried salt on the rocks, on the sharp stones at the foot of the old fig tree. The pale gray glimmer shines on the peaks of the rocky hills, gradually fading out the stars: the Goat, the Dog, the Snake, the Scorpion, and the three sister stars, Mintaka, Alnilam, Alnitak. Then the sky seems to invert, a large pearly veil covers it, snuffing out the last stars. In the dips of the dunes, the small prickly plants tremble slightly, while dewdrops form pearls in their down.

On Lalla's cheeks, the drops roll a little, like tears. The young woman awakens and moans quietly. She doesn't open her eyes yet, but her plaint rises, mingles with the unbroken sound of the sea, which is now in her ears again. The pain comes and goes in her belly, sending out signals which are closer and closer together, rhythmical like the sound of the waves.

Lalla raises herself up slightly on the bed of sand, but the pain is so sharp it takes her breath away. Then suddenly she realizes the time has come for the baby to be born, right now, here, on this beach, and a wave of fear runs through her, overwhelms her, because she knows she's alone, that no one will come to help her, no one. She wants to get up; she takes a few steps in the cold sand, staggering, but falls back down, and her moaning turns to a scream. Out here, there is nothing but the gray beach, and the dunes, which are still plunged in darkness, and before her, the heavy sea, gray and green, dark, still mingling with the black of night.

Lying on her side in the sand, knees curled up, Lalla is moaning again in rhythm with the sea. The pain comes in waves, in long regular rollers, whose highest crest moves over the dark surface of the water, catching a brief glint of pale light from time to time, until it breaks. Lalla follows the progress of her pain on the sea, each shudder stemming from far out on the horizon, from the dark area, where the night is still thick, and radiating slowly out till it reaches the shore on the eastern side, spreading slantwise, casting out layers of foam, while the swish of the water over the hard sand creeps up, engulfs her. Sometimes the pain is just too strong, as if her belly were tearing open, were emptying, and the moaning increases in her throat, covering over the crashing of the waves breaking on the sand.

Lalla rises onto her knees, tries to crawl along by the dune to get to the path. She makes such an intense effort that, in spite of the dawn chill, sweat streams down her face and body. She waits again, eyes fixed on the sea. She turns toward the path on the other side of the dunes, and cries, calls out: "Hartani! Hartani!" just as she used to in the old days, when she would go up on the plateau of stones, and he'd be hiding in the hollow of a rock. She tries to whistle too, like the shepherds, but her lips are chapped and trembling.

It won't be long before people start waking up in the houses of the Project; they'll throw back their covers, and the women will walk to the fountain to draw the morning water. Maybe the girls will wander around in the brush looking for twigs of dead wood for the fire, and the women will light the brazier, to grill a little meat, to heat up the oatmeal, the water for the tea. But all of that is far away, in another world. It's like a dream that continues to play out over there on the muddy plain where the people live at the mouth of the big river, or else, even farther away, across the sea, in the big city of beggars and thieves, the murderous city with white buildings and booby-trapped cars. The *fijar* has spread its cold white glow everywhere at the very same instant in which the elderly meet with death, in silence, in fear.

Lalla can feel her body emptying, and her heart starts beating very slowly, very painfully. The waves of pain are so close together now, there is only one continuous pain undulating and throbbing inside her belly. Slowly, in an immense effort, Lalla drags her body with her forearms along the dune. Before her, a few tugs away, the silhouette of the tree stands on the pile of rocks, very black against the white sky. The fig tree has never seemed so tall to her, so strong. Its wide trunk twists backward, its thick branches are tossed back, and the lovely laced leaves are stirring slightly in the cool wind, shining in the light of day. But the most beautiful and powerful thing is the smell. It envelops Lalla, it seems to be drawing her forward, it inebriates and nauseates her at the same time, it undulates with the waves of pain. Barely breathing, Lalla heaves her body slowly over the resisting sand. Her spread legs leave a trail behind her like a boat being hauled up to dry on the beach.

Slowly, laboriously, she drags the too-heavy load, groaning when the pain gets too strong. She doesn't take her eyes off the shape of the tree, the tall fig tree with the black trunk, with pale leaves shining in the morning light. As she approaches, the fig tree gets even taller, becomes immense, seems to fill the whole sky. Its shade spreads out all around like a dark lake in which the last colors of the night are still lingering. Slowly, pulling her body along, Lalla enters that shade, under the high powerful branches like the arms of a giant. That's what she wants, she knows he's the only one who can help her now. The powerful smell of the tree penetrates her, encompasses her, and soothes her tormented body, mingles with the odor of the sea and the kelp. The sand has left the rocks at the foot of the tall tree bare, rusted with the sea air, polished, worn with the wind and the rain. Between the rocks are the mighty roots, like arms of iron.

Clenching her teeth to keep from crying out, Lalla wraps her arms around the trunk of the fig tree, and slowly pulls herself up, gets in an upright position on her wobbly knees. The pain in her body is now like a wound that is gradually spreading open, tearing. Lalla can no longer think of anything but what she sees, what she hears, what she smells. Old Naman, the Hartani, Aamma, and even the photographer, who are they, what has become of them? The pain that is springing from the young woman's womb spreads out over the whole expanse of the sea, the whole expanse of the dune, all the way out to the pale sky, it is stronger than everything, it erases everything, empties everything. Pain fills her body, like a deafening sound, it makes her body as huge as a mountain lying stretched upon the earth.

Time has slowed down because of the pain, it is beating to the rhythm of her heart, to the rhythm of her breathing lungs, to the rhythm of the contractions of her uterus. Slowly, as if she were lifting an enormous weight, Lalla raises her body up against the trunk of the fig tree. She knows he is the only one that can help her, like the tree that helped her mother long ago, on the day of her birth. Instinctively, she repeats the ancestral motions, gestures whose significance goes beyond her, without needing anyone to teach them to her. Squatting at the foot of the tall dark tree, she unties the belt of her dress. Her brown coat is spread on the ground, over the rocky earth. She loops the belt around the first main branch of the fig tree, after having twisted the fabric to make it stronger. When she hangs from the cotton belt with both hands, the tree sways a little, letting dewdrops rain down. The virgin water runs over Lalla's face, and she drinks it in with delight, running her tongue over her lips.

In the sky, the *red* hour is beginning now. The last stains of night disappear, and the milky whiteness gives way to the blaze of the last dawn in the east, above the rocky hills. The sea grows darker, almost purple, while at the peaks of the waves, violet sparkles light up, and the sea foam glitters even whiter. Never has Lalla watched the coming of day so intently, eyes dilated, pained, face burning with the splendor of the light.

Just then the spasms suddenly become violent, unbearable, and the pain is like the huge blinding red light. To keep from screaming, Lalla bites the cloth of her dress on her shoulder, and her arms lifted over her head pull on the cotton belt so hard that the tree bends and her body lifts up. At each extreme pain, in rhythm, Lalla hangs from the branch of the tree. Sweat is running down her face now, blinding her; the blood-red color of the pain is before her, out on the sea, in the sky, in the foam of each wave rolling in. At times, in spite of herself, a cry escapes from between her clenched teeth, is drowned out by the sound of the sea. It's a cry of pain and of distress at the same time, due to all of that light, all of that loneliness. The tree bows down slightly at each spasm, making its wide leaves shimmer.

In short little gulps, Lalla breathes in its odor, the odor of sugar and sap, and it's like a familiar smell that reassures and soothes her. She pulls on the main branch, her lower back bumps against the trunk of the fig tree, the dewdrops continue to rain down on her hands, on her face, on her body. There are even very small black ants that are running along her arms as they cling to the belt, and making their way down her body to escape.

It lasts a long time, such a long time that Lalla feels the tendons in her arms have grown as hard as ropes, but her fingers are clenching the cotton belt so tightly that nothing could pry them away. Then suddenly, incredibly, she can feel her body emptying, while her arms pull fiercely on the belt. Very slowly, with the motions of a blind person, Lalla lets herself slip backwards along the cotton belt, her hips and back touch the roots of the fig tree. Air finally enters her lungs and at the same time, she hears the sharp scream of the child who is starting to cry.

On the beach, the red light has turned orange, then the color of gold. The sun must already be touching the rocky hills in the east, in the land of the shepherds. Lalla holds the child in her arms, she cuts the umbilical cord with her teeth, and knots it like a belt around the tiny belly that is jerking with sobs. Very slowly, she crawls over the hard sand toward the sea, kneels in the fluffy foam, and dips the screaming child into the saltwater; she bathes and cleans the baby carefully. Then she returns to the tree, lays the baby in the big brown coat. With the same instinctive gestures that she doesn't understand, she digs into the sand with her hands, near the roots of the fig tree, and buries the placenta.

Then she lies down at last at the foot of the tree, her head very close to the trunk which is so strong; she opens the coat, takes the baby in her arms, and brings it to her swollen breasts. When the child begins to suck, its tiny little face with closed eyes pushing up against her breast, Lalla stops resisting the fatigue. She looks briefly at the lovely light of day that has just begun, and at the deep blue sea, with its slanting waves like animals running. Her eyes close. She's not sleeping, but it's as if she were floating on the surface of the waters, for a long time. She can feel the warm little head pushing up against her breast, wanting to live, sucking her milk greedily. "Hawa, daughter of Hawa," Lalla thinks, only once, because it's funny, and makes her feel good, like a smile, after so much suffering. Then she waits, patiently, for someone from the plank and tarpaper Project to come, a young boy crab catcher, an old woman hunting for dead wood, or a little girl who simply loves to walk in the dunes to watch the seabirds. Someone always ends up coming out here, and the shade of the fig tree is so peaceful and cool.

Agadir, March 30, 1912

So they came for the last time, they appeared on the vast plain, near the sea, at the mouth of the river. They came from all directions, those from the north, the Ida ou Trouma, the Ida ou Tamane, the Aït Daoud, the Meskala, the Aït Hadi, the Ida ou Zemzen, the Sidi Amil, those from Bigoudine, from Amizmiz, from Ichemraren; those from the east, beyond Taroudant, those from Tazenakht, from Ouarzazate, the Aït Kalla, the Assarag, the Aït Kedif, the Amtazguine, the Aït Toumert, the Aït Youss, the Aït Zarhal, the Aït Oudinar, Aït Moudzit, those from the Sarhro Mountains, the Bani Mountains; those from the coast, from Essaouira to Agadir, the fortified city; those from Tiznit, from Ifni, from Aoreora, from Tan-Tan, from Goulimine, the Aït Meloul, the Lahoussine, the Aït Bella, Aït Boukha, the Sidi Ahmed ou Moussa, the Ida Gougmar, the Aït Baha; and above all, those from the far south, the free men of the desert, the Imraguen, the Arib, the Oulad Yahia, the Oulad Delim, the Aroussiyine, the Khalifiya, the Reguibat Sahel, the Sebaa, the peoples of the Chleuh language, the Ida ou Belal, Ida ou Meribat, the Aït ba Amrane.

They gathered together on the riverbed, so numerous they covered the whole valley. But they weren't warriors for the most part. They were women and children, wounded men, the elderly, all the people who had been fleeing endlessly over the dust tracks, driven by the arrival of the foreign soldiers, and who no longer knew where to go. The sea had stopped them there, before the great city of Agadir.

Most of them didn't know why they had come there, to the Souss riverbed. Perhaps it was simply hunger, weariness, despair that had led them there, to the mouth of the river, facing the sea. Where could they go? For months, years, they had been wandering in search of a land, a river, a well where they could set up their tents and make corrals for their sheep. Many had died, lost on the trails leading nowhere in the desert around the great city of Marrakech, or in the ravines of the Oued Tadla. Those who had succeeded in fleeing had gone back to the South, but the old wells had gone dry, and the foreign soldiers were everywhere. In the city of Smara, where Ma al-Aïnine's palace of red stones stood, the desert wind that wears everything away was now blowing. The soldiers of the Christians had slowly closed their wall around the free men of the desert; they occupied the wells of the holy valley of the Saguiet al-Hamra. What did these foreigners want? They wanted the entire earth; they wouldn't stop until they had devoured everything, that was certain.

The people of the desert had been there for days, south of the fortified city, and they were waiting for something. Ma al-Aïnine's last warriors, the Berik Allah were mixed in with the mountain tribes; their faces were marked with distress, with forlorn hope, due to the death of Ma al-Aïnine. There was a strange feverish, hungry sheen to their eyes. Each day, the men from the desert looked toward the citadel, where Moulay Sebaa, the Lion, was to appear along with his mounted warriors. But off in the distance, the red walls of the city remained silent; the gates were closed. And there was something threatening about that silence which had lasted for days. Big black birds circled in the blue sky, and at night, the yapping of jackals could be heard.

343

Nour was there too, alone in the crowd of defeated men. He had gotten used to that loneliness long ago. His father, his mother, and his sisters had gone back to the South, back to the endless trails. But he hadn't been able to go back, not even after the death of the sheik.

Every evening, lying on the cold earth, he thought of the path upon which Ma al-Aïnine had led his people northward, to new lands, the path the Lion would now follow, to become the true king. For two years now, his body had become hardened to hunger and exhaustion, and his whole being was filled with the desire to set out upon that path which would soon be opened.

Then, in the morning, the rumor spread through the camp: "Moulay Hiba, Moulay Sebaa, the Lion! Our king! Our king!" Shots cracked, and women and children cried out, making their voices quaver. The crowd turned toward the dusty plain, and Nour saw the sheik's horsemen engulfed in a red cloud.

The cries and the shots drowned out the sound of the horses' hooves. The red fog rose high into the morning sky, whirling over the river valley. The crowd of warriors ran out to meet the horsemen, firing their long-barreled rifles skyward. They were, for the most part, men from the mountains, Chleuhs wearing their homespun cloaks, wild men, disheveled, eyes blazing. Nour didn't recognize the warriors of the desert, the blue men who had followed Ma al-Aïnine until his death. Hunger and thirst had not left their mark on these men; they had not been burned by the desert for days and months; they had come from their fields, their villages, without knowing why or against whom they were going to fight.

All day long, the warriors ran across the valley, all the way up to the ramparts of Agadir, as the galloping horses of Moulay Sebaa, the Lion, raised the great red cloud. What did they want? They were just running and shouting, that was all, and the voices of the women and children quavered over the riverbed. At times, Nour caught a glimpse of the horsemen going by in their red cloud, surrounded by flashes of light: the Lion's horsemen were brandishing their spears.

"Moulay Hiba! Moulay Sebaa, the Lion!" the voices of the children were shouting all around him. Then the horsemen disappeared over on the other side of the plain, by the ramparts of Agadir.

That whole day the valley was filled with jubilation, and with the lip-scorching fire of the sun. The desert wind started blowing around evening time, covering the campsites in a golden fog, hiding the walls of the city. Nour sought shelter under a tree, wrapped in his cloak.

Gradually, the excitement fell, as night did. Cool darkness settled over the desiccate earth at prayer time, when the animals knelt down to protect themselves from the damp of night.

Nour thought again of the summer that would soon begin, of the drought, of the wells, of the slow herds his father would lead out to the salt flats on the other side of the desert, in Oualata, in Ouadane, in Chinchan. He thought of the loneliness of those boundless lands, so remote that all memory of the sea or the mountains is effaced. It had been so long since he had known rest. It was as if there were nothing anywhere but the expanses of dust and stones, ravines, dried rivers, rocks jutting up like knives, and most of all, fear, like a shadow hanging over everything one sees.

At mealtime, when he went to have some bread and millet porridge with the blue men, Nour watched the star-filled night covering the earth. Weariness burned his skin, fever too, throwing its long shivers down his body.

In their makeshift campsite, under the shelters of branches and leaves, the blue men no longer spoke, no

345

longer told the legend of Ma al-Aïnine, no longer sang. Wrapped in their ragged cloaks, they stared into the burning coals, blinking when the wind swept the smoke back. Maybe they weren't waiting for anything anymore, eyes blurred, hearts beating very slowly.

One after the other, the fires went out, and darkness flooded through the wide valley. In the distance, jutting into the black sea, the city of Agadir blinked weakly. Then Nour lay down on the ground, his head turned toward the lights, and as he did every evening, he thought of the great sheik Ma al-Aïnine, who had been buried in front of the ruined house in Tiznit. They had laid him in the grave, face turned toward the east; in his hands they had placed his only possessions, his holy book, his calamus, his ebony prayer beads. The loose earth tumbled over his body, the red dust of the desert, then they had put down large stones so the jackals wouldn't dig up the body; and the men had stamped on the earth with their bare feet until it became smooth and hard as a slab of stone. Near the tomb stood a young acacia with white thorns, like the one in front of the house of prayer in Smara.

Then, one after the other, the blue men of the desert, the Berik Allah, the last companions of the Goudfia had knelt on the grave, and had run their hands slowly over the smooth earth, then over their faces, as if to receive one last blessing from the great sheik.

Nour thought of that night, when all of the men had left the plain of Tiznit, and he had remained alone with Lalla Meymuna near the tomb. In the cold night, he had listened to the voice of the old woman crying interminably inside the ruined house, like a song. He had fallen asleep on the ground, lying next to the tomb, and his body had remained motionless, dreamless, as if he too were dead. The next morning, and the following days, he had hardly left the tomb, sitting on the burning earth, enveloped in his woolen cloak, his eyes and throat burning with fever. Already, the wind was blowing dust onto the smooth earth of the tomb, gently obliterating it. Then the fever had seized his whole body, and he had lost consciousness. Some women from Tiznit had taken him home and cared for him while he was delirious, on the verge of death. When he recovered, after several weeks, he walked back to the ruined house where Ma al-Aïnine had died. But no one was there; Lalla Meymuna had gone back to her tribe, and the wind had blown so hard, carrying so much sand, he wasn't able to find the grave.

Perhaps that was the way things were meant to be, thought Nour; perhaps the great sheik had gone back to his true domain, lost in the desert sands, swept away in the wind. Now Nour looked out on the vast stretch of the Souss River, in the night, barely lit by the haze of the galaxy, the great glow that is the mark of blood left by the angel Gabriel's lamb, according to what people say. It was the same silent land as that around Tiznit, and Nour sometimes thought he was hearing the long weeping chant of Lalla Meymuna, but it was probably the sound of a jackal yapping in the night. The spirit of Ma al-Aïnine was still alive there; it was covering the entire earth, mingling with the sand and the dust, hiding in the crevices or glimmering faintly on each sharp stone.

Nour could feel his gaze, out there in the sky, in the dark spots on the earth. He could feel his gaze upon him, as he had once before, in the square in Smara, and a shudder ran over his body. The gaze entered him, hollowing out its dizziness. What did he want to say? Maybe he was asking something, just like that, mutely, out on that plain, encompassing the men in his light. Maybe he was asking the men to come join him, where he was, mixed in with the gray earth, scattered in the wind,

347

turned to dust. . . Nour fell into a motionless, dreamless sleep, buoyed by the immortal gaze.

When they heard the sound of the cannons for the first time, the blue men and the warriors started running toward the hills, to look out on the sea. The noise shook the sky like thunder. Alone, off the coast of Agadir, a large battleship, like a monstrous slow animal, was spitting out flashes. The noise came a long time afterward, a long rumble, followed by the crashing sound of shells exploding inside the city. In a few minutes, the high walls of red stone were no more than a pile of rubble from which black smoke rose. Then the inhabitants spilled out of the broken walls, men, women, children, bloody and screaming. They filled the river valley, running away from the sea as fast as they could, in the throes of panic.

The short flame flashed several times from the cannons of the cruiser *Cosmao*, and the ripping sound of the shells exploding in the Kasbah of Agadir rolled out over the entire valley of the Souss River. The black smoke of the burning city rose high into the blue sky, covering the camp of nomads with its shadow.

Then the mounted warriors of Moulay Sebaa, the Lion, appeared. They crossed the riverbed, falling back toward the hills in front of the inhabitants of the city. In the distance, the cruiser *Cosmao* was immobile on the metal-colored sea, and its cannons turned slowly toward the valley where the people of the desert were fleeing. But the flame didn't flare again at the end of the cannons. There was a long silence, with only the sound of the people running and the cries of the animals, while the black smoke continued to rise into the sky.

When the soldiers of the Christians appeared before the crumbled ramparts of the city, no one understood at first who they were. Perhaps for a second even Moulay Sebaa and his men believed they were the warriors from the North that Moulay Hafid, the Leader of the Faithful, had sent for the holy war.

But it was Colonel Mangin's four battalions, having come on a forced march to the rebel city of Agadir – four thousand men wearing the uniforms of African infantrymen, Senegalese, Sudanese, Saharans, armed with Lebel rifles and a score of Nordenfeldt machine guns. The soldiers advanced slowly toward the bank of the river, fanning out in a half-circle, while on the other side of the river, at the foot of the rocky hills, Moulay Sebaa's cavalry of three thousand began turning in a circle, churning up a large whirling cloud, raising the red dust up into the sky. Moulay Sebaa, wearing his white cloak, standing at a distance from the cloud, anxiously watched the long line of enemy soldiers, like a column of insects marching over the dried earth. He knew that the battle was already lost, as in the past at Bou Denib, when the bullets of the black infantrymen had cut down more than a thousand of his mounted warriors from the South. Sitting still on his horse, which was quivering with impatience, he watched the foreigners advancing slowly toward the river, as if on maneuver. Several times, Moulay Sebaa tried to give the order to retreat, but the warriors from the mountains weren't listening to his orders. They were spurring their horses on to gallop in that frantic circle, drunk with dust and the smell of gunpowder, letting out cries in their savage language, invoking the names of their saints. When the circling was over, they would jump into the trap which had been laid for them; they were all going to die.

Moulay Sebaa could do nothing more then, and tears of pain were already filling his eyes. On the other side of the dried riverbed, Colonel Mangin had prepared the machine guns on either flank of his army, atop the rocky hills. When the Moorish cavalry charged toward the center, just when they were crossing the riverbed, the crossfire of the machine guns would decimate them, and then it would simply be a matter of finishing them off with bayonets.

There was another heavy silence, as the horsemen stopped circling on the plain. Colonel Mangin took a look with his binoculars, trying to understand: were they going to retreat? Then it would mean marching again for days over that deserted land, pursuing that fleeing, exasperating horizon. But Moulay Sebaa remained motionless on his horse, because he knew that the end was near. The mountain warriors, the sons of the tribal chieftains had come here to fight, not to flee. They had stopped circling to pray before the charge.

Then everything went very quickly in the cruel, noonday sun. The three thousand horsemen charged in close formation, as if for a cavalcade, brandishing their long spears. When they reached the riverbed, the non-commissioned officers in charge of the machine guns glanced at Colonel Mangin, who had raised his arm. He let the first horsemen through, then suddenly brought his arm down, and the steel barrels started firing their streams of bullets, six hundred a minute, with a sinister sound that hacked the air and echoed through the entire valley, all the way out to the mountains. Does time exist when a few minutes are enough to kill a thousand men, a thousand horses? When the horsemen realized they were trapped, that they would never get through that wall of bullets, they tried to retreat, but it was too late. The bursts of machine gun fire swept over the riverbed, and the bodies of men and horses continued to fall, as if a large invisible wave were mowing them down. Streams of blood ran over the smooth stones, mingled with the thin trickles of water. Then silence fell again, while the last horsemen escaped toward the hills, covered with blood, on their horses whose hair was bristling in fear.

Unhurriedly, the army of black soldiers began marching along the riverbed, company after company, with the officers and Colonel Mangin in the lead. They took the eastern trail, in the direction of Taroudant, Marrakech, in pursuit of Moulay Sebaa, the Lion. They left without even glancing at the site of the massacre, without looking at the broken bodies of the men sprawled on the shingles, or the horses on their backs, or the vultures that were already on the banks of the river. They didn't look at the ruins of Agadir either, the black smoke still rising into the blue sky. In the distance, the cruiser *Cosmao* was gliding slowly out on the metal-colored sea, heading northward.

Then the silence ceased, and the cries of the living could be heard, the wounded men and animals, the women, children, like a single interminable wail, like a song. It was a sound filled with horror and suffering that rose from all sides at once, on the plain and on the riverbed.

Now Nour was walking over the shingles, amongst the felled bodies. The voracious flies and wasps were already buzzing in black clouds above the cadavers, and Nour felt nausea tightening in his throat.

With very slow movements, as if they were emerging from a dream, women, men, children, drew back the brush and walked over the riverbed without speaking. All day long, until nightfall, they carried the bodies of the men to the riverbanks to bury them. When night came, they lit fires on each bank, to ward off the jackals and wild dogs. The women of the villages came, bringing bread and sour milk, and Nour ate and drank with relief. Then he slept, lying on the ground, without even thinking of death.

The next day, at the crack of dawn, the men and women dug more graves for the warriors, then they also buried their horses. Over the graves, they placed large rocks from the river.

When everything was finished, the last blue men started walking again, on the southern trail, the one that is so long that it seems to never end. Nour was walking with them, barefoot, with nothing but his woolen cloak and a little bread tied in a moist cloth. They were the last Imazighen, the last free men, the Taubalt, the Tekna, the Tidrarin, the Aroussiyine, the Sebaa, the Reguibat Sahel, the last survivors of the Berik Allah, those who are blessed by God. They had nothing but what their eyes saw, what their bare feet touched. Before them, the flat earth stretched out like the sea, glistening with salt. It undulated, created white cities with magnificent walls, with domes that burst like bubbles. The sun burned their faces and their hands, the light hollowed out its dizziness at the time of day when the shadows of men are like bottomless wells.

Each evening, their bleeding lips sought the cool wells, the brackish mud of alkaline rivers. Then, the cold night enveloped them, crushed their limbs and took their breath away, weighed down on their necks. There was no end to freedom, it was as vast as the wide world, beautiful and cruel as the light, gentle as the eyes of water. Each day, at the first light of dawn, the free men went back toward their home, toward the south, toward the place where no one else could live. Each day, with the same motions, they erased the traces of their fires, they buried their excrement. Turned toward the desert, they carried out their wordless prayer. They drifted away, as if in a dream, disappeared.

ABOUT THE AUTHOR

JEAN-MARIE GUSTAVE LE CLÉZIO, winner of the 2008 Nobel Prize in Literature, was born on April 13th, 1940 in Nice, a descendant of a family from Brittany that immigrated to Mauritius in the eighteenth century. He pursued his undergraduate studies at the Institut d'Études Littéraires in Nice and earned his doctoral degree in early Mexican history from the University of Perpignan. His first novel, Le procès-verbal *(The Interrogation), won the Prix Renaudot in 1963 and established his reputation as one of France's preeminent contemporary writers. He was awarded the Grand Prix Paul Morand by the Académie Française in 1980 for his novel* Désert. *He has published more than forty works of fiction and anthropology, as well as several books for children. Mr. Le Clézio has lived in France, Mauritius, Thailand, Mexico, Panama, the United States, and England. He and his wife currently divide their time between New Mexico, Nice, and the island of Mauritius.*

DESERT

has been set in Minion, a type designed by Robert Slimbach in 1990. An offshoot of the designer's researches during the development of Adobe Garamond, Minion hybridized the characteristics of numerous Renaissance sources into a single calligraphic hand. Unlike many faces developed exclusively for digital typesetting, drawings for Minion were transferred to the computer early in the design phase, preserving much of the freshness of the original concept. Conceived with an eye toward overall harmony, its capitals, lower case, and numerals were carefully balanced to maintain a well-groomed "family" appearance – both between roman and italic and across the full range of weights. A decidedly contemporary face, Minion makes free use of the qualities Slimbach found most appealing in the types of the fifteenth and sixteenth centuries. Crisp drawing and a narrow set width make Minion an economical and easygoing book type, and even its name reflects its adaptable, affable, and almost self-effacing nature, referring as it does to a small size of type, a faithful or devoted servant, and a kind of peach.

DESIGN & COMPOSITION BY CARL W. SCARBROUGH